THIS HEART
of MINE

THIS HEART

of MINE

Susan Elizabeth Phillips

 WILLIAM MORROW 75 YEARS OF PUBLISHING
An Imprint of HarperCollins*Publishers*

This is a work of fiction. Names, characters, places, and incidents either are the product of the author's imagination or are used fictitiously. Any resemblance to actual events, locales, organizations, or persons, living or dead, is entirely coincidental and beyond the intent of either the author or the publisher.

HarperCollins books may be purchased for educational, business, or sales promotional use. For information please write: Special Markets Department, HarperCollins Publishers Inc., 10 East 53rd Street, New York, NY 10022.

FIRST EDITION

Designed by Jessica Shatan

Printed on acid-free paper

Library of Congress Cataloging-in-Publication Data
Phillips, Susan Elizabeth.
This heart of mine / by Susan Elizabeth Phillips.
p.   cm.
ISBN 0-380-97572-6 (hc)
I. Title.
PS3566.H522 T48   2001
813'.54—dc21   00-062038

01 02 03 04 05 RRD 10 9 8 7 6 5 4 3 2 1

To Jill Barnett
for her talents as a matchmaker

Acknowledgments

Thank you to everyone who has rallied around me with handy facts and personal expertise, especially Steve Axelrod, Jill Barnett, Christine Foutris, Ann Maxwell, Bill Phillips, John Roscich, Betty Schulte, the Windy City RWA moms, and Chris Zars. Also the incomparable Creative Fest team of Jennifer Crusie, Jennifer Greene, Cathie Linz, Lindsay Longford, and Suzette Vann. Barbara Jepson has simplified my life immeasurably. Carrie Feron continues to earn my undying gratitude with wisdom, friendship, and editorial guidance. I am hugely indebted to all the people at Morrow/Avon who do so much for me. Thanks, Ty, for lending Molly your condo, and Zach, for writing Kevin and Molly such pretty love songs. Most of all, thanks to my readers for insisting that Kevin have his own story. In order to tell it, I've taken a few liberties with time passage and the ages of characters associated with the Chicago Stars football team. I hope those of you who care about this sort of thing will forgive me.

Susan Elizabeth Phillips
www.susanephillips.com

THIS HEART
of MINE

Daphne the Bunny was admiring her sparkly violet nail polish when Benny the Badger zoomed past on his red mountain bike and knocked her off her paws.

"Oh, you pesky badger!" she exclaimed. "Somebody needs to squeeze the air out of your tires."

—*Daphne Takes a Tumble*

The day Kevin Tucker nearly killed her, Molly Somerville swore off unrequited love forever.

She was dodging the icy places in the Chicago Stars headquarters parking lot when Kevin came roaring out of nowhere in his brand-new $140,000 fire-engine-red Ferrari 355 Spider. With tires shrieking and engine snarling, the low-slung car sprang around the corner, spewing slush. As the rear end flew toward her, she flung herself backward, hit the bumper of her brother-in-law's Lexus, lost her footing, and fell in a cloud of angry exhaust.

Kevin Tucker didn't even slow.

Molly gazed at the fading taillights, gritted her teeth, and picked herself up. Dirty snow and muck clung to one leg of her excruciatingly expensive Comme des Garçons pants, her Prada tote was a mess, and her Italian boots had a scratch. "Oh, you pesky quarterback," she muttered under her breath. "Somebody needs to castrate you."

He hadn't even *seen* her, let alone noticed that he'd nearly killed her! Of course, that was nothing new. Kevin Tucker had spent his entire career with the Chicago Stars football team not noticing her.

Daphne dusted off her fluffy white cottontail, rubbed the dirt from her shimmery blue pumps, and decided to buy herself the fastest pair of Rollerblades in the whole world. So fast she could catch up with Benny and his mountain bike . . .

Molly spent a few moments contemplating chasing Kevin in the chartreuse Volkswagen Beetle she'd bought used after she'd sold her Mercedes, but even her fertile imagination couldn't conjure up a satisfactory conclusion to that scene. As she headed toward the front entrance of Stars headquarters, she shook her head in self-disgust. The man was reckless and shallow, and he only cared about football. Enough was enough. She was finished with unrequited love.

Not that it was really love. Instead, she had a pathetic crush on the jerk, which might be excusable if she were sixteen, but was ludicrous for a twenty-seven-year-old woman with a near-genius IQ.

Some genius.

A blast of warm air hit her as she entered the lobby through a set of glass doors emblazoned with the team logo, consisting of three interlocking gold stars in a sky blue oval. She no longer spent much time at the Chicago Stars headquarters as she'd done when she was still in high school. Even then she'd felt like a stranger. As a dyed-in-the-wool romantic, she preferred reading a really good novel or losing herself in a museum to watching contact sports. Of course she was a dedicated Stars fan, but her loyalty was more a product of family background than natural inclination. Sweat, blood, and the violent clashing of shoulder pads were as foreign to her nature as . . . well . . . Kevin Tucker.

"Aunt Molly!"

"We've been waiting for you!"

"You'll never ever guess what happened!"

She smiled as her beautiful eleven-year-old nieces came flying into the lobby, blond hair streaming behind them.

Tess and Julie looked like miniature versions of their mother, Molly's older sister, Phoebe. The girls were identical twins, but Tess was enveloped in jeans and a baggy Stars sweatshirt, while Julie wore black capris and a pink sweater. Both were athletic but Julie loved ballet, and Tess triumphed at team sports. Their sunny, optimistic natures made the Calebow twins popular with their classmates but a trial to their parents, since it never occurred to either girl to turn down a challenge.

The twins screeched to a stop. Whatever they'd been about to tell Molly vanished as they stared at her hair.

"Omigod, it's red!"

"Really red!"

"That's so cool! Why didn't you tell us?"

"It was sort of an impulse," Molly replied.

"I'm gonna dye my hair just like it!" Julie announced.

"Not your best idea," Molly said quickly. "Now, what were you going to tell me?"

"Dad is like so mad," Tess declared, eyes wide.

Julie's eyes grew even larger. "Him and Uncle Ron have been fighting with Kevin again."

Molly's ears perked up, even though she'd turned her back forever on unrequited love. "What did he do? Other than nearly run me over."

"He did?"

"Never mind. Tell me."

Julie took a gulp of air. "He went skydiving in Denver the day before the Broncos game."

"Oh, boy . . . " Molly's heart sank.

"Dad just found out about it, and he fined him ten thousand dollars!"

"Wow." As far as Molly knew, this was the first time Kevin had ever been fined.

The quarterback's uncharacteristic recklessness had started just before training camp in July, when an amateur motorcycle dirt track racing event had left him with a sprained wrist. It was unlike him to do anything that could jeopardize his performance on the field, so everyone had been sympathetic, especially Dan, who considered Kevin the consummate professional.

Dan's attitude had begun to shift, however, after word reached him that during the regular season Kevin had gone paragliding in Monument Valley. Not long after, the quarterback bought the high-performance

Ferrari Spider that had knocked Molly over in the parking lot. Then last month the *Sun-Times* reported that Kevin had left Chicago after the Monday postgame meetings to fly out to Idaho for a day of heli-skiing in a secluded back bowl at Sun Valley. Since Kevin hadn't been injured, Dan had only given him a warning. But the recent skydiving incident had obviously pushed her brother-in-law over the edge.

"Dad yells all the time, but I never heard him yell at Kevin until today," Tess reported. "And Kevin yelled back. He said he knew what he was doing and he wasn't hurt and Dad should stay out of his private business."

Molly winced. "I'll bet your dad didn't like that."

"He really yelled then," Julie said. "Uncle Ron tried to calm them down, but Coach came in, and then he started yelling, too."

Molly knew that her sister Phoebe had an aversion to yelling. "What did your mom do?"

"She went to her office and turned up Alanis Morissette."

Probably a good thing.

They were interrupted by the pounding of sneakers as her five-year-old nephew, Andrew, came flying around the corner, much like Kevin's Ferrari. "Aunt Molly! Guess what?" He hurled himself against her knees. "Everybody yelled, and my ears hurt."

Since Andrew was blessed with not only his father's good looks but also Dan Calebow's booming voice, Molly sincerely doubted that. Still, she stroked his head. "I'm sorry."

He looked up at her with stricken eyes. "And Kevin was soooo mad at Daddy and Uncle Ron and Coach that he said the F word."

"He shouldn't have done that."

"Twice!"

"Oh, dear." Molly resisted a smile. Spending so much time inside the headquarters of a National Football League team office made it inevitable that the Calebow children heard more than their share of obscenities, but the family rules were clear. Inappropriate language in the Calebow household meant heavy fines, although not as heavy as Kevin's ten thousand dollars.

She couldn't understand it. One of the things she most hated about her crush—her *ex*-crush—on Kevin was the fact that her crush was on *Kevin,* the shallowest man on earth. Football was all that mattered to him. Football and an endless parade of blank-faced international models. Where did he find them? NoPersonality.com?

"Hi, Aunt Molly."

Unlike her siblings, eight-year-old Hannah walked toward Molly instead of running. Although Molly loved all four children equally, her heart held a special place for this vulnerable middle child who didn't share either her siblings' athletic prowess or their bottomless self-confidence. Instead, she was a dreamy romantic, a too-sensitive, overly imaginative bookworm with a talent for drawing, just like her aunt.

"I like your hair."

"Thank you."

Her perceptive gray eyes spotted what her sisters had missed, the grime on Molly's pants.

"What happened?"

"I slipped in the parking lot. Nothing serious."

Hannah took a nibble from her bottom lip. "Did they tell you about the fight Kevin and Dad had?"

She looked upset, and Molly had a pretty good idea why. Kevin showed up at the Calebow house from time to time, and like her foolish aunt, the eight-year-old had a crush on him. But unlike Molly, Hannah's love was pure.

Since Andrew was still wrapped around her knees, Molly held her arm out toward Hannah, who cuddled against her. "People have to take the consequences of their actions, sweetheart, and that includes Kevin."

"What do you think he'll do?" Hannah whispered.

Molly was fairly certain he'd console himself with another model who had a minimal mastery of the English language but maximum mastery of the erotic arts. "I'm sure he'll be fine once he gets over being angry."

"I'm afraid he'll do something foolish."

Molly brushed back a lock of Hannah's light brown hair. "Like skydiving the day before the Broncos game?"

"He prob'ly wasn't thinking."

She doubted that Kevin's small brain had the capacity to think about anything except football, but she didn't share that observation with Hannah. "I need to talk to your mom for a few minutes, and then you and I can leave."

"It's my turn after Hannah," Andrew reminded her as he finally released her legs.

"I haven't forgotten." The children took turns having overnights at her tiny North Shore condo. Usually they stayed with her on weekends instead of a Tuesday night, but the teachers had an in-service education day tomorrow, and Molly thought Hannah needed a little extra attention.

"Get your backpack. I won't be long."

She left them behind and headed down a corridor lined with photographs that marked the history of the Chicago Stars. Her father's portrait came first, and she saw that her sister had freshened up the black horns she'd long ago painted on his head. Bert Somerville, the founder of the Chicago Stars, had been dead for years, but his cruelties lived on in both his daughters' memories.

A formal portrait of Phoebe Somerville Calebow, the Stars' current owner, followed, and then a photograph of her husband, Dan Calebow, from the days when he'd been the Stars' head coach instead of the team's president. Molly regarded her temperamental brother-in-law with a fond smile. Dan and Phoebe had raised her from the time she was fifteen, and both of them had been better parents on their worst day than Bert Somerville on his best.

There was also a photo of Ron McDermitt, the Stars' longtime general manager and Uncle Ron to the kids. Phoebe, Dan, and Ron had worked hard to balance the all-consuming job of running an NFL team with family life. Over the years it had involved several reorganizations, one of which had brought Dan back to the Stars after being away for a while.

Molly made a quick detour into the restroom. As she draped her coat over the sink, she gazed critically at her hair. Although the jagged little cut complimented her eyes, she hadn't left well enough alone. Instead, she'd dyed her dark brown hair a particularly bright shade of red. She looked like a cardinal.

At least the hair color added some flash to her rather ordinary features. Not that she was complaining about her looks. She had an all-right nose and an all-right mouth. They went along with an all-right body, which was neither too thin nor too heavy, but healthy and functional, for which she was grateful. A glance at her bustline confirmed what she'd accepted long ago—as the daughter of a showgirl, she'd been shortchanged.

Her eyes were nice, though, and she liked to believe their slight tilt gave her a mysterious look. As a child she used to wear a half-slip over the bottom half of her face as a veil and pretend she was a beautiful Arabian spy.

With a sigh she swiped at the muck on her ancient Comme des Garçons pants, then wiped off her beloved but battered Prada tote. When she'd done her best, she picked up the quilted brown coat she'd bought on sale at Target and headed for her sister's office.

It was the first week of December, and some of the staff had begun to put up a few Christmas decorations. Phoebe's office door displayed a cartoon Molly had drawn of Santa dressed in a Stars uniform. She poked her head inside. "Aunt Molly's here."

Gold bangles clinked as her blond bombshell of an older sister threw down her pen. "Thank God. A voice of sanity is just what I— Oh, my God! What did you do to your hair?"

With her own cloud of pale blond hair, amber eyes, and drop-dead figure, Phoebe looked rather like Marilyn Monroe might have looked if she'd made it into her forties, although Molly couldn't imagine Marilyn with a smear of grape jelly on the front of her silk blouse. No matter what Molly did to herself, she'd never be as beautiful as her sister, but she didn't mind. Few people knew the misery Phoebe's lush body and vamp's beauty had once caused her.

"Oh, Molly . . . not again." The consternation in her sister's eyes made Molly wish she'd worn a hat.

"Relax, will you? Nothing's going to happen."

"How can I relax? Every time you do something drastic to your hair, we have another *incident.*"

"I outgrew *incidents* a long time ago." Molly sniffed. "This was purely cosmetic."

"I don't believe you. You're getting ready to do something crazy again, aren't you?"

"I am not!" If she said it frequently enough, maybe she'd convince herself.

"Only ten years old," Phoebe muttered to herself. "The brightest and best-behaved student at the boarding school. Then, out of nowhere, you hack off your bangs and plant a stink bomb in the dining hall."

"Nothing more than a gifted child's chemistry experiment."

"Thirteen years old. Quiet. Studious. Not a single misstep since the stink-bomb incident. Until you started combing grape Jell-O powder through your hair. Then presto change-o! You pack up Bert's college trophies, call a garbage company, and have them hauled away."

"You liked that one when I told you about it. Admit it."

But Phoebe was on a roll, and she wasn't admitting anything. "Four years go by. Four years of model behavior and high scholastic achievement. Dan and I have taken you into our home, into our *hearts.* You're a senior, on your way to being valedictorian. You have a stable home, people who love you . . . You're vice-president of the Student Council, so why should I worry when you put blue and orange stripes in your hair?"

"They were the school colors," Molly said weakly.

"I get the call from the police telling me that my sister—my studious, brainy, Citizen of the Month sister!—deliberately set off a fire alarm during fifth-period lunch! No more *little* mischief for our Molly! Oh, no . . . She's gone straight to a class-two *felony!*"

It had been the most miserable thing Molly had ever done. She'd betrayed the people who loved her, and even after a year of court supervision and many hours of community service, she hadn't been able to explain why. That understanding had come later, during her sophomore year at Northwestern.

It had been in the spring, right before finals. Molly had found herself restless and unable to concentrate. Instead of studying, she read stacks of romance novels, drew, or stared at her hair in the mirror and yearned for something pre-Raphaelite. Even using up her allowance on hair extensions hadn't made the restlessness go away. Then one day she'd walked out of the college bookstore and discovered a calculator that she hadn't paid for tucked in her purse.

Wiser than she'd been in high school, she'd rushed back inside to return it and headed for Northwestern's counseling office.

Phoebe interrupted Molly's thoughts by jumping to her feet. "And the last time . . . "

Molly winced, even though she'd known this was where Phoebe would end up.

" . . . the *last* time you did something this drastic to your hair—that awful crew cut two years ago . . . "

"It was trendy, not awful."

Phoebe set her teeth. "The last time you did something this drastic, you gave away *fifteen million dollars!*"

"Yes, well . . . Getting the crew cut was purely coincidental."

"*Ha!*"

For the fifteen millionth time, Molly explained why she'd done it. "Bert's money was strangling me. I needed to make a final break from the past so I could be my own person."

"A poor person!"

Molly smiled. Although Phoebe would never admit it, she understood exactly why Molly had given up her inheritance. "Look on the bright side. Hardly anybody knows I gave away my money. They just think that I'm eccentric for driving a used Beetle and living in a place the size of a closet."

"You adore that place."

Molly didn't even try to deny it. Her loft was her most precious possession, and she loved knowing she earned the money that paid her mortgage each month. Only someone who'd grown up without a home that was truly her own could understand what it meant to her.

She decided to change the subject before Phoebe could start in on her again. "The munchkins told me Dan hit Mr. Shallow with a ten-thousand-dollar fine."

"I wish you wouldn't call him that. Kevin's not shallow, he's just—"

"Interest-impaired?"

"Honestly, Molly, I don't know why you dislike him so much. The two of you couldn't have exchanged even a dozen words over the years."

"By design. I avoid people who speak only Gridiron."

"If you knew him better, you'd adore him as much as I do."

"Isn't it fascinating that he mainly dates women with limited English? But I guess it prevents a silly thing like conversation from interfering with sex."

Phoebe laughed in spite of herself.

Although Molly shared almost everything with her sister, she hadn't shared her own infatuation with the Stars' quarterback. Not only would it be humiliating, but Phoebe would confide in Dan, who'd go ballistic. Her brother-in-law was more than a little protective where Molly was concerned, and unless an athlete was happily married or gay, he didn't want Molly anywhere near him.

At that moment the subject of her thoughts burst into the room. Dan Calebow was big, blond, and handsome. Age had treated him kindly, and in the twelve years since Molly had known him, the added lines in that virile face had only given him character. His was the kind of presence that filled a room by reflecting the perfect self-confidence of someone who knew what he stood for.

Dan had been head coach when Phoebe had inherited the Stars. Unfortunately, she hadn't known anything about football, and he'd immediately declared war. Their early battles had been so fierce that Ron McDermitt had once suspended Dan for insulting her, but it wasn't long before their anger turned into something else entirely.

Molly considered Phoebe and Dan's love story the stuff of legend, and she'd long ago decided that—if she couldn't have what her sister and brother-in-law had together—she didn't want anything. Only a Great Love Story would satisfy Molly, and that was as likely as Dan rescinding Kevin's fine.

Her brother-in-law automatically wrapped an arm around Molly's shoulders. When Dan was with his family, he always had an arm around someone. A pang shot through her heart. Over the years she'd dated a lot of decent guys and even tried to convince herself she was in love with one or two of them, but she'd fallen out of love the moment she realized they couldn't come close to filling the giant shadow cast by her brother-in-law. She was beginning to suspect no one ever would.

"Phoebe, I know you like Kevin, but this time he's gone too far." His Alabama drawl always grew broader when he was upset, and now he was dripping molasses.

"That's what you said last time," Phoebe replied. "And you like him, too."

"I don't understand it! Playing for the Stars is the most important thing in his life. Why is he working so hard to screw that up?"

Phoebe smiled sweetly. "You could probably answer that better than either one of us, since you were a pretty big screw-up until I came along."

"You must have me confused with someone else."

Phoebe laughed, and Dan's glower gave way to the intimate smile Molly had witnessed a thousand times and envied just as many. Then his smile faded. "If I didn't know him better, I'd think the devil was chasing him."

"Devils," Molly interjected. "All with foreign accents and big breasts."

"It goes along with being a football player, which is something I don't ever want you to forget."

She didn't want to hear any more about Kevin, so she gave Dan a quick peck on the cheek. "Hannah's waiting. I'll have her back late tomorrow afternoon."

"Don't let her see the morning papers."

"I won't." Hannah brooded when the newspapers weren't kind to the Stars, and Kevin's fine was sure to be controversial.

Molly waved her good-byes, collected Hannah, kissed the sibs, and set off for home. The East-West Tollway was already backing up with rush-hour traffic, and Molly knew it would be well over an hour before she got to Evanston, the old North Shore town that was both the location of her alma mater and her current home.

"Slytherin!" she called out to the jerk who cut her off.

"Dirty, rotten Slytherin!" Hannah echoed.

Molly smiled to herself. The Slytherins were the bad kids in the Harry Potter books, and Molly had turned the word into a useful G-rated curse. She'd been amused when Phoebe, then Dan, had started to use it. As Hannah began to chatter about her day, Molly found herself thinking back to her conversation with Phoebe and those years right after she'd finally come into her inheritance.

Bert's will had left Phoebe the Chicago Stars. What remained of his estate after a series of bad investments had gone to Molly. Since Molly was a minor, Phoebe had tended the money until it had grown into fifteen million dollars. Finally, with the emancipation of being twenty-one, along with her brand-new degree in journalism, Molly had taken control of her inheritance and started living the high life in a luxury apartment on Chicago's Gold Coast.

The place was sterile and her neighbors much older, but she was slow to realize she'd made a mistake. Instead, she'd indulged herself in the designer clothes she adored and bought presents for her friends as well as an expensive car for herself. But after a year she'd finally admitted that the life of the idle rich wasn't for her. She was used to working hard, whether in school or at the summer jobs Dan had insisted she take, so she'd accepted a position at a newspaper.

The work kept her busy, but it wasn't creative enough to be fulfilling, and she began to feel as if she were playing at life instead of living it. Finally she decided to quit so she could work on the epic romantic saga she'd always fantasized about writing. Instead, she found herself tinkering with the stories she made up for the Calebow children, tales of a spunky little bunny who wore the latest fashions, lived in a cottage at the edge of Nightingale Woods, and couldn't stay out of trouble.

She'd begun putting the stories on paper, then illustrating them with the funny drawings she'd done all her life but never taken seriously. Using pen and ink, then filling in the sketches with bright acrylic colors, she watched Daphne and her friends come alive.

She'd been elated when Birdcage Press, a small Chicago publisher, bought her first book, *Daphne Says Hello*, even though the advance money barely covered her postage. Still, she'd finally found her niche. But her vast wealth made her work seem more like a hobby than a vocation, and she continued feeling dissatisfied. Her restlessness grew. She hated her apartment, her wardrobe, her hair . . . A jazzy little crew cut didn't help.

She needed to pull a fire alarm.

Since those days were behind her, she'd found herself seated in her attorney's office telling him she wanted all of her money put into a foundation that would help disadvantaged children. He'd been flabbergasted, but she'd felt completely satisfied for the first time since she'd turned twenty-one. Phoebe had been given the opportunity to prove herself when she'd inherited the Stars, but Molly had never had that chance. Now she would. When she signed the papers, she felt feather-light and free.

"I love it here." Hannah sighed as Molly unlocked the door of her tiny second-floor loft a few minutes' walk from downtown Evanston. Molly gave her own sigh of pleasure. Even though she hadn't been gone long, she always loved the moment when she walked inside her own home.

All the Calebow children regarded Aunt Molly's loft as the coolest place on earth. The building had been constructed in 1910 for a Studebaker dealer, then used as an office building and eventually a warehouse before being renovated a few years ago. Her condo had floor-to-ceiling industrial windows, exposed ductwork, and old brick walls that held some of her drawings and paintings. Her unit was both the smallest in the building and the cheapest, but the fourteen-foot ceilings gave it a spacious feeling. Every month when she made her mortgage payment, she kissed the envelope before she slipped it into the mailbox. A silly ritual, but she did it just the same.

Most people assumed that Molly still had a stake in the Stars, and only a few of her very closest friends knew she was no longer a wealthy heiress. She supplemented her small income from the Daphne books by writing articles freelance for a teen magazine called *Chik*. There wasn't much left at the end of the month for her favorite luxuries—great clothes and hardback books, but she didn't mind. She bargain-shopped and used the library.

Life was good. She might never have a Great Love Story like Phoebe's, but at least she was blessed with a wonderful imagination and an active fantasy life. She had no complaints and certainly no reason to be afraid that her old restlessness might be rearing its unpredictable head. Her new hairstyle was nothing more than a fashion statement.

Hannah threw off her coat and crouched down to greet Roo, Molly's small gray poodle, who'd scampered to the door to greet them. Both Roo and the Calebows' poodle, Kanga, were the offspring of Phoebe's beloved Pooh.

"Hey, stinker, did you miss me?" Molly tossed down her mail to plant a kiss on Roo's soft gray topknot. Roo reciprocated by swiping Molly's chin with his tongue, then crouching down to produce his very best growl.

"Yeah, yeah, we're impressed, aren't we, Hannah?"

Hannah giggled and looked up at Molly. "He still likes to pretend he's a police dog, doesn't he?"

"The baddest dog on the force. Let's not damage his self-esteem by telling him he's a poodle."

Hannah gave Roo an extra squeeze, then abandoned him to head for Molly's workspace, which took up one end of the open living area. "Have you written any more articles? I loved 'Prom-Night Passion.'"

Molly smiled. "Soon."

In keeping with the demands of the marketplace, the articles she freelanced to *Chik* were almost always published with suggestive titles, although their content was tame. "Prom-Night Passion" stressed the consequences of backseat sex. "From Virgin to Vixen" had been an article on cosmetics, and "Nice Girls Go Wild" followed three fourteen-year-olds on a camping trip.

"Can I see your new drawings?"

Molly hung up their coats. "I don't have any. I'm just getting started with a new idea." Sometimes her books began with idle sketches, other times with text. Today it had been real-life inspiration.

"Tell me! Please!"

They always shared cups of Constant Comment tea before they did anything else, and Molly walked into the tiny kitchen that sat opposite her work area to put water on to boil. Her minuscule sleeping loft was located just above, where it looked out over the living space below. Metal shelves on the downstairs walls overflowed with the books she adored: her beloved set of Jane Austen's novels, tattered copies of the works of Daphne Du Maurier and Anya Seton, all of Mary Stewart's early books, along with Victoria Holt, Phyllis Whitney, and Danielle Steel.

Narrower shelves held double-deep rows of paperbacks—historical sagas, romance, mysteries, travel guides, and reference books. Her favorite literary writers were also well represented, along with biographies of famous women and some of Oprah's less depressing book club selections, most of which Molly had discovered before Oprah shared them with the world.

She kept the children's books she loved on shelves in the sleeping loft. Her collection included all the Eloise stories and Harry Potter books, *The Witch of Blackbird Pond,* some Judy Blume, Gertrude Chandler Warner's *The Boxcar Children, Anne of Green Gables,* a little Sweet Valley High for fun, and the tattered Barbara Cartland books she'd discovered when she was ten. It was the collection of a dedicated bookworm, and all the Calebow children loved curling up on her bed with a whole stack piled around them while they tried to decide which one to read next.

Molly pulled out a pair of china teacups with delicate gold rims and a scatter of purple pansies. "I decided today that I'm calling my new book *Daphne Takes a Tumble.*"

"Tell me!"

"Well . . . Daphne is walking through Nightingale Woods minding her own business when, out of nowhere, Benny comes racing past on his mountain bike and knocks her off her feet."

Hannah shook her head disapprovingly. "That pesky badger."

"Exactly."

Hannah regarded her cagily. "I think somebody should steal Benny's mountain bike. Then he'd stay out of trouble."

Molly smiled. "Stealing doesn't exist in Nightingale Woods. Didn't we talk about that when you wanted somebody to steal Benny's jet ski?"

"I guess." Her mouth set in the mulish line she'd inherited from her father. "But if there can be mountain bikes and jet skis in Nightingale Woods, I don't see why there can't be stealing, too. And Benny doesn't mean to do bad things. He's just mischievous."

Molly thought of Kevin. "There's a thin line between mischief and stupidity."

"Benny's not stupid!"

Hannah looked stricken, and Molly wished she'd kept her mouth shut. "Of course he's not. He's the smartest badger in Nightingale Woods." She ruffled her niece's hair. "Let's have our tea, and then we'll take Roo for a walk by the lake."

Molly didn't get a chance to look at her mail until later that night, after Hannah had fallen asleep with a tattered copy of *The Jennifer Wish*. She put her phone bill in a clip, then absentmindedly opened a business-size envelope. She wished she hadn't bothered as she took in the letterhead.

Straight Kids for a Straight America

The radical homosexual agenda has targeted your children! Our most innocent citizens are being lured toward the evils of perversion by obscene books and irresponsible television shows that glorify this deviant and morally repugnant behavior . . .

Straight Kids for a Straight America, SKIFSA, was a Chicago-based organization whose wild-eyed members had been appearing on all the local talk shows to spew their personal paranoia. If only they'd turn their energies to something constructive, like keeping guns away from kids, and she tossed the letter in the trash.

L ate the next afternoon Molly lowered one hand from the steering wheel and ran her fingers through Roo's topknot. Earlier she'd returned Hannah to her parents, and now she was on her way to the Calebows' Door County, Wisconsin, vacation home. It would be late when she got there, but the roads were clear and she didn't mind driving at night.

She'd made the decision to travel north impulsively. Her conversation with Phoebe yesterday had exposed something she'd been doing her best to deny. Her sister was right. Having her hair dyed red was a symptom of a bigger problem. Her old restlessness was back.

True, she wasn't experiencing any compulsion to pull a fire alarm, and giving away her money was no longer an option. But that didn't mean that her subconscious couldn't find some new way to commit mayhem. She had the uneasy sensation she was being drawn back to a place she thought she'd left behind.

She remembered what the counselor had told her all those years ago at Northwestern.

"As a child, you believed you could make your father love you if you did everything you were supposed to. If you got the best grades, minded your manners, followed all the rules, then he'd give you the approval every child needs. But your father was incapable of that kind of love. Eventually something inside you snapped, and you did the worst thing you could think of. Your rebellion was actually healthy. It kept you functioning."

"That doesn't explain what I did in high school," she'd told him. "Bert was dead by then, and I was living with Phoebe and Dan. They both love me. And what about the shoplifting incident?"

"Maybe you needed to test Phoebe and Dan's love."

Something odd had fluttered inside her. "What do you mean?"

"The only way you can make certain their love is unconditional is to do something terrible and then see if they're still around for you."

And they had been.

So why was her old problem coming back to haunt her? She didn't want mayhem in her life anymore. She wanted to write her books, enjoy her friends, walk her dog, and play with her nieces and nephews. But she'd been feeling restless for weeks, and one look at her red hair, which really was awful, told her she might be on the verge of going off the deep end again.

Until that urge faded, she'd do the sensible thing and hide away in Door County for a week or so. After all, what possible trouble could she get into there?

Kevin Tucker had been dreaming about Red Jack Express, a quarter-back delayed sneak, when something woke him up. He rolled over, groaned, and tried to figure out where he was, but the bottle of scotch he'd befriended before he'd fallen asleep made that tough. Normally adrenaline was his drug of choice, but tonight alcohol had seemed like a good alternative.

He heard the sound again, a scratching at the door, and it all came back to him. He was in Door County, Wisconsin, the Stars weren't play-ing this week, and Dan had slapped him with a ten-thousand-dollar fine. After he'd done that, the son of a bitch had ordered him to go up to their vacation house and stay there till he got his head together.

There wasn't a damn thing wrong with his head, but there was defi-nitely a problem with the Calebows' high-tech security system—because somebody was trying to break in.

2

So what if he is the hottest guy at your school? It's the way he treats you that counts.

—"Is He Too Hot to Handle?"
Molly Somerville for *Chik*

Kevin suddenly remembered that he'd been too preoccupied with his scotch to set the house's security system. A lucky break. Now he had a shot at a little entertainment.

The house was cold and dark as sin. He threw his bare feet over the edge of the couch and bumped into the coffee table. Cursing, he rubbed his shin, then hopped toward the door. What did it say about his life that tangling with a burglar would be this week's bright spot? He just hoped the son of a bitch was armed.

He dodged a chunky shape that he thought might be an armchair and stepped on something small and sharp, probably one of the Legos he'd seen scattered around. The house was big and luxurious, set deep into the Wisconsin woods, with trees on three sides and the icy waters of Lake Michigan at the rear.

Damn, it was dark. He headed toward the scratching sound, and just as he reached it, heard the click of the latch. The door began to open.

He felt that adrenaline rush he loved, and in one smooth motion he shoved the door against the wall and grabbed the person on the other side.

The guy was a lightweight, and he came flying.

He was a pansy, too, from the sound of that scream as he hit the floor.

Unfortunately, he had a dog. A big dog.

The hair stood on the back of Kevin's neck as he heard the low, bloodcurdling growl of an attack dog. He had no time to brace himself before the animal clamped down on his ankle.

With the reflexes that were making him a legend, he lunged toward the switch, at the same time steeling himself for the crunch of his ankle bones. Light flooded the foyer, and he realized two things.

He wasn't being attacked by a rottweiler. And those panicked sounds weren't coming from a guy.

"Aw, shit . . . "

Lying on the slate floor at his feet was a small, screaming woman with hair the color of a 49ers jersey. And clamped to his ankle, ripping holes in his favorite jeans, was a small, gray . . .

His brain skidded away from the word.

The stuff she'd been carrying when he'd grabbed her lay strewn all around. As he tried to shake off the dog, he spotted lots of books, drawing supplies, two boxes of Nutter Butter cookies, and bedroom slippers with big pink rabbits' heads on the toes.

He finally shook off the snarling dog. The woman scrambled to her feet and assumed some kind of martial arts pose. He opened his mouth to explain, only to have her foot come up and catch him behind the knee. The next thing he knew, he'd been sacked.

"Damn . . . It took the Giants a good three quarters to do that."

She'd been wearing a coat when she hit the floor, but the only thing between him and the slate was a layer of denim. He winced and rolled to his back. The animal pounced on his chest, barking dog breath into his face and slapping him in the nose with the tails of the blue bandanna fastened around his neck.

"You tried to kill me!" she screamed, the fiery little wisps of 49er hair flashing around her face.

"Not on purpose." He knew he'd met her before, but he couldn't for the life of him remember who she was. "Could you call off your pit bull?"

Her panicked look was giving way to fury, and she bared her teeth just like the dog. "Come here, Roo."

The animal snarled and crawled off Kevin's chest. It finally hit him.

Oh, shit . . . "You're, uh, Phoebe's sister. Are you okay"—he searched for a name—"Miss Somerville?" Since he was the one lying on the slate floor with a bruised hip and puncture wounds in his ankle, he considered the question something of a courtesy.

"This is the second time in two days!" she exclaimed.

"I don't remember—"

"The *second* time! Are you demented, you stupid badger? Is that your problem? Or are you just an *idiot!*"

"As to that, I— Did you just call me a badger?"

She blinked. "A bastard. I called you a bastard."

"That's all right then." Unfortunately, his lame attempt at humor didn't make her smile.

The pit bull retreated to his mistress's side. Kevin pushed himself up off the slate and rubbed his ankle, trying to recall what he knew about his employer's sister, but he remembered only that she was an egghead. He'd seen her a few times at Stars headquarters with her head buried in a book, but her hair sure hadn't been this color.

It was hard to believe that she and Phoebe were related, because she wasn't even close to being a fox. Not that she was a dog either. She was just sort of ordinary—flat where Phoebe was curvy, small where Phoebe was large. Unlike her sister's, this one's mouth didn't look as if it had been designed to whisper dirty words under the sheets. Instead, Little Sis's mouth looked as if it spent its days shushing people in the library.

He didn't need the evidence of all those scattered books to tell him she was the kind of woman he least liked—brainy and way too serious. She was probably going to be a talker, too, an even bigger strike against her. In the spirit of fairness, though, he had to give Little Sis high marks for eye power. They were an unusual color, somewhere between blue and gray, and they had a sexy slant to them, just like her eyebrows, which he realized were almost meeting in the middle as she scowled at him. Damn it. Phoebe's sister! And he'd thought this week couldn't get any worse.

"Are you all right?" he asked.

Those blue-gray irises turned the exact color of an Illinois summer afternoon right before the tornado siren went off. He'd now managed to piss off every member of the Stars' ruling family, except maybe the kids. It was a gift.

He'd better mend his fences, and since charm was his long suit, he flashed a smile. "I didn't mean to scare you. I thought you were a burglar."

"What are you doing here?"

Even before her screech, he could see that the charm thing wasn't working.

He kept an eye on that kung fu leg of hers. "Dan suggested I come up here for a few days, to think things over . . . " He paused. "Which I didn't need to do."

She slapped the switch, and two sets of rustic iron wall sconces came on, filling the far corners with light.

The house was built of logs, but with six bedrooms and ceilings that soared up two stories to the exposed roof beams, the place didn't bear any resemblance to a frontier log cabin. Big windows made the woods seem part of the interior, and the huge stone fireplace that dominated one end of the room could have roasted a buffalo. All the furniture was big, overstuffed, and comfortable, designed to take the abuse of a large family. Off to the side a wide staircase led to a second floor complete with a small loft at one end.

Kevin bent over to pick up her things. He examined the rabbit slippers. "Don't you get nervous wearing these during hunting season?"

She snatched them from his hand. "Give them to me."

"I wasn't planning on wearing them. It'd be a little hard to keep the guys' respect."

She didn't smile as he handed them over. "There's a lodge not too far from here," she said. "I'm sure you can find a room for the night."

"It's too late to throw me out. Besides, I was invited."

"It's my house. You're uninvited." She tossed her coat on one of the couches and headed for the kitchen. The pit bull curled his lip, then stuck his pompon straight up, just as if he were giving Kevin the finger. Only when the dog was certain his message had been delivered did he trot after her.

Kevin followed them. The kitchen was roomy and comfortable, with

Craftsman cabinets and a daylight view of Lake Michigan through every window. She dropped her packages on a pentagon-shaped center island surrounded by six stools.

She had an eye for fashion, he'd give her that. She wore close-fitting charcoal pants and a funky, oversize metallic-gray sweater that put him in mind of a suit of armor. With that short flaming hair, she could be Joan of Arc right after the match had been struck. Her clothes looked expensive but not new, which was odd, since he remembered hearing that she'd inherited Bert Somerville's fortune. Even though Kevin was wealthy himself, he'd come into his money long after his character had been formed. In his experience, people who'd grown up wealthy didn't understand hard work, and he hadn't met many of them he liked. This snobby rich girl was no exception.

"Uh, Miss Somerville? Before you kick me out . . . I'll bet you didn't let the Calebows know you were coming up here, or they'd have told you the place was already occupied."

"I have dibs. It's understood." She threw the cookies in a drawer and slammed it shut. Then she studied him, all uptight and mad as hell. "You don't remember my name, do you?"

"Sure I know your name." He searched his mind and couldn't come up with a thing.

"We've been introduced at least three times."

"Which was totally unnecessary, since I've got a great memory for names."

"Not mine. You've forgotten."

"Of course I haven't."

She stared at him for a long moment, but he was used to operating under pressure, and he didn't have any trouble waiting her out.

"It's Daphne," she said.

"Why are you telling me something I already know? Are you this paranoid with everyone, Daphne?"

She pursed her lips and muttered something under her breath. He could swear he heard the word "badger" again.

Kevin Tucker didn't even know her name! *Let this be a lesson,* Molly thought as she gazed at all that dangerous gorgeousness.

Right then she knew she had to find a way to protect herself from him. Okay, so he was drop-dead good-looking. So were a lot of men. Granted, not many of them had that particular combination of dark blond hair and brilliant green eyes. And not many had a body like his, which was trim and sculpted rather than bulky. Still, she wasn't stupid enough to be taken in by a man who was nothing more than a great body, a pretty face, and an on/off charm switch.

Well, she *was* stupid enough—witness her late, unlamented crush on him—but at least she'd known she was being stupid.

One thing she wouldn't do was come across as a fawning groupie. He was going to see her at her absolute snottiest! She conjured up Goldie Hawn in *Overboard* for inspiration. "You're going to have to leave, Ken. Oh, excuse me, I mean *Kevin.* It is Kevin, right?"

She must have gone too far because the corner of his mouth kicked up. "We've been introduced at least three times. I'd think you'd remember."

"There are just so many football players, and you all look alike."

One of his eyebrows arched.

She'd made her point, and it was late, so she could afford to be generous, but only in the most condescending way. "You can stay tonight, but I came here to work, so you'll have to vacate tomorrow morning." A glance out the back windows showed his Ferrari parked by the garage, which was why she hadn't seen it when she'd pulled up in front.

He deliberately settled on a stool, as if to show her he wasn't going anywhere. "What kind of work do you do?" He sounded patronizing, which told her he didn't believe it was anything too arduous.

"*Je suis auteur.*"

"An author?"

"*Soy autora,*" she added in Spanish.

"Any reason you've given up English?"

"I thought you might be more comfortable with a foreign language." A vague wave of her hand. "Something I read . . . "

Kevin might be shallow, but he wasn't stupid, and she wondered if she'd crossed the line. Unfortunately, she was on a roll. "I'm almost certain Roo has recovered from his little problem with rabies, but you might want to get some shots, just to be on the safe side."

"You're still mad about the burglar thing, aren't you?"

"I'm sorry, I can't hear you. Probably a concussion from the fall."

"I said I was sorry."

"So you did." She moved aside a pile of crayons the kids had left on the counter.

"I think I'll head upstairs to bed." He rose and started toward the door, then paused for another look at her awful hair. "Tell me the truth. Was it some kind of football bet?"

"Good night, Kirk."

A s Molly entered her bedroom, she realized she was breathing hard. Only a thin wall separated her from the guest room where Kevin would be sleeping. Her skin tingled, and she felt an almost uncontrollable urge to take the scissors to her hair, even though there wasn't much left to cut. Maybe she should dye it back to its natural color tomorrow, except she couldn't give him the satisfaction.

She'd come here to hide out, not sleep next to the lion's den, and she grabbed her things. With Roo following, she hurried down the hall to the big, dormitory-style corner room the three girls shared and locked the door.

She sagged against the jamb and tried to settle down by taking in the room's sloping ceiling and the cozy dormers designed for daydreaming. Two of the walls displayed a Nightingale Woods mural that she'd painted while everyone in the family got in her way. She'd be all right, and in the morning he'd be gone.

Sleep, however, was impossible. Why hadn't she let Phoebe know she was driving up here, as she usually did? Because she hadn't wanted more lectures about her hair or warnings about "incidents."

She tossed and turned, watched the clock, and finally flicked on the light to sketch some ideas for her new book. Nothing worked. Usually the sound of the winter wind battering the solid log house soothed her, but tonight that wind urged her to throw off her clothes and dance, to leave the studious, good girl behind and cross over to the wild side.

She tossed back the covers and jumped out of bed. The room was chilly, but she felt flushed and feverish. She wished she were home. Roo lifted one sleepy eyelid, then closed it again as she made her way to the padded bench in the nearest dormer.

Frost feathers decorated the windowpanes, and snow swirled in thin, dancing ribbons through the trees. She tried to concentrate on the night beauty, but she kept seeing Kevin Tucker. Her skin prickled, and her breasts tingled. It was so demeaning! She was a bright woman—brilliant, even—but, despite her denial, she was as obsessed as a sex-starved groupie.

Maybe this was a perverse form of personal growth. At least she was obsessing over sex instead of the Great Love Story she wouldn't ever have.

She decided it was safer to obsess over the Great Love Story. Dan had saved Phoebe's life! It was the most romantic thing Molly could imagine, but she supposed it had also given her unrealistic expectations.

She gave up on the Great Love Story and went back to obsessing over sex. Did Kevin speak English while he was doing it or had he memorized a few handy foreign phrases? With a groan, she buried her face in the pillow.

After only a few hours' sleep she awakened to a cold, gray dawn. When she looked out, she saw that Kevin's Ferrari was gone. *Good!* She took Roo outside, then showered. While she dried off, she forced herself to hum a little ditty about Winnie the Pooh, but as she pulled on a well-worn pair of gray pants and the Dolce & Gabbana sweater she'd bought before she gave away her money, the pretense of pretending she was happy faded.

What was wrong with her? She had a wonderful life. She was healthy. She had good friends, a terrific family, and an entertaining dog. Although she was nearly always broke, she didn't mind because her loft was worth every penny it cost her. She loved her work. Her life was perfect. More than perfect, now that Kevin Tucker was gone.

Disgusted with her moodiness, she shoved her feet into the pink slippers the twins had given her for her birthday and padded down to the kitchen, the bunny heads on the toes waggling. A quick breakfast, then she'd get to work.

She'd arrived too late last night to pick up groceries, so she pulled a box of Dan's Pop-Tarts from the cupboard. Just as she was slipping one into the toaster, Roo began to bark. The back door opened, and Kevin came in, his arms loaded with plastic grocery bags. Her idiotic heart skipped a beat.

Roo snarled. Kevin ignored him. "Morning, Daphne."

Her instinctive burst of pleasure gave way to annoyance. *Slytherin!*

He dumped the bags on the center island. "Supplies were running low."

"What difference does it make? You're leaving, remember? *Vous partez. Salga.*" She enunciated the foreign words and was gratified to see that she'd annoyed him.

"Leaving isn't a good idea." He gave a hard twist to the cap on the milk. "I'm not making any more waves with Dan right now, so you'll need to go instead."

Exactly what she should do, but she didn't like his attitude, so she let her inner bitch take over. "That's not going to happen. As an athlete, you won't understand this, but I need peace and quiet because *I* actually have to *think* when I work."

He definitely caught the insult but chose to ignore it. "I'm staying here."

"So am I," she replied, just as stubbornly.

She could see that he wanted to toss her out but couldn't do it because she was his boss's sister. He took his time filling his glass, then settled his hips against the counter. "It's a big house. We'll share."

She started to tell him to forget it, that she'd leave after all, when something stopped her. Maybe sharing wasn't as crazy as it sounded. The quickest way to get over her fixation would be to see the Slytherin beneath the real man. It had never been Kevin as a human being who attracted her because she had no idea who he really was. Instead, it was the illusion of Kevin—gorgeous body, sexy eyes, valiant leader of men.

She watched him drain the glass of milk. One belch. That's all it would take. Nothing disgusted her more than a man who belched . . . or scratched his crotch . . . or had gross table manners. Or what about the losers who tried to impress women by pulling out a fat roll of bills held together with one of those garish money clips?

Maybe he wore a gold chain. Molly shuddered. That would do it for sure. Or was a gun nut. Or said, *"You duh man."* Or in any of a hundred ways couldn't measure up to the standard set by Dan Calebow.

Yes, indeed, there were a million pitfalls awaiting Mr. Kevin I'm-too-sexy-for-my-Astroturf-green-eyes Tucker. One belch . . . one crotch scratch . . . even the slightest glimmer of gold around that gorgeous neck . . .

She realized she was smiling. "All right. You can stay."

"Thanks, Daphne." He drained the glass but didn't burp.

She narrowed her eyes and told herself that as long as he kept calling her Daphne, she was halfway home.

She found her laptop computer and carried it up to the loft, where she set it on the desk, along with her sketch pad. She could work on either *Daphne Takes a Tumble* or the article "Making Out—How Far to Go?"

Very far.

It was definitely the wrong time to work on an article about any kind of sex, even the teenage variety.

She heard the sound of game film being played below and realized Kevin had brought video with him so he could do his homework. She wondered if he ever cracked a book or went to an art film or did anything that wasn't connected with football.

Time to get her mind back on her work. She propped one foot on Roo and gazed out the window at the angry whitecaps rolling over the gray, forbidding waters of Lake Michigan. Maybe Daphne should return to her cottage late at night only to find everything dark. And when she walked inside, Benny could jump out and—

She had to stop making her stories so autobiographical.

Okay . . . She flipped open her sketch pad. Daphne could decide to put on a Halloween mask and scare— No, she'd already done that in *Daphne Plants a Pumpkin Patch.*

Definitely time to phone a friend. Molly picked up the phone next to her and dialed Janine Stevens, one of her best writing pals. Although Janine wrote for the young adult market, they shared the same philosophy about books and frequently brainstormed together.

"Thank God you called!" Janine cried. "I've been trying to reach you all morning."

"What's wrong?"

"Everything! Some big-haired woman from SKIFSA was on the local news this morning ranting and raving about children's books being a recruiting tool for the homosexual lifestyle."

"Why don't they get a life?"

"Molly, she held up a copy of *I Miss You So* and said it was an example of the kind of filth that lures children into perversion!"

"Oh, Janine . . . that's awful!" *I Miss You So* was the story of a thirteen-year-old girl trying to come to terms with the persecution of an artistic older brother who'd been branded as gay by the other kids. It was beautifully written, sensitive, and heartfelt.

Janine blew her nose. "My editor called this morning. She said they've decided to wait until the heat dies down, and they're going to postpone my next book for a *year!*"

"You finished it almost a year ago!"

"They don't care. I can't believe it. My sales were finally starting to take off. Now I'm going to lose all my momentum."

Molly consoled her friend as best she could. By the time she hung up, she'd decided that SKIFSA was a bigger menace to society than any book could ever be.

She heard footsteps below and realized that the game film was no longer running. The only good thing about her conversation with Janine was that it had distracted her from thinking about Kevin.

A deep male voice called up to her. "Hey, Daphne! Do you know if they've got an airfield around here?"

"An airfield? Yes. There's one in Sturgeon Bay. It's—" Her head shot up. "*Airfield!*"

She vaulted out of her chair and made a rush for the railing. "You're going skydiving again!"

He tilted his head to gaze up at her. Even with his hands in his pockets, he looked as tall and dazzling as a sun god.

Will you please burp!

"Why would I go skydiving?" he said mildly. "Dan's asked me not to."

"Like that's going to stop you."

Benny pumped the pedals of his mountain bike faster and faster. He didn't notice the rain falling on the road that led through Nightingale Woods or the big puddle just ahead.

She raced down the stairs, even though she knew she should stay as far away from him as possible. "Don't do it. There were flurries all night. It's too windy."

"Now you're tantalizing me."

"I'm trying to explain that it's dangerous!"

"Isn't that what makes anything worth doing?"

"No plane's going to take you up on a day like today." Except that celebrities like Kevin could get people to do just about anything.

"I don't think I'd have too much trouble finding a pilot. If I did plan to go skydiving."

"I'll call Dan," she threatened. "I'm sure he'll be interested to hear just how lightly you've taken your suspension."

"Now you're scaring me," he drawled. "I'll bet you were one of those bratty little girls who tattled to the teacher when the boys misbehaved."

"I didn't go to school with boys until I was fifteen, so I missed the opportunity."

"That's right. You're a rich kid, aren't you?"

"Rich and pampered," she lied. "What about you?" Maybe if she distracted him with conversation, he'd forget about skydiving.

"Middle class and definitely not pampered."

He still looked restless, and she was trying to think of something to talk about when she spotted two books on the coffee table that hadn't been there earlier. She looked more closely and saw that one was the new Scott Turow, the other a rather scholarly volume on the cosmos that she'd tried to get into but set aside for something lighter. "You *read*?"

His mouth twitched as he slouched into the sectional sofa. "Only if I can't get anybody to do it for me."

"Very funny." She settled at the opposite end of the couch, unhappy with the revelation that he enjoyed books. Roo moved closer, ready to guard her in case Kevin took it into his mind to tackle her again.

You wish.

"Okay, I'll concede that you're not quite as . . . intellectually impaired as you appear to be."

"Let me put that in my press kit."

She'd set her trap quite nicely. "That being the case, why do you keep doing such stupid things?"

"Like what?"

"Like skydiving. Skiing from a helicopter. Then there's that dirt-track racing you did right after training camp."

"You seem to know a lot about me."

"Only because you're part of the family business, so don't take it personally. Besides, everybody in Chicago knows what you've been up to."

"The media make a big deal out of nothing."

"It's not exactly nothing." She kicked off her rabbit's-head slippers and tucked her feet under her. "I don't get it. You've always been the poster boy for pro athletes. You don't drive drunk or beat up women. You show up early for practice and stay late. No gambling scandals, no grandstanding, not even much trash talk. Then all of a sudden you freak out."

"I haven't freaked out."

"What else can you call it?"

He cocked his head. "They sent you up here to spy on me, didn't they?"

She laughed, even though it compromised her role as a rich bitch. "I'm the last person any of them would trust with team business. I'm sort of a geek." She made an X over her heart. "Come on, Kevin. Cross my heart, I won't say a thing. Tell me what's going on."

"I enjoy a little excitement, and I'm not apologizing for it."

She wanted more, so she continued her exploring mission. "Don't your lady friends worry about you?"

"If you want to know about my love life, just ask. That way I can have the pleasure of telling you to mind your own business."

"Why would I want to know about your love life?"

"You tell me."

She regarded him demurely. "I was just wondering if you find your women in international catalogs? Or maybe on the Web? I know there are groups that specialize in helping lonely American men find foreign women because I've seen the pictures. 'Twenty-one-year-old Russian beauty. Plays classical piano in the nude, writes erotic novels in her spare time, wants to share her dandy with a Yankee doodle.'"

Unfortunately, he laughed instead of being offended. "I date American women, too."

"Not many, I'll bet."

"Did anybody ever mention that you're nosy?"

"I'm a writer. It goes with the profession." Maybe it was her imagination, but he didn't look as restless as when he'd sat down, so she decided to keep poking. "Tell me about your family."

"Not much to tell. I'm a PK."

Prize kisser? "Pathetic klutz?"

He grinned and crossed his ankles on the edge of the coffee table. "Preacher's kid. Fourth generation, depending on how you count."

"Oh, yes. I remember reading that. Fourth generation, huh?"

"My father was a Methodist minister, son of a Methodist minister, who was the grandson of one of the old Methodist circuit riders who carried the gospel into the wilderness."

"That must be where your daredevil blood comes from. The circuit rider."

"It sure didn't come from my father. A great guy, but not exactly what you'd call a risk taker. Pretty much an egghead." He smiled. "Like you. Except more polite."

She ignored that. "He's no longer alive?"

"He died about six years ago. He was fifty-one when I was born."

"What about your mother?"

"I lost her eighteen months ago. She was older, too. A big reader, the head of the historical society, into genealogy. Summers were the high-light of my parents' lives."

"Skinny-dipping in the Bahamas?"

He laughed. "Not quite. We all went to a Methodist church camp-ground in northern Michigan. It's been in my family for generations."

"Your family owned a campground?"

"Complete with cabins and a big old wooden Tabernacle for church services. I had to go with them every summer until I was fifteen, and then I rebelled."

"They must have wondered how they hatched you."

His eyes grew shuttered. "Every day. What about you?"

"An orphan." She said the word lightly, the way she always did when anyone asked, but it felt lumpy.

"I thought Bert only married Vegas showgirls." The way his eyes swept from her crimson hair to linger on her modest chest told her he didn't believe she could have sequins in her gene pool.

"My mother was in the chorus at The Sands. She was Bert's third wife, and she died when I was two. She was flying to Aspen to celebrate her divorce."

"You and Phoebe didn't have the same mother?"

"No. Phoebe's mother was his first wife. She was in the chorus at The Flamingo."

"I never met Bert Somerville, but from what I've heard, he wasn't an easy man to live with."

"Fortunately, he sent me off to boarding school when I was five. Before that, I remember a stream of very attractive nannies."

"Interesting." He dropped his feet from the coffee table and picked up the pair of silver-framed Rēvo sunglasses he'd left there. Molly gazed at them with envy. Two hundred and seventy dollars at Marshall Field's.

Daphne set the sunglasses that had fallen from Benny's pocket on her own nose and bent over to admire her reflection in the pond. *Parfait!* (She believed French was the best language for contemplating personal appearance.)

"Hey!" Benny called out from behind her.

Plop! The sunglasses slid from her nose into the pond.

Kevin rose from the couch, and she could feel his energy filling the room. "Where are you going?" she asked.

"Out for a while. I need some fresh air."

"Out where?"

He folded in the stems of his sunglasses, the motion deliberate. "It's been nice talking to you, but I think I've had enough questions from management for now."

"I told you. I'm not management."

"You've got a financial stake in the Stars. In my book that makes you management."

"Okay. So management wants to know where you're going."

"Skiing. Do you have a problem with that?"

No, but she was fairly sure Dan would. "There's just one alpine ski area around here, and the drop is only a hundred and twenty feet. That's not enough challenge for you."

"Damn."

She concealed her amusement.

"I'll go cross-country, then," he said. "I've heard there are some world class trails up here."

"Not enough snow."

"I'm going to find that *airfield*!" He shot toward the coat closet.

"No! We'll—we'll hike."

"Hike?" He looked as if she'd suggested bird watching.

She thought fast. "There's a really treacherous path along the bluffs. It's so dangerous that it's closed off when there's wind or even a hint of snow, but I know a back way to get to it. Except you need to be really sure you want to do this. It's narrow and icy, and the slightest misstep could send you plunging to your death."

"You're making this up."

"I don't have that much imagination."

"You're a writer."

"Children's books. They're completely nonviolent. Now, if you want to stand around and talk all morning, that's up to you. But I'd like a little adventure."

She'd finally caught his interest.

"Let's get to it, then."

They had a good time on their hike, even though Molly never quite managed to locate the treacherous path she'd promised Kevin—maybe because she'd invented it. Still, the bluff they crossed was bitterly cold and windy, so he didn't complain too much. He even reached out to take her hand on an icy stretch, but she wasn't that foolish. Instead, she gave him a snooty look and told him he'd have to manage on his own because she wasn't going to prop him up every time he saw a little ice and got scared.

He'd laughed and climbed up on a slippery pile of rocks. The sight of him facing the winter-gray water, head thrown back, wind tearing through that dark blond hair had stolen her breath.

For the rest of their walk she'd forgotten to be obnoxious, and they had far too much fun. By the time they returned to the house, her teeth were chattering from the cold, but every womanly part of her burned.

He shrugged out of his coat and rubbed his hands. "I wouldn't mind using your hot tub."

And she wouldn't mind using his hot body. "Go ahead. I have to get back to work." As Molly rushed toward the loft, she found herself remembering what Phoebe had once said to her.

When you're raised as we were, Moll, casual sex is a snake pit. We need a love that's soul-deep, and I'm here to testify that you don't find it by bed-hopping.

Although Molly had never bed-hopped, she knew that Phoebe was right. Except what was a twenty-seven-year-old woman with a healthy body, but no soul-deep love, supposed to do? If only Kevin had acted shallow and stupid on their walk . . . but he hadn't talked about football once. Instead, they'd talked about books, living in Chicago, and their mutual passion for *This Is Spinal Tap.*

She couldn't concentrate on Daphne, so she flipped open her laptop to work on "Making Out—How Far to Go?" The subject depressed her even more.

By her junior year at Northwestern she'd grown sick of waiting for her Great Love Story to come along, so she'd decided to forget about soul-deep love and settle for soul-deep caring with a boy she'd been dating for a month. But losing her virginity had been a mistake. The affair had left her depressed, and she knew that Phoebe had been right. She wasn't made for casual sex.

A few years later she'd convinced herself she finally cared enough about a man to try again. He'd been intelligent and charming, but the wrenching sadness following the affair had taken months to fade.

She'd had a number of boyfriends since then, but no lovers, and she'd done her best to sublimate her sex drive with hard work and good friends. Chastity might be old-fashioned, but sex was an emotional quagmire for a woman who hadn't known love until she was fifteen. So why did she keep thinking about it, especially with Kevin Tucker in the house?

Because she was only human, and the Stars quarterback was a delectable piece of body candy, a walking aphrodisiac, a grown-up toy boy. She moaned, glared at her keyboard, and forced herself to concentrate.

At five she heard him leave the house. By seven "Making Out—How Far to Go?" was nearly done. Unfortunately, the subject had left her edgy and more than a little aroused. She called Janine, but her friend wasn't home, so she went downstairs and stared at herself in the small kitchen mirror. It was too late for the stores to be open, or she could have run out for hair color. Maybe she'd just cut it. That crew cut a few years ago hadn't been so bad.

She was lying to herself. It had been horrible.

She grabbed a Lean Cuisine instead of the scissors and ate at the kitchen counter. Afterward she dug the marshmallows out of a carton of Rocky Road ice cream. Finally she grabbed her drawing pad and settled in front of the fireplace to sketch. But she hadn't slept well, and before long her lids grew heavy. Kevin's arrival sometime after midnight made her bolt up.

"Hey, Daphne."

She rubbed her eyes. "Hello, Karl."

He hung his coat on the back of a chair. It reeked of perfume. "This thing needs to air out."

"I'll say." Jealousy gnawed at her. While she'd been drooling over Kevin's body and obsessing about her own hang-ups, she'd ignored one important fact: He hadn't shown the slightest interest in her. "You must have been busy," she said. "It smells like more than one brand. All of them domestic, or did you find an au pair somewhere?"

"I wasn't that lucky. The women were unfortunately American, and they all talked too much." His pointed look said she did, too.

"And I'll bet lots of the words had more than one syllable, so you probably have a headache." She needed to stop this. He wasn't nearly as dumb as she wanted him to be, and if she didn't watch herself, he was going to figure out exactly how much interest she took in his personal life.

He looked more aggravated than angry. "I happen to like to relax when I'm on a date. I don't want to debate world politics or discuss global warming or be forced to listen to people with unpredictable personal hygiene recite bad poetry."

"Gee, and those are all my favorite things."

He shook his head, then rose and stretched, lengthening that lean body vertebra by vertebra. He was already bored with her. Probably because she hadn't entertained him by reciting his career statistics.

"I'd better turn in," he said. "I'm taking off first thing tomorrow, so if I don't see you, thanks for the hospitality."

She managed a yawn. "*Ciao,* babycakes." She knew he had to get back for practice, but that didn't ease her disappointment.

He smiled. "Night, Daphne."

She watched him mount the stairs, the denim tightening around those lean legs, molding his narrow hips, muscles rippling beneath his T-shirt.

Oh, God, she was drooling! And she was Phi Beta Kappa!

She was also aching and restless, blazingly dissatisfied with everything in her life.

"Damn it!" She knocked her sketch pad to the floor, jumped to her feet, and made a beeline for the bathroom to stare at her hair. She was going to shave it off!

No! She didn't want to be bald, and this time she wouldn't let herself act crazy.

She moved purposefully to the video center and pulled out the remake of *The Parent Trap*. Her inner child loved watching the twins get their parents back together, and her outer child loved Dennis Quaid's smile.

Kevin had that same crooked smile.

Resolutely, she took his game film from the VCR, put in *The Parent Trap*, and settled back to watch.

By two o'clock in the morning, Hallie and Annie had reunited their parents, but Molly was more restless than ever. She began surfing through old movies and infomercials, only to pause as she heard the familiar theme song of the old show, *Lace, Inc.*

"*Lace is on the case, oh yeah . . . Lace can solve the case, oh yeah . . .*" Two beautiful women ran across the screen, the sexy detectives Sable Drake and Ginger Hill.

Lace, Inc. had been one of Molly's favorite shows as a child. She'd wanted to be Sable, the smart brunette, played by actress Mallory McCoy. Ginger was the redheaded sexpot karate expert. *Lace, Inc.* had been a jiggle show, but Molly hadn't cared about that. She'd simply enjoyed watching women beat up the bad guys for a change.

The opening credits showed Mallory McCoy first, then Lilly Sherman, who'd played Ginger Hill. Molly sat up straighter as she remembered a fragment of conversation she'd once overheard at Stars' headquarters indicating that Lilly Sherman had some sort of connection with Kevin. She hadn't wanted anyone to know she was interested, so she didn't ask any questions. She studied the actress more carefully.

She wore her trademark tight pants, tube top, and high heels. Her long red hair curled around her shoulders, and her eyes batted seduc-

tively at the camera. Even with a dated hairstyle and big gold hoop ear-
rings, she was a knockout.

Sherman must be in her forties by now, surely a little old to be one of
Kevin's women, so what was their connection? A photograph she'd seen
of the actress a few years ago showed that she'd gained weight since the
television show. She was still a beautiful woman, though, so it was possible they'd had a fling.

Molly stabbed the remote, and a cosmetics commercial came on.
Maybe that's what she needed. A complete makeover.

She flipped off the TV and headed upstairs. Somehow she didn't
think a makeover would fix what was wrong with her.

After a hot shower she slipped into one of the Irish linen nightgowns
she'd bought when she was rich. It still made her feel like a heroine in a
Georgette Heyer novel. She carried her notepad to bed so she could
think more about Daphne, but the surge of creativity she'd experienced
that afternoon had vanished.

Roo snored softly at the foot of the bed. Molly told herself she was
getting sleepy. She wasn't.

Maybe she could finish polishing her article, but as she made her way
to the loft to get her laptop, she glanced into the guest bathroom. It had
two doors—the one she was standing in and a second one across from
it that led directly into the bedroom where he slept. That door was ajar.

Her restless, twitchy legs carried her onto the tile.

She saw a Louis Vuitton shaving kit sitting on the counter. She
couldn't imagine Kevin buying it for himself, so it must have been a gift
from one of his international beauties. She moved closer and saw a red
toothbrush with crisp white bristles. He'd put the cap back on the tube
of Aquafresh.

She brushed her fingertip over the lid of a column of deodorant, then
reached for a frosted glass bottle of very expensive aftershave. She
unscrewed the stopper and drew it to her nose. Did it smell like Kevin?
He wasn't one of those men who drowned himself in cologne, and she
hadn't gotten close enough to know for sure, but something familiar
about the scent made her close her eyes and inhale more deeply. She
shivered and set it down, then glanced into the open shaving kit.

Lying next to a bottle of ibuprofen and a tube of Neosporin was Kevin's Super Bowl ring. She knew he'd earned it in the early days of his career as Cal Bonner's backup. It surprised her to see a championship ring tossed so carelessly in the bottom of a shaving kit, but then everything she knew about Kevin said he wouldn't want to wear a ring that had been earned when someone else was in charge.

She began to move away, only to pause as she saw what else lay in the shaving kit.

A condom.

No big deal. Of course he'd carry condoms with him. He probably had a whole crate of them. She picked it up and studied it. It seemed to be an ordinary condom. So why was she staring at it?

This was insane! All day she'd been acting like a woman obsessed. If she didn't pull herself together, she'd be boiling a bunny just like crazy Glenn Close.

She winced. *Sorry, Daphne.*

One peek. That was it. She'd just take one peek at him sleeping and then she'd leave.

She moved toward the bedroom door and slowly pushed it open.

3

Late that night Daphne sneaked into Benny's badger den with the scary Halloween mask fastened around her head . . .
—*Daphne Plants a Pumpkin Patch*

A dim wedge of light from the hallway fell across the carpet. Molly could make out a large shape beneath the bedcovers. Her heart hammered with the excitement of the forbidden. She took a tentative step inside.

The same dangerous energy shot through her that she'd felt when she was seventeen, right before she'd pulled the fire alarm. She moved closer. Just one look and then she'd leave.

He lay on his side, turned away from her. The sound of his breathing was deep and slow. She remembered old Westerns where the gunslinger woke up at the slightest sound, and she envisioned a rumple-haired Kevin pointing a Colt .45 at her belly.

She'd pretend she was sleepwalking.

He'd left his shoes on the floor, and she pushed one of them aside with her foot. It made a slight rustle as it brushed over the carpet, but he didn't move. She pushed aside its mate, but he didn't react to that either. So much for the Colt .45.

Her palms grew damp. She rubbed them on her gown. Then she bumped ever so gently against the end of the bed.

He was dead to the world.

Now that she knew what he looked like asleep, she'd leave.

She tried to, but her feet took her to the other side of the bed instead, where she could see his face.

Andrew slept like this. Fireworks could explode next to her nephew, and he wouldn't stir. But Kevin Tucker didn't look at all like Andrew. She took in his amazing profile—strong forehead, angled cheekbones, and straight, perfectly proportioned nose. He was a football player, so he must have broken it a few times, but there was no bump.

This was a terrible invasion of his privacy. Inexcusable. But as she gazed down at his rumpled dark blond hair, she could barely resist brushing it back from his brow.

One perfectly sculpted shoulder rose above the covers. She wanted to lick it.

That's it! She'd lost her mind. And she didn't care.

The condom was still in her hand and Kevin Tucker lay under the blankets—naked, if that bare shoulder was any indication. What if she crawled in with him?

It was unthinkable.

But who would know? He might not even wake up. And if he did? He'd be the last person to tell the world he'd been with the owner's oversexed sister.

Her heart was beating so fast she was lightheaded. Was she really thinking about doing this?

There'd be no emotional aftermath. How could there be when she didn't harbor even the illusion of a soul-deep love? As for what he'd think of her . . . He was used to having women throw themselves at him, so he'd hardly be surprised.

She could see the fire alarm hanging on the wall right in front of her, and she told herself not to touch it. But her hands tingled, and her breath came fast and shallow. She'd run out of willpower. She was tired of her restlessness, her twitchy feet. Tired of mutilating her hair because she didn't know how to fix herself. Fed up from too many years trying to be perfect. Her skin was damp with desire and a growing sense of horror as she watched herself slide off her bunny slippers.

Put those right back on!

But she didn't. And the fire alarm clanged in her head.

She reached for the hem of her nightgown . . . pulled it over her head . . . stood naked and trembling. Appalled, she watched her fingers curl around the covers and tug. Even as the blankets fell back, she told herself she wasn't going to do it. But her breasts were tingling, her body crying out with need.

She set her hip on the mattress, then slowly slipped her legs beneath the covers. Oh, God, she was really doing this. She was naked, and she'd climbed into bed with Kevin Tucker.

Who let out a soft snore and rolled over, taking most of the covers with him.

She stared at his back and knew she'd just been given a divine sign telling her to leave. She had to get out of his bed right this minute!

Instead, she curled around him, pressed her breasts against his back, breathed him in. There . . . that whiff of musky aftershave. It had been so long since she'd touched a man like this.

He stirred, shifted, muttered something as if he were dreaming.

The shriek of the fire alarm grew louder. She slid her arm around him and stroked his chest.

Only for a minute, she told herself. And then she'd leave.

Kevin felt his old girlfriend Katya's hand on his chest. He'd been standing in his garage with the first car he'd ever owned and Eric Clapton. Eric had been giving him a guitar lesson, but instead of a guitar, Kevin kept trying to play a leaf rake. Then he looked up, and Eric was gone. He was in this weird log room with Katya.

She kept stroking his chest, and he realized that she was naked. He forgot about Eric's guitar lesson as blood rushed to his groin.

He'd broken it off with Katya months ago, but now he had to have her. She used to wear bad perfume. Too strong. It was a stupid reason to break up with a woman, because now she smelled like cinnamon rolls.

Good smell. Sexy smell. Made him sweat. He couldn't remember being this turned on by her when they were together. No sense of humor. Too much time putting on makeup. But now he needed her right away. Right that moment.

He rolled toward her. Curled his hand around her bottom. It felt different. Fleshier. More to squeeze.

He ached, and she smelled so good. Like oranges now. And her breasts were full against his chest—warm, soft, juicy oranges—and her mouth was on his, and her hands were all over him. Playing. Stroking. Finding their way to his cock.

He groaned as she caressed him. He smelled her woman's smell and knew he wouldn't last long. His arm didn't want to move, but he had to feel her.

She was slick, wet honey.

He moaned and rolled over. On top of her. Pushed inside her. It didn't happen easily. Strange.

The dream began to fade, but not his lust. He was feverish with it. The smell of soap, shampoo, and woman enflamed him. He thrust again and again, dragged open his eyes, and . . . couldn't believe what he saw!

He was buried inside Daphne Somerville.

He tried to say something, but he was long past talking. His blood pounded, his heart raced. There was a roaring in his head. He exploded.

At that moment everything inside Molly went cold. *No! Not yet!*

She felt his shudder. His weight crushed her, driving her into the mattress. Much too late, her sanity returned.

He went slack. Dead weight on top of her. Useless dead weight.

It was over. *Already!* And she couldn't even blame him for being the worst lover in history because she'd gotten exactly what she deserved. Nothing at all.

He jerked his head to clear it, then pulled out of her and erupted from the covers. *"What in the hell are you doing?"*

She wanted to yell at him for being such a disappointment, wanted to yell at herself even more. Once again she'd been caught pulling the fire alarm, but she wasn't seventeen any longer. She felt old and defeated.

Humiliation burned through her. "S-s-sleepwalking?"

"Sleepwalking, *my ass!*" He vaulted out of bed and stalked toward the bathroom. "Don't you dare move!"

Too late she remembered that Kevin had a reputation for holding grudges. Last year it had turned a rematch against the Steelers into a bloodbath, and the year before that he'd gone after a three-hundred-pound Viking defensive tackle. She scrambled from the bed and looked frantically for her nightgown.

A stream of obscenities erupted from the bathroom.

Where was her gown?

He shot back out, naked and furious. "Where the hell did you get that condom?"

"From your—your shaving kit." She spotted her linen gown, snatched it up, and clutched it to her breasts.

"My shaving kit?" He rushed back into the bathroom. "You pulled it from my— Shit!"

"It was . . . an impulse. A—a sleepwalking accident." She edged toward the hall door, but he reappeared before she could get there, charging across the carpet and grabbing her arm, giving her a shake.

"Do you know how long that thing was in there?"

Not nearly long enough! And then she realized he was talking about the condom. "What are you trying to say?"

He dropped her arm and pointed toward the bathroom. "I'm trying to say that it's been in there forever, and the son of a bitch *broke!*"

Exactly three seconds ticked by. Then her knees gave out. She sagged into the chair across from the bed.

"Well?" he barked.

Her fuzzy brain started working again. "Don't worry about it." Too late she grew conscious of the dampness between her thighs. "It's the wrong time of the month."

"There isn't any wrong time of the month." He flipped on the floor lamp, exposing more than she wanted him to see of her very ordinary, very naked body.

"There is for me. I'm as regular as a clock." She didn't want to talk to him about her period. She clutched her nightgown and tried to figure out how to get it back on without showing more of herself than she already had.

He didn't seem the slightest bit interested in either her nudity or his. "What the hell were you doing poking around in my shaving kit?"

"It, uh, was open, and I just happened to look in, and . . ." She cleared her throat. "If it was so old, why were you still carrying it around?"

"I forgot about it!"

"That's a stupid reason."

Those Astroturf-green eyes were murderous. "Are you trying to blame this on me?"

She drew a deep breath. "No. No, I'm not." It was time to stop acting like a coward and face the music. She stood up and pulled the night-gown over her head. "I'm sorry, Kevin. Really. I've been acting crazy lately."

"You're not telling me a damn thing."

"I apologize. I'm embarrassed." Her voice quivered. "Actually, I'm beyond embarrassment. I'm completely humiliated. I—I hope you can forget about this."

"Not likely." He grabbed a pair of dark green boxers from the floor and shoved his legs in.

"I'm sorry." She deserved to grovel, but since that didn't appear to be working, she reverted to being the world-weary, spoiled heiress. "The truth is, I was lonesome and you were available. You have a—reputation as a playboy. I didn't think you'd mind."

"I was *available*?" The air crackled. "Let's think about this. Let's think about what this would be called if the situation was reversed?"

"I don't know what you're talking about."

"What would this situation be called, for example, if I'd decided to crawl in bed with you—a nonconsenting female!"

"It's—" Her fingers fidgeted with the skirt of her nightgown. "Uh, yes, I see what you mean."

His eyes narrowed, and his voice grew low and dangerous. "It would be called rape."

"You're not seriously trying to say that I—I raped you?"

He regarded her coldly. "Yeah, I think I am."

This was far worse than she'd imagined. "That's ridiculous. You—you weren't nonconsenting!"

"Only because I was asleep and I thought you were someone else."

That stung. "I see."

He didn't back off. If anything, his jaw hardened. "Contrary to what you seem to think, I like having a relationship before I have sex. And I don't let anybody use me."

Which was exactly what she'd done. She wanted to cry. "I'm sorry, Kevin. Both of us know my behavior was outrageous. Could we forget about this?"

"I don't have much choice." He bit off his words. "It's not something I want to read about in the papers."

She backed toward the door. "I hope you realize I'll never say anything."

He regarded her with disgust.

Her face crumpled. "I'm sorry. Really."

4

Daphne jumped off her skateboard and crouched down in the long weeds so she could peer into the nest.

—*Daphne Finds a Baby Rabbit*
(preliminary notes)

K evin dropped back into the pocket. Sixty-five thousand screaming fans were on their feet, but a perfect stillness cocooned him. He didn't think about the fans, the TV cameras, about the *Monday Night Football* crew in the booth. He didn't think about anything except what he'd been born to do—play the game that had been invented just for him.

Leon Tippett, his favorite receiver, ran the pattern perfectly and broke free, ready for that sweet moment when Kevin would drill the ball into his hands.

Then, in an instant, the play turned to crap. Their safety came out of nowhere, ready to pick off the pass.

Adrenaline flooded Kevin's body. He was deep behind the line of scrimmage, and he needed another receiver, but Jamal was down, and Stubs had double coverage.

Briggs and Washington broke through the Stars' line and bore down. Those same fire-breathing monsters, disguised as Tampa Bay defensive ends, had dislocated his shoulder last year, but Kevin wasn't about to throw the ball away. With the recklessness that had been causing him so much trouble lately, he looked to the left . . . and then made a sharp, blind, *insane* cut to the right. He needed a hole in that wall of white jerseys. He willed it to be there. And found it.

With the agility that had become his trademark, he slipped through, leaving Briggs and Washington grabbing air. He spun and shook off a defender who outweighed him by eighty pounds.

Another cut. A jitterbug. Then he put on the steam.

Off the field he was a big man, six feet two and 193 pounds of muscle, but here in the Land of Mutant Giants he was small, graceful, and very fast. His feet conquered the artificial turf. The lights in the dome turned his gold helmet into a meteor, his aqua jersey into a banner woven from the heavens. Human poetry. God-kissed. Blessed among men. He carried the ball across the goal line into the end zone.

And when the official signaled the touchdown, Kevin was still standing.

The postgame party was at Kinney's house, and from the moment Kevin walked in the door, women started to grab him.

"Fabulous game, Kevin."

"Kevin, *querido,* over here!"

"You were awesome! I'm hoarse from screaming!"

"Were you excited when you took it in? God, I know you were excited, but how did it really feel?"

"*¡Felicitación!*"

"Kevin, *chéri!*"

Charm came easily to Kevin, and he flashed his smile while he untangled himself from all but two of the most persistent.

"You like your women beautiful and silent," his best friend's wife had said the last time they'd talked. "But most women aren't silent, so you home in on foreign babes with limited English. A classic case of intimacy avoidance."

Kevin remembered giving her a lazy once-over. "Is that so? Well, listen up, Dr. Jane Darlington Bonner. I'll be intimate with you anytime you want."

"Over my dead body," her husband, Cal, had responded from across the dinner table.

Even though Cal was his best friend, Kevin enjoyed giving him a hard time. It had been that way since the days he'd been the old man's resentful backup. Now, however, Cal was retired from football and beginning his residency in internal medicine at a hospital in North Carolina.

Kevin couldn't resist needling him. "It's a matter of principle, old man. I need to prove a point."

"Yeah, well, prove it with your own woman, and leave mine alone."

Jane had laughed, kissed her husband, given their daughter, Rosie, a napkin, and picked up their new son, Tyler. Kevin smiled as he remembered Cal's response when he'd asked about the Post-it notes he kept seeing on Ty's diapers.

"It's because I won't let her write on his legs anymore."

"Still at it, is she?"

"Arms, legs—the poor kid was turning into a walking scientific notebook. But it's gotten better since I started tucking Post-its in all her pockets."

Jane's habit of absentmindedly jotting down complex equations on unorthodox surfaces was well known, and Rosie Bonner piped up.

"Once she wrote on my foot. Didn't you, Mommy? And another time—"

Dr. Jane pushed a drumstick into her daughter's mouth.

Kevin smiled at the memory, only to be interrupted as the beautiful Frenchwoman on his right shouted over the music. "*Tu es fatigué, chéri?*"

Kevin had a facility with languages, but he'd learned to keep it hidden. "Thanks, but I don't want anything to eat right now. Hey, let me introduce you to Stubs Brady. I think you two might have a lot in common. And—Heather, is it?—my buddy Leon has been watching you with lascivious intent all evening."

"What kind of tent?"

Definitely time to shed a few females.

He'd never admit to Jane that she was right about his preference in women. But unlike some of his teammates, who paid lip service to the notion of giving all they had to the game, Kevin really did. Not only his body and mind but his heart as well, and you couldn't do that with a high-maintenance female in your life. Beautiful and undemanding, that's what he wanted, and foreign women fit the bill.

Playing for the Stars was everything that mattered to him, and he wouldn't let anybody get in the way of that. He loved wearing the aqua and gold uniform, taking the field in the Midwest Sports Dome, and most of all, working for Phoebe and Dan Calebow. Maybe it was the result of a childhood spent as a preacher's kid, but there was honor in being a Chicago Star, something that couldn't be said for every NFL team.

When you played for the Calebows, respect for the game was more important than the bottom line. The Stars weren't the team for thugs or prima donnas, and during the course of his career Kevin had seen some brilliant talent traded because those players hadn't measured up to Phoebe and Dan's standards of character. Kevin couldn't imagine playing for anyone else, and when he no longer got the job done for the Stars on the field, then he'd retire to coaching.

Coaching the Stars.

But two things had happened this season to jeopardize his dreams. One was his own fault—the crazy recklessness that had hit him right after training camp. He'd always had a reckless streak but, until now, he'd restricted it to off season. The other was Daphne Somerville's midnight visit to his bedroom. That had done more to jeopardize his career than all the skydiving and dirt-bike racing in the world.

He was a sound sleeper, and it hadn't been the first time he'd awakened in the middle of making love, but up until then he'd always chosen his partners. Ironically, if it hadn't been for her family connections, he might have thought about choosing her. Maybe it was the appeal of forbidden fruit, but he'd had a great time with her. She'd kept him on his toes and made him laugh. Although he'd been careful not to let her see it, he'd found himself watching her. She moved with a rich girl's confidence he'd found sexy. Her body might not be flashy, but everything was in the right place, and he'd definitely noticed.

Even so, he'd kept his distance. She was the boss's sister, and he never fraternized with women connected with the team—no coaches' daughters, front-office secretaries, or even teammates' cousins. Despite that, look what had happened.

Just thinking about it made him angry all over again. Not even a hotshot quarterback was more important to the Calebows than family, and if they ever found out what had happened, he was the one they'd be coming after for explanations.

His conscience was going to force him to call her soon. Just once to make certain there hadn't been any consequences. There wouldn't be, he told himself, and he wasn't going to worry about it, especially now, when he couldn't afford any distractions. On Sunday, they were playing in the AFC Championship, and his game had to be flawless. Then his ultimate dream would come true. He'd be taking the Stars to the Super Bowl.

But six days later his dream was snatched away. And he had no one to blame but himself.

By working day and night, Molly finished *Daphne Takes a Tumble* and put it in the mail the same week the Stars lost the AFC Championship. With fifteen seconds left on the clock, Kevin Tucker had refused to play it safe and thrown into double coverage. His pass was intercepted, and the Stars had lost by a field goal.

Molly fixed herself a cup of tea to ward off the chill of the January evening and took it over to her worktable. She had an article due for *Chik,* but instead of turning on her laptop, she picked up the legal pad she'd left on the couch to jot down some ideas she had for a new book, *Daphne Finds a Baby Rabbit.*

The telephone rang just as she sat down. "Hello."

"Daphne? It's Kevin Tucker."

Tea splashed into the saucer, and the breath went out of her. Once she'd had a crush on this man. Now just the sound of his voice terrified her.

She forced in air. Since he was still calling her Daphne, he must not have talked to anyone about her. That was good. She didn't want him talking about her, didn't even want him to think of her. "How did you get my number?"

"I made you give it to me."

She'd managed to forget. "I, uh . . . What can I do for you?"

"With the season over, I'm getting ready to leave town for a while. I wanted to be sure there weren't any . . . unfortunate consequences from . . . what happened."

"No! No consequences at all. Of course not."

"That's good."

Beneath his chilly response, she heard relief. At the same time she saw a way to make things easier, and she jumped at it. "I'm coming, darling!" she called out to an imaginary person.

"I take it you're not alone."

"No, I'm not." Again the raised voice. "I'm on the phone, Benny! I'll be there in a moment, sweetheart." She winced. Couldn't she have thought of a better name?

Roo trotted in from the kitchen to see what was up. She clutched the receiver tighter. "I appreciate your call, Kevin, but there was no need."

"As long as everything's—"

"Everything's wonderful, but I have to go. Sorry about the game. And thanks for calling." Her hand was still trembling when she disconnected.

She had just talked with the father of her unborn baby.

Her palm settled over her flat abdomen. She still hadn't completely absorbed the fact that she was pregnant. When her period hadn't arrived on schedule, she'd convinced herself that stress was the cause. But her breasts had grown increasingly tender, she'd begun to feel nauseated, and two days ago, she'd finally bought a home pregnancy test. The result had left her so panic-stricken she'd rushed out and bought another one.

There was no mistake. She was going to have Kevin Tucker's baby.

But her first thoughts hadn't been of him. They'd been of Dan and Phoebe. Family was the center of their existence, and neither of them would be able to imagine raising a child without the other. This was going to devastate them.

When she'd finally considered Kevin, she'd known she had to make certain he never found out. He'd been her unwilling victim, and she would bear the consequences alone.

It wouldn't be all that difficult to keep him in the dark. With the season over, there was little chance she'd run into him, and she'd simply stay away from Stars headquarters when they started practice in the summer. Except for a few of Dan and Phoebe's team parties, she'd never socialized much with the players. Eventually Kevin might hear that she'd had a baby, but this morning's phone call would make him believe there had been another man in her life.

She gazed through the windows of her loft into the winter sky. Although it wasn't even six o'clock, it was already dark. She stretched out on the couch.

Until two days ago she'd never considered single motherhood. She hadn't thought much about motherhood at all. Now she couldn't think of anything else. The restlessness that had always seemed like a back-beat to her life had vanished, leaving her with the unfamiliar feeling that everything was exactly as it should be. She'd finally have a family of her own.

Roo licked the hand she was dangling over the side of the couch. She closed her eyes and wove the daydreams that had taken over her imagi-nation now that her initial shock had worn off. A little boy? A girl? It didn't matter. She'd spent enough time with her nieces and nephew to know that she'd be a good mother regardless, and she'd love this baby enough for two parents.

Her baby. Her family.

Finally.

She stretched, content to the tips of her toes. This was what she'd been searching for all these years, a family of her very own. She couldn't remember ever feeling so peaceful. Even her hair was peaceful, no longer brutally short and back to its natural dark brown color. Just right for her.

Roo nudged her hand with his wet nose.

"Hungry, buddy?" She rose and was on her way to the kitchen to feed him when the phone rang again. Her pulse raced, but it was only Phoebe.

"Dan and I had a meeting in Lake Forest. We're on the Edens now, and he's hungry. Want to go to Yoshi's with us for dinner?"

"I'd love to."

"Great. See you in about half an hour."

As Molly hung up, the knowledge of how much she was going to hurt them hit hard. They wanted her to have exactly what they did—a deep, unconditional love that formed the foundation of both their lives. But most people weren't that lucky.

She slipped into her threadbare Dolce & Gabbana sweater and a skinny, ankle-length charcoal skirt she'd bought last spring for half off at Field's. Kevin's phone call had unsettled her, so she flipped on the television. Lately she'd gotten into the habit of watching reruns of *Lace, Inc.* The show was nostalgic for her, a link to one of the few pleasant parts of her childhood.

She still wondered about Kevin's connection to Lilly Sherman. Phoebe might know, but Molly was afraid to mention his name, even though Phoebe had no idea Molly had been with him at the Door County house.

"Lace is on the case, oh yeah . . . Lace can solve the case, oh yeah . . . "

Commercials followed the credits, and then Lilly Sherman as Ginger Hill bounced across the screen in a pair of tight white shorts, her breasts overflowing a bright green bikini top. Auburn hair billowed around her face, gold hoops brushed her cheekbones, and her seductive smile promised untold sensual delights.

The camera angle widened to show both detectives at the beach. In contrast to Ginger's skimpier apparel, Sable wore a high-cut maillot. Molly remembered there'd been an offscreen friendship between the two actresses.

The buzzer from the lobby sounded. She turned off the television and, a few minutes later, opened the door for her sister and brother-in-law.

Phoebe kissed her cheek. "You look pale. Are you all right?"

"It's January in Chicago. Everybody's pale." Molly squeezed her a moment longer than necessary. Celia the Hen, a motherly resident of Nightingale Woods who clucked over Daphne, had been created just for her sister.

"Hey, Miz Molly. We've missed you." Dan gave her his customary rib-crushing bear hug.

As she hugged him back, she thought how lucky she was to have them both. "It's only been two weeks since New Year's."

"And two weeks since you've been home. Phoebe gets cranky." He tossed his jacket over the back of the couch.

As Molly took Phoebe's coat, she smiled. Dan still considered their house Molly's real home. He didn't understand how she felt about her condo. "Dan, do you remember the first time we met? I tried to convince you Phoebe was beating me."

"Hard to forget something like that. I still remember what you told me. You said she wasn't entirely evil, just mildly twisted."

Phoebe laughed. "The good old days."

Molly gazed fondly at her sister. "I was such a little prig, it's a wonder you *didn't* beat me."

"Somerville girls had to find their own ways to survive."

One of us still does, Molly thought.

Roo adored Phoebe and pounced into her lap the moment she sat. "I'm so glad I got to see the illustrations for *Daphne Takes a Tumble* before you sent them off. The expression on Benny's face when his mountain bike slips in the rain puddle is priceless. Any ideas for a new book?"

She hesitated. "Still in the thinking stages."

"Hannah was delirious when Daphne bandaged Benny's paw. I don't think she expected Daphne to forgive him."

"Daphne is a very forgiving rabbit. Although she did use a pink lace ribbon for his bandage."

Phoebe laughed. "Benny needs to be more in touch with his feminine side. It's a wonderful book, Moll. You always manage to stick in one of life's important lessons and still be funny. I'm so glad you're writing."

"It's exactly what I always wanted to do. I just didn't know it."

"Speaking of that . . . Dan, did you remember—" Phoebe broke off as she realized Dan wasn't there. "He must have gone to the bathroom."

"I haven't cleaned in there for a couple of days. I hope it's not too—" Molly sucked in her breath and whirled around.

But it was too late. Dan was walking back in with the two empty boxes he'd seen in the wastebasket. The pregnancy test kits looked like loaded grenades in his big hands.

Molly bit her lip. She hadn't wanted to tell them yet. They were still dealing with the loss of the AFC Championship, and they didn't need another disappointment.

Phoebe couldn't see what her husband was holding until he dropped one of the boxes into her lap. She slowly picked it up. Her hand traveled to her cheek. "Molly?"

"I know you're twenty-seven years old," Dan said, "and we both try to respect your privacy, but I've got to ask about this."

He looked so upset that Molly couldn't bear it. He loved being a father, and he was going to have a harder time accepting this than Phoebe would.

Molly took the boxes and set them aside. "Why don't you sit down?"

He slowly folded his big body onto the couch next to his wife. Phoebe's hand instinctively crept into his. The two of them together against the world. Sometimes watching the love they had for each other made Molly feel lonely to the bottom of her soul.

She took the chair across from them and managed a shaky smile. "There's no easy way to tell you this. I'm going to have a baby."

Dan flinched, and Phoebe leaned against him.

"I know it's a shock, and I'm sorry for that. But I'm not sorry about the baby."

"Tell me there's going to be a wedding first."

Dan's lips had barely moved, and she was once again reminded of exactly how unbending he could be. If she didn't hold her ground now, he'd never give her any peace. "No wedding. And no daddy. That's not going to change, so you need to make peace with it."

Phoebe looked even more distressed. "I—I didn't know you were see-ing anyone special. You usually tell me."

Molly couldn't let her probe too deeply. "I share a lot with you, Phoeb, but not everything."

A muscle had started to tic in Dan's jaw, definitely a bad sign. "Who is he?"

"I'm not going to tell you," she said quietly. "This was my doing, not his. I don't want him in my life."

"You damn well wanted him in your life long enough to get pregnant!"

"Dan, don't." Phoebe had never been intimidated by Dan's hot temper, and she looked far more concerned about Molly. "Don't make a decision too quickly, Moll. How far along are you?"

"Only six weeks. And I'm not going to change my mind. There'll be just the baby and me. And both of you, I hope."

Dan shot up and began to pace. "You have no idea what you're getting yourself into."

She could have pointed out that thousands of single women had babies every year and that he was a bit old-fashioned in his outlook, but she knew him too well to waste her breath. Instead, she concentrated on practicalities.

"I can't stop either of you from worrying, but you need to remember that I'm better equipped than most single women to have a child. I'm nearly thirty, I love children, and I'm emotionally stable." For the first time in her life she felt as if that might be true.

"You're also broke most of the time." Dan's lips were tight.

"Daphne sales are going up slowly."

"Very slowly," he said.

"And I can do more freelancing. I won't even have to pay for child care because I work at home."

He regarded her stubbornly. "Children need a father."

She rose and walked to him. "They need a good man in their life, and I hope you'll be there for this baby because you're the best there is."

That got to him, and he hugged her. "We just want you to be happy."

"I know. That's why I love you both so much."

I just want her to be happy," Dan repeated to Phoebe as the two of them drove home that night after a strained dinner.

"We both do. But she's an independent woman, and she's made up her mind." Her brow knit with worry. "I suppose all we can do now is support her."

"It happened sometime around the beginning of December." Dan's eyes narrowed. "I promise you one thing, Phoebe. I'm going to find the son of a bitch who did this to her, and then I'm going to take his head off."

But finding him was easier said than done, and as one week slipped into another, Dan came no closer to discovering the truth. He made up excuses to phone Molly's friends and shamelessly pumped them for information, but no one remembered her dating anyone at the time. He pumped his own children with no more success. Out of desperation he finally hired a detective, a fact he neglected to mention to his wife, who would have ordered him to mind his own business. All he ended up with was a big bill and nothing he didn't already know.

In mid-February Dan and Phoebe took the kids to the Door County house for a long weekend of snowmobiling. They invited Molly to come along, but she said she was on deadline for *Chik* and couldn't stop work. He knew the real reason was that she didn't want any more lectures from him.

On Saturday afternoon he'd just brought Andrew inside to warm up from snowmobiling when Phoebe found him in the mudroom where they were taking off their boots.

"Have fun, pookie?"

"Yes!"

Dan grinned as Andrew flew across the wet floor in his socks and threw himself into her arms, something he generally did when he was separated from either one of them for more than an hour.

"I'm glad." She buried her lips in his hair, then gave him a nudge toward the kitchen. "Get your snack. The cider's hot, so let Tess pour it for you."

As Andrew ran off, Dan decided Phoebe looked particularly delectable in a pair of gold jeans with a soft brown sweater. He was just starting to reach for her when she held out a yellow credit card receipt. "I found this upstairs."

He glanced at it and saw Molly's name.

"It's a receipt from the little drugstore in town," Phoebe said. "Look at the date at the top."

He found it, but he still didn't understand why she seemed upset. "So what?"

She sagged against the washer. "Dan, that's when Kevin stayed here."

Kevin left the sidewalk café and began walking along the Cairns Esplanade toward his hotel. Palm trees swayed in the sunny February breeze, and boats bobbed in the harbor. After spending five days diving in the Coral Sea with the sharks that swam near the North Horn site of Australia's Great Barrier Reef, it was nice being back in civilization.

The city of Cairns on the northeastern coast of Queensland was the diving expedition's home port. Since the town had good restaurants and a couple of five-star hotels, Kevin had decided to stay around for a while. The city was far enough from Chicago that he wasn't in much danger of running into a Stars fan who wanted to know why he threw into double coverage late in the fourth quarter of the AFC Championship. Instead of giving the Stars the victory that would have taken them to the Super Bowl, he'd let his teammates down, and even swimming with a school of hammerheads wasn't making him forget that.

An Aussie hottie in a halter top and tight white shorts give him the twice-over, followed by an inviting smile. "Need a tour guide, Yank?"

"Thanks, not today."

She looked disappointed. He probably should take her up on her invitation, but he couldn't work up enough interest. He'd also ignored the seductive overtures of the sexy blond doctoral candidate who'd cooked on the dive boat, but that had been more understandable. She was one of the smart, high-maintenance women.

This was the heart of Queensland's monsoon season, and a splatter of raindrops hit him. He decided to work out at the hotel health club for a while, then head over to the casino for a few games of blackjack.

He'd just changed into his gym clothes when a sharp knock sounded at the door. He walked over and opened it. "Dan? What are you doing—"

That was as far as he got before Dan Calebow's fist came up to meet him.

Kevin staggered backward, caught the corner of the couch, and fell.

Adrenaline rushed through him, hot and fast. He shot back up, ready to take Dan apart. Then he hesitated, not because Dan was his boss but because the raw fury in his expression indicated that something was drastically wrong. Since Dan had been more understanding than Kevin had deserved about the game, Kevin knew it didn't have anything to do with that ill-advised pass.

It went against his grain not to fight back, but he forced himself to lower his fists. "You'd better have a good reason for that."

"You son of a bitch. Did you really think you were going to walk away?"

Seeing such contempt on the face of a man he respected made his gut clench. "Walk away from what?"

"It didn't mean anything to you, did it?" Dan sneered.

Kevin waited him out.

Dan came forward, his lip curled. "Why didn't you tell me you weren't alone when you stayed at my house in December?"

The hair on the back of Kevin's neck prickled. He chose his words carefully. "I didn't think it was up to me. I thought it was Daphne's business to tell you she'd been there."

"*Daphne?*"

Enough was enough, and Kevin's own temper snapped. "It wasn't my fault your nutcase of a sister-in-law showed up!"

"You don't even know her fucking *name?*"

Dan looked as if he was getting ready to spring again, and Kevin was angry enough to hope he would. "Stop right there! She told me her name was Daphne."

"Yeah, right," Dan scoffed. "Well, her name is Molly, you son of a bitch, and she's pregnant with your baby!"

Kevin felt as if he'd taken the sack of his life. "What are you talking about?"

"I'm talking about the fact that I've had a stomachful of high-priced athletes who think they have a God-given right to scatter illegitimate kids around like so much trash."

Kevin felt sick. She'd told him there hadn't been any consequences when he'd called. She'd even had her boyfriend with her.

"You could at least have had the decency to use a goddamn rubber!"

His brain started working again, and there was no way he'd take the blame for this. "I talked to Daph—to your sister-in-law before I left Chicago, and she said everything was fine. Maybe you'd better have this conversation with her boyfriend."

"She's a little preoccupied to have a boyfriend right now."

"She's holding out on you," he said carefully. "You made this trip for nothing. She's going with a guy named Benny."

"Benny?"

"I don't know how long they've been together, but I'm guessing he's the one responsible for her current condition."

"Benny's not her boyfriend, you arrogant son of a bitch! He's a fricking *badger*!"

Kevin stared at him, then headed for the wet bar. "Maybe we'd better start over from the beginning."

M olly parked her Beetle behind Phoebe's BMW. As she got out of the car, she dodged a mound of dingy, ice-crusted snow. Northern Illinois was in the grip of a frigid spell that showed every sign of lingering, but she didn't mind. February was the best time of year for curling up with a warm computer and a sketchbook, or just for daydreaming.

> Daphne couldn't wait until the baby rabbit was big enough to play with. They'd dress up in skirts with sparkly beads and say, "Oo-la-la! You look divine!" Then they'd drop water balloons on Benny and his friends.

Molly was glad her speech at the literacy luncheon was over and that Phoebe had come along for moral support. Although she loved visiting schools to read to children, giving speeches to adults made her nervous, especially with an unpredictable stomach.

A month had passed since she'd discovered she was pregnant, and every day the baby became more real to her. She hadn't been able to resist buying a tiny pair of unisex denim overalls, and she couldn't wait to start wearing maternity clothes, although, since she was only two and a half months along, that wasn't necessary yet.

She followed her sister inside the rambling stone farmhouse. It had been Dan's before he and Phoebe were married, and he hadn't uttered a word of complaint when Molly had moved in along with his new bride.

Roo raced out to growl hello, while his more mannerly sister, Kanga, trotted behind. Molly had left him here while she was at the luncheon, and as soon as she hung up her coat, she leaned over to greet both dogs. "Hey, Roo. Hello, Kanga, sweetie."

Both poodles rolled over to get their tummies scratched.

As Molly complied, she watched Phoebe slip the Hermès scarf she'd been wearing into the pocket of Andrew's jacket.

"What's with you?" Molly asked. "All afternoon you've been distracted."

"Distracted? What do you mean?"

Molly retrieved the scarf and held it out to her sister. "Andrew gave up cross-dressing when he turned four."

"Oh, dear. I guess—" She broke off as Dan appeared from the back of the house.

"What are you doing here?" Molly asked. "Phoebe told me you were traveling."

"I was." He kissed his wife. "Just got back."

"Did you sleep in those clothes? You look awful."

"It was a long flight. Come in the family room, will you, Molly?"

"Sure."

The dogs trailed behind her as she made her way toward the back of the house. The family room was part of the addition that had been built as the Calebow family had grown. It had lots of glass and comfortable seating areas, some with armchairs for reading, another with a table for doing homework or playing games. A state-of-the-art stereo system held everything from Raffi to Rachmaninoff.

"So where did you go anyway? I thought you were—" Molly's words died as she saw the large man with dark blond hair standing in the corner of the room. The green eyes she'd once found so alluring regarded her with undiluted hostility.

Her heart began to hammer. His clothes were as wrinkled as Dan's, and stubble covered his jaw. Although he had a fresh suntan, he didn't look like someone who'd come off a relaxing vacation. Instead, he looked dangerously wired and ready to detonate.

Molly remembered Pheobe's distraction that afternoon, her furtive expression when she'd slipped into the back of the room right after Molly's speech to take a call on her cell phone. There was nothing coincidental about this meeting. Somehow Phoebe and Dan had unearthed the truth.

Phoebe spoke with quiet determination. "Let's all sit down."

"I'll stand," Kevin said, his lips barely moving.

Molly felt sick and angry and panicked. "I don't know what's going on here, but I won't have any part of it." She spun around, only to have Kevin step forward and block her way.

"Don't even think about it."

"This has nothing to do with you."

"That's not what I hear." His cold eyes cut into hers like shards of green ice.

"You heard wrong."

"Molly, let's sit down so we can discuss this," Phoebe said. "Dan flew all the way to Australia to find Kevin, and the least you—"

Molly whirled toward her brother-in-law. "You flew to Australia?"

He gave her the same stubborn look she'd seen on his face when he'd refused to let her go to a co-ed sleepover after her high school prom. The same look she'd seen when he wouldn't let her postpone college to backpack through Europe. But she hadn't been a teenager for years, and something inside her snapped.

"You had no right!" Without planning it, she found herself hurtling across the room to get to him.

She wasn't a violent person. She wasn't even hot-tempered. She liked rabbits and fairy tale forests, china teapots and linen nightgowns. She'd never struck anyone, let alone someone she loved. Even so, she felt her hand curling into a fist and flying toward her brother-in-law.

"How could you?" She caught Dan in the chest.

"Molly!" her sister cried.

Dan's eyes widened in astonishment. Roo began to bark.

Guilt, anger, and fear coalesced into an ugly ball inside Molly. Dan backed away, but she went after him and landed another blow. "This isn't your business!"

"Molly, stop it!" Phoebe exclaimed.

"I'll never forgive you." She swung again.

"Molly!"

"It's my life!" she cried over Roo's frenzied barks and her sister's protests. "Why couldn't you stay out of it!"

A strong arm caught her around the waist before she could land another blow. Roo howled. Kevin drew her back against his chest. "Maybe you'd better calm down."

"Let me go!" She jabbed him with her elbow.

He grunted but didn't release her.

Roo clamped onto his ankle.

Kevin yelped, and Molly jabbed him again.

Kevin started to swear.

Dan joined in.

"Oh, for Pete's sake!" A shrill noise split the air.

5

Sometimes you need a friend really badly, but everyone's gone away for the day.

—*Daphne's Lonesome Day*

Molly's eardrums rang from the blast of the toy whistle clamped between Phoebe's teeth.

"That's enough!" Her sister marched forward. "Molly, you are off-side! Roo, let go! Kevin, get your hands off her. Now, everybody *sit down!*"

Kevin dropped his arm. Dan rubbed his chest. Roo released Kevin's pant leg.

Molly felt sick. Exactly what had she hoped to accomplish? She couldn't bear looking at anyone. The idea that her sister and brother-in-law must know by now how she'd attacked Kevin while he slept was beyond humiliating.

But she was accountable for what had happened, and she couldn't run away. Taking a cue from Daphne's fans, she grabbed her lovey for comfort and carried him to an armchair as far away from the rest of them as she could get. He gave her a sympathetic lick on the chin.

Dan took a seat on the couch. He wore the same stubborn expression that had unglued her. Phoebe perched next to him looking like a worried Vegas showgirl wearing mommy clothes. And Kevin . . .

His anger filled the room. He stood next to the fireplace, arms crossed over his chest, hands locked beneath his armpits, as if he didn't trust himself not to use them on her. How could she ever have had a crush on someone who was so dangerous?

That's when it sank in. Phoebe, Dan, Kevin . . . and her. The creator of Daphne the Bunny was up against the NFL.

Her only strategy lay in a strong offense. She'd look like a bitch, but it was the kindest thing she could do for Kevin. "Let's make it snappy. I have things to do, and this is just too boring for words."

A dark blond eyebrow shot to the middle of his forehead.

Phoebe sighed. "It's not going to work, Molly. He's too tough to scare off. We know Kevin is the father of your baby, and he's here to talk about the future."

She whirled toward Kevin. He hadn't told them! Phoebe would never be talking like this if she knew what Molly had done.

His eyes gave nothing away.

Why had he kept silent? Once Phoebe and Dan knew the truth, he'd be off the hook.

She turned toward her sister. "The future doesn't involve him. The truth is, I—"

Kevin sprang away from the fireplace. "Get your coat," he snapped. "We're going for a walk."

"I don't really—"

"Now!"

As much as she hated facing him, talking with Kevin alone would be easier than dealing with him in front of the Calebow Mafia. She set her lovey on the carpet and rose. "Stay here, Roo."

Phoebe picked up the poodle as he began to whine.

With her spine ramrod straight, Molly marched out of the room. Kevin caught up with her in the kitchen, gripped her arm, and hauled her into the laundry room. There he shoved Julie's pink and lavender ski jacket at her and snagged Dan's brown duffel coat from a hook for himself. He threw open the back door and gave her a none-too-gentle nudge outside.

Molly pulled on the coat and tugged at the zipper, but it didn't come close to meeting in the front, and the wind cut through her silk blouse.

Kevin didn't bother fastening Dan's coat, even though he only wore a summer weight knit shirt and khakis. The heat of his fury was keeping him warm.

She reached nervously into Julie's pocket and found an old knit cap with a faded Barbie patch. The remnants of a glittery silver pompon hung by a few threads at the top. She yanked it on over her hair. He pulled her to a flagstone path that led to the woods. She could feel the anger rolling off him.

"You weren't going to tell me," he said.

"There was no need. But I'm going to tell *them*! You should have done that when Dan showed up and spared yourself a long trip."

"I can just imagine his reaction. This isn't my fault, Dan. Your perfect little sister-in-law raped me. I'm sure he'd have believed that."

"He'll believe it now. I'm sorry you had to be . . . inconvenienced this way."

"Inconvenienced?" The word was a whiplash to her. "This is a hell of a lot more than an inconvenience!"

"I know that. I—"

"This might be an *inconvenience* in your rich-girl's life, but in the real world—"

"I understand! You were a victim." She hunched her shoulders against the cold and tried to fit her hands into the pockets. "This is my situation to deal with, not yours."

"I'm not anybody's victim," he snarled.

"You were mine, and that makes me responsible for the consequences."

"The consequences, as you call them, add up to a human life."

She stopped walking and looked up at him. The wind snatched a lock of his hair and slapped it against his forehead. His face was rigid, his too-handsome features uncompromising.

"I know that," she said. "And you have to believe that I didn't plan any of this. But now that I'm pregnant, I want this baby very much."

"I don't."

She winced. Logically, she understood. Of course he wouldn't want a baby. But his anger was so fierce that she crossed her arms protectively over her waist. "Then we haven't got a problem. I don't need you, Kevin. Really. And I'd very much appreciate it if you'd forget all about this."

"Do you really think I'm going to do that?"

To her this was personal, but she had to remember this was a professional crisis for him. Kevin's passion for the Stars was well known. Phoebe and Dan were his bosses and two of the most powerful people in the NFL.

"As soon as I tell my sister and Dan what I did, you'll be off the hook. This won't affect your career at all."

His eyes narrowed. "You aren't telling them anything."

"Of course I am!"

"Keep your mouth shut."

"Is this your pride talking? You don't want anyone to know you were a victim? Or are you that afraid of them?"

His lips barely moved. "You don't know anything about me."

"I know the difference between right and wrong! What I did was wrong, and I won't compound it by bringing you any further into this. I'm going back inside, and—"

He caught her arm and gave her a shake. "Listen up, because I'm jet-lagged and I don't want to have to say this more than once. I've been guilty of a lot of things in my life, but I've never left behind an illegitimate kid, and I don't intend to start now."

She drew away and clutched herself tighter. "I'm not getting rid of this baby, so don't even suggest it."

"I'm not." His lips tightened into a bitter line. "We're getting married."

She was flabbergasted. "I don't want to get married."

"That makes two of us, and we won't stay that way for long."

"I won't—"

"Don't waste your breath. You screwed me over, lady, and now I'm making the calls."

Normally Kevin enjoyed the dance club, but now he wished he hadn't come. Even though his confrontation with the Calebow clan had taken place yesterday afternoon, he still wasn't fit to be around other people.

"Kevin! Over here!"

A girl with glitter on her eyelids and a cellophane dress called to him above the noise. They'd dated for a couple of weeks last summer. Nina? Nita? He no longer remembered or cared.

"Kevin! Hey, buddy, come on over here and let me buy you a drink!"

He pretended he didn't hear either of them and made his way back through the crowd in the direction he'd just come. This had been a mistake. He couldn't deal with friends now, let alone fans eager to talk about the championship game he'd lost.

He claimed his coat but didn't button it, and the cold air of Dearborn Street hit him like a fist. On his drive into the city, the car radio had announced that the mercury had dipped to three below. Winter in Chicago. The valet spotted him and went to get his car, which was parked in a prominent space less than twenty feet away.

In another week he'd be a married man. So much for keeping his personal life separate from his career. He handed the valet a fifty, then slid behind the wheel of his Spider and pulled away.

You have to set an example, Kevin. People expect the children of clergy to do the right thing.

He shook off the voice of the good Reverend John Tucker. Kevin was doing this to protect his career. Okay, so the idea of an illegitimate child made his skin crawl, but that would bother anybody. This sure as hell wasn't some leftover preacher's kid thing. It was all about the game.

Phoebe and Dan weren't expecting a love match, and the fact that the marriage wasn't going to last long wouldn't surprise them. At the same time, he'd be able to hold up his head around them. As for Molly Somerville, with her important connections and her careless morality, he'd never hated anyone more. So much for marrying the silent, undemanding woman Jane Bonner loved to taunt him about. Instead, he had a snooty egghead who'd take big bites out of him if he gave her the chance. Luckily, he didn't intend to give her one.

Kevin, there's right and there's wrong. You can either walk through your life in the shadows or you can stay in the light.

He ignored John Tucker and accelerated onto Lake Shore Drive. This had nothing to do with right and wrong. It was career damage control.

Not quite, a small voice whispered inside him. He shot into the left lane, then the right, then the left again. He needed speed and danger, but he wasn't going to get either on Lake Shore Drive.

A few days after Phoebe and Dan's ambush, Molly met Kevin to take care of the wedding license. Afterward, they drove separately downtown to the Hancock Building where they signed the legal papers that would separate their finances. Kevin didn't know that Molly had no finances to separate, and she didn't tell him. It would only make her look loonier than he already thought she was.

Molly tuned out as the attorney explained the documents. She and Kevin hadn't said a word about what role he'd take in her child's life, and she was too dispirited to bring it up. One more thing they needed to work out.

Leaving the office, Molly gathered her courage and tried once more to talk to him. "Kevin, this is crazy. At least let me tell Dan and Phoebe the truth."

"You swore to me you'd keep your mouth shut."

"I know, but—"

His green eyes chilled her to the bone. "I'd like to believe you can be honorable about something."

She looked away, wishing she hadn't given him her word. "These aren't the 1950s. I don't need marriage to raise this child. Single women do it all the time."

"Getting married won't be anything more than a minor inconvenience for either one of us. Are you so self-centered you can't give up a few weeks of your life to try to set this straight?"

She didn't like the contempt in his voice or being called self-centered, especially when she knew he was doing this only to keep himself on good terms with Dan and Phoebe, but he walked away before she could respond. She finally gave up. She could fight one of them, but not all three.

The wedding took place a few days later in the Calebow living room. Molly wore the winter-white midcalf dress her sister had bought her. Kevin wore a deep charcoal suit with a matching tie. Molly thought it made him look like a gorgeous mortician.

They'd both refused to invite any of their friends to the ceremony, so only Dan, Phoebe, the children, and the dogs were there. The girls had decorated the living room with white crepe-paper streamers and tied bows on the dogs. Roo wore his around his collar, and Kanga's perched crookedly on her topknot. She flirted shamelessly with Kevin, shaking her topknot to get his attention and batting her tail. Kevin ignored her just as he ignored Roo's growling, so Molly knew he was one of those men who believed that a poodle threatened his masculinity. Why hadn't she considered that in Door County instead of looking for burps, gold chains, and "You duh man"?

Hannah's eyes shone, and she gazed at Kevin and Molly as if they were the central figures in a fairy tale. Because of her, Molly pretended to be happy when all she wanted to do was throw up.

"You look so beautiful." Hannah sighed. Then she turned to Kevin, her heart in her eyes. "You look beautiful, too. Like a prince."

Tess and Julie let out whoops of laughter. Hannah turned crimson.

But Kevin didn't laugh. He smiled instead and squeezed her shoulder. "Thanks, kiddo."

Molly blinked her eyes and looked away.

The judge conducting the ceremony stepped forward. "Let's begin."

Molly and Kevin moved toward him as if they were passing through a force field.

"Dearly beloved . . . "

Andrew wiggled loose from his mother's side and shot forward to wedge himself between the bride and groom.

"Andrew, come back here." Dan reached out to retrieve him, but Kevin and Molly simultaneously snatched his sticky little hands to keep him right where he was.

And that was how they got married—underneath a makeshift bower of mismatched crepe paper streamers with a five-year-old planted firmly between them and a gray poodle glaring at the groom.

Not once did Molly and Kevin look at each other, not even during the kiss, which was dry, fast, and closemouthed.

Andrew looked up at them and grimaced. "Yucky, mush, mush."

"They're supposed to kiss, you baby," Tess said from behind.

"I'm not a baby!"

Molly leaned down to hug him before he could get worked up. Out of the corner of her eye she saw Dan shake Kevin's hand and Phoebe give him a quick embrace. It was awkward and awful, and Molly couldn't wait to get away. Except that was a problem all in itself.

They made a play of sipping a few drops of champagne, but neither of them managed to eat more than a bite of the small white wedding cake. "Let's get out of here," Kevin finally growled in her ear.

Molly didn't have to fabricate a headache. She'd been feeling increasingly ill all afternoon. "All right."

Kevin murmured something about getting on the road before it snowed.

"A good idea," Phoebe said. "I'm glad you're taking us up on our offer."

Molly tried to look as if the prospect of spending a few days in Door County with Kevin weren't her worst nightmare.

"It's the best thing to do," Dan agreed. "The house is far enough away that you'll avoid the worst of the media stir when we make the announcement."

"Besides," Phoebe said with phony cheer, "it'll give you a chance to get to know each other better."

"Can't wait for that," Kevin muttered.

They didn't bother changing their clothes, and ten minutes later Molly was kissing Roo good-bye. Under the circumstances she thought it best to leave her dog with her sister.

As Molly and Kevin drove off in his Ferrari, Tess and Julie wrapped crepe-paper streamers around Andrew while Hannah cuddled up to her father.

"My car's at an Exxon station a couple of miles from here. Turn left when you get to the highway." The idea of being closed up together for the seven-and-a-half-hour trip to northern Wisconsin had been more than her nerves could handle.

Kevin slipped on his silver-framed Rēvos. "I thought we'd agreed on the Door County plan."

"I'll drive there in my own car."

"Suits me."

Kevin followed her directions and pulled into the service station a few minutes later. His arm pressed her waist as he leaned across her to open the passenger door. Molly took the keys from her purse and climbed out.

He roared off without a word.

She cried all the way to the Wisconsin border.

K evin made a detour to his home in one of Oak Brook's gated communities, where he changed into jeans and a flannel shirt. He picked up a couple of CDs by a Chicago jazz group he liked, along with a book about climbing Everest that he'd forgotten to stick in his suitcase. He thought about fixing himself something to eat since he wasn't in any hurry to get back on the road, but he'd lost his appetite along with his freedom.

As he headed north into Wisconsin on I-94, he tried to remember the way he'd felt when he'd swum with the reef sharks only a little over a week ago, but he couldn't recapture the sensation. Rich athletes were a target for predatory women, and the notion that she might have gotten pregnant on purpose had occurred to him. But Molly didn't need the money. No, she'd been after kicks instead, and she hadn't bothered to consider the consequences.

North of Sheboygan his cell phone rang. When he answered, he heard the voice of Charlotte Long, a woman who'd been his parents' friend for as long as he could remember. Like his parents, she'd spent her summers at his family's campground in northern Michigan, and she still returned there every June. He'd been out of contact with her until his mother's death.

"Kevin, your Aunt Judith's attorney just called me again."

"Terrific," he muttered. He remembered Charlotte talking with his father and mother after the daily service in the Tabernacle. Even in his earliest memories they'd all seemed ancient.

At the time of his birth his parents' well-ordered lives had centered on the Grand Rapids church where his father had been pastor, the books they'd loved, and their scholarly hobbies. They had no other children, and they didn't have a clue what to do with a lively little boy they loved with all their hearts but didn't understand.

Please try to sit still, sweetheart.

How did you get so dirty?

How did you get so sweaty?

Not so fast.

Not so loud.

Not so fierce.

Football, son? I believe my old tennis racket is stored in the attic. Let's try that instead?

Even so, they'd attended his games because that's what good parents did in Grand Rapids. He still remembered looking up into the stands and catching sight of their anxious, mystified faces.

They must have wondered how they hatched you.

That's what Molly had said when he'd told her about them. She might be wrong about everything else, but she sure had been right about that.

"He said you haven't called him." The note of accusation was strong in Charlotte's voice.

"Who?"

"Your Aunt Judith's attorney. Pay attention, Kevin. He wants to talk about the campground."

Even though Kevin had known what Charlotte was going to say, his hands tightened on the steering wheel. Conversations about the Wind Lake Campground always made him tense, which was why he avoided them. It was the place where the gap between himself and his parents had been the most painful.

The campground had been established by his great-grandfather on some land he'd bartered for in remote northeastern Michigan during the late 1800s. From the beginning it had served as a summer gathering place for Methodist religious revivals. Since it was located on an inland lake instead of on the ocean, it never acquired the fame of campgrounds like Ocean Grove, New Jersey, or Oak Bluffs on Martha's Vineyard, but it had the same gingerbread cottages, as well as a central tabernacle where services had been held.

Growing up, Kevin had been forced to spend summers there as his father conducted daily services for the dwindling number of elderly people who came back each year. Kevin was always the only child.

"You realize the campground is yours now that Judith has died," Charlotte said unnecessarily.

"I don't want it."

"Of course you do. It's been passed down through the Tucker family for over a hundred years. It's an institution, and you certainly don't want to be the one to end that."

Oh, yes, he did. "Charlotte, the place is a sinkhole for money. With Aunt Judith dead, there's no one to look after it."

"You're going to look after it. She's taken good care of everything. You can hire someone to run it."

"I'm selling it. I have a career to concentrate on."

"You can't! Really, Kevin, it's part of your family history. Besides, people still come back every year."

"I'll bet that makes the local undertaker happy."

"What was that? Oh, dear . . . I have to go or I'll be late to my watercolor class."

She hung up before he could tell her about his marriage. Just as well. Talking about the campground darkened an already black mood.

God, those summers had been agonizing. While his friends at home played baseball and hung out, he was stuck with a bunch of old people and a million rules.

Not so much splashing when you're in the water, dear. The ladies don't like getting their hair wet.

Worship starts in half an hour, son. Get cleaned up.

Were you throwing your ball against the Tabernacle again? There are marks all over the paint.

When he'd turned fifteen, he'd finally rebelled and nearly broken their hearts.

I'm not going back, and you can't make me! It's so damn boring there! I hate it! I'll run away if you try to make me go back! I mean it!

They'd given in, and he'd spent the next three summers in Grand Rapids with his friend Matt. Matt's dad was young and tough. He'd played college football for the Spartans, and every evening he threw the ball around with them. Kevin had worshipped him.

Eventually John Tucker had grown too old to minister, the Tabernacle had burned down, and the religious purpose of the campgrounds had come to an end. His Aunt Judith had moved into the bleak old house on the grounds where Kevin and his parents used to stay, and she'd continued to rent out the cottages in the summer. Kevin had never returned.

He didn't want to think anymore about those endless, boring summers filled with old people shushing him, so he cranked up the volume on his new CD. But just as he left the interstate behind, he spotted a familiar chartreuse Beetle on the shoulder of the road. Gravel clicked against the undercarriage as he pulled over. It was Molly's car, all right. She was leaning against the steering wheel.

Great. Just what he needed. A hysterical female. What right did she have to be hysterical? He was the one who should be howling.

He debated driving away, but she'd probably already spotted him, so he got out and walked toward the car.

The pain stole her breath, or maybe it was the fear. Molly knew she had to get to a hospital, but she was afraid to move. Afraid if she moved, the hot, sticky wetness that had already seeped through the skirt of her white woolen wedding dress would become a flood that would sweep away her baby.

She'd attributed the first cramps to hunger pangs from forgetting to eat all day. Then a spasm had gripped her that was so strong she'd barely been able to pull the car over.

She folded her hands over her stomach and curled in on herself. *Please don't let me lose this baby. Please, God.*

"Molly?"

Through the haze of her tears, she saw Kevin peering through the car window. When she didn't move, he rapped on the glass. "Molly, what's wrong?"

She tried to respond but couldn't.

He jiggled the handle. "Unlock the door."

She began to reach for it, but another cramp hit. She whimpered and wrapped her arms around her thighs to hold them together.

He rapped again, harder this time. "Hit the lock! Just hit it!"

Somehow she managed to do as he asked.

A wave of bitterly cold air struck her as he jerked open the door, and his breath made a frosty cloud in the air. "What's wrong?"

Fear clogged her throat. All she could do was bite her lip and squeeze her thighs more tightly.

"Is it the baby?"

She managed a jerky nod.

"Do you think you're having a miscarriage?"

"*No!*" She fought the pain and tried to speak more calmly. "No, it's not a miscarriage. Just—just some cramps."

She could see that he didn't believe her, and she hated him for it.

"Let's get you to a hospital."

He ran to the other side of the car, opened the door, and reached through to shift her into the passenger seat, but she couldn't let him do that. If she moved . . . "No! Don't . . . don't move me!"

"I have to. I won't hurt you. I promise."

He didn't understand. It wasn't she who'd be hurt. "No . . . "

But he didn't listen. She gripped her thighs tighter as he reached beneath her and awkwardly shifted her into the other seat. The effort left her gasping.

He raced back to his car and returned moments later with his cell phone and a wool stadium blanket that he tossed over her. Before he slid behind the wheel, he threw a jacket on the seat. Covering up her blood.

As he pulled back onto the highway, she willed her arms to keep their strength as she clamped her legs together. He was talking to someone on the phone . . . locating a hospital. The tires on her tiny Bug squealed as they hurtled down the highway and around a bend. Reckless, dare-devil driving. *Please, God . . .*

She had no idea how long it took to reach the hospital. She knew only that he was opening the door next to her and getting ready to pick her up again.

She tried to blink away her tears as she gazed up at him. "Please . . . I know you hate me, but . . . " She gasped against another cramp. "My legs . . . I have to keep my legs together."

He studied her for a moment, then slowly nodded.

She felt as though she weighed nothing as he slipped his arms beneath the skirt of her wedding dress and lifted her so effortlessly. He pressed her thighs tightly against his body and carried her through the door.

Someone came forward with a wheelchair, and he hurried toward it.

"No . . . " She tried to grip his arm, but she was too weak. "My legs . . . If you set me down . . . "

"Right here, sir," the attendant called out.

"Just show me where to take her," Kevin said.

"I'm sorry, sir, but—"

"Get moving!"

She rested her cheek against his chest and for a moment felt as if she and her baby were safe. The moment evaporated as he carried her into a curtained cubicle and carefully set her on the table.

"We'll take care of her while you go to registration, sir," the nurse said.

He squeezed Molly's hand. For the first time since he'd come back from Australia, he looked concerned instead of hostile. "I'll be right back."

As she gazed into the flickering fluorescent light above her, she wondered how he'd fill out the paperwork. He didn't know her birthday or her middle name. He knew nothing about her.

The nurse was young, with a soft, sweet face. But when she tried to help Molly off with her bloody panties, Molly refused. She'd have to ease open her legs to do that.

The nurse stroked her arm. "I'll be very careful."

But in the end it didn't do any good. By the time the emergency room doctor arrived to examine her, Molly had already lost her baby.

K evin refused to let them dismiss her until the next day, and because he was a celebrity, he got his wish. Through the window of the private room she saw a parking lot and a line of barren trees. She shut her eyes against the voices.

One of the doctors was talking to Kevin, using the deferential tone people adopted when they spoke with someone famous. "Your wife is young and healthy, Mr. Tucker. She'll need to be checked by her own physician, but I don't see any reason why the two of you won't be able to have another child."

Molly saw a reason.

Someone took her hand. She didn't know if it was a nurse, the doctor, or Kevin. She didn't care. She pulled her hand away.

"How are you feeling?" Kevin whispered.

She pretended to be asleep.

He stayed in her room for a long time. When he finally left, she rolled over and reached for the telephone.

Her head was fuzzy from the pills they'd given her, and she had to dial twice before she finally got through. When Phoebe answered, Molly started to cry. "Come get me. Please . . . "

D an and Phoebe appeared in her room sometime after midnight. Molly thought Kevin had left, but he must have been sleeping in the lounge because she heard him talking to Dan.

Phoebe stroked her cheek. Fertile Phoebe, who'd given birth to four children without mishap. One of her tears dropped onto Molly's arm. "Oh, Moll . . . I'm so sorry."

When Phoebe left her bedside to talk to the nurse, Kevin took her place. Why wouldn't he go away? He was a stranger, and no one wanted a stranger around when her life was falling apart. Molly turned her head into the pillow.

"You didn't need to call them," he said quietly. "I would have driven you back."

"I know."

He'd been kind to her, so she made herself look at him. She saw concern in his eyes, as well as fatigue, but she couldn't see even the smallest shadow of grief.

As soon as she got back home, she tore up *Daphne Finds a Baby Rabbit* and carried it out to the trash.

The next morning the story of her marriage hit the newspapers.

6

Melissa the Wood Frog was Daphne's best friend. Most days she liked to dress in pearls and organdy. But every Saturday she added a shawl and pretended she was a movie star.

—*Daphne Gets Lost*

Our Chicago Celebrity of the Week spotlight turns to wealthy football heiress Molly Somerville. Unlike her flamboyant sister, Chicago Stars owner Phoebe Calebow, Molly Somerville has kept a low profile. But while no one was looking, sly Miss Molly, who dabbles at writing children's books, scooped up Chicago's most eligible bachelor, the delectable Stars quarterback Kevin Tucker. Even close friends were shocked when the couple was married in a very private ceremony at the Calebow home just last week."

The gossip reporter rearranged her plastic expression into a look of deep concern. *"But it looks like there's no happy ending for the newly-weds. Sources now report the couple suffered a miscarriage almost immediately after the wedding ceremony, and they've since separated. A spokesman for the Stars would say only that the couple was working through their troubles privately and would make no comments to the media."*

Lilly Sherman snapped off the Chicago television station, then took a deep breath. Kevin had married a spoiled Midwestern heiress. Her hands trembled as she closed the French doors that looked out over the garden of her Brentwood home, then picked up the coffee-colored pashmina shawl that lay at the foot of her bed. Somehow she had to steady herself before she reached the restaurant. Although Mallory McCoy was her best friend, this secret was Lilly's own.

She tossed the pashmina over the shoulders of her latest St. John knit, a creamy suit with gold buttons and exquisite braided trim. Then she picked up a brightly wrapped gift bag and set off for one of Beverly Hills' newest restaurants. After she'd been shown to her table, she ordered a blackberry kir. Ignoring the curious gazes of a couple at the next table, she studied the décor.

Subdued lighting glazed the oyster-white walls and illuminated the restaurant's small but fine display of original art. The carpet was aubergine, the linens crisp and white, the silver a sleek Art Deco design. A perfect place to celebrate an unwelcome birthday. Her fiftieth. Not that anyone knew. Even Mallory McCoy thought they were celebrating Lilly's forty-seventh.

Lilly hadn't been given the room's best table, but she'd grown so accustomed to playing the diva that no one would have known it. Two of the top men at ICM occupied the prime spot, and she momentarily contemplated walking over and introducing herself. They would know who she was, of course. Only a rare man didn't remember Ginger Hill from *Lace, Inc.* But nothing was less welcome in this town than an overweight former sex kitten celebrating a fiftieth birthday.

She reminded herself that she didn't look her age. Her eyes were the same brilliant green the camera had always loved, and although she wore her auburn hair shorter now, Beverly Hills' top colorist made certain it hadn't lost any of its luster. Her face was barely lined, her skin still smooth, thanks to Craig, who wouldn't let her lie in the sun when she was younger.

The twenty-five-year age difference between her husband and herself, along with Craig's good looks and his role as her manager, had invited inevitable comparisons to Ann-Margret and Roger Smith, as well as to Bo and John Derek. And it was true that Craig had been her Svengali. When she'd arrived in L.A. over thirty years ago, she hadn't even possessed a high school diploma, and he'd taught her how to dress, walk, and speak. He'd exposed her to culture and transformed her from an awkward teenager into one of the eighties' hottest sex symbols.

Because of Craig, she was well read and culturally literate, with a particular passion for art.

Craig had done everything for her. Too much. Sometimes she'd felt as if she'd been swallowed up by the demanding force of his personality. Even when he was dying, he'd been dictatorial. Still, he'd truly loved her, and she only wished, at the end, that she'd been able to love him more.

She distracted herself with the paintings on the restaurant's walls. Her eyes drifted past a Julian Schnabel and a Keith Haring to take in an exquisite Liam Jenner oil. He was one of her favorite artists, and just looking at the painting calmed her.

She glanced at her watch and saw that Mallory was late as usual. During the six years they'd filmed *Lace, Inc.,* Mallory had always been the last to arrive on the set. Normally Lilly didn't mind, but now it gave her too much time to think about Kevin and the fact that he'd separated from his heiress wife before the ink was dry on the wedding license. The reporter said Molly Somerville had suffered a miscarriage. Lilly wondered how Kevin had felt about that, or even if the baby had been his. Famous athletes were prime targets for unscrupulous women, including rich ones.

Mallory came dashing toward the table. She was still the same size four she'd been during their days on *Lace, Inc.,* and unlike Lilly, she'd been able to keep her career alive by becoming the queen of the miniseries. Even so, Mallory didn't have Lilly's presence in person, and no one took note of her arrival. Lilly had nagged her about this countless times, *Attitude, Mallory! Walk like you're getting twenty mil a picture.*

"Sorry I'm late," Mallory chirped. "Happy, happy, you adorable person! Present later."

They exchanged social kisses just as if Mallory hadn't held Lilly in her arms more than once through the ordeal of Craig's long illness and death two years ago.

"Do you hate me for being late for your birthday dinner?"

Lilly smiled. "I know you'll be surprised to hear this, but after twenty years of friendship I've gotten used to it."

Mallory sighed. "We've been together longer than either of my marriages lasted."

"That's because I'm nicer than your ex-husbands."

Mallory laughed. The waiter appeared to take her drink order, then pressed them to try an *amuse-bouche* of ratatouille tart with goat cheese while they contemplated the menu. Lilly briefly considered the calories before she agreed to the tart. It was her birthday, after all.

"Do you miss it a lot?" Mallory inquired when the waiter left.

Lilly didn't have to ask what Mallory meant, and she shrugged. "When Craig was sick, caring for him took so much of my energy that I didn't think about sex. Since he died, there's been too much to do." *And I'm so fat I'd never let any man see my body.*

"You're so independent now. Two years ago you didn't have a clue what was in your financial portfolio, let alone know how to manage it. I can't tell you how much I admire the way you've taken charge."

"I didn't have any choice." Craig's financial planning had left her wealthy enough that she no longer needed work to support herself, only to give her life purpose. In the past year she'd had a small part as the sexy mother of the male star in a halfway decent movie. She'd been able to carry it off because she was a pro, but the whole time they were filming, she'd had to struggle against a sense of the ridiculous. For a woman of her size and age still to be playing sexpots, even aging ones, seemed somehow absurd.

She didn't like having her sense of identity wrapped up in a profession for which she no longer had a passion, but acting was all she knew, and with Craig's death she needed to keep busy or she'd think too much about the mistakes she'd made. If only she could peel away the years and go back in time to that crucial point where she'd lost her way.

The waiter returned with Mallory's drink, the *amuse-bouche,* and a lengthy explanation of the menu's many courses. After they'd made their selections, Mallory lifted her champagne flute. "To my dearest friend. Happy birthday, and I'll kill you if you don't love your present."

"Gracious as always."

Mallory laughed and pulled a flat, rectangular box from the tote she'd set at the side of her chair. The package was professionally wrapped in paisley paper tied with a burgundy bow. Lilly opened it to find an exquisite antique shawl of gold lace.

Her eyes stung with sentimental tears. "It's beautiful. Where ever did you find it?"

"A friend of a friend who deals in rare textiles. It's Spanish. Late nineteenth century."

The symbolism of the lace made it hard for her to speak, but there was something she needed to say, and she reached across the table to touch her friend's hand. "Have I ever told you how dear you are to me?"

"Ditto, sweetie. I've got a long memory. You held me together through my first divorce, through those awful years with Michael . . . "

"Don't forget your face-lift."

"Hey! I seem to remember a little eye job you had a few years ago."

"I have no idea what you're talking about."

They exchanged smiles. Plastic surgery might seem vain to much of the world, but it was a necessity for actresses who'd built their reputations on sex appeal. Although Lilly wondered why she'd bothered with an eye job when she couldn't manage to lose even twenty pounds.

The waiter set a gold-rimmed Versace plate in front of Lilly with a tiny square of aspic containing slivers of poached lobster surrounded by a trail of saffron sauce that had been whipped into a creamy froth. Mallory's plate held a wafer-thin slice of salmon accented with capers and a few transparent slices of julienned apple. Lilly mentally compared calories.

"Stop obsessing. You worry so much about your weight that you've lost sight of how gorgeous you still are."

Lilly deflected the well-meaning lecture she'd heard before by reaching behind her chair and coming up with the gift bag. The waterfall of French ribbon she'd tied around the handles brushed her wrist as she handed it over.

Mallory's eyes lit up with delight. "It's *your* birthday, Lilly. Why are you giving me a present?"

"Coincidence. I finished it this morning, and I couldn't wait any longer."

Mallory tore at the ribbons. Lilly sipped her kir as she watched, trying not to show how much Mallory's opinion meant.

Her friend pulled out the quilted pillow. "Oh, sweetie . . . "

"The design might be too strange," Lilly said quickly. "It's just an experiment."

She'd taken up quilting during Craig's illness, but the traditional patterns hadn't satisfied her for long, and she'd begun to experiment with designs of her own. The pillow she'd made for Mallory had a dozen shades and patterns of blue swirling together in an intricate design, while a trail of delicate gold stars peeped out from unexpected places.

"It's not strange at all." Mallory smiled at her. "I think it's the most beautiful thing you've done so far, and I'll always treasure it."

"Really?"

"You've become an artist."

"Don't be silly. It's just something to do with my hands."

"You keep telling yourself that." Mallory grinned. "Is it coincidence that you used the colors of your favorite football team?"

Lilly hadn't even realized it. Maybe it was a coincidence.

"I've never understood how you turned into such a sports fan," Mallory said. "And not even a West Coast team."

"I like the uniforms."

Lilly managed a shrug and turned the conversation in another direction. Her thoughts, however, remained stuck.

Kevin, what have you done?

Chef Rick Bayless's cutting-edge Mexican cuisine made the Frontera Grill one of Chicago's favorite spots for lunch, and before Molly had given away her money, she'd frequently eaten here. Now she ate at this North Clark Street restaurant only when someone else was picking up the check, in this case Helen Kennedy Schott, her editor at Birdcage Press.

" . . . we're all very committed to the Daphne books, but we do have some concerns."

Molly knew what was coming. She'd submitted *Daphne Takes a Tumble* in mid-January, and she should have given Helen at least an idea about her next book by now. But *Daphne Finds a Baby Rabbit* had gone into the trash, and Molly had a devastating case of writer's block.

In the two months since her miscarriage she hadn't been able to write a word, not even for *Chik*. Instead, she'd kept busy with school book talks and a local tutoring program for preschoolers, forcing herself to focus on the needs of living children instead of the baby she'd lost. Unlike the adults Molly met, the children didn't care that she was the about-to-be-ex-wife of the city's most famous quarterback.

Just last week the town's favorite gossip column had once again turned the media spotlight on her:

Heiress Molly Somerville, the estranged wife of Stars quarterback Kevin Tucker, has been keeping a low profile in the Windy City. Has it been boredom or a broken heart over her failed marriage to Mr. Football? No one has seen her at any of the city's nightspots, where Tucker still shows up with his foreign lovelies in tow.

At least the column hadn't said Molly "dabbled at writing children's books." That had stung, although lately she hadn't even been able to dabble. Every morning she told herself this would be the day she'd come up with an idea for a new Daphne book or even an article for *Chik,* and every morning she'd find herself staring at a blank piece of paper. In the meantime her financial situation was deteriorating. She desperately needed the second part of the advance payment she was due to receive for *Daphne Takes a Tumble,* but Helen still hadn't approved it.

The restaurant's colorful décor suddenly seemed too bright, and the lively chatter jangled her nerves. She'd told no one about her block, especially not the woman sitting across from her. Now she spoke carefully. "I want this next book to be really special. I've been tossing around a number of ideas, but—"

"No, no." Helen held up her hand. "Take your time. We understand. You've been through a lot lately."

If her editor wasn't concerned about not getting a manuscript, why had she invited her to lunch? Molly rearranged one of the tiny corn masa boats on her plate. She'd always loved them, but she'd been having trouble eating since the miscarriage.

Helen touched the rim of her margarita glass. "You should know that we've had some inquiries from SKIFSA about the Daphne books."

Helen mistook Molly's stunned expression. "Straight Kids for a Straight America. They're an antigay organization."

"I know what SKIFSA is. But why are they interested in the Daphne books?"

"I don't think they would have looked at them if there hadn't been so much press about you. The news reports apparently caught their attention, and they called me several weeks ago with some concerns."

"How could they have concerns? Daphne doesn't have a sex life!"

"Yes, well, that didn't stop Jerry Falwell from outing Tinky Winky on the *Teletubbies* for being purple and carrying a purse."

"Daphne's allowed to carry a purse. She's a girl."

Helen's smile seemed forced. "I don't think the purse is the issue. They're . . . concerned about possible homosexual overtones."

It was a good thing Molly hadn't been eating, because she would have choked. "In my books?"

"I'm afraid so, although there haven't been any accusations yet. As I said, I think your marriage caught their attention, and they saw a chance for publicity. They asked for an advance look at *Daphne Takes a Tumble,* and since we didn't foresee any problems, we sent them a copy of the mock-up. Unfortunately, that was a mistake."

Molly's head was beginning to ache. "What possible concerns could they have?"

"Well . . . they mentioned that you use a lot of rainbows in all of your books. Since that's a symbol for gay pride . . . "

"It's become a crime to use rainbows?"

"These days it seems to be," Helen said dryly. "There are a few other things. They're all ridiculous, of course. For example, you've drawn Daphne giving Melissa a kiss in at least three different books, including *Tumble.*"

"They're best friends!"

"Yes, well . . . " Like Molly, Helen had given up any pretense of eating, and she crossed her arms on the edge of the table. "Also, Daphne and Melissa are holding hands and skipping down Periwinkle Path. There's some dialogue."

"A song. They're singing a song."

"That's right. The lyrics are 'It's spring! It's spring! We're gay! We're gay!' "

Molly laughed for what seemed the first time in two months, but her editor's tight-lipped smile sobered her. "Helen, you're not seriously telling me they think Daphne and Melissa are getting it on?"

"It's not just Daphne and Melissa. Benny—"

"Hold it right there! Even the most paranoid person couldn't accuse Benny of being gay. He's so macho that he—"

"They've pointed out that he borrows a lipstick in *Daphne Plants a Pumpkin Patch.*"

"He uses it to make his face scary so he can frighten Daphne! This is so ludicrous it doesn't even deserve a response."

"We agree. On the other hand, I'd be less than truthful if I didn't admit we're a little edgy about this. We think SKIFSA wants to use you to raise their profile, and they're going to do it by zeroing in on *Daphne Takes a Tumble.*"

"So what? When the fringe groups started accusing J. K. Rowling of Satanism in the Harry Potter books, her publisher ignored it."

"Forgive me, Molly, but Daphne isn't quite as well known as Harry Potter."

And Molly didn't have either J. K. Rowling's clout or her money. The possibility of Helen's authorizing the rest of her advance seemed to be growing more remote by the minute.

"Look, Molly, I know this is ridiculous, and Birdcage is standing behind the Daphne books one hundred percent—there's no question about that. But we're a small company, and I thought it was only fair to tell you that we're getting a fair amount of pressure about *Daphne Takes a Tumble.*"

"I'm sure it'll disappear as soon as the press lets go of the story about . . . about my marriage."

"That may take a while. There's been so much speculation . . . " She let her words trail off, subtly hinting for details.

Molly knew it was the air of mystery around her marriage that was keeping the press interested, but she refused to comment on it, and so did Kevin. His courteous, formal calls to check up on her had finally stopped at her insistence. From the time he'd learned of her pregnancy right through her miscarriage, his behavior had been faultless, and the resentment she felt whenever she thought of him made her ashamed, so she stopped thinking about him.

"We think it's a good idea to be cautious now." Her editor slipped an envelope from the folder she had at her side and passed it across the table. Unfortunately, it was too large to contain a check.

"Luckily, *Daphne Takes a Tumble* hasn't gone into final production yet, and that gives us a chance to make a few of the changes they're suggesting. Just to avoid any misunderstanding."

"I don't want to make changes." The muscles tightened in a painful band around Molly's shoulders.

"I understand, but we think—"

"You told me you loved the book."

"And we're totally committed. The changes I'm suggesting are very minor. Just look through them and think about it. We can talk more next week."

Molly was furious when she left the restaurant. By the time she got home, however, her anger had faded, and the bleak sense of emptiness she couldn't shake off settled over her once again. She tossed aside the envelope with Helen's suggestions and went to bed.

Lilly wore the shawl Mallory had given her to the J. Paul Getty Museum. She stood on one of the curved balconies that made the museum so wonderful and gazed out over the hills of Los Angeles. The May day was sunny, and if she turned her head a bit, she could see Brentwood. She could even make out the tile roof of her house. She'd loved the house when she and Craig first found it, but now all the walls seemed to be closing in on her. Like so much else in her life, it was more Craig's than hers.

She slipped back inside the museum, but she paid little attention to the old masters on the wall. It was the Getty itself she loved. The cluster of ultramodern buildings with their wonderful balconies and unpredictable angles formed a work of art that pleased her far more than the precious objects inside. A dozen times since Craig's death she'd ridden the sleek white tram that carried visitors to the hilltop museum. The way the buildings enfolded her made her feel as if she'd become part of the art—frozen in time at the moment of perfection.

People magazine had showed up on the stands today with a two-page story about Kevin and his mystery marriage. She'd fled here to escape a nearly overwhelming urge to pick up the phone and call Charlotte Long, the woman who was her only inside source of information about Kevin. It was May, and the marriage and separation had taken place three months ago, but she didn't know anything more now than she had then. If only she could call Charlotte Long without worrying that she'd tell Kevin.

As she headed down the staircase and into the courtyard, she tried to figure out how to keep herself busy for the rest of the day. No one was banging on her door begging her to star in a new film. She didn't want to start another quilting project because it would give her too much time to think, and she'd had more than enough of that lately. The breeze loosened a lock of hair and whipped it against her cheek. Maybe she should stop worrying about the consequences and just give in to the urge to call Charlotte Long. But how much pain did she want to put herself through when she couldn't see any possibility of a happy ending?

If only she could see him.

7

Should I overdose on pills? Daphne asked herself. Or jump
from the top of a very tall tree? Oh, where was that handy carbon
monoxide leak when a girl needed it?
—*Daphne's Nervous Breakdown*
(notes for a never-to-be-published manuscript)

I'm fine," Molly told her sister every time they talked.
"Why don't you come out to the house this weekend? I promise, you
won't find a single copy of *People* around. The irises are beautiful, and I
know how much you love May."

"This weekend's not good. Maybe next."

"That's what you said the last time we talked."

"Soon, I promise. It's just that I've got so many things going right
now."

It was true. Molly had painted her closets, pasted photos in albums,
cleaned out files, and groomed her sleepy poodle. She did everything
but work on the revisions she'd finally been forced to agree to do
because she needed the rest of her advance money.

Helen wanted some dialogue changed in *Daphne Takes a Tumble* as well
as three new drawings. Two would show Daphne and Melissa standing
farther apart, and in the third, Benny and his friends were to be eating
cheese sandwiches instead of hot dogs. Everyone had scoured Daphne
with the most lascivious of adult minds. Helen had also asked Molly to
make changes in the text of two older Daphne books that were going back

to press. But Molly had done none of it, not out of principle, although she wished that were the case, but because she couldn't concentrate.

Her friend Janine, who was still stung over SKIFSA'S condemnation of her own book, was upset that Molly hadn't told Birdcage to go to hell, but Janine had a husband who made their mortgage payment every month.

"The kids miss you," Phoebe said.

"I'll call them tonight. I promise."

She did call them, and she managed to do all right with the twins and Andrew. But Hannah broke her heart.

"It's because of me, isn't it, Aunt Molly?" she whispered. "That's why you don't want to come over anymore. It's because the last time you were here, I said I was sad that your baby died."

"Oh, sweetheart . . . "

"I didn't know I wasn't supposed to talk about the baby. I promise, I won't ever, ever say anything again."

"You didn't do anything wrong, love. I'll come over this weekend. We'll have a great time."

But the trip only made her feel worse. She hated being responsible for the worry that clouded Phoebe's face, and she couldn't bear the soft, considerate way Dan spoke to her, as if he were afraid she would shatter. Being with the children was even more painful. As they looped their arms around her waist and demanded she come with them to see their newest projects, she could barely breathe.

The family was tearing her apart with their love. She left as soon as she could.

May slid into June. Molly sat down a dozen times to work on the drawings, but her normally agile pen refused to move. She tried to come up with an idea for a *Chik* article, but her mind was as empty as her bank account. She could make her mortgage payments through July, but that was all.

As one June day slipped into the next, little things began to get away from her. One of her neighbors set a sack of mail he'd pulled from her overflowing mailbox outside her door. Her laundry piled up, and dust settled over her normally tidy condo. She got a cold and had trouble shaking it off.

One Friday morning her head ached so badly she called in sick for her volunteer tutoring and went to bed. Other than dragging herself outside long enough for Roo to do his business and occasionally forcing down a piece of toast, she slept all weekend.

When Monday came, her headache was gone, but the aftereffects of the cold had sapped her energy, so she phoned in sick again. Her bread box was empty, and she was out of cereal. She found some canned fruit in the cupboard.

On Tuesday morning as she dozed in bed, her sleep was disturbed by the buzzer from the lobby. Roo hopped to attention. Molly burrowed deeper into her covers, but just when she was falling back asleep, someone began pounding on her door. She pulled a pillow over her head, but it didn't block out the deep, familiar voice clearly audible over the sound of Roo's yips.

"Open up! I know you're in there!"

That awful Kevin Tucker.

She sneezed and stuck her fingers in her ears, but Roo kept barking and Kevin kept banging. Miserable dog. Reckless, scary quarterback. Everyone in the building was going to complain. Cursing, she dragged herself out of bed.

"What do you want?" Her voice sounded creaky from lack of use.

"I want you to open the door."

"Why?"

"Because I need to talk to you."

"I don't want to talk." She grabbed a tissue and blew her nose.

"Tough. Unless you'd like everyone in this building to know your private business, I suggest you open up."

Reluctantly, she flipped the lock. As she opened the door, she wished she were armed.

Kevin stood on the other side, dazzling and perfect with his healthy body, gleaming blond hair, and blazing green eyes. Her head pounded. She wanted to hide behind dark glasses.

He pushed his way past her snarling poodle and shut the door. "You look like hell."

She stumbled over to the couch. "Roo, be quiet."

The dog gave Molly an offended sniff as she lay down.

"Have you seen a doctor?"

"I don't need a doctor. My cold is almost gone."

"How about a shrink?" He walked over to the windows and began opening them.

"Stop that." It was bad enough that she had to endure his arrogance and the threatening glare of his good looks. She didn't have to tolerate fresh air, too. "Will you go away?"

As he gazed around at her condo, she noticed the dirty dishes littering the kitchen counter, the bathrobe hanging over the end of the couch, and the dusty tabletops. He was an uninvited guest, and she didn't care.

"You blew off the appointment with the attorney yesterday."

"What appointment?" She shoved a hand into her ratty hair, then winced as it caught on a snarl. Half an hour ago she'd stumbled into the bathroom to brush her teeth, but she couldn't remember taking a shower. And her shabby gray Northwestern nightshirt smelled like poodle.

"The annulment?" He glanced toward the pile of unopened mail spilling out of the white Crate & Barrel shopping bag next to the door and said sarcastically, "I guess you didn't get the letter."

"I guess. You'd better leave. I might still be contagious."

"I'll take my chances." He wandered over to the windows and gazed down at the parking lot. "Nice view."

She closed her eyes to sneak in a nap.

Kevin didn't think he'd ever seen anyone more pathetic. This pasty-faced, stringy-haired, musty-smelling, sniffling, sad-eyed female was his wife. Hard to believe she was the daughter of a showgirl. He should have let his attorney take care of this, but he kept seeing the raw desperation in her eyes when she'd begged him to hold her legs together, as if brute strength alone could keep that baby inside her.

I know you hate me, but . . .

He couldn't quite hate her any longer, not after he'd watched her fruitless struggle to hold on to that baby. But he did hate the way he felt, as if he had some sort of responsibility for her. Training camp started in less than two months. He needed to be focusing all his energy on getting ready for next season. He gazed at her resentfully.

You have to set an example, Kevin. Do the right thing.

He moved away from the windows and stepped over her worthless, pampered dog. Why did someone with her millions live in such a small place? Convenience, maybe. She probably had at least three other addresses, all of them in warm climates.

He sank down on the sectional couch at the opposite end from where she was lying and studied her critically. She must have dropped ten pounds since the miscarriage. Her hair had grown longer, nearly to her jawline, and it had lost that silky sheen he remembered from their wedding day. She hadn't bothered with makeup, and the deep bruises under those exotic eyes made her look as if she'd been somebody's punching bag.

"I had an interesting conversation with one of your neighbors."

She settled her wrist over her eyes. "I promise I'll call your attorney first thing in the morning if you'll just leave."

"The guy recognized me right away."

"Of course he did."

She wasn't too tired for sarcasm, he noticed. His resentment simmered.

"He was more than happy to gossip about you. Apparently you stopped emptying your mailbox a few weeks ago."

"Nobody sends me anything interesting."

"And the only time you've left your apartment since Thursday night is to take out your pit bull."

"Stop calling him that. I'm recovering from a cold, that's all."

He could see her red nose, but somehow he didn't think a cold was the only thing wrong with her. He rose. "Come on, Molly. Holing up like this isn't normal."

She peered at him from beneath her wrist. "Like you're an expert on normal behavior? I heard you were swimming with sharks when Dan found you in Australia."

"Maybe it's depression."

"Thank you, Dr. Tucker. Now, get out."

"You lost a baby, Molly."

He'd made a statement of fact, but it was as if he'd shot her. She sprang up from the couch, and the way her expression turned feral told him more than he wanted to know.

"Get out of here before I call the police!"

All he had to do was walk through the door. God knew he had enough aggravation on his plate right now with the publicity the *People* article had kicked up. And just being with her was making his gut churn. If only he could forget the way she'd looked when she'd been trying to hold on to that baby.

Even as the words were coming out of his mouth, he tried to cut them off. "Get dressed. You're coming with me."

Her rage seemed to frighten her, and he watched her struggle to make light of it. The best she could manage was a pitiful croak. "Been smoking a little too much weed, have you?"

Furious with himself, he stomped up the five steps that led to her bedroom loft. Her pit bull shadowed him to make sure he didn't steal the jewelry. He looked down at her from over the top of the kitchen cabinets. God, he hated this. "You can either get yourself dressed or go with me the way you are. Which will probably get you quarantined by the Health Department."

She lay back on the couch. "You're so wasting your breath."

It would be for only a few days, he told himself. He was already in a foul mood about being forced to drive up to the Wind Lake Campground. Why not make himself completely miserable by bringing her along?

He'd never intended to go back there, but he couldn't avoid it. For weeks he'd been telling himself he could sell off the property without seeing it again. But when he couldn't answer any of the questions his business manager had posed, he'd known he had to bite the bullet and see exactly how run-down it had become.

At least he'd be getting rid of two ugly duties at the same time. He'd settle the campground and badger Molly into getting her butt moving again. Whether it worked or not would be up to her, but at least his conscience would be clean.

He unearthed a suitcase from the back of her closet and yanked open her drawers. Unlike her messy kitchen, here everything was neatly arranged. He tossed shorts and tops in the suitcase, then threw in some underwear. He found jeans along with sandals and a pair of sneakers. A couple of sundresses caught his eye. He threw them on top. Better to take too much than have her sulk because she didn't have what she wanted.

The suitcase was full, so he grabbed what looked like her old college backpack and glanced around for the bathroom. He found it downstairs, near the front door, and began dumping in various cosmetics and toiletries. Succumbing to the inevitable, he headed for the kitchen and loaded up on dog food.

"I hope you're planning to put all that back." She was standing by the refrigerator, the pit bull in her arms, her rich-girl's eyes weary.

He'd like nothing better than to put it back, but she looked too damn pathetic. "You want to take a shower first, or do we drive with the windows down?"

"Are you deaf? I'm not some rookie you can order around."

He propped one hand on the edge of the sink and gave her the same stony look he used on those rookies. "You've got two choices. Either you can go with me right now, or I'm taking you over to your sister's house. Somehow I don't think she'll like what she sees."

Her expression told him he'd just thrown a Hail Mary.

"Please leave me alone," she whispered.

"I'll look through your bookshelves while you take a shower."

8

A smart girl never accepts a ride from a stranger, even if he is a hottie.

"Hitchhiking Hell"
—article for *Chik* magazine

Molly crawled with Roo into the backseat of the snappy SUV Kevin was driving instead of his Ferrari. She propped up the pillow she'd brought along and tried to go to sleep, but it wasn't possible. As they sped east past the urban blight of Gary, then took I-94 toward Michigan City, she kept asking herself why she hadn't opened her mail. All she'd needed to do was show up at the attorney's office. Then she wouldn't have been body-snatched by a mean-tempered quarterback.

Her refusal to talk to him was beginning to seem childish. Besides, her headache was better, and she wanted to know where they were going. She stroked Roo. "Do you have a destination in mind, or is this a make-it-up-as-you-go kidnapping?"

He ignored her.

They drove for another hour in silence before he pulled over for gas near Benton Harbor. While he was filling the tank, a fan spotted him and asked for an autograph. She clipped a leash on Roo and took him into the grass, then slipped into the bathroom. As she washed her hands, she caught a glimpse of herself in the mirror. He was right. She did look like hell. She'd washed her hair, but she hadn't done anything more than drag her fingers through it afterward. Her skin was ashen, her eyes sunken.

She began to reach into her purse for a lipstick, then decided it took too much effort. She thought about phoning one of her friends to come get her, but Kevin's implied threat to talk to Phoebe and Dan about her physical condition made her hesitate. She couldn't stand causing them more worry than she already had. Better to go along with him for now.

He wasn't in the car when she returned. She debated getting into the backseat again, but doubted he'd talk to her unless she was in his face, so she put Roo there instead and climbed in the front. He emerged from the service station with a plastic bag and a Styrofoam coffee cup. After he got inside, he stuck the coffee in the cup holder, then pulled a bottle of orange juice from the sack and handed it to her.

"I'd rather have coffee."

"Too bad."

The cold bottle felt good in her hands, and she realized she was thirsty, but when she tried to open it, she discovered she was too weak. Her eyes filled unexpectedly with tears.

He took it without comment, unscrewed the lid, and returned it to her.

As he pulled away from the pump, she choked back the tightness in her throat. "At least you muscle boys are good for something."

"Be sure to let me know if you want any beer cans crushed."

She was startled to hear herself laugh. The orange juice slid in a cool, sweet trickle down her throat.

He pulled out onto the interstate. Sand dunes stretched on their left. She couldn't see the water, but she knew there would be cruisers on the lake, probably some freighters on their way to Chicago or Ludington. "Would you mind telling me where we're going?"

"Northwest Michigan. A hole called Wind Lake."

"There goes my fantasy of a Caribbean cruise."

"The campground I told you about."

"The place where you told me you spent your summers when you were a kid?"

"Yeah. My aunt inherited it from my father, but she died a few months back, and I was unlucky enough to end up with it. I'm going to sell it, but I have to check out the condition first."

"I can't go to a camp. You'll have to turn around and take me home."

"Believe me, we won't be there for long. Two days at the most."

"Doesn't matter. I don't do camp anymore. I had to go every summer when I was a kid, and I promised myself I'd never go back."

"What was so bad about camp?"

"All that organized activity. Sports." She blew her nose. "There was no time to read, no time to be alone with your thoughts."

"Not much of an athlete?"

One summer she'd sneaked out of her cabin in the middle of the night and gathered up every ball in the equipment shed—volleyballs, soccer, tennis, softballs. It had taken her half a dozen trips to carry them all to the lake and throw them in the water. The counselors had never discovered the culprit. Certainly no one had suspected quiet, brainy Molly Somerville, who'd been named Most Cooperative despite spraying her bangs green.

"I'm a better athlete than Phoebe," she said.

Kevin shuddered. "The guys are still talking about the last time she played softball at the Stars picnic."

Molly hadn't been there, but she could imagine.

He swung into the left lane and said, with an edge, "I wouldn't think spending a few weeks every summer at some rich-kid's camp damaged you too much."

"I suppose you're right."

Except she never went for a few weeks. She went all summer, every summer, from the time she was six.

When she'd been eleven, there was a measles outbreak and all the campers were sent home. Her father had been furious. He couldn't find anyone to stay with her, so he'd been forced to take her with him to Vegas, where he'd set her up in a suite separate from his own with a change girl as a baby-sitter, even though Molly kept telling him she was too old for one. During the day the girl watched the soaps, and at night she crossed the hall to sleep with Bert.

They'd been the best two weeks of Molly's childhood. She'd read the complete works of Mary Stewart, ordered cherry cheesecake from room service, and made friends with the Spanish-speaking maids. Sometimes she'd announce to her sitter that she was going down to the pool, but instead, she'd wander around near the casino until she found a family with a lot of kids. Then she'd stay as close as she could and pretend she belonged to them.

Normally, the memories of her childish attempts to create a family made her smile, but now she felt another prickle of tears and swallowed. "Have you noticed there's a speed limit?"

"Making you nervous?"

"You should be, but I'm numb from too many years of riding with Dan." Besides, she didn't care that much. It shocked her—the realization that she had no interest in the future. She couldn't even muster the energy to worry about her finances or the fact that her editor at *Chik* had stopped calling.

He backed off on the accelerator. "Just so you know, the campground is in the middle of nowhere, the cottages are so old they're probably in ruins by now, and the place is more boring than elevator music because nobody under the age of seventy ever goes there." He tilted his head toward the sack of food he'd picked up at the service station. "If you're done with that orange juice, there are some cheese crackers inside."

"Yummy, but I think I'll pass."

"You seem to have passed on a lot of meals lately."

"Thanks for noticing. I figure if I lose another sixty pounds, I might be as skinny as some of your *chères amies.*"

"Feel free to concentrate on that nervous breakdown of yours. At least it'll keep you quiet."

She smiled. One thing she'd say for Kevin, he didn't handle her with kid gloves like Phoebe and Dan. It was nice to be treated as an adult. "Maybe I'll just take a nap instead."

"You do that."

But she didn't sleep. Instead, she closed her eyes and tried to make herself think about her next book, but her mind refused to take a single step into the cozy byways of Nightingale Woods.

After they got off the interstate, Kevin stopped at a roadside store with a smokehouse attached and returned carrying a brown paper bag that he tossed into her lap. "Michigan lunch. Do you think you can make some sandwiches?"

"Maybe if I concentrate."

Inside she found a generous piece of smoked whitefish, a hunk of sharp cheddar cheese, and a loaf of dark pumpernickel bread, along with a plastic knife and a few paper napkins. She mustered enough energy to put together two crude, open-faced sandwiches for him and a smaller one for herself, all but a few bites of which she ended up feeding to Roo.

They headed east toward the middle of the state. Through half-closed eyes she saw orchards coming into bloom and neat farms with silos. Then, as the afternoon light began to fade, they made their way north toward I-75, which stretched all the way to Sault Ste. Marie.

They didn't talk much. Kevin listened to the CDs he'd brought with him. He liked jazz, she discovered, everything from forties bebop to fusion. Unfortunately, he also liked rap, and after fifteen minutes of trying to ignore Tupac's views of women, she hit the eject button, grabbed the disk, and tossed it out the car window.

His ears turned red, she discovered, when he yelled.

It was getting dark when they reached the northern part of the state. Just beyond the pretty town of Grayling they left the freeway for a two-lane highway that seemed to lead nowhere. Before long they were driving through dense woods.

"Northeastern Michigan was nearly stripped of timber by the lumber industry during the 1800s," he said. "What you're seeing now is second- and third-growth forest. Some of it is pretty wild. Towns in this area are small and scattered."

"How much farther?"

"Only a little over an hour, but the place is run-down, so I don't want to get there after dark. There's supposed to be a motel not far from here, but don't expect the Ritz."

Since she couldn't imagine him worrying about the dark, she suspected he was stalling, and she curled deeper into the seat. The headlights of an occasional oncoming car flickered across his features, casting dangerous shadows beneath those male underwear model cheekbones. She felt a shiver of foreboding, so she closed her eyes and pretended she was alone.

She didn't open them again until he pulled up in front of an eight-unit roadside motel made of white aluminum siding and fake brick. As he got out of the car to register, she thought about making sure he understood that she wanted a separate unit, but common sense intervened.

Sure enough, he returned from the office with two keys. His unit, she noticed, was at the opposite end from hers.

Early the next morning she awakened to door pounding and poodle barking. "Slytherins," she grumbled. "This is getting to be a bad habit."

"We're leaving in half an hour," Kevin called from the other side. "Get the lead out."

"Hut, hut," she muttered into her pillow.

She dragged herself into the cramped shower and even managed to run a comb through her hair. Lipstick, however, was beyond her. She felt as if she had a colossal hangover.

When she finally emerged, he was pacing near the car. The lemony patch of sunlight that splashed over him revealed a grim mouth and unfriendly expression. As Roo took advantage of the shrubbery, Kevin grabbed her suitcase and tossed it into the back of the car.

Today he'd decorated his muscles with an aqua Stars T-shirt and light gray shorts. They were ordinary clothes, but he wore them with the confidence of those who were born beautiful.

She fumbled in her purse for her sunglasses, then glared at him resentfully. "Don't you ever turn it off?"

"Turn what off?"

"Your basic ugliness," she muttered.

"Maybe I should just drop you off at a funny farm instead of taking you to Wind Lake."

"Whatever. Is coffee too much to hope for?" She shoved on her glasses, but they didn't do a whole lot to shut out the blinding glare of his irritating beauty.

"It's in the car, but it took you so long to get ready that it's probably cold by now."

It was piping hot, and as they pulled back out onto the road, she took a long, slow sip.

"Fruit and doughnuts were the best I could do for breakfast. They're in that bag." He sounded as grouchy as she felt. She wasn't hungry, and she concentrated on the scenery.

They might have been in the wilds of the Yukon instead of a state that made Chevrolets, Sugar Pops, and soul music. From a bridge crossing the Au Sable River she saw rocky cliffs rising on one shore and dense woods stretching on the other. An osprey soared down over the water. Everything seemed wild and remote.

Occasionally they passed a farm, but this was clearly timber country. Maple and oak competed with pine, birch, and cedar. Here and there, golden straws of sunlight penetrated the canopy formed by the trees. It was wonderfully serene, and she tried to feel peaceful, but she was out of practice.

Kevin swore and jerked the wheel to avoid a squirrel. Getting closer to their destination definitely hadn't improved his mood. She spotted a metal highway sign that indicated the turnoff for Wind Lake, but he flew past it. "That's the town," he grunted. "The campground is on the far side of the lake."

They drove for another few miles before a decorative green-and-white sign with a Chippendale top edged in gilt came into sight.

WIND LAKE COTTAGES
Bed & Breakfast
Established 1894

Kevin frowned. "That sign looks new. And nobody said anything to me about a bed-and-breakfast. She must have used the old house to take in guests."

"Is that bad?"

"The place is musty and dark as sin. I can't believe anybody would want to stay there." He turned onto a gravel lane that wound through the trees for about half a mile before the campground emerged.

He stopped the car, and Molly caught her breath. She'd expected to see rough cabins decaying on their foundations. Instead, they'd driven into a storybook village.

A shady rectangular Common sat at the center, surrounded by small gingerbread cottages painted in colors that could have spilled from a box of bonbons: mint with tangerine and toffee, mocha touched with lemon and cranberry, peach with blueberry and brown sugar. Wooden lace dripped from tiny eaves, and fanciful spindles bordered front porches no larger than a trundle bed. At one end of the Common sat a charming gazebo.

A closer inspection showed that the flower beds in the Common were overgrown, and the loop of road that surrounded it needed fresh gravel. Everything bore an air of neglect, but it seemed recent rather than long-term. Most of the cottages were tightly shuttered, although a few had been opened up. An elderly couple emerged from one of them, and Molly spotted a man with a cane walking near the gazebo.

"These people shouldn't be here! I had all the summer rentals canceled."

"They must not have gotten the word." As Molly gazed around, she experienced the oddest sense of familiarity. Since she'd never been anywhere like this, she couldn't explain it.

Across the road from the center of the Common was a small picnic area with a sandy, crescent-shaped beach directly behind it and, beyond that, a sliver of the blue-gray water of Wind Lake against the backdrop of a tree-lined shore. Several canoes and a few rowboats were overturned near a weathered dock.

She wasn't surprised that the beach was deserted. Although the early-June morning was sunny, this was a North Woods lake, and the water would still be too chilly for all but the hardiest swimmers.

"Notice the complete absence of anyone under the age of seventy!" Kevin exclaimed as he stepped on the accelerator.

"It's early. A lot of schools aren't out yet."

"It'll look this way at the end of July. Welcome to my childhood." He swung away from the Common onto a narrower lane that ran parallel to the lake. She saw more cottages, all of them built in the same Carpenter Gothic style. Presiding over them was a beautiful two-story Queen Anne.

This couldn't be the dark, musty place he'd described. The house was painted a light cocoa with salmon, maize, and moss green accents decorating the gingerbread trim above the porch, over the gables, and on the porch spindles. A round turret curved on the left of the house, and the broad porch extended around two sides. Petunias bloomed in clay pots by the double front doors, which held matching panels of frosted glass etched with a design of vines and flowers. Ferns spilled over brown wicker stands, and old-fashioned wooden rockers held cheery checked pillows in colors that matched the trim. Once again she had the sense of being plunged into an earlier time.

"I don't frickin' believe this!" Kevin vaulted out of the car. "This place was a wreck the last time I saw it."

"It sure isn't a wreck now. It's beautiful."

She winced as he slammed the door, then got out herself. Roo broke free and headed for the shrubs. Kevin gazed up at the house, his hands planted on his hips.

"When the hell did she turn this into a bed-and-breakfast?"

Just then the front door opened, and a woman who appeared to be in her late sixties emerged. She had faded blond-and-gray hair caught up in a clip with strands escaping here and there. She was tall and big-boned, and her mouth was wide, topped by prominent cheekbones and bright blue eyes. A flour-dusted blue apron protected her khaki slacks and short-sleeved white blouse.

"Kevin!" She hurried down the steps and gave him a vigorous hug. "You sweet boy! I knew you'd come!"

To Molly, Kevin's hug in return seemed perfunctory.

The woman gave her an assessing look. "I'm Charlotte Long. My husband and I came here every summer. He died eight years ago, but I still stay in Loaves and Fishes. Kevin was always losing balls in my rosebushes."

"Mrs. Long was a good friend of my parents and my aunt," Kevin said.

"My, I miss Judith. We met when my family first came here." Her sharp blue eyes returned to Molly. "And who's this?"

Molly extended her hand. "Molly Somerville."

"Well, now . . . " Her lips pursed as she turned back to Kevin. "You can't read a magazine without hearing about that marriage of yours. Isn't it a little early to be seeing someone else? I'm sure Pastor Tucker would be disappointed that you aren't trying harder to make things work with your wife."

"Uh, Molly is my . . . " The word seemed to stick in his throat. Molly sympathized, but she wasn't going to be the one to say it.

"Molly's my . . . wife." He finally managed to get it out.

Once again Molly found herself under the scrutiny of those blue eyes. "Well, that's good, then. But why are you calling yourself Somerville? Tucker's a good, proud name. Pastor Tucker, Kevin's father, was one of the finest men I ever knew."

"I'm sure he was." She'd never liked disappointing people. "Somerville's also my professional name. I write children's books."

Her disapproval vanished. "I've always wanted to write a children's book. Well, now, isn't this nice? You know, when Kevin's mother was alive, she was afraid he'd marry one of those supermodels who go around smoking dope and having sexual relations with everybody."

Kevin choked.

"Here now, pup, you get out of Judith's lobelia." Charlotte patted her thigh, and Roo abandoned the flowers to trot over. Charlotte reached down to chuck his chin. "Better keep an eye on him. We've got some coyotes around here."

Kevin's expression turned calculating. "Big ones?"

Molly gave him a reproachful gaze. "Roo sticks close to home."

"Too bad."

"Well, I'm off! There's a list of guests and dates on Judith's computer. The Pearsons should be here any time. They're birdwatchers."

Kevin turned pale beneath his tan. "Guests? What do you—"

"I had Amy freshen up Judith's old room for you, the one your parents used. The other bedrooms are rented."

"Amy? Wait a—"

"Amy and Troy Anderson, he's the handyman. They just got married, even though she's only nineteen and he's twenty. I don't know why they were in such a hurry." Charlotte reached back to untie the apron. "Amy's supposed to take care of the cleaning, but they're so gaga over each other that they're worthless. You'll have to keep after them." She handed the apron to Molly. "It's a good thing you're here, Molly. I never was much of a cook, and the guests are complaining."

Molly stared down at the apron. Kevin shot forward as the older woman began to walk away. "Wait a minute! The campground's closed. All the reservations were canceled."

She regarded him with disapproval. "How could you even think to do that, Kevin? Some of these people have been coming here for forty years. And Judith spent every penny she had sprucing up the cottages and turning the house into a bed-and-breakfast. Do you have any idea how much it costs to advertise in *Victoria* magazine? And that Collins boy in town charged her almost a thousand dollars to set up a Web site."

"A *Web site*?"

"If you're not familiar with the Internet, I suggest you look into it. It's a wonderful thing. Except for all that porno."

"I'm familiar with the Internet!" Kevin exclaimed. "Now, tell me why people are still coming here after I closed the place down."

"Why, because I told them to. Judith would have wanted it. I kept trying to explain that to you. Do you know that it took me nearly a week to get hold of everyone?"

"You called them?"

"I used that E-mail, too," she said proudly. "It didn't take me long to get the hang of it." She patted his arm. "Don't be nervous, Kevin. You and your wife will do just fine. As long as you put out a nice, big breakfast, most people are happy. The menus and recipes are in Judith's blue notebook in the kitchen. Oh, and get Troy to look at the toilet in Green Pastures. It's leaking."

She headed off down the lane.

Kevin looked sick. "Tell me this is a bad dream."

As Mrs. Long disappeared, Molly watched a late-model Honda

Accord turn into the lane and head toward the B&B. "As a matter of fact, I think you're wide awake."

Kevin followed the direction of her gaze and swore as the car stopped in front of the B&B. Molly was too tired to stand any longer, so she sank down on the top step to watch the entertainment. Roo yipped a greeting at the couple who came up the sidewalk.

"We're the Pearsons," a thin, round-faced, sixtyish woman said. "I'm Betty and this is my husband, John."

Kevin looked as if he'd taken a direct hit to the head, so Molly replied for him. "Molly Somerville. This is Kevin, the new owner."

"Oh, yes. We heard about you. You play baseball, don't you?"

Kevin sagged against the gas lamppost.

"Basketball," Molly said. "But he's really too short for the NBA, so they're cutting him."

"My husband and I aren't much for sports. We were sorry to hear about Judith. Lovely woman. Very knowledgeable about the local bird population. We're on the trail of Kirtland's warbler."

John Pearson outweighed his wife by nearly two hundred pounds, and his double chins wiggled. "We hope you're not planning on making too many changes in the food. Judith's breakfast spread is famous. And her cherry chocolate cake . . . " He paused, and Molly half expected him to kiss his fingertips. "Is afternoon tea still at five o'clock?"

Molly waited for Kevin to respond, but he seemed to have lost the power of speech. She cocked her head at them. "I have a feeling tea might be a little late today."

9

Daphne lived in the prettiest cottage in Nightingale Woods. It sat off by itself in a great grove of trees, which meant she could play her electric guitar whenever she wanted and no one complained.

—*Daphne Gets Lost*

Kevin had his cell phone pressed to one ear, the B&B's phone pressed to the other as he paced the entrance hall barking orders to his business manager and somebody who was either a secretary or a housekeeper. Behind him an imposing walnut staircase rose half a flight, then turned at a right angle. The spindles were dusty, and the richly patterned carpet on the treads needed vacuuming. An urn filled with drooping peacock feathers topped a pilaster on the landing.

His pacing was wearing her out, so Molly decided to explore while he talked. With Roo trotting after her, she moved slowly into the front parlor. The pincushion settee and pleasing jumble of chairs were upholstered in pretty buttercup and rose fabrics. Botanical prints and pastoral scenes hung in gilded frames on the cream-colored walls, while lace curtains framed the windows. Brass candlesticks, a Chinese jardiniere, and some crystal boxes ornamented the mantel above the fireplace. Unfortunately, the brass was tarnished, the crystal dull, and the tabletops dusty. A lint-flecked Oriental carpet contributed to the overall air of neglect.

The same was true of the music room, where the traditional pineapple-patterned wallpaper served as a background for rose-patterned reading chairs and a spinet piano. A writing desk in the corner held ivory stationery, along with an old-fashioned fountain pen and a bottle of ink. A pair of tarnished silver candlesticks sat on top, near an old toby jug.

A Queen Anne table and ten matching high-backed chairs graced the dining room across the hallway. The room's dominant feature was a square, cutaway bay window that provided a generous view of lake and woods. Molly suspected that the tall crystal vases on the sideboard had held fresh flowers when his Aunt Judith was alive, but now the marble top was cluttered with the remains of breakfast serving dishes.

She walked through a door at the back into an old-fashioned country kitchen warmed by blue-and-white tiles as well as wooden cabinets topped with a collection of chintzwear china pitchers. In the center a sturdy farm table with a marble slab served as a workspace, but now dirty mixing bowls, eggshells, measuring cups, and an open jar of dried cranberries littered the surface. The very modern restaurant-size stove needed cleaning, and the dishwasher door hung open.

A round oak table for informal dining sat in front of the windows. Printed pillows covered the seats of the farmhouse chairs, and a punched-tin chandelier hung above. Behind the house the yard sloped down to the lake, with woods on each side.

She peeked into a large, well-stocked pantry that smelled of baking spices, then entered a small connecting room, where the very modern computer resting on an old tavern table signaled that this was the office. She was tired of walking, so she sat down and booted it up. Twenty minutes later she heard Kevin.

"Molly! Where the hell are you?"

Slytherin rudeness didn't deserve a response, so she ignored him and opened another file.

For a normally graceful man, he had an unusually heavy step that morning, and she heard his approach long before he located her. "Why didn't you answer me?"

She repositioned the mouse as he came up behind her, deciding it was time to face up to him. "I don't answer roars."

"I wasn't roaring! I was—"

When he didn't finish, she looked up to see what had distracted him. Outside the window a very young woman in skimpy black shorts and a tight, scoop-neck top flew across the garden, followed by an equally young man. She turned and ran backward, laughing and taunting him. He called out something to her. She grabbed the hem of her top and tugged it up, flashing her bare breasts.

"Whoa . . . " Kevin said.

Molly felt her skin grow hot.

The man caught her around the waist and dragged her into the woods so that they weren't visible from the road, although Kevin and Molly could see them clearly. He leaned against the trunk of an old maple. She immediately jumped on him and wrapped her legs around his waist.

Molly felt the slow pulse of dormant blood stirring as she watched the young lovers begin to devour each other. He cupped her bottom. She pressed her breasts to his chest, then, resting her elbows on his shoulders, caught his head to steady it, as if she weren't already kissing him deeply enough.

Molly heard Kevin move behind her, and her body gave a sluggish throb. She could feel his height looming over her, his warmth penetrating her thin top. How could someone who made his living with sweat smell so clean?

The young man turned his lover so that her back was against the tree. He pushed a hand under her T-shirt and covered her breast.

Molly's own breasts tingled. She wanted to look away, but she couldn't manage it. Apparently Kevin couldn't either, because he didn't move, and his voice sounded vaguely husky.

"I think we've just caught our first glimpse of Amy and Troy Anderson."

The young woman dropped to the ground. She was petite but leggy, with dishwater-blond hair pulled up in a purple scrunchy. His hair was darker and cut close to his head. He was thin and quite a bit taller than the girl.

Her hands slipped between their bodies. It took Molly only a moment to realize what she was doing.

Unzipping his jeans.

"They're going to do it right in front of us," Kevin said softly.

His comment jerked Molly out of her trance. She bolted up from the computer and turned her back to the window. "Not in front of me."

His eyes drifted from the window to her, and for a moment he didn't say anything. He just gazed at her. Again that sluggish pulsing in her bloodstream. It reminded her that even though they'd been intimate, she didn't know him.

"Getting a little hot for you?"

She was definitely warmer than she wanted to be. "Voyeurism isn't my thing."

"Now, that surprises me. This should be right up your alley, since you seem to like preying on the unsuspecting."

Time hadn't diminished the embarrassment she felt. She opened her mouth to apologize once again, only to have something calculating in his expression stop her. With a shock she realized that Kevin wasn't interested in groveling. He wanted to be entertained with an argument.

He deserved her very best, but her brain had been inactive for so long, it was hard to come up with a response. "Only when I'm drunk."

"Are you saying you were drunk that night?" He glanced out the window, then back at her.

"Totally wasted. Stoli on ice. Why else do you think I behaved like that?"

Another look out the window, this one lasting a bit longer. "I don't remember you being drunk."

"You were asleep."

"What I remember is that you told me you were sleepwalking."

She managed a huffy sniff. "Well, I hardly wanted to confess that I had a problem with alcohol."

"Recovered now, are you?" Those green eyes were much too perceptive.

"Even the thought of Stoli makes me nauseous."

His gaze raked a slow, steady path over her body. "You know what I think?"

She swallowed. "I'm not interested."

"I think I was just irresistible to you."

She searched her imaginative brain for a scorching comeback, but the best she could come up with was a rather pitiful "Whatever makes you happy."

He shifted his position to get a better view of the scene outside. Then he winced. "That's got to hurt."

She wanted to look so badly she could barely stand it. "That's sick. Don't watch them."

"It's interesting." He tilted his head slightly. "Now, that's a new way to go about it."

"Stop it!"

"And I don't even think *that's* legal."

She couldn't stand it any longer, and she whirled around, only to realize that the lovers had vanished.

His chuckle had an evil edge. "If you run outside, you might be able to catch them before they're done."

"You think you're funny."

"Fairly amusing."

"Well, then, this should really entertain you. I dipped into Aunt Judith's computer records, and the B&B seems to be booked solid into September. Most of the cottages, too. You won't believe how much people are willing to pay to stay here."

"Let me see that." He pushed past her to get to the computer.

"Enjoy yourself. I'm going to find someplace to stay."

He was busy scanning the screen, and he didn't respond, not even when she reached over him to pick up the piece of notepaper she'd used to jot down the names of the vacant cottages.

A pegboard hung on the wall next to the desk. She found the appropriate keys, stuck them in her pocket, and made her way through the kitchen. She hadn't eaten that day, and on the way she picked up a leftover slice of Charlotte Long's cranberry bread. The first bite told her that Mrs. Long had been right when she'd said she wasn't much of a cook, and she dropped it in the trash.

When she reached the hallway, curiosity won out over her fatigue, and she climbed the steps to see the rest of the house. Roo trotted at her

side as she peered into the guest rooms, each of which had been indi-
vidually decorated. There were book-filled nooks, pretty views from the
windows, and the homey decorating touches people expected at an
upscale B&B.

She spotted a bird's nest filled with antique glass marbles on top of a
stack of vintage hatboxes. An arrangement of apothecary bottles sat
near a wire birdcage. Pieces of embroidery in oval frames, old wooden
signs, and wonderful stoneware vases that should have held fresh flowers were tucked here and there. She also saw unmade beds, overflowing
trash cans, and grubby bathtubs draped with discarded towels. Clearly
Amy Anderson would rather cavort in the trees with her new husband
than clean.

At the end of the hallway she opened the door into the only room
that hadn't been rented out. She knew because it was tidy. Judging from
the family photos propped on the dressing table, the room had
belonged to Judith Tucker. It occupied the corner of the house, including the turret. She visualized Kevin sleeping beneath the carved headboard. He was so tall, he'd have to lie across the mattress.

An image of the way he'd looked the night she'd slipped into his bed
came back to her. She shook it off and made her way downstairs. As she
stepped out onto the front porch, she smelled pine, petunias, and the
lake. Roo stuck his nose in a flowerpot.

She wanted nothing more than to sink into one of the rockers and
take a nap, but since she wasn't going to join Kevin in Aunt Judith's bedroom, she needed to find a place to stay. "Come on, Roo. Let's go visit
the empty cottages."

One of the computer files had contained a diagram that marked the
location of each cottage. As she approached the Common, she noticed
the small, hand-painted signs near the front doors: GABRIEL'S TRUMPET,
MILK AND HONEY, GREEN PASTURES, GOOD NEWS.

As she passed Jacob's Ladder, a handsome, rawboned man came
through the woods. He looked as if he were in his early to mid-fifties,
significantly younger than the other residents she'd spotted. She nodded and received a brusque nod in response.

She headed in the opposite direction, toward Tree of Life, a coral cottage with plum and lavender trim. It was empty, as was Lamb of God. They were both charming, but she decided she'd like more privacy than the cottages on the Common afforded, so she turned away and walked back toward the more isolated ones that perched along the lane that paralleled the lake.

An odd sense of déjà vu came over her. Why did this place seem so familiar? As she passed the B&B, Roo pranced ahead of her, stopping to sniff at a clump of chickweed, then discovering an alluring patch of grass. When she came to the end of the lane, she saw exactly what she wanted nestled in the trees. Lilies of the Field.

The tiny cottage had been freshly painted the softest of creamy yellows with its spindles and lacy wooden trim accented in palest blue and the same dusty pink as the inside of a seashell. Her chest ached. The cottage looked like a nursery.

She mounted the steps and discovered that the screen door squeaked, just as it should. She found the proper key in her pocket and turned it in the lock. Then she stepped inside.

The cottage was decorated in authentic shabby chic instead of the kind that was trendy. The white-painted walls were old and wonderful. Underneath a dustcover she found a couch upholstered in a faded print. The battered wooden trunk in front of it served as a coffee table. A scrubbed pine chest sat along one wall, a brass swing-arm lamp next to it. Despite the musty smell, the cottage's white walls and lace curtains made everything feel airy.

Off to the left, the tiny kitchen held an old-fashioned gas stove and a small drop-leaf table with two farmhouse chairs similar to the ones she'd seen in the B&B's kitchen. A glance inside the painted wooden cupboard showed wonderfully mismatched pottery and china plates, more pressed glass, and sponge-painted mugs. Something ached inside her as she spotted a child's set of Peter Rabbit dishes, and she turned away.

The bathroom had a claw-foot tub along with an ancient pedestal sink. A rag rug covered the rough-planked floor in front of the tub, and someone had stenciled a chain of vines near the ceiling.

Two bedrooms occupied the back, one tiny and the other large enough for a double bed and a painted chest of drawers. The bed, covered in a faded quilt, had a curved iron headboard painted a soft yellow with a flower basket motif worked in the center. A small milk glass lamp rested on the bedside table.

In the back of the cottage, nestling into the woods, was a screened porch. Bent-willow chairs leaned against the wall, and a hammock hung across one corner. She'd done more today than she'd done in weeks, and just looking at the hammock made her realize how tired she was.

She lowered herself into it. Above her the beaded-board ceiling was painted the same creamy yellow as the exterior of the house, with subtle dusty pink and blue accents along the moldings. What a wonderful place. Just like a nursery.

She closed her eyes. The hammock rocked her like a cradle. She was asleep almost instantly.

The Klingon greeted Kevin at the cottage door with a growl and bared teeth. "Don't start. I'm not in the mood."

He walked past the dog to the bedroom and set down Molly's suitcase, then made his way to the kitchen. She wasn't there, but Charlotte Long had seen her disappear inside, and he found her on the porch, asleep in the hammock. Her watchdog scampered past him to do guard duty. Kevin gazed down at her.

She looked small and defenseless. One hand curled under her chin, and a lock of dark brown hair fell over her cheek. Her lashes were thick, but not thick enough to hide the shadows under her eyes, and he felt guilty for the way he'd been bullying her. At the same time, something told him she wouldn't react well to coddling. Not that he could have coddled her anyway. He still had too much resentment.

His eyes skimmed along her body, then lingered. She wore bright red capri jeans and a rumpled yellow sleeveless blouse with one of those Chinese collars. When she was awake and being her normal smart-ass self, it was hard to see her showgirl ancestry, but asleep it was a different story. Her ankles were trim, her legs slim, and her hips had a nice soft curve. Beneath her blouse, her breasts rose and fell, and, through the open V, he caught a glimpse of black lace. His hand itched to pop open the buttons and see more.

His reaction disgusted him. As soon as he got back to Chicago, he'd better call an old girlfriend because it had clearly been too long since he'd had sex.

The Klingon must have been reading his mind because he started to growl at him, then barked.

Roo awakened her. Molly eased her eyes open, then sucked in her breath as she saw the shadow of a man looming over her. She tried to sit up too quickly, and the hammock tipped.

Kevin caught her before she could fall and set her on her feet. "Don't you ever think first?"

She brushed the hair from her eyes and tried to blink herself awake. "What do you want?"

"Next time tell me when you're going to disappear."

"I did." She yawned. "But you were too busy gaping at Mrs. Anderson's breasts to pay attention."

He pulled a bent-willow chair away from the wall and sat down on it. "That couple is completely worthless. The minute you turn your back on them, they're climbing all over each other."

"They're newlyweds."

"Yeah, well, so are we."

There was nothing she could say to that. She sank down on the metal glider, which was missing its cushions and very uncomfortable.

His expression grew calculating. "One thing I'll say about Amy, at least she supports her husband."

"The way he was holding her against the tree—"

"It's the two of them against the world. Working side by side. Helping each other out. A team."

"If you think you're being subtle, you're not."

"I need some help."

"I can't hear a word you're saying."

"Apparently I'm stuck with this place for the summer. I'll get somebody in here to run it as soon as I can, but until then . . . "

"Until then nothing." She rose from the glider. "I'm not doing it. The sex-crazy newlyweds can help you. And what about Charlotte Long?"

"She says she hates to cook, and she was only doing it because of Judith. Besides, a couple of the guests came looking for me, and all of them take a dim view of her efforts." He rose and started to pace, his restless energy buzzing like a bug zapper. "I offered them a refund, but when it comes to their vacations, people are completely unreasonable. They want the refund plus everything they were promised in that *Virginia* magazine."

"*Victoria.*"

"Whatever. The point is, we're going to have to stay in this godforsaken place a little longer than I planned."

It wasn't godforsaken to her. It was charming, and she tried to make herself feel happy that they'd be here longer, but all she felt was empty.

"While you were taking your beauty rest, I went into town to put a Help Wanted ad in the local paper. I find out the place is so damn small the paper's a weekly, and it just came out today, so the next issue is seven days off! I put out the word with some of the locals, but I don't know how effective that's going to be."

"You think we'll be here a week?"

"No, I'll talk to people." He looked ready to take a bite out of something. "But I guess there's a chance if I can't find anyone until the ad's out. Not a big chance, but I suppose it could happen."

She sat on the glider. "I guess you'll be running a B&B until then."

He narrowed his eyes. "You seem to have forgotten that you took a vow to support me."

"I did not!"

"Did you pay any attention to those wedding vows you were saying?"

"I tried not to," she admitted. "I'm not in the habit of making promises I know I'm not going to keep."

"Neither am I, and so far I've kept my word."

"To love, honor, and obey? I don't think so."

"Those weren't the vows we took." He tucked his hands under his arms and watched her.

She tried to figure out what he was talking about, but her only memories of the ceremony were of the poodles and the way she'd held on to Andrew's sticky little hand for dear life. A sense of uneasiness crept through her. "Maybe you'd better refresh my memory."

"I'm talking about the vows Phoebe wrote for us," he said quietly. "Are you sure she didn't mention it to you?"

She'd mentioned it, but Molly'd been so miserable she hadn't paid attention. "I guess I wasn't listening."

"Well, I was. I even fixed a couple of the sentences to make them more realistic. Now, I might not have this exactly right—you can call your sister to verify—but the gist of it is that you, Molly, promised to accept me, Kevin, as your husband, at least for a while. You promised to give me your respect and consideration from that day forward. Notice there was no mention of love and honor. You promised not to speak badly of me to others." He eyed her. "And to support me in everything we share together."

Molly bit her lip. It was just like Phoebe to have written something like that. Of course she'd done it to protect the baby.

She pulled herself together. "Okay, you're a great quarterback. I can do the respect part. And if you don't count Phoebe, Dan, and Roo, I never speak badly of you to others."

"My eyes are tearing up from emotion. How about the other part? That 'support' thing?"

"That was supposed to be about— You know what it was about." She blinked her eyes and took a deep breath. "Phoebe certainly wasn't trying to force me into helping you run a B&B."

"Don't forget the cottages, and a sacred vow is just that."

"You kidnapped me yesterday, and now you're trying to manipulate me into forced labor!"

"It'll only be for a couple of days. A week at the most. Or maybe that's too much to ask from a rich girl."

"This is your problem, not mine."

He stared at her for a long moment, then that cold look settled over his face. "Yeah, I guess it is."

Kevin wasn't someone who asked for help easily, and she regretted her peevishness, but she couldn't be around people now. Still, she should have been more tactful about refusing him. "I just—I haven't been in great shape lately, and—"

"Forget it," he snapped. "I'll manage on my own." He stalked across the porch and out through the back door.

She stomped around the cottage for a while, feeling ugly and out of sorts. He'd brought in her suitcase. She unzipped it, only to go back out on the porch and stare at the lake.

Those wedding vows . . . She'd been prepared to break the traditional ones. Even couples who loved each other had a hard time living up to those. But these vows—the ones Phoebe had written—were different. These were vows that an honorable person should be able to keep.

Kevin had.

"Damn."

Roo looked up.

"I don't want to be with a lot of people now, that's all."

But she wasn't telling herself the whole truth. She mainly didn't want to be around *him.*

She glanced at her watch and saw that it was five o'clock. With a grimace she gazed down at her poodle. "I'm afraid we have some personal character building to do."

Ten guests had gathered in the buttercup and rose parlor for afternoon tea, but somehow Molly couldn't imagine *Victoria* magazine giving the occasion its seal of approval. The inlaid table at the side of the room held an open bag of Oreos, a can of grape Hi-C, a coffeepot, Styrofoam cups, and a jar that looked as if it contained powdered tea. Despite the fare, the guests seemed to be enjoying themselves.

The bird-watching Pearsons stood behind a pair of elderly women perched on the pincushion settee. Across the room two white-haired couples chatted. The women's gnarled fingers flashed with old diamonds and newer anniversary rings. One of the men had a walrus mustache, the other lime green golf slacks with white patent leather shoes. Another couple was younger, in their early fifties perhaps, prosperous baby boomers who could have stepped out of a Ralph Lauren ad. It was

Kevin, however, who dominated the room. As he stood by the fireplace, he looked so much like the lord of the manor that his shorts and Stars T-shirt might have been jodhpurs and a riding jacket.

" . . . so the president of the United States is sitting on the fifty-yard line, the Stars are down by four points, there are only seven seconds left on the clock, and I'm pretty sure I just sprained the heck out of my knee."

"That must have been painful," the boomer woman cooed.

"You don't notice the pain until later."

"I remember this game!" her husband exclaimed. "You hit Tippett on a fifty-yard post pattern, and the Stars won by three."

Kevin shook his head modestly. "I got lucky, Chet."

Molly rolled her eyes. Nobody made it to the top of the NFL trusting in luck. Kevin had gotten where he was by being the best. His good ol' boy act might charm the guests, but she knew the truth.

Still, as she watched him she knew she was seeing self discipline in action, and she begrudgingly gave him her respect. No one suspected he hated being here. She'd forgotten that he was a minister's son, but she shouldn't have. Kevin was a man who did his duty, even though he hated it. Just as he'd done when he'd married her.

"I can't believe it," Mrs. Chet cooed. "When we chose a bed-and-breakfast in the wilds of northeastern Michigan, we never imagined our host would be the famous Kevin Tucker."

Kevin graced her with his aw-shucks expression. Molly wanted to tell her not to bother flirting with him, since she didn't have a foreign accent.

"I'd love to hear your take on the draft." Chet readjusted the navy cotton sweater he'd tossed around the shoulders of his kelly green polo shirt.

"How about the two of us share a beer out on the front porch later on tonight?"

"I wouldn't mind joining you," walrus mustache interjected, while lime green pants nodded in agreement.

"We'll all do it," Kevin said graciously.

John Pearson polished off the last of the Oreos. "Now that Betty and

I know you personally, we'll have to start following the Stars. You, uh, wouldn't happen to have located one of Judith's lemon–poppy seed cakes in the freezer, would you?"

"I have no idea," Kevin said. "And that reminds me, I'd better apologize in advance for tomorrow's breakfast. Pancakes from a mix is the best I can do, so if you decide to leave, I'll understand. That offer for double your refund still stands."

"We wouldn't think about leaving such a charming place." Mrs. Chet gave Kevin a look that had adultery written all over it. "And don't worry about breakfast. I'll be glad to pitch in."

Molly did her part to protect the Ten Commandments by forcing herself out of the doorway and into the room. "That won't be necessary. I know Kevin wants you to relax while you're here, and I think I can promise that the food will be a little better tomorrow."

Kevin's eyes flickered, but if she expected him to fall at her feet from gratitude, he quickly disabused her of the notion with his introduction. "This is my estranged wife, Molly."

"She doesn't look strange," walrus mustache's wife said in a too-loud whisper to her friend.

"That's because you don't know her," Kevin murmured.

"My wife's a bit hard of hearing." Like the others, Mr. Mustache was obviously taken aback by Kevin's introduction. Several of those in the room regarded her curiously. The *People* spread . . .

Molly tried to be annoyed, but it was a relief not having to pretend they were a happily married couple.

John Pearson stepped forward hastily. "Your husband has quite a sense of humor. We're delighted you'll be cooking for us, Mrs. Tucker."

"Please call me Molly. Now, if you'll excuse me, I need to check the supplies in the kitchen. And I know your rooms aren't as orderly as they should be, but Kevin will clean them up himself before bedtime." As she headed down the hallway, she decided Mr. Tough Guy didn't always have to have the last word.

Her satisfaction faded the moment she opened the kitchen door and saw the young lovers having sex against Aunt Judith's refrigerator. She stepped backward only to bump into Kevin's chest.

He peered over her head. "Awww, for Pete's sake."

The lovers sprang apart. Molly was ready to avert her eyes, but Kevin stalked into the kitchen. He glared at Amy, whose scrunchy had come out of her hair and who was doing up her buttons wrong. "I thought I asked you to get those dishes cleaned up."

"Yeah, well, uh . . . "

"Troy, you're supposed to be mowing the Common."

He struggled with his zipper. "I was just getting ready to—"

"I know exactly what you were getting ready to do, and believe me, that won't get the grass cut!"

Troy looked sulky and muttered under his breath.

"Did you say something?" Kevin's bark must be the same one he used on rookies.

Troy's Adam's apple worked. "There's, uh, too much work to do around here for what we're getting paid."

"And what's that?"

Troy told him, and Kevin doubled it on the spot. Troy's eyes gleamed. "Cool."

"But there's a catch," Kevin said smoothly. "You're going to have to actually do some work for that money. Amy, sweetheart, don't even think about leaving tonight until those guest rooms are spick-and-span. And, Troy, you've got an appointment with the lawn mower. Any questions?"

As they shook their heads warily, Molly saw matching hickeys on their necks. Something uncomfortable stirred in the pit of her stomach.

Troy moved toward the door, and Amy's longing gaze reminded Molly of Ingrid Bergman bidding Humphrey Bogart a final farewell on that Casablanca runway.

What would it feel like to be that much in love? Again she felt that unpleasant quivering in her stomach. Only after the lovers had parted did she realize it was jealousy. They had something she seemed destined never to experience.

10

"It's much too dangerous," said Daphne.
"That's what makes it fun," Benny replied.

—*Daphne Gets Lost*

A few hours later Molly stepped back to admire the homey space she'd created for herself on the nursery cottage's screened porch. She'd put the blue-and-yellow striped cushions on the glider and the chintz-patterned ones on the bent-willow chairs. The small, drop-leaf kitchen table with its chipped white paint now sat against one side of the screen with two of the unmatched farmhouse chairs. Tomorrow she'd find some flowers to put in the old copper watering can she'd stuck on top.

With some of the essentials she'd transferred from the B&B to the cottage, she fixed toast and a scrambled egg and carried them out to the table. While Roo snoozed nearby, she watched daylight begin to fade over the wedge of lake visible through the trees. Everything smelled of pine and the dank, distant scent of the water. She heard something that sounded distinctly human rustling outside. At home she would have been alarmed. Here she settled back in the chair and waited to see who would appear. Unfortunately, it was Kevin.

She hadn't thrown the latch on the screen door, and she wasn't surprised when he walked inside without an invitation. "The brochure says breakfast is from seven to nine. What kind of people want to eat that early when they're on vacation?" He set an alarm clock on the table, then glanced at the remnants of her scrambled egg. "You could have gone into town with me and had a burger," he said begrudgingly.

"Thanks, but I don't do burgers."

"So you're a vegetarian like your sister?"

"I'm not as strict. She won't eat anything with a face. I won't eat anything with a cute face."

"This I've got to hear."

"Actually, it's a pretty good system for healthy eating."

"I take it you think cows are cute." He couldn't have sounded more skeptical.

"I love cows. Definitely cute."

"How about pigs?"

"Does the movie *Babe* ring a bell?"

"I won't even ask about lamb."

"I'd appreciate it if you didn't. Or rabbit." She shuddered. "I'm not too attracted to chickens and turkey, so I do occasionally indulge. I also eat fish since I can avoid my favorite."

"Dolphin, I'll bet." He settled into the old wooden chair across from her and gazed down at Roo, who'd stirred enough to snarl. "You might have latched on to something here that I could get into. There are certain animals, for example, I find positively repulsive."

She gave him her silkiest smile. "It's well known that men who don't like poodles are the same ones who grind up human body parts in garbage disposals."

"Only if I'm bored."

She laughed, then caught herself as she realized he'd turned the charm-thing on her, and she'd nearly gotten caught up in it. Was this supposed to be her reward for agreeing to help him out? "I don't understand why you dislike it here so much. The lake is beautiful. There's swimming, boating, hiking. What's so bad about that?"

"When you're the only kid, and you have to go to a church service every day, it loses its charm. Besides, there's a limit to the size motor you can put on a boat, so there's no water skiing."

"Or Jet Skis."

"What?"

"Nothing. Weren't there ever other children around?"

"Sometimes a grandkid would show up for a few days. That was the highlight of my summer." He grimaced. "Of course, half the time that grandkid was a girl."

"Life's a bitch."

He leaned back in his chair until it rested on two legs. She waited for it to tilt over, but he was too well coordinated for that to happen. "Do you really know how to cook, or were you just winging it in front of the guests?"

"I was winging it." She lied hoping to make him nervous. Her everyday cooking might leave something to be desired, but she loved to bake, especially for her nieces and nephews. Sugar cookies with bunny ears were her specialty.

"Terrific." The legs of the chair banged to the floor. "God, this place is boring. Let's take a walk along the lake before it gets dark."

"I'm too tired."

"You haven't done enough today to make yourself tired." He was full of restless energy with no place to go, so she shouldn't have been startled when he grabbed her wrist and tugged her from her seat. "Come on, I haven't been able to work out for two days. I'm going stir crazy."

She pulled away. "Go work out now. Nobody's stopping you."

"I have to meet my fan club on the front porch soon. You need the exercise, so stop being stubborn. Stay here, Godzilla." He opened the screen and gave Molly a gentle push, then firmly closed in a yapping Roo.

She didn't offer any real resistance, even though she was exhausted and she knew it wasn't a good idea to be alone with him. "I'm not in the mood, and I want my dog."

"If I said grass was green, you'd argue with me." He tugged her along the path.

"I refuse to be nice to my kidnapper."

"For somebody who was kidnapped, you're not trying too hard to get away."

"I like it here."

He glanced back at the cozy nest she'd made for herself on the porch. "Next thing you'll be hiring a decorator."

"We rich girls like our comforts, even if it's only for a few days."

"I guess."

The path widened as it got closer to the lake, then wound along the shore for a while before narrowing again and making a sharp incline up a rocky bluff that overlooked the water. Kevin pointed in the opposite direction. "There are some wetlands over there, and behind the campgrounds there's a meadow with a brook."

"Bobolink Meadow."

"What?"

"It's a— Nothing." It was the name of the meadow on the edge of Nightingale Woods.

"You can get a good view of the town from that bluff."

She gazed up the steep path. "I don't have enough energy for the climb."

"Then we won't go all the way."

She knew he was lying. Still, her legs didn't feel as wobbly as they'd been yesterday, so she set off with him. "How do the people in the town support themselves?"

"Tourism mainly. The lake has good fishing, but it's so isolated that it hasn't been overdeveloped like a lot of other places. There's a decent golf course, and the area has some of the best cross-country trails in the state."

"I'm glad nobody's spoiled it with a big resort."

The path was beginning to angle uphill, and she needed all her breath for the climb. She wasn't surprised when he left her behind. What surprised her was the fact that she kept on going.

He called down to her from the top of the bluff. "Not exactly a walking advertisement for physical fitness, are you?"

"Just skipped a few"—she gasped—"Tae-Bo classes."

"You want me find an oxygen tank?"

She was breathing too hard to respond.

She was glad she'd made the effort when she caught the view from the top. There was still enough light to see the town at the far end of the lake. It looked quaint and rustic. Boats bobbed in the harbor, and a church steeple peeked through the trees against a rainbow candy sky.

Kevin pointed toward a cluster of luxury houses closer to the bluff. "Those are vacation homes. The last time I was here, that was all woods, but nothing else seems to have changed much."

She took in the vista. "It's so pretty."

"I guess." He'd moved toward the edge of the bluff, where he gazed down at the water. "I used to dive off here in the summer."

"A little dangerous for a kid by himself, wasn't it?"

"That's what made it fun."

"Your parents must have been saints. I can't imagine how many gray hairs you—" She stopped as she realized he was kicking off his shoes instead of paying attention to her.

Pure instinct made her take a quick step forward, but she was too late. He threw himself into space, clothes and all.

She gasped and rushed to the edge just in time to watch the sharp, clean line of his body hit the water. There was barely a splash.

She waited, but he didn't come up. Her hand flew to her mouth. She searched the water but couldn't spot him. "Kevin!"

Then the surface rippled, and his head emerged. She released her breath, then caught it again as he turned his face to the evening sky. Water ran in rivulets over those clean planes, and something triumphant shone in his expression.

She clenched her fists and shouted down at him. "*You idiot!* Are you completely crazy?"

Treading water, he looked up at her, his teeth gleaming. "Are you going to tattle to your big sister?"

She was shaking so much that she stomped her foot. "You had no idea whether that water was deep enough for diving!"

"It was deep enough the last time I dove in."

"And how long ago was that?"

"About seventeen years." He flipped to his back. "But there's been a lot of rain."

"You're a moron! Have all those concussions scrambled your brain cells?"

"I'm alive, aren't I?" He flashed a daredevil grin. "Come on in, bunny lady. The water's real warm."

"Are you out of your mind? I'm not diving off this cliff!"

He flipped to his side, took a few lazy strokes. "Don't you know how to dive?"

"Of course I do. I went to summer camp for *nine* years!"

His voice lapped at her, a low, lazy taunt. "I'll bet you stink."

"I do not!"

"Then are you chicken, bunny lady?"

Oh, God. It was as if a fire alarm had gone off inside her head, and she didn't even kick off her sandals. She just curled the toes over the edge of the rock and threw herself off the bluff, following him into insanity.

All the way down she tried to scream.

She hit harder than he had and there was a lot more splash. When she came up, water dripped over the stunned expression on his face.

"Jesus." He spoke on a softly expelled breath that sounded more like a prayer than a curse. And then he started to yell. "*What the hell do you think you're doing?*"

The water was so cold she couldn't catch her breath. Even her bones were shriveling. "It's *freezing*! You lied to me!"

"If you ever do anything like that again . . . "

"You dared me!"

"If I'd dared you to drink poison, would you have been stupid enough to do that, too?"

She didn't know if she was angrier with him for goading her into being so reckless or at herself for taking the bait. Water flew as she slapped it with her arm. "Look at me! I act like a normal person when I'm around other people!"

"Normal?" He blinked the splash from his eyes. "Is that why I found you holed up in your apartment looking like spoiled shrimp?"

"At least I was safe there, instead of catching pneumonia here!" Her teeth began to chatter, and her icy, waterlogged clothes pulled at her. "Or maybe making me jump off a cliff is your idea of therapy?"

"I didn't think you'd do it!"

"I'm nuts, remember?"

"Molly . . . "

"Crazy Molly!"

"I didn't say—"

"That's what you're thinking. Molly the fruitcake! Molly the lunatic!

Off her rocker! Certifiable! The tiniest little miscarriage, and she flips out!"

She choked. She hadn't meant to say that, hadn't ever intended to mention it again. But the same force that had made her jump off the cliff had pushed out the words.

A thick, heavy silence fell between them. When he finally broke it, she heard his pity. "Let's go in now so you can get warmed up." He turned away and began swimming toward the shore.

She had started to cry, so she stayed where she was.

He reached the bank, but he didn't try to climb out. Instead, he looked back at her. The water lapped at his waist, and his voice was a gentle ripple. "You need to get out. It'll be dark soon."

The cold had numbed her limbs, but it hadn't numbed her heart. Grief overwhelmed her. She wanted to sink under the surface and never come up. She gulped for air and whispered words she'd never intended to say. "You don't care, do you?"

"You're just trying to pick a fight," he said softly. "Come on. Your teeth are chattering."

Words slid through the tightness in her throat. "I know you don't care. I even understand."

"Molly, don't do this to yourself."

"We had a little girl," she whispered. "I made them find out and tell me."

The water lapped the bank. His hushed words drifted across the smooth surface. "I didn't know."

"I named her Sarah."

"You're tired. This isn't a good time."

She shook her head. Looked up into the sky. Spoke the truth, not to condemn him, just to point out why he could never understand how she felt. "Losing her didn't mean anything to you."

"I haven't thought about it. The baby wasn't real to me like it was to you."

"*She*! The baby was a *she,* not an *it*!"

"I'm sorry."

The unfairness of attacking him silenced her. It was wrong to condemn him for not sharing her suffering. Of course the baby hadn't been real to him. He hadn't invited Molly into his bed, hadn't wanted a child, hadn't carried the baby inside him.

"I'm the one who's sorry. I didn't mean to yell. My emotions keep getting away from me." Her hand trembled as she pushed a strand of wet hair from her eyes. "I won't bring this up again. I promise you."

"Come on out now," he said quietly.

Her limbs were clumsy from the cold, and her clothes heavy as she swam toward the bank. By the time she got there, he'd climbed out onto a low, flat rock.

He crouched down and pulled her up beside him. She landed on her knees, a cold, dripping, miserable wreck.

He tried to lighten the mood. "At least I kicked off my shoes before I dove in. Yours flew off when you hit the water. I'd have gone after them, but I was in shock."

The rock had retained some of the day's heat, and a little of it seeped through her clammy shorts. "It doesn't matter. They were my oldest sandals." Her last pair of Manolo Blahniks. Given the current state of her finances, she'd have to replace them with rubber shower thongs.

"You can pick up another pair in town tomorrow." He rose. "We'd better head back before you get sick. Why don't you start walking? I'll catch up with you as soon as I rescue my own shoes."

He headed back up the path. She hugged herself against the evening chill and put one foot in front of the other, trying not to think. She hadn't gone far before he came up next to her, T-shirt and shorts sticking to his body. They walked in silence for a while.

"The thing is . . . "

When he didn't go on, she looked up at him. "What?"

He looked troubled. "Forget it."

The woods rustled around them with evening sounds. "All right."

He shifted his shoes from one hand to the other. "After it was over . . . I just . . . I didn't let myself think about her."

She understood, but it made her feel even lonelier.

He hesitated. She wasn't used to that. He always seemed so certain.

"What do you think she—" He cleared his throat. "What do you think Sarah would have been like?"

Her heart constricted. A fresh wave of pain swept over her, but it didn't throb in the same way as her old pain. Instead, it stung like antiseptic on a cut.

Her lungs expanded, contracted, expanded again. She was startled to realize she could still breathe, that her legs could still move. She heard the crickets begin their evening jam. A squirrel scuffled in the leaves.

"Well . . . " She was trembling, and she wasn't sure whether the sound that slipped from her was a choked laugh or a leftover sob. "Gorgeous, if she took after you." Her chest ached, but instead of fighting the pain, she embraced it, absorbed it, let it become part of her. "Extremely smart, if she took after me."

"And reckless. I think today pretty much proves that. Gorgeous, huh? Thanks for the compliment."

"Like you don't know." Her heart felt a little lighter. She wiped at her runny nose with the back of her hand.

"So how come you think you're so smart?"

"Summa cum laude. Northwestern. What about you?"

"I graduated."

She smiled, but she wasn't ready to stop talking about Sarah. "I'd never have sent her to summer camp."

He nodded. "I'd never have made her go to church every day during the summer."

"That's a lot of church."

"Nine years is a lot of summer camp."

"She might have been clumsy and a slow learner."

"Not Sarah."

A little capsule of warmth encircled her heart.

He slowed. Looked up into the trees. Slipped one hand into his pocket. "I guess it just wasn't her time to be born."

Molly took a breath and whispered back, "I guess not."

11

"Company's coming!" Celia the Hen clucked. "We'll bake cakes and tarts and custard pies!"

—*Daphne Makes a Mess*

M olly set the alarm clock Kevin had left for five-thirty, and by seven o'clock the smell of blueberry muffins filled the downstairs of the B&B. In the dining room, the sideboard held a stack of pale yellow china plates with a ginkgo leaf at each center. Dark green napkins, pressed-glass water goblets, and pleasantly mismatched sterling completed the setting. A pan of sticky buns from the freezer baked in the oven while the marble slab on the work table held a brown pottery baking dish filled with thick slices of bread soaking in an egg batter fragrant with vanilla and cinnamon.

For the first time in months Molly was ravenous, but she hadn't found time to eat. Preparing breakfast for a house full of paying guests was a lot more challenging than making smiley-face pancakes for the Calebow kids. As she moved Aunt Judith's recipe notebook away from the French toast batter, she tried to work up some resentment against Kevin, who was still asleep upstairs, but she couldn't. By acknowledging the baby last night, he'd given her a gift.

The burden of the miscarriage no longer felt as if it were hers alone to bear, and her pillow hadn't been tear-soaked when she'd awakened. Her depression wasn't going to vanish instantly, but she was ready to entertain the possibility of being happy again.

Kevin straggled in after she'd given John Pearson his second serving of French toast. His eyes were bleary, and he bore the look of a man suffering from a lethal hangover. "Your pit bull tried to corner me in the hallway."

"He doesn't like you."

"So I've noticed."

She realized something was missing, but it took her a moment to figure out what it was. His hostility. The anger Kevin had been holding against her finally seemed to have faded.

"Sorry I overslept," he said. "I told you last night to kick me out of bed if I wasn't up when you got here."

Not in a million years. Nothing would make her enter Kevin Tucker's bedroom, especially now that he was no longer looking at her as if she were his mortal enemy. She tilted her head toward the empty liquor bottles in the trash. "It must have been quite a party last night."

"They all wanted to talk about the draft, and one topic led to another. I'll say one thing for that generation, they sure know how to drink."

"It didn't affect Mr. Pearson's appetite."

He gazed at the French toast that was turning golden brown on the griddle. "I thought you didn't know how to cook."

"I phoned Martha Stewart. If people want bacon or sausage, you'll have to fry it."

"The *Babe* thing?"

"And proud of it. You're also waiting tables." She shoved the coffeepot at him, then turned the French toast.

He gazed at the coffeepot. "Ten years in the NFL, and this is what it all comes down to."

Despite his complaints, Kevin was surprised how quickly the next hour passed. He poured coffee, carried food back and forth, entertained the guests, and swiped some of Molly's pancakes for himself. She was a great cook, and he got sparks out of her by telling her he'd decided he'd let her keep the job.

Seeing those eyes flash felt good. Last night's confrontation seemed to have lifted some of her depression, and she had a little of the sparkle back that he remembered from Door County. He, on the other hand, had stared at the bedroom ceiling until dawn. Never again would he be able to think about the baby as an abstraction. Last night had given her a name. *Sarah.*

He blinked and grabbed the coffeepot for another round of refills.

Charlotte Long peeked in to see how Molly was doing and ended up eating two muffins. The sticky buns had gotten a little burned at the corners, but the French toast was good, and Molly didn't hear any complaints. She'd just downed her own breakfast standing up when Amy appeared.

"Sorry I'm late," she muttered. "I didn't get out of here until like eleven last night."

Molly spotted a fresh hickey on her neck, this one just above her collarbone. She was ashamed to feel another pang of jealousy. "You did a good job. The house already looks better. Why don't you get started on those dishes?"

Amy wandered over to the sink and began loading the dishwasher. Clips with tiny pink starfish on them held her hair away from her face. She'd outlined, shadowed, and mascaraed her eyes, but either she hadn't bothered with lipstick or Troy had already eaten it off.

"Your husband's really cute. I don't watch football, but even I know who he is. That's so cool. Troy says he's like the third-best quarterback in the NFL."

"First-best. He just needs to control his talent better."

Amy stretched, hiking her purple top above her navel and forcing her shorts even lower on her hipbones. "I heard you just got married, too. Isn't it great?"

"A dream come true," Molly said dryly. Apparently Amy didn't read *People.*

"We've been married like three and a half months."

Just about the same as Kevin and Molly. Except Kevin and Molly weren't having any trouble keeping their hands off each other.

Amy resumed loading the dishwasher. "Everybody said we were too young—I'm nineteen and Troy's twenty—but we couldn't wait any longer. Me and Troy are Christians. We don't believe in sex before marriage."

"So now you're making up for lost time?"

"It's so cool." Amy grinned, and Molly smiled back.

"It might be better if you didn't try to make up for any more of that lost time during working hours."

Amy rinsed out a mixing bowl. "I guess. It's just so hard."

"The slave driver will probably be checking up on you today, so why don't you get the bedrooms done as soon as you're finished here?"

"Yeah . . . " She sighed. "If you see Troy outside, will you like tell him I love him and everything?"

"I don't think so."

"Yeah, I guess that's immature. My sister says I should be a little more standoffish or he'll take me for granted."

Molly remembered the adoration on Troy's youthful face. "I don't think you have to worry about that yet."

Kevin had disappeared by the time Molly was done in the kitchen, probably tending to his hangover. She made iced tea, then phoned Phoebe to tell her where she was. Her sister's confusion didn't surprise her, but she couldn't explain how Kevin had blackmailed her into going with him without revealing too much about her physical and emotional condition. Instead, she just said that Kevin needed some help and she'd wanted to get away from the city. Phoebe started clucking just like Celia the Hen, and Molly got off the phone as quickly as possible.

She was tired by the time she finished baking Aunt Judith's citrus Bundt cake for afternoon tea, but she couldn't resist sprucing up the parlor a little. As she filled a cut-glass bowl with potpourri, Roo began barking. She went outside to investigate and saw a woman emerge from a dusty burgundy Lexus and turn to gaze out over the Common. Molly wondered if Kevin had checked the computer to see if any new guests were arriving. They needed to get better organized.

Molly took in the woman's oyster-white tunic, bronze capris, and sculpted sandals. Everything about her was stylish and expensive. She turned, and Molly immediately recognized her: Lilly Sherman.

Molly had met a lot of celebrities over the years, so she was seldom awed by famous people, but Lilly Sherman made her feel starstruck. Everything about her radiated glamour. This was a woman accustomed to snarling traffic, and Molly half expected some paparazzi to jump out of the pine trees.

The stylish sunglasses on top of her head held the rich auburn hair that had been her trademark away from her face. Her hair was shorter than it had been in her days as Ginger Hill, but it still had a sexy, tumbled look. Her complexion was pale and porcelain-smooth, her figure voluptuous. Molly thought of all the girls she'd known with eating disorders that had left them cadaverously thin. In earlier times women had aspired toward Lilly's figure, and they'd probably been better for it.

As Lilly headed up the path toward the house, Molly saw that her eyes were an unusually vibrant shade of green, even more vivid than on television. A faint web of lines fishtailed from the corners, but she looked barely forty. The large diamond on her left hand sparkled as she bent down to greet Roo. It took Molly a few moments to accept the fact that her poodle's stomach was being rubbed by Lilly Sherman.

"This place is a bitch to get to." Lilly's voice had the same husky quality Molly remembered from her days as Ginger Hill, but now it was a shade more sultry.

"It's a little isolated."

Lilly straightened and came closer, regarding Molly with the neutral politeness celebrities adopted to keep people at a distance. Then her attention sharpened, and her eyes frosted. "I'm Lilly Sherman. Would you have someone bring in my suitcases?"

Uh-oh. She'd recognized Molly from the *People* article. This woman wasn't her friend.

Molly stepped aside as Lilly climbed the steps to the porch. "We're sort of reorganizing at the moment. Do you happen to have a reservation?"

"I'd hardly come all this way without one. I spoke with Mrs. Long two days ago, and she said you had a room."

"Yes, we probably do. I'm just not exactly sure where. I'm a big fan, by the way."

"Thank you." Her reply was so cool that Molly wished she hadn't mentioned it.

Lilly gazed at Roo, who was trying to impress her with his Bruce

Willis sneer. "My cat's in the car. Mrs. Long said it wouldn't be a problem to bring her, but your dog seems a little fierce."

"It's all show. Roo might not like having a cat around, but he won't
hurt her. Introduce them if you like while I go inside to check on your
room."

Lilly Sherman's star might have faded, but she was still a star, and
Molly expected her to object to being kept waiting, but she said nothing.

As Molly headed inside, she wondered if Kevin knew about this. Had
they been lovers? Lilly seemed too intelligent, not to mention that she
spoke flawless English. Still . . .

Molly hurried upstairs and found Amy bent over one of the tubs, her
tight black shorts forming a world-class wedgie.

"A guest just arrived, and I don't know where to put her. Is anybody
leaving?"

Amy straightened and gazed at Molly strangely. "No, but there's the
attic. No one's stayed up there this season."

"The attic?"

"It's pretty nice."

Molly couldn't imagine sticking Lilly Sherman in an attic.

Amy settled back on her heels. "Uh, Molly, if you ever want to talk
about, you know, things with me, you can . . . "

"Things?"

"I mean, I noticed when I cleaned Kevin's room that you didn't sleep
there last night."

Molly found it irritating to be pitied by someone with connect-the-
dots hickeys. "We're estranged, Amy. Nothing for you to worry about."

"I'm really sorry. I mean, like, if it's about sex or anything, I could
maybe answer any questions or, you know, give you some advice."

Molly had become an object of pity for a nineteen-year-old Dr. Ruth.
"Not necessary."

She hurried upstairs to the attic and found the room surprisingly
spacious, despite its sloping ceiling and dormers. The antique furniture
was homey and the four poster double bed seemed to have a comfortable mattress. A large window had been added at one end to give more
light. Molly threw it open for fresh air, then investigated the tiny, old-

fashioned bathroom at the opposite end. Barely adequate, but at least it was private, and if Lilly Sherman didn't like it, she could leave.

Just the thought of it raised her spirits.

She asked Amy to get the room ready, then rushed downstairs. There was still no sign of Kevin. She returned to the front porch.

Lilly stood near the railing stroking the enormous marmalade cat in her arms while Roo sulked beneath one of the wooden rockers. He hopped up as Molly opened the front door, gave her an injured look, and scurried inside. She arranged her face in a pleasant expression. "I hope your cat will be gentle with him."

"They kept their distance." Lilly rubbed her thumb over the cat's chin. "This is Marmalade, commonly known as Marmie."

The longhaired cat was nearly the size of a raccoon, with gold eyes, enormous paws, and a large head. "Hey, Marmie. Go easy on Roo, will you?" The cat meowed.

"I'm afraid the only empty room is the attic. It's nice, but it's still an attic, and the bathroom leaves something to be desired. You may want to reconsider staying or maybe you'd rather take one of the cottages. They're not all filled yet."

"I prefer the house, and I'm sure this will be fine."

Since Lilly had Four Seasons written all over her, Molly couldn't imagine anything about it would be fine. Still, manners were manners. "I'm Molly Somerville."

"Yes, I recognized you," she said coldly. "You're Kevin's wife."

"We're estranged. I'm just helping him out for a few days."

"I see." Her expression said she didn't see at all.

"I'll get you some iced tea while you're waiting."

Molly raced through her preparations and was just returning to the porch when she spotted Kevin crossing the Common toward the house. Since breakfast he'd changed into faded jeans, a pair of battered sneakers, and an old black T-shirt with the sleeves ripped out so that ravelings draped his biceps. The hammer protruding from his pocket indicated either that he'd recovered from his hangover or had a high tolerance for pain. Remembering the hits he'd taken over the years, she suspected it was the latter. Since he disliked the place so much, she wondered why he was putting himself out to do repairs. Boredom, she suspected, or maybe that preacher's kid's sense of duty that kept complicating his life.

"Hey, Daphne! You want to go into town with me to pick up some supplies?"

She smiled to hear him call her Daphne again. "We have a new guest."

"That's great," he said unenthusiastically. "Just what we need."

The rocker banged against the wall, and she turned to see Lilly stand up. The diva had disappeared, and in her place was a vulnerable, ashen-faced woman. Molly set down the iced tea tumbler. "Are you all right?"

In a barely perceptible motion she shook her head.

Kevin's foot hit the bottom porch step, and he looked up. "I thought we might—" He froze.

They'd had a love affair. Now Molly was certain of it. Despite the age disparity, Lilly was a beautiful woman—her hair, those green eyes, that voluptuous body. She'd come to find Kevin because she wanted him back. And Molly wasn't ready to give him away. The idea shocked her. Was her old crush sneaking back?

He stayed where he was. "What are you doing here?"

Lilly didn't flinch from his rudeness. She almost seemed to be expecting it. "Hello, Kevin." Her arm fluttered at her side, as if she wanted to touch him but couldn't. Her eyes drank in his face.

"I'm here on vacation." Her throaty voice sounded breathless and very uncertain.

"Forget it."

Molly watched as Lilly pulled herself together. "I have a reservation. I'm staying."

Kevin turned on his heel and stalked from the house.

Lilly pressed her fingers to her mouth, smearing her soft taupe lipstick. Her eyes shimmered with tears. Pity stirred inside Molly, but Lilly wouldn't tolerate it, and she rounded on her with a hiss. "I'm staying!"

Molly gazed uncertainly toward the Common, but Kevin had disappeared. "All right." She had to know if they'd been lovers, but she couldn't just blurt out something like that. "You and Kevin seem to have a history."

Lilly sank back down in the rocker, and the cat jumped into her lap. "I'm his aunt."

Molly's relief was followed almost immediately by a weird sense of protectiveness toward Kevin. "Your relationship seems to leave something to be desired."

"He hates me." Lilly suddenly looked too fragile to be a star. "He hates me, and I love him more than anyone on earth." She seemed to pick up the iced tea tumbler as a distraction. "His mother, Maida, was my older sister."

The intensity in her voice made the small of Molly's back tingle. "Kevin told me his parents were elderly."

"Yes. Maida married John Tucker the same year I was born."

"A big age difference."

"She was like a second mother to me. We lived in the same town when I was growing up, practically next door."

Molly had the sense that Lilly was telling her this not because she wanted Molly to know but simply to keep from falling apart. Her curiosity made her take advantage of it. "I remember reading you were very young when you went to Hollywood."

"Maida moved when John was assigned to a church in Grand Rapids. My mother and I didn't get along, and things went downhill fast, so I ran away and ended up in Hollywood."

She fell silent.

Molly had to know more. "You did very well for yourself."

"It took a while. I was wild, and I made a lot of mistakes." She leaned back in the rocker. "Some of them can't be undone."

"My older sister raised me, too, but she didn't come into my life until I was fifteen."

"Maybe it would have been better for me that way. I don't know. I guess some of us were just born to raise hell."

Molly wanted to know why Kevin was so hostile, but Lilly had turned her head away, and just then Amy popped out onto the porch. She was either too young or too self-absorbed to recognize their celebrity guest. "The room's ready."

"I'll show you upstairs. Amy, would you get Miss Sherman's suitcase from her car?"

When Molly let Lilly into the attic, she expected her to object to such humble quarters, but Lilly said nothing. Molly pointed out the general direction of the beach from the window. "There's a nice walk along the lake, but maybe you know all this. Have you been here before?"

Lilly set her purse on the bed. "I wasn't invited."

The uncomfortable prickling Molly had been feeling at the back of her neck intensified. As soon as Amy appeared with the suitcase, Molly excused herself.

Instead of heading back to the cottage for a nap, she wandered into the music room. She touched the old fountain pen at the desk, then the ink bottle, then the ivory and rose stationery with WIND LAKE BED & BREAKFAST engraved at the top. Finally she stopped fidgeting and sat down to think.

By the time the small gold anniversary clock chimed the hour, she'd made up her mind to find Kevin.

She started her search at the beach, where she found Troy repairing some boards that had come loose on the dock. When she asked him about Kevin, he shook his head and adopted the same pitiful expression Roo had just used when Molly had left the house without him. "He hasn't been around for a while. Have you seen Amy?"

"She's finishing the bedrooms."

"We're, uh, trying to get everything done so we can go home early."

Where you'll rip off each other's clothes and fall into bed. "I'm sure that'll be fine."

Troy looked as grateful as if she'd scratched him under the chin.

Molly headed for the Common, then followed the sound of an angry hammer to the rear of a cottage named Paradise. Kevin was crouched on the roof taking out his frustration on a new set of shingles.

She tucked her thumbs in the back pockets of her shorts and tried to figure out how to go about this. "Are you still planning a trip into town?"

"Maybe later." He stopped hammering. "Did she leave?"

"No."

His hammer thwacked the shingles. "She can't stay here."

"She had a reservation. I couldn't really kick her out."

"Damn it, Molly!" *Thwack!* "I want you to . . . " *Thwack!* " . . . get rid of her!" *Thwack!*

She didn't appreciate being thwacked at, but she still had enough warm feelings left over from last night to treat him gently. "Would you come down for a minute?"

Thwack! "Why?"

"Because it's hurting my neck to look up at you, and I'd like to talk."

"Don't look up!" *Thwack! Thwack!* "Or don't talk!"

She sat on a stack of shingles, letting him know she wasn't going anywhere. He tried to ignore her, but he finally blasted out an obscenity and put aside his hammer.

She watched him come down the ladder. Lean, muscular legs. Great butt. What was it about men and their butts that was so enticing? He glared at her when he reached the ground, but it was more annoyance than hostility. "Well?"

"Would you tell me about Lilly?"

He narrowed those green eyes. "I don't like her."

"So I gathered." The suspicion that had been eating at her wouldn't go away. "Did she forget to send you a Christmas present when you were growing up?"

"I don't want her here, that's all."

"She doesn't look like she's going anywhere."

He braced his hands on his hips, his elbows jutting out in angry wings. "That's her problem."

"Since you don't want her here, it seems to be yours, too."

He headed back to the ladder. "Can you handle that damned tea by yourself today?"

Once again the base of her neck prickled. Something was very wrong. "Kevin, wait."

He turned to look at her, his expression impatient.

She told herself this wasn't any of her business, but she couldn't let it go. "Lilly said she's your aunt."

"Yeah, so what?"

"When she looked at you, I got this strange feeling."

"Spit it out, Molly. I've got things to do."

"Her heart was in her eyes."

"I seriously doubt that."

"She loves you."

"She doesn't even know me."

"I've got this weird feeling about why you're so upset." She bit her lip and wished she hadn't started this, but some powerful instinct wouldn't let her back off. "I don't think Lilly's your aunt, Kevin. I think she's your mother."

12

"Fudge!" Benny smacked his lips. "I love fudge!"
—*Daphne Says Hello*

K evin looked as though she'd punched him. "How did you know? *Nobody* knows that!"

"I guessed."

"I don't believe you. She told you. Damn her!"

"She didn't say a thing. But the only other person I've seen with eyes that exact color of green is you."

"You knew just by looking at her eyes?"

"There were a couple of other things." The longing Molly had witnessed on Lilly's face when she gazed at Kevin had been too intense for an aunt. And Lilly had given her clues.

"She told me how young she was when she left home, and she said she'd gotten into trouble. I knew your parents were older. It was just a hunch."

"A damn good hunch."

"I'm a writer. Or at least I used to be. We tend to be fairly intuitive."

He flung down his hammer. "I'm getting out of here."

And she was going with him. He hadn't abandoned her last night, and she wouldn't abandon him now. "Let's go cliff diving," she blurted out.

He stopped and stared at her. "You want to go cliff diving?"

No, I don't want to go cliff diving! Do you think I'm an idiot? "Why not?"

He gazed at her for a long moment. "Okay, you're on."

Exactly what she'd been afraid of, but it was too late to back out now. If she tried, he'd just call her "bunny lady" again. That was what the kindergarten children called her when she read them her stories, but, from him, it didn't sound as innocent.

An hour and a half later she lay on a flat rock near the edge of the bluff trying to catch her breath. As the heat from the rocks seeped through her wet clothes, she decided the diving hadn't been the worst part. She was a good diver, and it had even been sort of fun. The worst part was hauling her body back up that path so she could throw herself off again.

She heard him coming up the path, but unlike her, he wasn't breathing hard. She shut her eyes. If she opened them, she'd just see what she already knew, that he'd stripped down to a pair of navy blue boxers before his first dive. It was painful to look at him—all those ripples, planes, and smooth long muscles. She'd been terrified—hopeful?—the boxers would come off in the dive, but he'd somehow managed to keep them on.

She reined in her imagination. This was exactly the kind of fantasizing that had gotten her in such terrible trouble. And maybe it was time she reminded herself that Kevin hadn't exactly been the most memorable lover. In point of fact, he'd been a dud.

That wasn't fair. He'd been operating under a double disadvantage. He'd been sound asleep, and he wasn't attracted to her.

Some things hadn't changed. Although he seemed to have worked past his contempt for her, he hadn't sent out any signals that he found her sexually irresistible—or even remotely appealing.

The fact that she could think about sex was upsetting but also encouraging. The first crocus seemed to have popped up in the dark winter of her soul.

He flopped down next to her and stretched out on his back. She smelled heat, lake, and devil man.

"No more somersaults, Molly. I mean it. You were too close to the rocks."

"I only did one, and I knew exactly where the edge was."

"You heard me."

"Jeez, you sound like Dan."

"I'm not even going to think about what he'd say if he saw you do that."

They lay there for a while in silence that was surprisingly companionable. Every one of her muscles felt achy but relaxed.

> Daphne lay sunning herself on a rock when Benny came racing up the path. He was crying.
>
> "What's the matter, Benny?"
>
> "Nothing. Go away!"

Her eyes flicked open. It had been nearly four months since Daphne and Benny had held an imaginary conversation in her head. Probably just a fluke. She rolled toward Kevin. Although she didn't want to ruin the good time they'd been having, he needed help dealing with Lilly just as she needed help dealing with the loss of Sarah.

His eyes were closed. She noticed that his lashes were darker than his hair, which was already drying at the temples. She rested her chin on her hand. "Did you always know that Lilly was your birth mother?"

He didn't open his eyes. "My parents told me when I was six."

"They did the right thing not trying to keep it a secret." She waited, but he didn't say anything more. "She must have been very young. She hardly looks forty now."

"She's fifty."

"Wow."

"She's a Hollywood type. A ton of plastic surgery."

"Did you get to see her a lot when you were young?"

"On television."

"But not in person?" A woodpecker drummed not far away, and a hawk soared above the lake. She watched the rise and fall of his chest.

"She showed up once when I was sixteen. Must have been a slow time in Tinsel Town." He opened his eyes and sat up. Molly expected him to get up and walk away, but he gazed out at the lake. "As far as I'm concerned, I had one mother, Maida Tucker. I don't know what game the bimbo queen thinks she's playing by coming here, but I'm not playing it with her."

The word "bimbo" stirred old memories inside Molly. That used to be what people thought of Phoebe. Molly remembered what her sister had told her years ago. *Sometimes I think "bimbo" is a word men made up so they could feel superior to women who are better at survival than they are.*

"The best thing might be to talk to her," Molly said now. "Then you can find out what she wants."

"I don't care." He rose, grabbed his jeans, and shoved his legs in. "What a shitty week this is turning out to be."

Maybe for him, but not for her. This was turning out to be the best week she'd had in months.

He pushed his fingers through his damp hair and spoke more gently. "Do you still want to go into town?"

"Sure."

"If we go now, we can make it back by five o'clock. You'll take care of tea for me, won't you?"

"Yes, but you know you'll have to deal with her sooner or later."

She watched the play of hard emotion over his face. "I'll deal with her, but I'm choosing the time and the place."

Lilly stood at the attic window and watched Kevin drive away with the football heiress. Her throat tightened as she remembered his contempt. Her baby boy . . . The child she'd given birth to when she was barely more than a child herself. The son she'd handed over to her sister to raise as her own.

She knew it had been the right thing to do—the unselfish thing—and the success he'd made of his life proved that. What chance would he have had as the child of an undereducated, screwed-up seventeen-year-old who dreamed of being a star?

She let go of the curtain and sat on the edge of the bed. She'd met the boy the same day she'd gotten off the bus in L.A. He was a teenager fresh from an Oklahoma ranch and looking for stunt work. They'd shared a room in a fleabag hotel to save money. They'd been young and randy, hiding their fear of a dangerous city behind fumbling sex and tough talk. He'd disappeared before he knew she was pregnant.

She'd been lucky to find work waiting tables. One of the older waitresses, a woman named Becky, had taken pity on her and let her sleep on her couch. Becky had been a single mother with no patience left at the end of a long workday for the demands of her three year old child. Watching the little girl cringe from her mother's harsh words and occasional slaps had been a cold dose of reality. Two weeks before Kevin was born, Lilly had called Maida and told her about the baby. Her sister and John Tucker immediately drove to L.A.

They'd stayed with her through Kevin's birth and even told her she could return to Michigan with them. But she couldn't go back, and she knew by the way they looked at each other that they didn't want her to.

At the hospital, Lilly held her baby boy every chance she got and tried to whisper a lifetime of love to him. She watched the love blossoming on her sister's face whenever she picked him up, and saw John's expression soften with longing. Their absolute worthiness to raise her child couldn't have been more apparent, and she'd loved and hated them for it. Watching them drive away with her baby boy had been the worst moment of her life. Two weeks later, she'd met Craig.

Lilly knew she'd done the right thing by giving Kevin up, but the price had still been too high. For thirty-two years she'd lived with a gaping hole in her heart that neither her career nor her marriage could fill. Even if she'd been able to have more children, that hole would still have been there. Now she wanted to heal it.

When she'd been seventeen, the only way she could fight for her son was to give him up. But she wasn't seventeen anymore, and it was time to find out, once and for all, if she could ever have a place in his life. She'd take whatever he'd give her. A Christmas card once a year. A smile. Something to tell her he'd stopped hating her. The fact that he didn't want her near him had been brutally apparent each time she'd tried to contact him since Maida's death, and it had been even more apparent today. But maybe she just hadn't tried hard enough.

She thought of Molly and felt a chill. Lilly had no respect for females who preyed on famous men. She'd seen it happen dozens of times in

Hollywood. Bored, wealthy young things with no life of their own tried to define themselves by snaring famous men. Molly had trapped him with her pregnancy and her position as the sister of Phoebe Calebow.

Lilly got up from the bed. During Kevin's growing up years, she hadn't been able to protect him when he needed it, but now she had a chance to make up for that.

Wind Lake was a typical resort village—quaint at its center and a bit shabby at the edges. The main street ran along the lake and featured a few restaurants and gift shops, a marina, an upscale clothing boutique for the tourists, and the Wind Lake Inn.

Kevin parked and Molly got out of the car. Before they'd left the campground, she'd showered, conditioned her hair, used a little eye makeup and her M.A.C. Spice lipstick. Since she only had sneakers, her sundress wasn't an option, so she'd slipped into light gray drawstring shorts and a black cropped top, then consoled herself by noticing that she'd lost enough weight to let the shorts ride below her belly button.

As he came around the front of the car, his eyes skimmed over her, then studied her more closely. She felt an unwelcome tingle and wondered if he liked what he saw, or if he was making an unfavorable comparison with his United Nations companions.

So what if he was? She liked her body and her face. They might not be memorable to him, but she was happy with them. Besides, she didn't care what he thought.

He gestured toward the boutique. "They should have sandals in there if you want to replace the ones you lost in the lake."

Boutique sandals were way out of her price range. "I'll try the beach shop instead."

"Their stuff is pretty cheap."

She pushed her sunglasses higher on her nose. Unlike his Rēvos, hers had cost nine dollars at Marshall's. "I have simple tastes."

He regarded her curiously. "You're not one of those penny-pinching multimillionaires, are you?"

She thought for a moment, then decided not to play any more games with him about this. It was time for him to see who she was, insanity and all. "I'm not actually a multimillionaire."

"It's fairly common knowledge that you're an heiress."

"Yes, well . . . " She bit her lip.

He sighed. "Why do I think I'm going to hear something really wacky?"

"I guess that depends on your perspective."

"Go on. I'm still listening."

"I'm broke, okay?"

"Broke?"

"Never mind. You wouldn't understand in a million years." She walked away from him.

As she crossed the street toward the beach shop, he came up next to her. It irritated her to see that he looked disapproving, although she should have expected it from Mr. I'll-Take-the-High-Road, who could be the poster boy for grown-up preachers' kids, even though he was in denial about it.

"You blew all that money the first chance you got, didn't you? That's why you live in such a small place."

She turned on him in the middle of the street. "No, I didn't blow it. I splurged a little the first year, but believe me, there was plenty left."

He took her arm and pulled her out of the traffic onto the curb. "Then what happened?"

"Don't you have something better to do than harass me?"

"Not really. Bad investments? Did you put everything you had in vegetarian crocodile meat?"

"Very funny."

"You cornered the market in bunny slippers?"

"How about this?" She stopped in front of the beach shop. "I bet everything I had on the Stars in the last game, and some dickhead threw into double coverage."

"That was low."

She took a deep breath and pushed her sunglasses to the top of her head. "Actually, I gave it all away a few years ago. And I'm not sorry."

He blinked, then laughed. "You gave it away?"

"Having trouble with your hearing?"

"No, really. Tell me the truth."

She glared at him and went inside the shop.

"I don't believe this. You really did." He came up behind her. "How much was there?"

"A lot more than you have in your portfolio, sonny boy."

He grinned. "Come on. You can tell me."

She headed for a bin of footwear, then wished she hadn't, since it was filled with neon plastic sandals.

"More than three million?"

She ignored him and reached for the plainest ones, a disgusting pair with silver glitter imbedded in the vamp.

"Less than three?"

"I'm not saying. Now, go away and don't bother me."

"If you tell me, I'll take you over to that boutique, and you can put whatever you want on my credit card."

"You're on." She threw down the silver glitter sandals and made for the door.

He moved ahead of her to open it. "Don't you want me to twist your arm a little so you can hold on to your pride?"

"Did you see how ugly those sandals were? Besides, I know how much you earned last season."

"I'm glad we signed that prenuptial agreement. Here I thought we were protecting your fortune, but son of a gun, in one of those ironic twists life sometimes throws at you, it turns out we were really protecting mine." His grin grew bigger. "Who'd have figured?"

He was enjoying himself way too much, so she picked up her stride. "I'll bet I can max out your credit card in half an hour."

"Was it more than three million?"

"I'll tell you *after* I've finished shopping." She smiled at an elderly couple.

"If you lie, I'm taking everything back."

"Isn't there a mirror someplace where you can go admire yourself?"

"I never knew a woman so hung up on my good looks."

"*All* your women are hung up on your good looks. They just *pretend* it's your personality."

"I swear, somebody needs to spank you."

"You are, like, so not the man to do it."

"You are, like, such a damned brat."

She smiled and headed into the boutique. Fifteen minutes later she emerged with two pairs of sandals. Only as she put her sunglasses back on did she notice that Kevin also carried a shopping bag. "What did you buy?"

"You need a bathing suit."

"You bought me one?"

"I guessed at the size."

"What kind of bathing suit?"

"Jeez, if somebody bought me a present, I'd be happy about it instead of acting so suspicious."

"If it's a thong, it goes back."

"Now, would I insult you that way?" They began wandering down the street.

"A thong is probably the only kind of suit you know exists. I'm sure that's what all your girlfriends wear."

"You think you can distract me, but it's not going to work." They passed a sweet shop called Say Fudge. Next to it was a tiny public garden, little more than a few hydrangea bushes and a pair of benches. "It's reckoning time, Daphne." He indicated one of the benches, then settled beside her. His arm brushed her shoulder as he propped it along the back. "Tell me all about the money. Didn't you have to wait till you were twenty-one to get your hands on it?"

"Yes, but I was still in school, and Phoebe wouldn't let me touch a penny. She said if I wanted into the accounts before I graduated, I'd have to sue her."

"Smart lady."

"She and Dan kept me on a pretty tight leash, so once I graduated and she finally handed it over, I did everything you'd expect. I bought a car, moved into a luxury apartment, bought loads of clothes—I do miss those clothes. But after a while the life of a trust-fund baby lost its luster."

"Why didn't you just get a job?"

"I did, but the money kept hanging over me. I hadn't earned a penny of it. Maybe if it had come from someone other than Bert Somerville, I wouldn't have had such a hard time with it, but it felt as if he'd poked his nasty head back in my life, and I didn't like it. Finally I decided to set up a foundation and give it all away. And if you tell anybody, I swear I'll make you regret it."

"You gave away all of it?"

"Every penny."

"How much?"

She fiddled with the drawstring on her shorts. "I don't want to tell you. You already think I'm nuts."

"It's going to be so easy for me to return those sandals."

"Fifteen million, all right!"

He looked as if he'd been face-masked. "You gave away fifteen million dollars!"

She nodded.

He threw back his head and laughed. "You *are* nuts!"

She remembered the somersault dive she'd made off the cliff. "Probably. But I haven't regretted it for a moment." Although now she wouldn't mind having some of it back so she could keep paying her mortgage.

"You really don't miss it?"

"No. Except for the clothes, which I believe I already mentioned. And thank you for the sandals, by the way. I love them."

"My pleasure. Matter of fact, I've enjoyed your story so much, I'll add a new outfit the next time you're in town."

"Done!"

"God, it's heartbreaking to see a woman fight so hard to hang tough."

She laughed.

"Kevin! Hello!"

Molly heard a distinctly Germanic accent and looked up to see a willowy blonde hurrying toward them with a small white box in her hand. The woman wore a blue-and-white-striped apron over black slacks and a V-neck top. She was pretty. Lots of hair, brown eyes, good makeup. She was probably a couple of years older than Molly, nearer Kevin's age.

"Hey, there, Christina." Kevin gave the woman a smile that was way too sexy as he rose to greet her.

She extended the white cardboard box, and Molly spotted a blue seal on the side with SAY FUDGE embossed on it. "You seemed to enjoy the fudge last night, *ja*? This is a small present to welcome you to Wind Lake. Our sample box."

"Thanks a lot." He looked so pleased that Molly wanted to remind him it was just candy, not a Super Bowl ring! "Christina, this is Molly. Christina owns that fudge shop over there. I met her yesterday when I came into town to grab a burger."

Christina was more slender than a woman who owned a fudge shop should be. That struck Molly as a crime against nature.

"Pleasure to meet you, Molly."

"Nice meeting you, too." Molly could have ignored the curiosity in her expression, but she wasn't that good a person. "I'm Kevin's wife."

"Oh." Her disappointment was just as blatant as her mission with the fudge box.

"Estranged wife," Kevin cut in. "Molly writes children's books."

"*Ach so?* I've always wanted to write a children's book. Maybe you could give me a few suggestions sometime."

Molly kept her expression pleasant but noncommittal. Just once she'd like to meet someone who *didn't* want to write a children's book. People assumed they were easy to write because they were short. They had no idea what went into writing a successful book, one that children genuinely enjoyed and learned from, not just something adults had decided a child should enjoy.

"I'm sorry you're going to sell the campground, Kevin. We'll miss you." Before Christina could drool over him any more, she spotted a woman heading into the fudge shop. "I have to go. Stop by the next time you're in town so you can sample my cherry chocolate."

The minute she was out of earshot, Molly turned on him. "You can't sell the campground!"

"I told you from the beginning that's what I was doing."

True, but it hadn't meant anything at the time. Now she couldn't bear the idea that he would throw it away. The campground was a permanent part of him, part of his family, and in a strange way she couldn't analyze, it was beginning to feel like part of her.

He misunderstood her silence. "Don't worry. We won't have to stay around that long. The minute I find someone to take over, we're out of here."

All the way back to the campground, Molly tried to sort out her thoughts. The only deep roots Kevin had left were here. He'd lost his parents, he had no siblings, and he didn't seem inclined to let Lilly into his life. The house where he'd grown up belonged to the church. He had nothing to connect him with his past except the campground. It would be wrong to give that up.

The Common came into sight, and her jumbled thoughts gave way to a feeling of peace. Charlotte Long was sweeping her front porch, an elderly man rode by on a three-wheel bike, and a couple chatted on a bench. Molly drank in the storybook cottages and shady trees.

No wonder she'd experienced a sense of familiarity the moment she'd arrived here. She'd stepped through the pages of her books right into Nightingale Woods.

Instead of heading along the lake where she might meet someone, Lilly followed a narrow path that led into the woods beyond the Common. She'd changed into a pair of slacks and a square-neck, tobacco-brown top, but she was still hot, and she wished she were thin enough to wear shorts. Those little white ones that had been a permanent part of her wardrobe on *Lace, Inc.* They'd barely covered her bottom.

Weeds brushed her legs as the trees opened into a meadow. Her toes felt pleasantly gritty inside her sandals, and some of the tension she'd been carrying all day began to ease. She heard running water from a stream and turned to look for it only to see something so out of place that she blinked.

A chrome diner's chair with a red vinyl seat.

Lilly couldn't imagine what it was doing in the middle of the meadow. As she began to walk toward it, she saw a creek with ferns growing among the reeds and mossy rocks. The chair sat on a lichen-encrusted boulder. Its red vinyl seat sparkled in the sunlight, and there was no visible rust, so it had been put there recently. But why? Its perch was precarious, and it wobbled as she touched it.

"Leave that alone!"

She spun around to see a big bear of a man crouched in bars of sunlight at the edge of the meadow.

Her hand flew to her throat.

Behind her the chair splashed into the creek.

"Damn it!" The man jumped to his feet.

He was huge, with shoulders as wide as twelve lanes of L.A. freeway and a scowling, rough-hewn face that belonged on the villain in an old B Western. *I got ways of makin' a woman like you talk.* The only thing missing was a week's worth of stubble on that grim jaw.

His hair was a Hollywood stylist's nightmare or daydream, she wasn't sure which. Thick and graying at the temples, it grew too long at the collar, where it looked as if he might have swiped at it with the knife he undoubtedly kept in his boot. Except he wore a pair of battered running shoes instead, with socks that slouched around his ankles. And his eyes—mysteriously dark in that deeply tanned, dangerously lined face.

Every casting agent in Hollywood would salivate over him.

All those thoughts were scrambling through Lilly's head instead of the one thought that should have been there: *Run!*

He strode toward her. Beneath his khaki shorts his legs were brown and strong. He wore an old blue denim work shirt with the sleeves rolled up to reveal muscular forearms dusted with dark hair. "Do you know how long it took me to get that chair right where I wanted it?"

She backed away from him. "Maybe you have too much leisure time."

"Do you think that's funny?"

"Oh, no." She kept backing. "Not funny. Definitely not."

"Does it amuse you to spoil a whole day's work?"

"Work?"

His eyebrows shot together. "What are you doing?"

"Doing?"

"Stand still, damn it, and stop cowering!"

"I'm not cowering!"

"For God's sake, I'm not going to hurt you!" Grumbling under his breath, he stalked back to where he'd been sitting and picked up something off the ground. She took advantage of his distraction to edge closer to the path.

"I told you not to move!"

He was holding some kind of notebook, and he no longer seemed sinister, just incredibly impolite. She regarded him with all the imperiousness of Hollywood royalty. "Someone's forgotten his manners."

"Waste of energy. I come here for privacy. Is that too much to ask?"

"Not at all. I'm leaving right now."

"Over there!" He pointed an angry finger toward the creek.

"Pardon me?"

"Sit over there."

She was no longer frightened, just annoyed. "I don't think so."

"You ruined an afternoon's work. Sitting for me is the least you can do to make up for it."

He was holding a sketch pad, she realized, not a notebook. He was an artist. "Why don't I just leave instead?"

"I told you to sit!"

"Has anyone ever mentioned that you're rude?"

"I work hard at it. Sit on that boulder and face the sun."

"Thanks, but I don't do sun. Bad for the complexion."

"Just once I'd like to meet a beautiful woman who isn't vain."

"I appreciate the compliment," she said dryly, "but I passed the beautiful woman mark a good ten years and forty pounds ago."

"Don't be infantile." He whipped a pencil from his shirt pocket and began to sketch, not bothering to argue with her any longer, or even to sit down on the small camp stool she spotted a few feet away. "Tilt your chin. God, you really are beautiful."

He uttered the compliment so dispassionately that it didn't seem flattering. She resisted the urge to tell him he should have seen her in her prime. "You're right about my vanity," she said, just to needle him. "Which is why I'm not going to stand here in the sun any longer."

The pencil continued to fly over his sketch pad. "I don't like models talking when I'm working."

"I'm not your model."

Just as she was about to turn away for the last time, he jabbed his pencil in the pocket of his work shirt. "How do you expect me to concentrate when you won't stand still?"

"Pay attention: I don't care whether you concentrate or not."

His brow furrowed, and she had the feeling he was trying to make up his mind whether he could bully her into staying. Finally he flipped his sketch pad shut. "We'll meet here tomorrow morning then. Let's say seven. That way the sun won't be too hot for you."

Her irritation turned to amusement. "Why not make it six-thirty?"

His eyes narrowed. "You're patronizing me, aren't you?"

"Rude and astute. A fascinating combination."

"I'll pay you."

"You couldn't afford me."

"I seriously doubt that."

She smiled and turned onto the path.

"Do you know who I am?" he called out.

She glanced back. His expression couldn't have been more threatening. "Should I?"

"I'm Liam Jenner, damn it!"

She sucked in her breath. Liam Jenner. The J. D. Salinger of American painters. My God . . . What was he doing here?

He could see that she knew exactly who he was, and his scowl turned smug. "We'll compromise on seven then."

"I—" *Liam Jenner!* "I'll think about it."

"You do that."

What an obnoxious man! He'd done the world a favor by being so reclusive. But still . . .

Liam Jenner, one of the most famous painters in America, wanted her to sit for him. If only she were twenty and beautiful again.

13

Daphne put down her hammer and hopped back to admire the sign she'd nailed to her front door. It read NO BADGERS ALLOWED (AND THIS MEANS VOUS!). She'd painted it herself just that morning.

—*Daphne's Lonesome Day*

"Use the stepstool to check that top shelf, will you, Amy?" Kevin said from the pantry. "I'm going to move these boxes out of the way."

As soon as they'd returned from town, Kevin had enlisted Amy's help taking inventory of their food supplies. For the past ten minutes she'd been darting assessing glances between the pantry where he was working and the kitchen counter where Molly was preparing for the tea. Finally, she couldn't hold back any longer.

"It's sort of interesting, isn't it, that you and Molly got married about the same time as me and Troy."

Molly set the first slice of Bundt cake on the Victorian cake platter and listened to Kevin dodge. "Molly said she was going to need more brown sugar. Anything up there?"

"I see two bags. There's this book I read about marriage . . . "

"What else?"

"Some raisin boxes and a thingy of baking powder. Anyway, this book said that sometimes couples who, like, have just got married have a hard time adjusting and everything. Because it's such a big change."

"Is there any oatmeal? She said she needed that, too."

"There's a box, but it's not a big one. Troy, like, thinks being married is awesome."

"What else?"

"Pans and stuff. No more food. But if you're having trouble adjusting or anything, I mean, you could talk to Troy."

Molly smiled at the long silence that followed. Eventually, Kevin said, "Maybe you'd better see what's left in the freezer."

Amy emerged from the pantry and gave Molly a pitying glance. There was something about the teenager's sympathy and those hickeys that was getting under her skin.

Tea wasn't nearly as much fun without Kevin. Mrs. Chet—actually Gwen—didn't try to hide her disappointment when Molly said he had another commitment. She might have cheered up if she'd known that Lilly Sherman was staying there, but Lilly didn't appear, and Molly wasn't going to announce her presence.

She was setting out the pottery mixing bowls so she'd be ready for breakfast the next morning when Kevin came in through the back carrying groceries. He dodged Roo, who was trying to make a meal of his ankles, and set the bags on the counter. "Why are you doing that? Where's Amy?"

"Stop it, Roo. I just let her go. She was starting to whimper from Troy-deprivation."

No sooner had she said it than she spotted Amy flying across the yard toward her husband, who must have sniffed her on the wind, because he'd appeared out of nowhere.

"There they go again," Kevin said.

Their reunion was more passionate than a perfume commercial. Molly watched Troy dip his mouth to the top of Amy's exposed breast. She threw back her head. Arched her neck.

Another hickey.

Molly smacked a Tupperware lid back on its container. "She's going to end up needing a blood transfusion if he doesn't stop that."

"She doesn't seem to mind it too much. Some women like it when a man puts his mark on them."

Something in the way he looked at her made her breasts prickle. She didn't like her reaction. "And some women see it for what it is—the pathetic attempt of an insecure man to dominate a woman."

"Yeah, there's always that." He gave her a lazy smile and headed back out the side door for the rest of the groceries.

While he unloaded, he asked Molly if she wanted to go into town for dinner, but she declined. There was only so much Kevin temptation she wanted to expose herself to at one time. She headed back to the cottage, feeling good about her self-discipline.

The sun looked like a big lemon cookie in the sky, which made Daphne hungry. Green beans! she thought. With a nice topping of dandelion leaves. And strawberry cheesecake for dessert.

This was the second time today the critters had popped into her head. Maybe she was finally ready to get back to work—if not to write, then at least to do the drawings Helen wanted and free up the rest of her advance.

She let herself into the cottage and found a well-stocked refrigerator and a cupboard stacked with supplies. She had to give Kevin credit. He was doing his best to be considerate. She wasn't crazy about the fact that she was starting to like him so much, and she tried to work up some anger by reminding herself he was a shallow, egotistical, overpriced, Ferrari-driving, kidnapping, poodle-hating womanizer. Except she hadn't seen any evidence of womanizing. None at all.

Because he didn't find her attractive.

She grabbed her hair and let out a muffled scream at her own utter patheticness. Then she fixed a huge dinner and ate every bite.

That evening she sat on the porch gazing down at the pad of paper she'd found in a drawer. Would it hurt to move Daphne and Melissa just a little farther apart? After all, it was only a children's book. It wasn't as if America's civil liberties rested on how close Daphne and Melissa were standing to each other.

Her pencil began to move, at first hesitantly, and then more quickly.

But the sketch that appeared wasn't the one she'd planned. Instead, she found herself drawing Benny in the water, fur dripping into his eyes, his mouth agape, as he looked up at Daphne, who was diving off the top of a cliff. Her ears streamed behind her, the beaded collar of her denim jacket flapped open, and a pair of very stylish Manolo Blahniks flew from her paws.

She frowned and thought of all the accounts she'd read of young people being permanently paralyzed from diving into unfamiliar water. What kind of safety message would this send small children?

She ripped the paper from the pad and crumpled it. This was the sort of problem all those people who wanted to write a children's book never considered.

Her brain had dried up again. Instead of thinking about Daphne and Benny, she found herself thinking about Kevin and the campground. This was his heritage, and he should never sell it. He said he'd been bored here as a child, but he didn't have to be bored now. Maybe he just needed a playmate. Her brain skittered away from thinking about exactly what playing with Kevin would involve.

She decided to walk to the Common. Maybe she'd sketch some of the cottages just for fun. On the way there, Roo trotted over to greet Charlotte Long and impress her with his dead dog imitation. Although fewer than half the cottages were occupied, most of the residents seemed to be out for an evening stroll, and long, cool shadows fell like whispers across the grass. Life passed more slowly here in Nightingale Woods . . .

The gazebo caught Molly's attention.

> I'll have a tea party! I'll invite my friends, and we'll wear fabulous hats and eat chocolate frosting and say, "*Ma chère*, have you ever seen such a bee-you-tee-ful day?"

She settled cross-legged on the beach towel she'd brought with her and began to sketch. Several couples strolled by and stopped to observe, but they were members of the last generation with manners, and they didn't interrupt her. As she drew, she found herself thinking about all her years at summer camp. The frailest thread of an idea began to form in her mind, not about a tea party but about—

She closed her notebook. What was the use of thinking so far ahead? Birdcage had contractual rights to two more Daphne books, neither of which they'd accept until she'd made the revisions they'd demanded of *Daphne Takes a Tumble*.

The lights were on when she returned to the cottage. She hadn't left them that way, but she wasn't too worried.

Roo immediately started barking and made a dash for the bathroom door. It wasn't latched, and the dog bumped it open a few inches with his head.

"Calm down, poochy." Molly pushed it open the rest of the way and saw Kevin, all bare-naked beautiful, stretched out in the old-fashioned tub, legs crossed and propped on the rim, a book in his hands, and a small cigar clamped in the corner of his mouth.

"What are you doing in my bathtub?" Although the water came all the way to the top, there weren't any soap bubbles to hide him, so she didn't go closer.

He pulled the cigar from the corner of his mouth. No smoke curled from it, and she realized it wasn't a cigar but a stick of candy—chocolate or root beer.

He had the gall to sound irritated. "Now, what do you think I'm doing? And would you mind knocking before you barge in?"

"Roo barged in, not me." The dog ambled out, his job done, and headed for his water bowl. "Why aren't you using your own tub?"

"I don't like sharing a bathroom."

She didn't point out what had to be obvious—that he seemed to be sharing this one with her. She noticed that his chest looked just as good wet as it did dry. Even better. Something about the way he was watching her made her feel edgy. "Where did you get that candy?"

"In town. And I only bought one."

"Nice going."

"All you had to do was ask."

"Like I knew you were going to buy candy? And I'll just bet there's a box of the beautiful fräulein's fudge tucked away somewhere."

"Close the door on your way out. Unless you want to get naked and climb in here with me?"

"Thanks so much, but it looks a little small."

"Small? I don't think so, sweetheart."

"Oh, grow up!"

His chuckle followed her as she spun around and slammed the door. *Slytherin!* She headed for the small bedroom. Sure enough, his suitcase was there. She sighed and pressed her fingers to her temple. Her old headache was coming back.

> Daphne put down her electric guitar and opened her door. Benny stood on the other side.
> "Can I use your bathtub, Daphne?"
> "Why do you want to?"
> He looked scared. "I just do."

She poured herself a glass of sauvignon blanc from the bottle she found chilling in the refrigerator, then carried it out to the porch. Her black cropped top wasn't warm enough for the evening chill, but she didn't bother going inside to get a sweater.

She was rocking in the glider when he appeared. He wore a pair of gray sweat socks with a silky-looking robe that had dark maroon and black vertical stripes. It was the kind of robe a woman would buy for a man she loved sleeping with. Molly hated it.

"Let's host a tea in the gazebo before we leave," she said. "We'll make an event of it and invite everyone in the cottages."

"Why would we want to do that?"

"For fun."

"Sounds like a real thrill ride." He sat on the chair next to her and stretched his legs. The hair on his calves lay damp against his skin. He smelled like Safeguard and something expensive—a Brinks truckload of broken female hearts.

"I'd rather you didn't stay here, Kevin."

"I'd rather I did." He took a sip of wine from the glass he'd brought out with him.

> "Can I sleep at your house, Daphne?"
> "I guess. But why do you want to?"
> "Because mine has a ghost."

"You can't hide from Lilly forever," she said.

"I'm not hiding. Just picking my own time."

"I don't know much about getting annulments, but it seems as though this might compromise ours."

"It was compromised from the beginning," he said. "The way my attorney explained it, the grounds for a legal annulment are misrepresentation or duress. I figured you could claim duress. I sure wasn't going to argue."

"But the fact that we're together now makes that doubtful."

"Big deal. We'll get a divorce instead. It might take a little longer, but it'll accomplish the same thing."

She rose from the glider. "I still don't want you to stay here."

"It's my cottage."

"I have renter's rights."

His voice slid over her, soft and sexy. "I think being around me just makes you nervous."

"Yeah, right." She managed a yawn.

Amused, he nodded toward her wineglass. "You're drinking. Aren't you afraid you'll attack me again in my sleep?"

"Oops. Relapse. And I didn't even realize it."

"Or maybe you're afraid I'll attack you."

Something licked at her deep inside, but she played Ms. Cool, wandering over to the table to wipe up a few bread crumbs with the napkin she'd left there. "Why should I be? You're not attracted to me."

He waited just long enough before he replied to make her nervous. "How do you know who I'm attracted to?"

Her heart did a provoking little skipper-dee. "Oh, my gosh! And here I thought my command of the English language would drive us apart."

"You're such a wise-ass."

"Sorry, but I like my men with more depth of character."

"Are you trying to say you think I'm shallow?"

"As a sidewalk puddle. But you're rich and gorgeous, so it's okay."

"I am not shallow!"

"Fill in the blank: The most important thing in Kevin Tucker's life is—"

"Football is my career. That hardly makes me shallow."

"The second, third, and fourth most important things in Kevin Tucker's life are football, football, and oh my god, football."

"I'm the best at what I do, and I'm not apologizing."

"The fifth most important thing in Kevin Tucker's life is— Oh, wait now, that would be women, wouldn't it?"

"Quiet ones, so that leaves you out!"

She was halfway to a great comeback when it hit her. "I get it. All the foreign women ... " He looked wary. "You don't want someone you can truly communicate with. That might get in the way of your primary obsession."

"You have no idea what you're talking about. I keep telling you: I date lots of American women."

"And I'll bet they're interchangeable. Beautiful, not too bright, and— as soon as they turn demanding—out the door."

"The good old days."

"I insulted you, in case you didn't realize it."

"I insulted you back, in case you didn't realize it."

She smiled. "I'm sure you don't want to stay under the same roof with someone who's so demanding."

"You're not getting rid of me that easily. As a matter of fact, living together could have some advantages." He rose from the glider and gazed at her with an expression that conjured up images of sweaty bodies and messy sheets. Then he reached into the pocket of his robe, breaking the spell which had probably all been in her imagination anyway.

He pulled out a crumpled sheet of paper. It took her only a moment to recognize the drawing she'd made of Daphne diving into the water.

"I found this in the trash." He smoothed it out as he came toward her, then pointed down at Benny. "This guy? He's the badger?"

She nodded slowly, wishing she hadn't discarded the drawing where he could find it.

"So why did you throw it away?"

"Safety issues."

"Uhm . . ."

"Sometimes I use incidents in my own life for inspiration."

His mouth quirked. "I can see that."

"I'm really more a cartoonist than an artist."

"This is a little too detailed for a cartoon."

She shrugged and held out her hand to take it back, but he shook his head. "It's mine now. I like it." He slipped it his pocket, then turned back toward the kitchen door. "I'd better get dressed."

"Good, because staying here won't work."

"Oh, I'm staying here. I'm just going into town for a while." He paused and gave her a crooked smile. "You can come along if you'd like."

Her brain sounded a warning. "Thanks anyway, but my German's rusty, and too much chocolate makes my skin break out."

"If I didn't know better, I'd say you were jealous."

"Just remember, *liebling*, the alarm goes off at five-thirty tomorrow morning."

She heard him come in sometime after one, so it was a pleasure banging on his bedroom door at dawn. There had been rain overnight, but as they walked silently down the lane, they were both too groggy to appreciate the freshly washed, rosy-gray sky. While Kevin yawned, she concentrated on putting one foot in front of the other and avoiding puddles. Only Roo was happy to be up and about.

Molly fixed blueberry pancakes, and Kevin sliced uneven chunks of fruit into a blue pottery bowl. As he worked, he grumbled that someone with a 65-percent pass completion record shouldn't have to do kitchen duty. His complaining stopped, however, when Marmie strolled in.

"Where did that cat come from?"

Molly dodged his question. "She showed up yesterday. That's Marmie."

Roo whimpered and crawled under the table. Kevin grabbed a tea towel to dry his hands. "Hey, girl." He knelt and stroked the animal. Marmie immediately curled against him.

"I thought you didn't like animals."

"I love animals. Where did you get that idea?" Marmie put her paws on his leg, and he picked her up.

"From my dog?"

"That's a dog? Jeez, I'm sorry. I thought it was an industrial-waste accident." His long, lean fingers slid through the cat's fur.

"Slytherin." She slapped the lid back onto the flour container. What kind of man liked a cat more than he liked an exceptionally fine French poodle?

"What did you call me?"

"It's a literary reference. You wouldn't understand."

"Harry Potter. And I don't appreciate name calling."

His reply irritated her. It was getting harder and harder to convince herself he was just a pretty face.

The Pearsons were their first customers. John Pearson consumed half a dozen pancakes and a serving of scrambled eggs while he updated Kevin on the couple's so-far-fruitless search for Kirtland's warbler. Chet and Gwen were leaving that day, and when Molly peered into the dining room, she saw Gwen casting come-hither glances at Kevin. A little later she heard a commotion from the front of the house. She turned off the heat and rushed into the foyer, where the forbidding man she'd seen on the Common the day she'd arrived was growling at Kevin.

"She's a redhead. Tall—five feet nine. And beautiful. Somebody said they saw her here yesterday afternoon."

"What do you want with her?" Kevin asked.

"We had an appointment."

"What kind of an appointment?"

"Is she here or not?"

"I thought I recognized that snarl." Lilly appeared at the top of the stairs. Somehow she managed to make her simple periwinkle linen camp shirt and matching walking shorts look glamorous. She began to descend, every inch the queen of the screen, then stalled awkwardly as she spotted Kevin. "Good morning."

He gave her a brusque nod and disappeared into the dining room.

Lilly retained her composure. The man who'd come to see her stared toward the dining room, and Molly realized he was the one she'd passed coming out of the woods her first day here. How did Lilly know him?

"It's eight-thirty," he grumbled. "We were supposed to meet at seven."

"I mulled it over for a few seconds and decided I'd rather sleep in."

He glared at her like a surly lion. "Let's get going. I'm losing the light."

"If you search hard enough, I'm sure you'll be able to find it. In the meantime I'm eating breakfast."

His brow furrowed.

Lilly turned to Molly, her expression frosty. "Would it be possible for me to eat in the kitchen instead of the dining room?"

Molly told herself to rise above Lilly's hostility, then decided the heck with it. Two could play this game. "Of course. Maybe you'd *both* like to eat there. I've made blueberry pancakes."

Lilly looked miffed.

"Do you have coffee?" he barked.

Molly had always been drawn to individuals who didn't care about earning the approval of others—probably because she'd spent so much time trying to earn her father's. This man's outrageous crankiness fascinated her. She also noticed that he was very sexy for someone his age. "All the coffee you can drink."

"Well, all right then."

Molly felt a little guilty and returned her attention to Lilly. "Feel free to use the kitchen anytime you want. I'm sure you'd rather avoid facing your fans first thing in the morning."

"What kind of fans?" he demanded.

"I'm fairly well known," Lilly said.

"Oh." He dismissed her celebrity. "If you insist on eating, could you hurry up about it?"

Lilly addressed Molly, but only to aggravate him, she was certain.

"This unbelievably self-absorbed man is Liam Jenner. Mr. Jenner, this is Molly, my . . . nephew's wife."

For the second time in two days Molly found herself starstruck. "Mr. Jenner?" She gulped. "I can't tell you what a pleasure this is. I've admired your work for years. I can't believe you're here! I just— You have long hair in that photograph they always print of you. I know it was taken years ago, but— I'm sorry. I'm babbling. It's just that your work has meant a lot to me."

Jenner glowered at Lilly. "If I'd wanted her to know my name, I'd have told her myself."

"Lucky us," Lilly said to Molly. "We finally have a winner for our Mr. Charm pageant."

Molly tried to catch her breath. "That's all right. I understand. I'm sure lots of people try to violate your privacy, but—"

"Maybe you could skip the adulation and just lead the way to those pancakes."

She gulped some air. "Right this way. Sir."

"Perhaps you should fix crab cakes instead," Lilly said.

"I heard that," he muttered.

In the kitchen Molly pulled herself together enough to direct Lilly and Liam Jenner to the round table that sat in the bay. She raced to rescue the scrambled eggs she'd abandoned and toss them on a plate.

Kevin came through the door and glanced toward Lilly and Jenner but apparently decided not to ask any questions. "Are those eggs ready yet?"

She handed him the plates. "They're overdone. If Mrs. Pearson complains, charm her out of it. Would you bring in some coffee? We have kitchen guests. This is Liam Jenner."

Kevin nodded at the artist. "I heard in town that you had a house on the lake."

"And you're Kevin Tucker." For the first time Jenner smiled, and Molly was startled by the transformation of those craggy features. Very sexy indeed. Lilly noticed, too, although she didn't seem as impressed as Molly.

He stood and extended his hand. "I should have recognized you right away. I've been following the Stars for years."

As the two men shook, Molly watched the temperamental artist turn into a football fan. "You had a pretty good season."

"Could have been better."

"I guess you can't win them all."

As the conversation turned to the Stars, Molly gazed at the three of them. What an odd group of people to have come together in this isolated place. A football player, an artist, and a movie star.

Here on Gilligan's Isle.

She smiled and took the plates from Kevin, who seemed to be enjoying the conversation, then plopped them on a tray and delivered them to the dining room. Luckily there were no complaints about the eggs. She filled two mugs from the coffee urn, picked up an extra cream and sugar, and carried it all back to the kitchen.

Kevin was leaning against the pantry door ignoring Lilly while he spoke to Jenner. " . . . heard in town that lots of people are visiting Wind Lake hoping to catch a glimpse of you. Apparently you've been a boon to local tourism."

"Not by choice." Jenner took the coffee Molly set in front of him and leaned back in his chair. He looked easy in his skin, she thought. Solidly built, a little grizzled, an artist disguised as a rugged outdoorsman. "As soon as word got around that I'd built a house here, all kinds of idiots started showing up."

Lilly accepted the spoon Molly handed her and began stirring her coffee. "You don't seem to think much of your admirers, Mr. Jenner."

"They're impressed by my fame, not my work. They start babbling about how they're so honored to meet me, but three-quarters of them wouldn't know one of my paintings if it bit 'em on the ass."

As one who'd babbled, Molly couldn't let that pass. "*Mamie in Earnest,* painted in 1968, a very early watercolor." She poured out the batter onto the griddle. "An emotionally complex work with a deceptive simplicity of line. *Tokens,* painted around 1971, a dry brush watercolor. The critics hated it, but they were wrong. From 1996 to

1998 you concentrated on acrylics with the *Desert Series*. Stylistically, those paintings are a pastiche—postmodern eclecticism, classicism, with a nod toward the Impressionists that only you could have pulled off."

Kevin smiled. "Molly's summa cum laude. Northwestern. She writes bunny books. My personal favorite of your paintings is a landscape—don't have a clue when you painted it or what the critics had to say about it—but there's this kid in the distance and I like it."

"I love *Street Girl*," Lilly said. "A solitary female figure on an urban street, worn-down red shoes, a hopeless expression on her face. Ten years ago it sold for twenty-two thousand dollars."

"Twenty-four."

"Twenty-two," she said smoothly. "I bought it."

For the first time Liam Jenner seemed to be at a loss for words. But not for long. "What do you do for a living?"

Lilly took a sip of coffee before she spoke. "I used to solve crimes."

Molly briefly debated letting Lilly's evasion go, but she was too curious to see what would happen. "This is Lilly Sherman, Mr. Jenner. She's quite a famous actress."

He leaned back in his chair and studied her before he finally murmured, "That silly poster. Now I remember. You were wearing a yellow bikini."

"Yes, well, the poster days are obviously long behind me."

"Praise God for that. The bikini was obscene."

Lilly looked surprised, then indignant. "There was nothing obscene about it. Compared to today it was modest."

His heavy brows drew together. "Covering your body with anything was obscene. You should have been nude."

"I'm outta here." Kevin headed back to the dining room.

Wild horses couldn't have dragged Molly from that kitchen, and she slipped a plate of pancakes in front of each of them.

"Nude?" Lilly's cup clattered into the saucer. "Not in this lifetime. I once passed up a fortune to pose for *Playboy*."

"What does *Playboy* have to do with it? I'm talking about art, not titillation." He tucked into the pancakes. "Excellent breakfast, Molly. Leave here and come cook for me."

"I'm actually a writer, not a cook."

"The children's books." His fork paused in midair. "I've thought about writing a children's book . . . " He speared one of Lilly's uneaten pancakes from her plate. "Probably not much of a market for my ideas."

Lilly sniffed. "Not if they involve nudes."

Molly giggled.

Jenner shot her a quelling gaze.

"Sorry." Molly bit her lip, then gave an unladylike snort.

Jenner's frown grew more ferocious. She was ready to apologize again when she spotted a small quiver at the corner of his mouth. So Liam Jenner wasn't quite the curmudgeon he pretended to be. This was getting more and more interesting.

He gestured toward Lilly's half-filled mug. "You can take that with you. What's left of your breakfast, too. We need to go."

"I never said I'd sit for you. I don't like you."

"Nobody does. And of course you'll sit for me." His voice deepened with sarcasm. "People stand in line for the honor."

"Paint Molly. Just look at those eyes."

Jenner studied her. Molly blinked self-consciously. "They're quite extraordinary," he said. "Her face is becoming interesting, but she hasn't lived in it long enough for it to be really fascinating."

"Hey, don't talk about me when I'm listening."

He lifted a dark eyebrow at Molly, then returned his attention to Lilly. "Is it just me, or are you this stubborn with everyone?"

"I'm not being stubborn. I'm simply protecting your reputation for artistic infallibility. Perhaps if I were twenty again, I'd pose for you, but—"

"Why would I be interested in painting you when you were twenty?" He seemed genuinely perplexed.

"Oh, I think that's obvious," Lilly said lightly.

He studied her for a moment, his expression difficult to read. Then he shook his head. "Of course. Our national obsession with emaciation. Aren't you a little old to be still buying into that?"

Lilly planted a perfect smile on her face as she got up from her chair. "Of course. Thank you for breakfast, Molly. Good-bye, Mr. Jenner."

His gaze followed her as she swept from the kitchen. Molly wondered if he noticed the tension she was carrying in her shoulders.

She left him to his own thoughts while he finished his coffee. Finally he picked up the plates from the table and carried them over to the sink. "Those were the best pancakes I've had in years. Tell me what I owe you."

"Owe me?"

"This is a commercial establishment," he reminded her.

"Oh, yeah. But there's absolutely no charge. It was my pleasure."

"I appreciate it." He turned to leave.

"Mr. Jenner."

"Just Liam."

She smiled. "Come for breakfast anytime you want. You can slip in through the kitchen."

He nodded slowly. "Thanks. I just might do that."

14

"Come closer to the water, Daphne," Benny said. "I won't get you wet."

—*Daphne Makes a Mess*

Any ideas for a new book?" Phoebe asked early the next afternoon over the phone.

An unwelcome subject, but since Molly had spent the first ten minutes of their conversation dodging Celia the Hen's nosy questions about Kevin, anything was an improvement. "A few. But remember that *Daphne Takes a Tumble* is the first book on a three-book contract. Birdcage won't accept another manuscript until I finish making the changes they want." No need to tell her sister she still hadn't started on those changes, although she'd borrowed Kevin's car after breakfast and gone into town to buy some art supplies.

"SKIFSA is a joke."

"Not a very funny one. I don't have a TV in the cottage. Have they popped up lately?"

"Last night. The new gay rights legislation in Congress has bought them a lot of local airtime." Phoebe's hesitation wasn't a good sign. "Moll, they mentioned Daphne again."

"I can't believe it! Why are they doing this? It's not like I'm a big-time children's author."

"This is Chicago, and you're the wife of the city's most famous quarterback. They're using that connection to get airtime. You *are* still Kevin's wife, aren't you?"

Molly didn't want to get into that discussion again. "Temporarily. Next time remind me to find a publisher with a little backbone." She wished she hadn't said that, since her publisher wasn't the only one who needed some backbone. Once again she reminded herself that she didn't have any choice, not if she wanted to pay her bills.

As if Phoebe had read her mind, she said, "How are you doing for money? I know you haven't—"

"I'm doing fine. No problem." As much as Molly loved her sister, she sometimes wished that everything Phoebe touched hadn't turned to gold. It made Molly feel so inadequate. Phoebe was wealthy, beautiful, and emotionally stable. Molly was poor, merely attractive, and she'd been a lot closer to a nervous breakdown than she'd ever admit. Phoebe had overcome enormous odds to become one of the most powerful owners in the NFL, but Molly couldn't even defend her fictional bunny from a real-life attack.

After she hung up, she chatted with some of the guests, then put fresh towels in the bathrooms while Kevin checked a retired couple from Cleveland into one of the cottages. Afterward she headed to her own cottage so she could change into the red suit he'd bought her and go for a swim.

As she pulled the two-piece suit from the bag, she discovered that the bottom wasn't quite a thong, but since it was held together by only a narrow tie on each side, it was a little skimpier than she liked. The top, however, had an underwire that pushed her up in all the right places, and Roo seemed to approve.

Although the air temperature was in the low eighties, the lake still hadn't warmed up, and the beach was deserted when she got there. She hissed against the cold as she waded in. Roo got his paws wet, then backed off and chased the herons instead. When she couldn't stand the torture any longer, she dove under.

She came up gasping, then began a vigorous sidestroke to keep warm as she caught sight of Kevin standing on the Common. Nine years of summer camp had taught her the importance of the buddy system, but he was near enough that he'd hear her yell if she started to drown.

She flipped to her back and swam for a while, avoiding the deeper water because, no matter what Kevin said, she was an extremely sensible person when it came to water safety. The next time she looked toward the Common, he was standing exactly where he'd been before.

He looked bored.

She waved her arm to catch his attention. He gave her a desultory wave back.

This wasn't good. This wasn't good at all.

She dove under and began to think.

Kevin watched Molly in the water while he waited for the garbage company to show up with the new Dumpster. He spotted a flash of crimson as she jackknifed, then dove beneath the surface. Buying that particular swimsuit for her had been a big mistake. It showed way too much of the tempting little body he was having an increasingly hard time ignoring. But the suit's color had caught his eye yesterday in the boutique because it was almost the same shade her hair had been the first time they'd met.

Her hair didn't look that way now. It had only been four days, but she was taking care of herself again, and her hair was the same rich color as the maple syrup he'd poured over the pancakes she'd made. He felt as if he were watching her come back to life. Her skin had lost its pasty look, and her eyes had begun to sparkle, especially when she wanted to give him a hard time.

Those eyes . . . That wicked slant shouted to the world that she was up to no good, but he seemed to be the only one who got the message. Phoebe and Dan saw brainy Molly, the lover of children, bunnies, and ridiculous dogs. Only he seemed to understand that Molly Somerville's veins had trouble rushing through them instead of blood.

On the flight back from Chicago, Dan had lectured him about how seriously she'd always taken everything. How as a kid she never did anything wrong. What a good student she'd been, a model citizen. He'd said that Molly was twenty-seven going on forty. Twenty-seven going on *seven* was more like it. No wonder she'd made a career as a children's book author. She was entertaining her peer group!

It galled him that she had the audacity to call him reckless. He'd never have given away fifteen million dollars. As far as he could tell, she didn't know anything about playing it safe.

He saw another flash of red in the water. All those years of summer camp had made her a good swimmer with a steady, graceful stroke. And a nice, neat body . . . But the last thing he wanted to do was start thinking about her body again, so he thought about the way she made him laugh.

Which didn't mean she wasn't a pain in the butt. She had a lot of nerve trying to poke around in his head, since it was screwed on a lot tighter than hers ever would be.

His eyes flicked back over the lake, but he couldn't see her. He waited for a flash of red. And waited . . . His shoulders grew tense as the surface remained smooth. He took a step forward. Then her head bobbed up, little more than a dot in the distance. Just before it disappeared again, she managed to shout one faint word.

"*Help!*"

He started to run.

Molly held her breath as long as she could, then resurfaced to fill her lungs. Sure enough, he'd just thrown himself into the water with a very nice racing dive.

This should get his adrenaline pumping.

She flailed around until she was sure he'd spotted her, then went under again, diving deep and swimming off to her right. It was a rotten thing to do, but it was for the greater good. A bored Kevin was an unhappy Kevin, and it was long past time he had some fun at the Wind Lake Campground. Maybe then, he wouldn't be so anxious to sell it.

She surfaced again. Thanks to her crafty underwater change of direction, he was heading too far to the left. She caught another breath and went back under.

As Daphne went under for the third time, Benny swam—

Delete that.

> As Benny went under for the third time, Daphne swam faster
> and faster . . .

Being rescued by Daphne would serve Benny right, Molly thought virtuously. He shouldn't have gone swimming without a buddy.

She opened her eyes underwater, but the lake was murky from all the rain, and she couldn't see much. She remembered how squeamish some of her campmates used to be about swimming in a lake instead of a pool—*What if a fish bites me?*—but Molly had grown used to it after her first summer, and she felt right at home.

Her lungs were starting to burn, and she came up for more air. He was about fifteen yards to her left. She refused to think about the boy and the wolf as she made her next move.

"*Help!*"

He pivoted in the water, wet blond hair sticking to that superb forehead. "Hold on, Molly!"

"Hurry! I've got a"—*hole in my head*—"a cramp!" Down she went.

She cut to the right, swam the pattern, headed for the sideline—made ol' Number Eleven work for it.

Her lungs were burning again. Time to resurface near the goal line.

He'd spent two decades picking out receivers in a crowd, and he spotted her instantly. His stroke was powerful, and she got so caught up watching the way he churned through the water that she nearly forgot to go under again.

His hand brushed her thigh, then fastened around the skimpy bottom of her bathing suit.

His hand. On her butt. She should have thought farther ahead.

He jerked hard on the suit to pull her to him, and the skimpy pair of ties that were holding it on snapped. He clamped his arm around her and pulled her to the surface.

The bottom part of the suit didn't come along.

As it trailed away in the water, she could only wonder how she'd gotten herself into this situation. Was this going to be her reward for doing a little good in the world?

"Are you all right?"

She glimpsed his face just before he started hauling her toward the shore. She'd really scared him. Part of her felt guilty, but she still remembered to cough and gasp for air as he dragged her through the water. At the same time she struggled with her modesty.

He wasn't even breathing heavily, and for a moment she let herself relax against him and enjoy the sensation of his body doing the work for hers. But it was hard to be both relaxed and bare-butt naked. "I—I had a cramp."

"Which leg is it?" His own leg brushed her hip, but he didn't seem to notice anything was missing.

"Stop—stop for a minute, will you?"

He slowed in the water and turned her in his arms without letting her go. She saw that anger had replaced his concern. "You shouldn't have been in the water by yourself! You could have drowned."

"It was . . . stupid."

"Which leg?"

"My . . . left. But it's better. I can move it now."

He let go of one arm to reach for her leg.

"No!" she squeaked, afraid of what he'd encounter on the way.

"Is it cramping again?"

"Not . . . exactly."

"Let's get to shore. I'll look at it there."

"I'm fine now. I can—"

He didn't pay any attention. Instead, he started hauling her toward the beach again.

"Uh, Kevin . . . " She coughed as she caught a mouthful.

"Keep still, damn it!"

Nice way for a PK to talk, especially to a drowning victim. She did her best to keep her lower half away from his lower half, but he kept sliding against her. Slip sliding . . . slip sliding . . . She groaned against a rush of sensation.

His rhythm changed, and she realized he'd touched bottom. She tried to disengage herself. "Let me go. I can walk now."

He swam farther in before he loosened his grip and stood. She dropped her feet.

The water came to her chin, but it was below his shoulders. Wet strands of hair plastered his forehead, and he looked grumpy. "You could be a tad more grateful, you know. I just saved your annoying life."

At least he didn't looked bored any longer. "Thank you."

He still had her arm, and he began moving toward the shore. "Have you ever had a cramp like this before?"

"Never. It took me completely by surprise."

"Why are you dragging your feet?"

"I'm cold. Probably a little shocky. Would you lend me your T-shirt?"

"Sure." He kept heading toward the beach.

She dragged her heels. "Could I have it now, please?"

"Now?" He stopped. The water lapped at her breasts. The red top had pushed them up quite nicely, and his gaze lingered. She noticed that his lashes had formed aggressive little spikes over those sharp green eyes, and she fought a sudden wobbliness in her knees.

"I'd like to put it on before we get out of the water," she said as pleasantly as she could.

He pulled his gaze from her breasts and started moving again. "It'll be easier to get you warm on the beach."

"Stop! Will you just stop!"

He did, but he was looking at her as if she'd sprung a fresh leak in the head.

She took a nibble out of her bottom lip. No good deed went unpunished, and she was going to have to tell him. "I have a slight problem . . . "

"I'll say. You don't have any sense. That Northwestern diploma you're so proud of should have read 'summa cum loony.'"

"Just give me your T-shirt. Please."

He made no move to take it off. Instead, he grew suspicious. "What kind of problem?"

"I seem to have . . . I'm really cold. Aren't you cold?"

He waited, that stubborn expression clearly indicating he wasn't going anywhere until she'd 'fessed up. She mustered her dignity. "I seem to have . . . " She cleared her throat. "Left the bottom half of my swimsuit . . . on the bottom."

Naturally, the first thing he did was stare straight down into the murky water.

"Stop that!"

As he gazed back up at her, his eyes looked less like jade daggers and more like happy green jelly beans. "How did you do that?"

"*I* didn't do it. *You* did. When you rescued me."

"I pulled off your suit?"

"You did."

He grinned. "I've always been damn good with women."

"Never mind. Just give me your stupid T-shirt!"

Was it accidental that his thigh brushed her hip? He gazed down into the water again, and she was possessed with a sudden crazy wish for all the murkiness to clear away. She heard something husky and seductive in his voice.

"So what you're telling me is that you're bare-ass naked under the water."

"You know exactly what I'm telling you."

"Now, this makes for an interesting dilemma."

"There's no dilemma."

He stroked the corner of his mouth with his thumb, and his smile was as soft as smoke. "We're up against the essence of true capitalism right here, right now, you and me, God bless America for the great country it is."

"What are you—"

"Pure capitalism. I have a commodity that you want—"

"My leg is starting to cramp again."

"The question is"—he lingered over his words, his eyes grazing her breasts—"what are you going to give me for that commodity?"

"I've been giving you my services as a cook," she said quickly.

"I don't know. Those sandals yesterday were pretty expensive. I think I've already paid for at least three days of cooking."

He was making her insides purr, and she didn't like it. "I won't be around for another day if you don't take that stupid shirt off your stupid overdeveloped chest right this second!"

"I never met such an ungrateful woman in my life." He started to pull it off, stalled to rub his arm, tugged on it again, inched it over his chest, flexed his gorgeous muscles . . .

"That's twenty yards for delay of game!"

"It's a five-yard penalty," he pointed out from under the T-shirt.

"Not today!"

He finally got it off, and she snatched it from him before he took it into his head to play keep-away, a game she was fairly certain an NFL quarterback could win against a bunny-book author.

"Bare-ass naked . . . " His smile grew broader.

She ignored him and struggled to put on the shirt, but handling all that wet cotton in bust-deep frigid water wasn't exactly easy. Naturally, he didn't help.

"Maybe it would work better if you climbed out of the water before you did that."

His humor was too infantile to merit a response. She finally got the T-shirt on inside out, but a huge air pocket left it billowing around her. She pushed it down and marched toward the shore, which was mercifully empty of guests.

Kevin stayed where he was and watched Molly emerge from the water. The view from behind was making it hard for him to take a good solid breath. It didn't seem to have occurred to her that white T-shirts pretty much turned to tissue paper when they got wet. First that trim little waist emerged, then curvy hips, then her legs, as sturdy and pretty as any he'd ever seen.

He swallowed hard at the sight of that sweet little bottom. The glaze of white T-shirt made it look as if it had been sponged with wet sugar.

He licked his lips. It was a good thing the water was cold enough for an iceberg, because the sight of her striding toward the beach had set him on fire. That small round bottom . . . the dark, seductive crevice. And he hadn't even caught the view from the front.

A circumstance he was about to change.

Molly heard Kevin splashing behind her. Then he was next to her, taking giant steps in the water. He pulled ahead, back muscles rippling as he pumped his arms. He hit the beach and turned around to face her.

Exactly what did he think was so interesting?

She began to feel nervous. One of his hands moved. He tugged absentmindedly on the front of his wet, low-riding jeans. "Maybe it's not so hard to believe your mother was a showgirl after all."

She glanced down at herself and yelped. Then she grabbed the T-shirt fabric, pulled it away from her body, and turned to rush back to the cottage.

"Uh . . . Molly? The view's pretty interesting from the back, too. And we've got company coming."

Sure enough, the Pearsons were approaching in the distance. They were barely visible behind beach chairs, tote bags, and a cooler.

Molly wasn't going to rely on Kevin's cooperation to get back to the cottage, so she headed toward the woods, holding the T-shirt away from her body in the front and back, while she stretched it to make it longer.

"If anybody throws you a fish," he called after her, "it's because you're waddling like a penguin."

"If anybody asks you to bray, it's because you're acting like an—"

"Save your sweet talk for later, Daphne. The garbage guys just drove up with the new Dumpster."

"Shut the lid after you climb in." She picked up her waddle and somehow managed to reach the cottage without further mishap. Once inside, she pressed her hands to her hot cheeks and laughed.

But Kevin wasn't laughing. As he stood on the Common gazing in the direction of the cottage, he knew he couldn't keep going on like this. It was ironic. He was a married man, but he wasn't taking advantage of the principal advantage marriage offered.

The question was, what did he intend to do about it?

15

Daphne sprayed her favorite perfume, Eau de Strawberry Shortcake, in a big squirty puff around her head. Then she fluffed her ears, straightened her whiskers, and put on her brand-new tiara.

—*Daphne Plants a Pumpkin Patch*

After her dip in the lake, Molly showered and changed, then found herself walking out to the porch and gazing toward the table where she'd left the sack of art supplies she'd bought in town that morning. It was long past time to start work on the drawings.

Instead of settling at the table, however, she sat on the glider and picked up the pad she'd used yesterday to sketch Daphne diving off the cliff. She gazed off into the distance. Finally she began to write.

"Mrs. Mallard is building a summer camp on the other side of Nightingale Woods," Daphne announced one afternoon to Benny, Melissa, Celia the Hen, and Benny's pal Corky the Raccoon. "And we all get to go!"

"I don't like summer camp," Benny grumbled.

"Can I wear my movie star sunglasses?" Melissa asked.

"What if it rains?" Celia clucked.

By the time Molly set aside the notepad, she'd written the beginning of *Daphne Goes to Summer Camp*. Never mind that she'd barely covered two pages, and never mind that her brain might dry up at any minute or that her publisher wouldn't buy this book until she did what they wanted to *Daphne Takes a Tumble*. At least she'd written, and for now she was happy.

The scent of lemon furniture polish greeted her as she walked into the B&B. The rugs had been vacuumed, the windows gleamed, and the tea table in the sitting room held a stack of Dresden rose china dessert plates with matching cups and saucers. Kevin's strategy of keeping the lovers separated until they'd finished their work seemed to be effective.

Amy emerged from the back with a pile of fresh white towels and took in the inexpensive canary-yellow sundress Molly had customized with four rows of colorful ribbon trim at the hem. "Wow! You look really cool. Nice makeup. I bet this'll get Kevin's attention."

"I'm not trying to get Kevin's attention."

Amy caressed the luscious little bruise at the base of her throat. "I've got this new perfume in my purse. It drives Troy nuts if I dab a little on my . . . well, you know. Do you want to borrow some?"

Molly avoided strangling her by making a dash for the kitchen.

It was too early to put out the apricot scones and oatmeal-butterscotch bread she'd made that morning, so she picked up her lovey and settled down with him on one of the kitchen chairs near the bay window. He tucked his topknot under her chin and rested his paw on her arm. She drew him closer. "Do you like it here as much as I do, pooch?"

He gave her an affirmative lick.

She gazed down the sloping yard toward the lake. These past few days in what she now thought of as Nightingale Woods had brought her back to life. She stroked Roo's warm belly and admitted that being with Kevin was a big part of it. He was stubborn and cocky—maddening beyond belief—but he'd made her feel alive again.

For all his talk about how smart *she* was, he didn't have any trouble keeping up with her. Like a few other jocks she knew—Dan sprang to mind, along with Cal Bonner and Bobby Tom Denton—Kevin's passion for athletics ran side by side with a keen intellect that his doofus behavior couldn't hide.

Not that she'd ever compare Kevin with Dan. Look at the way Dan loved dogs, for example. And kids. And most of all, look at the way Dan loved Phoebe.

She sighed again and let her gaze wander toward the gardens in the back, where Troy had finally cleared away the winter debris. The lilacs were in bloom, and a few irises displayed their purple ruffles, while a peony bush prepared to open.

A flicker of movement caught Molly's eye, and she saw Lilly sitting off to the side on an iron bench. At first Molly thought she was reading, but then she realized she was sewing instead. She thought about Lilly's coolness toward her and wondered if she were reacting personally or to the bad publicity from the wedding? . . . *the Chicago Stars football heiress who dabbles in writing children's books* . . . Molly hesitated, then rose and let herself out the back door.

Lilly sat near a small herb garden. Molly found it odd that someone who played the diva so convincingly hadn't objected to being stuck away in an attic. And despite that Armani sweater tossed so casually around her shoulders, she seemed remarkably content simply sitting by an overgrown garden and sewing. She was a puzzle. It was hard for Molly to warm up to someone who was so cold to her, but she couldn't quite dislike Lilly and not just because of her old affection for *Lace, Inc.* It took courage to stick around in the face of Kevin's hostility.

Marmie lay at Lilly's feet next to a large sewing basket. Roo ignored the cat to trot over and greet her owner, who leaned down to pat him. Molly realized she was working on a piece of a quilt, but it didn't look like anything she'd ever seen. The design wasn't a neatly arranged geometric, but a subtly shaded medley of curves and swirls in various patterns and shades of green, with touches of lavender and a surprising dab of sky blue.

"That's beautiful. I didn't know you were an artist."

The familiar hostility that formed in Lilly's eyes gave the summer afternoon a January chill. "This is just a hobby."

Molly decided to ignore the freeze-out. "You're very good. What's it going to be?"

"Probably a real quilt," she said reluctantly. "Usually I do smaller pieces like pillows, but this garden seems to demand something more dramatic."

"You're doing a quilt of the garden?"

Lilly's inherent good manners forced her to respond. "Just the herb garden. I started experimenting with it yesterday."

"Do you work from a drawing?"

Lilly shook her head, attempting to put an end to the conversation. Molly considered letting her do it, but she didn't want to. "How can you make something this complicated without a drawing?"

Lilly took her time responding. "I start putting scraps together that appeal to me, and then I pull out my scissors and see what happens. Sometimes the results are disastrous."

Molly understood. She created from bits and pieces, too—a few lines of dialogue, random sketches. She never knew what her books were about until she was well into them. "Where do you get your fabrics?"

Roo had propped his chin on one of Lilly's pricey Kate Spade sandals, but Molly's persistence seemed to bother her more. "I always have a box of scraps in my trunk," she said brusquely. "I buy a lot of remnants, but this project needs fabrics with some history. I'll probably try to find an antique store that sells vintage clothing."

Molly gazed back at the herb garden. "Tell me what you see."

She expected a rebuff, but, again, Lilly's good manners won out. "I was drawn to the lavender first. It's one of my favorite plants. And I love the silver of that sage behind it." Lilly's enthusiasm for her project began to overcome her personal dislike. "The spearmint needs to be weeded out. It's greedy, and it'll take over. That little tuft of thyme is fighting to survive against it."

"Which one is the thyme?"

"Those tiny leaves. It's vulnerable now, but it can be as aggressive as spearmint. It just goes about it more subtly." Lilly lifted her eyes, and her gaze held Molly's for a moment.

Molly got the message. "You think the thyme and I have something in common?"

"Do you?" she asked coolly.

"I have a lot of faults, but subtlety isn't one of them."

"I suppose that remains to be seen."

Molly wandered to the edge of the garden. "I'm trying hard to dislike you as much as you seem to dislike me, but it's tough. You were my heroine when I was a little girl."

"How nice." Icicles dripped.

"Besides, you like my dog. And I have a feeling that your attitude has less to do with my personality than it has to do with your concerns about my marriage."

Lilly stiffened.

Molly decided she had nothing to lose by being blunt. "I know about your real relationship with Kevin."

Lilly's fingers stalled on her needle. "I'm surprised he told you. Maida said he never spoke about it."

"He didn't. I guessed."

"You're very astute."

"You've taken a long time to come see him."

"After abandoning him, you mean?" Her voice had a bitter edge.

"I didn't say that."

"You were thinking it. What kind of woman abandons her child then tries to worm her way back into his life?"

Molly spoke carefully. "I doubt that you abandoned him. You seem to have found him a good home."

She gazed at the garden, but Molly suspected the peace she'd felt here earlier had vanished. "Maida and John had always wanted a child, and they loved him from the day he was born. But as torturous as it was to make my decision, I still gave him up too easily."

"Hey, Molly!"

Lilly tensed as Kevin came around the corner with Marmie lolling fat and happy in his arms. He stopped abruptly when he saw Lilly, and, as Molly watched, the charmer gave way to a hard-eyed man with a grudge.

He approached Molly as if she were alone in the garden. "Somebody let her out."

"I did," Lilly said. "She was with me until a few minutes ago. She must have heard you coming."

"This is your cat?"

"Yes."

He put her on the ground, almost as if she'd gone radioactive, then turned to walk away.

Lilly came up off the bench. Molly saw something both desperate and touching in her expression. "Do you want to know about your father?" Lilly blurted out.

Kevin stiffened. Molly's heart went out to him as she thought of all the questions she'd had over the years about her own mother. Slowly he turned.

Lilly clutched her hands. She sounded breathless, as if she'd just run a long distance. "His name was Dooley Price. I don't think that was his real first name, but it was all I knew. He was eighteen, a tall, skinny farm kid from Oklahoma. We met at the bus station the day we arrived in L.A." She drank in Kevin's face. "His hair was as light as yours, but his features were broader. You look more like me." She dipped her head. "I'm sure you don't want to hear that. Dooley was athletic. He'd ridden in rodeos—earned some prize money, I think—and he was convinced he could get rich doing stunts in the movies. I don't remember any more about him—another black mark you can chalk up against me. I think he smoked Marlboros and loved candy bars, but it was a long time ago, and that could have been someone else. We'd broken up by the time I discovered I was pregnant, and I didn't know how to find him." She paused and seemed to brace herself. "A few years later I read in the paper that he'd been killed doing some kind of stunt with a car."

Kevin's expression remained stony. He wouldn't let anyone see that this meant anything to him. Oh, Molly understood all about that.

Roo was sensitive to people's distress. He got up and rubbed against Kevin's ankles.

"Do you have a picture of him?" Molly asked because she knew Kevin wouldn't. The only photograph she had of her mother was her most treasured possession.

Lilly made a helpless gesture and shook her head. "We were only kids—two screwed-up teenagers. Kevin, I'm sorry."

He regarded her coldly. "There's no place for you in my life. I don't know how I can make that any clearer. I want you to leave."

"I know you do."

Both animals got up and followed him as he walked away.

Lilly's eyes glistened with fierce tears as she spun on Molly. "I'm not leaving!"

"I don't think you should," Molly replied.

Their eyes locked, and Molly thought she saw a faint crack forming in the wall between them.

Half an hour later, as Molly slipped the last of her apricot scones into a wicker basket, Amy appeared to announce that she and Troy would be staying in the upstairs bedroom Kevin had abandoned when he'd moved into Molly's cottage. "Somebody has to sleep here at night," Amy explained, "and Kevin said he'd pay us extra to do it. Isn't that cool?"

"That's great."

"I mean, we won't be able to make noise, but—"

"Get the jam, will you?" Molly couldn't bear hearing any more details of Amy and Troy's Super Bowl sex life.

But Amy wouldn't give up, and the buttery late-afternoon sunlight splashed her love-bitten neck as she regarded Molly earnestly. "It looks like things with you and Kevin could still work out if you just, maybe, tried a little harder. I'm serious about the perfume. Sex is real important to men, and if you'd just use a little—"

Molly shoved the scones at her and made a dash for the sitting room.

Later, when she got back to the cottage, Kevin was already there. He sat on the droopy old couch in the front room with Roo lolling on the cushion next to him. His feet were propped up, and a book lay open in his lap. Although he looked as if he didn't have a care in the world, Molly knew better.

He glanced up at her. "I like this Benny guy."

Her heart sank as she realized he was reading *Daphne Says Hello*. The other four books in the series lay nearby.

"Where did you get those?"

"Last night when I went into town. There's a kids' store—mainly clothes, but the owner sells some books and toys, too. She had these in the window. When I told her you were here, she got pretty excited about it." He tapped the page with his index finger. "This Benny character—"

"Those are children's books. I can't imagine why you'd bother reading them."

"Curiosity. You know, there are a couple of things about Benny that seem kind of familiar. For example—"

"Really? Well, thank you. He's entirely imaginary, but I do try to give all my characters qualities that readers can identify with."

"Yeah, well, I can identify with Benny, all right." He gazed down at a drawing of Benny wearing sunglasses that looked very much like his silver-rimmed Rēvos. "One thing I don't understand . . . The store owner said she'd gotten some pressure from one of her customers to take the books off the shelf because they were pornographic. Tell me what I'm missing."

Roo finally hopped off the couch and came over to greet her. She leaned down to pat him. "Have you ever heard of SKIFSA? Straight Kids for a Straight America?"

"Sure. They get their kicks going after gays and lesbians. The women all have big hair, and the men show too much teeth when they smile."

"Exactly. And right now they're after my bunny."

"What do you mean?" Roo trotted back to Kevin.

"They're attacking the Daphne series as homosexual propaganda."

Kevin started to laugh.

"I'm not kidding. They hadn't paid any attention to my books until we got married, but after all the stories about us appeared in the press, they decided to jump on the publicity bandwagon and go after me." She found herself telling him about her conversation with Helen and the changes Birdcage wanted in the Daphne books.

"I hope you told her exactly what she could do with her changes."

"It's not that easy. I have a contract, and they're keeping *Daphne Takes a Tumble* off the publication schedule until I send them the new illustrations." She didn't mention the rest of the advance money they owed her. "Besides, it's not as if moving Daphne and Melissa a few inches farther apart affects the story."

"Then why haven't you done the drawings?"

"I've had some troubles with . . . with writer's block. But it's gotten a lot better since I've been here."

"So now you're going to do them?"

She didn't like the disapproval she detected in his voice. "It's easy to stand on principle when you have a few million dollars in the bank, but I don't."

"I guess."

She got up and headed into the kitchen. As she pulled out a bottle of wine, Roo rubbed against her ankles. She heard Kevin come up behind her.

"We're drinking again, are we?"

"You're strong enough to fight me off if I get out of hand."

"Just don't make me hurt my passing arm."

She smiled and poured. He took the glass she handed him, and by unspoken agreement they walked together out onto the porch. The glider squeaked as he eased down next to her and took a sip of wine.

"You're a good writer, Molly. I can see why kids like your books. When you were drawing Benny, did you happen to notice how much—"

"What's with you and my pooch?"

"Damned if I know." He glared down at the poodle, who'd collapsed over one of his feet. "He followed me back here from the B&B. Believe me, I didn't encourage it."

Molly remembered the way Roo had picked up on Kevin's distress in the garden with Lilly. Apparently they had bonded, only Kevin didn't know it yet.

"How's your leg?" he asked.

"Leg?"

"Any aftereffects from that cramp?"

"It's . . . a little sore. Very sore. Sort of this dull throb. Pretty painful, actually. I'll have to take some Tylenol. But I'm sure it'll be better by tomorrow."

"No more swimming alone, okay? I'm serious. It was a stupid thing to do." He propped his arm along the back of the cushions and gave her his I-mean-business-you-lowlife-rookie look. "And while we're at it, don't get too cozy with Lilly."

"I don't think you have to worry about that. In case you didn't notice, she's not too fond of me. Still, I think you need to hear her out."

"That's not going to happen. This is my life, Molly, and you don't understand anything about it."

"That's not exactly true," she said carefully. "I'm an orphan, too."

He withdrew his arm. "You don't get to call yourself an orphan if you're over twenty-one."

"The point is, my mother died when I was two, so I know something about feeling disconnected from your roots."

"Our circumstances aren't anything alike, so don't try to make comparisons." He gazed out into the woods. "I had two great parents. You didn't have any."

"I had Phoebe and Dan."

"You were a teenager by then. Before that, you seem to have raised yourself."

He was deliberately turning the conversation away from himself. She understood that, too, and she let him do it. "Me and Danielle Steel."

"What are you talking about?"

"I was a fan, and I knew she had lots of kids. I used to pretend I was one of them." She smiled at his amusement. "Now, some might find that pathetic, but I think it was pretty creative."

"It's definitely original."

"Then I'd fantasize a mercifully painless death for Bert, at which point it would be magically revealed that he wasn't my father at all. My real father was—"

"Let me guess. Bill Cosby."

"I wasn't that well adjusted. It was Bruce Springsteen. And no comments, okay?"

"Why should I comment when Freud already did the job?"

Molly wrinkled her nose at him. They sat in surprisingly companionable silence, broken only by Roo's rhythmic snores. But Molly'd never been good at leaving well enough alone. "I still think you need to hear her out."

"I can't come up with a single reason why."

"Because she won't go away until you do. And because this will keep hovering over you for the rest of your life."

He set down his glass. "Maybe the reason you're so obsessed with analyzing my life is so you won't get depressed thinking about your own neuroses."

"Probably."

He rose from the glider. "What do you say we go into town for some dinner?"

She'd already spent far too much time with him today, but she couldn't stand the idea of staying here alone tonight while he painted the town German chocolate. "I suppose. Let me get a sweater."

As she headed back to her bedroom, she told herself what she already knew. Going out to dinner with him was a lousy idea, just as lousy as the two of them sitting around on the porch drinking wine together. Almost as lousy as not insisting he sleep under another roof.

Even though she didn't care about impressing him, she decided a shawl would make a better fashion statement with her sundress than a sweater, and she whipped out the bright red tablecloth she'd discovered in the bottom drawer of the dresser. As she unfolded it, she spotted something strange on the table next to her bed, something that hadn't been there earlier and that definitely didn't belong to her. "Aarrrggghhhh!"

Kevin shot into the room. "What's wrong?"

"Look at that!" She pointed at the small bottle of drugstore perfume. "That meddling little . . . trollop!"

"What are you talking about?"

"Amy stuck that perfume there!" She rounded on him. "Bite me!"

"Why are you mad at me? I didn't do it."

"No! Bite me. Give me a hickey right here." She jabbed her finger at a spot a few inches above her collarbone.

"You want me to give you a hickey?"

"Are you deaf?"

"Just thunderstruck."

"There's no one else I can ask, and I can't stand spending another day getting marital advice from a nineteen-year-old nymphomaniac. This'll put a stop to it."

"Did anybody ever mention you might be a few french fries short of a Happy Meal?"

"Go ahead. Make fun of me. She doesn't condescend to you the same way she does to me."

"Forget it. I'm not giving you a hickey."

"Fine. I'll get someone else to do it."

"You will not!"

"Desperate times call for desperate measures. I'll ask Charlotte Long."

"That's disgusting."

"She knows how the lovebirds behave. She'll understand."

"The image of that woman chomping on your neck just took away my appetite. And don't you think it'll be a little embarrassing showing off your bruise when other people are around?"

"I'll wear something with a collar, and I'll flip it up."

"Then push it right back down when you see Amy."

"Okay, I'm not proud of myself. But if I don't do something, I'm going to strangle her."

"She's just a teenager. Why do you care?"

"Fine. Forget it."

"And have you run off to Charlotte Long?" His voice dropped a husky note. "I don't think so."

She swallowed. "You'll do it?"

"I guess I have to."

Oh, boy . . . She squeezed her eyes shut and tilted her neck toward him. Her heart started to pound. What did she think she was doing?

Not a thing, apparently, because he didn't touch her.

She opened her eyes and blinked. "Could you, uh, hurry up?"

He didn't touch her, but neither did he move away. Oh, God, why did he have to be so gorgeous? Why couldn't he have wrinkly skin and a big potbelly instead of being a walking advertisement for hard bodies? "What are you waiting for?"

"I haven't given a girl a hickey since I was fourteen."

"I'm sure it'll come back if you concentrate."

"Concentration isn't my problem."

The gleam in those smoky green eyes indicated that her behavior had put her right on the border between eccentric and insane. Her burst of temper had faded. She had to extricate herself. "Oh, never mind."

She spun around to leave, but he caught her arm. The feel of his fingers on her skin made her shiver. "I didn't say I wouldn't. I just need to warm up a little."

Even if her feet had caught fire, she couldn't have moved.

"I can't just lunge and bite." His thumb stroked her arm. "It's not in my nature." Goose bumps quivered over her skin as he lifted his hand and trailed a finger over the curve of her neck.

Her voice developed a really annoying rasp. "It's all right. Go ahead and lunge."

"I'm a professional athlete." His words were a seductive caress as he traced a lazy S to the base of her throat. "Lack of a proper warm-up leads to injuries."

"That's the point, isn't it? An . . . injury?"

He didn't reply, and she stopped breathing as his mouth came closer. She felt a shock when his lips brushed the corners of hers.

He hadn't even made a direct hit, but her bones melted. She heard a soft, indecipherable sound and realized it had come from her, the easiest woman on planet earth.

He pulled her against him, a gentle movement, but the contact sizzled. Hard bone and warm flesh. She wanted all of his mouth, and she turned her head to find it, but he altered course. Instead of giving her the kiss she yearned for, he touched the opposite corner of her mouth.

Her blood pounded. His lips trailed from her jaw to her neck. Then he got ready to do exactly as she'd asked.

I've changed my mind! Please don't bite!

He didn't. He played at her throat until her breathing came fast and shallow. She hated him for teasing her, but couldn't make herself push away. And then he put an end to the game and kissed her for real.

The world spun, and everything turned upside down. His arms cradled her as if she really belonged inside them. She didn't know whose lips parted first, but their tongues touched.

It was a kiss made in lonely dreams. A kiss that took its time. A kiss that felt so right she couldn't remember all the reasons it was wrong.

His hand plowed through her hair, and those hard hips pressed against hers. She felt what she'd done to him and loved it. Her breast tingled as he covered it with his palm.

He yelped and snatched his hand away. "Damn it!"

She sprang back and instinctively checked to see if her breast had grown teeth. But it wasn't her breast.

He glared down at Roo, whose sharp, canine nails were digging into his leg. "Go away, mutt!"

Reality crashed back in on her. Just what did she think she was doing playing kissy-face with Mr. I'm Too Sexy? And she couldn't even blame him for letting things get out of hand because she was the one who'd started it.

"Stop it, Roo." Shaken, she pulled the dog away.

"Don't you ever trim the Klingon's toenails?"

"He wasn't attacking you. He just wanted to play."

"Yeah? Well, so did I!"

A long silence quivered between them.

She wanted him to be the first to look away, but he didn't, so she looked right back. It was unnerving. While she felt like hiding under the bed, he seemed perfectly willing to stand there all evening and think things over. The breast he'd touched still felt warm.

"This is getting complicated," he finally said.

She was messing with the NFL, so she ignored her rubbery legs. "Not for me. You're an okay kisser, by the way. So many athletes gnaw."

The corners of his eyes crinkled. "You just keep fighting, Daphne. Now, are we going to get dinner, or should we get back to work on that hickey you want so bad?"

"Forget the hickey. Sometimes the cure is worse than the disease."

"And sometimes bunny ladies turn into chickens."

She wasn't going to win this game, so she stuck her nose in the air like the rich heiress she wasn't, then grabbed the red tablecloth and swirled it around her shoulders.

The North Woods décor made the dining room of the Wind Lake Inn feel like an old hunting lodge. Indian-blanket-print curtains hung at the long, narrow windows, and the rustic walls displayed a collection of snowshoes and antique animal traps, along with the mounted heads of deer and elk. Molly focused on the birchbark canoe hanging from the rafters instead of those staring glass eyes.

Kevin was getting good at reading her mind, and he nodded toward the dead animals. "There used to be this restaurant in New York that specialized in exotic game—kangaroo, tiger, elephant steaks. One time some friends took me there for lionburgers."

"That's revolting! What kind of sick person would eat Simba?"

He chuckled and returned to his trout. "Not me. I had hash browns and pecan pie instead."

"You're messing with me. Stop it."

His eyes took a few lazy tango steps over her body. "You didn't mind earlier."

She toyed with the stem of her wineglass. "It was the alcohol."

"It was the sex we're not having."

She opened her mouth to cut him off at the knees, but he cut her off first. "Save your breath, Daph. It's time you faced a few important facts. Number one, we're married. Number two, we're living under the same roof—"

"Not by my choice."

"And number three, we're both celibate at the moment."

"You can't be celibate for a moment. It's a long-term lifestyle. Believe me, I know." She hadn't meant to say the last part out loud. Or maybe she had. She speared a carrot coin she didn't want to eat.

He set down his fork to study her more closely. "You're kidding, aren't you?"

"Of course I'm kidding." She gobbled up the carrot. "Did you think I was serious?"

He rubbed his chin. "You aren't kidding."

"Do you see the waiter? I think I'm ready for dessert."

"Care to elaborate?"

"No."

He bided his time.

She fiddled with another piece of carrot, then shrugged. "I've got issues."

"So does *Time* magazine. Stop hedging."

"First tell me where you think this conversation is going."

"You know where. Straight to the bedroom."

"Bedrooms," she emphasized, wishing he didn't look so grim about it. "His and hers. And it has to stay that way."

"A couple of days ago I'd have agreed with you. But both of us know that if it hadn't been for Godzilla's toenails, we'd be naked right now."

She shivered. "You don't know that for a fact."

"Listen, Molly, the newspaper ad doesn't come out until next Thursday. Today's only Saturday. It'll take another couple of days for interviews. Then another day or so to train whoever I hire. That's a lot of nights."

She'd wimped around long enough, and she abandoned all pretense of eating. "Kevin, I don't do casual sex."

"Now, that's weird. I seem to remember a night last February . . . "

"I had a crush on you, all right? A stupid crush that got out of hand."

"A crush?" He leaned back in the chair, beginning to enjoy himself. "What are you, twelve?"

"Stop being a jerk."

"So you had a crush on me?"

His crooked smile looked exactly like Benny's when he thought he had Daphne right where he wanted her. The bunny didn't like it, and neither did Molly.

"I had crushes on you and Alan Greenspan both at the same time. I can't imagine what I was thinking of. Although the crush I had on

Greenspan was a lot worse. Thank God I didn't run into him with that sexy briefcase."

He ignored that bit of folderol. "Interesting that Daphne seems to have a crush on Benny, too."

"She does not! He's horrible to her."

"Maybe if she'd put out, he'd be nicer."

"That's more disgusting than me and Charlotte Long!" She needed to sidetrack this conversation. "You can get sex anywhere, but we have a friendship, and that's more important."

"A friendship?"

She nodded.

"Yeah, I guess we do. Maybe that's what makes this exciting. I've never had sex with a friend before."

"It's nothing more than a fascination with the forbidden."

"I don't see why it's forbidden to you." He frowned. "I have a lot more to lose."

"Exactly how do you figure that?"

"Come on. You know how I feel about my career. Your closest family members happen to be my employers, and I'm on shaky ground with them at the moment. This is exactly why I always keep my female relationships separate from the team. I've never even dated one of the Star Girl cheerleaders."

"Yet here you are, all ready to get jiggy with the boss's sister."

"I've got everything to lose. You don't have anything."

Just this fragile little heart of mine.

He ran his thumb along the stem of his wineglass. "The truth is, a few nights of sexual dalliance might help your writing career."

"I can't wait to hear this."

"It'll reprogram your subconscious so you don't send out any more secret homosexual messages in your books."

She rolled her eyes.

He grinned.

"Give me a break, Kevin. If we were back in Chicago, it wouldn't occur to you to even think about having sex with me. How flattering is that?"

"It sure as hell would occur to me if we were together all the time like we are here."

He was deliberately missing the point, but before she could tell him that, the waitress appeared to see if there was anything wrong with the meals they weren't eating.

Kevin assured her there wasn't. She gave him a full-blast smile and began chatting with him as if he were her best friend. Since people reacted the same way to Dan and Phoebe, Molly was used to this kind of interruption, but the waitress was cute and curvy, so she found it annoying.

When the woman finally left, Kevin settled back in his chair and picked up the one part of their conversation she most wished he'd forgotten. "This celibacy thing . . . how long has that been going on?"

She took her time cutting a small piece of chicken. "A while."

"Any particular reason?"

She chewed slowly, as if she were thinking over his question instead of trying to find a way out. There wasn't any, so she attempted to sound grand and mysterious. "A choice I made."

"Is this one more part of that good girl thing everybody in the world believes about you except me?"

"I am a good girl!"

"You're a brat."

She sniffed, a little pleased, but not letting on. "Why should a virtuous woman have to justify herself? Or semivirtuous any way, so don't think I was a virgin before I lost my mind with you." But in some ways she was a virgin. Although she knew about sex, neither of her two affairs had taught her anything about making love, and neither had that awful night with Kevin.

"Because we're friends, remember? Friends tell each other things. You already know a lot more about me than almost anybody."

She didn't like being more embarrassed about this disclosure than she'd been when she told him she'd given away her inheritance, so she tried her best to look pious by putting her elbows on the table and making little prayer hands. "Being sexually discriminating is nothing to be ashamed about."

In some ways he understood her better than her own family, and his raised eyebrow told her she hadn't impressed him.

"I'm just—I know a lot of people treat sex casually, but I can't do that. I think it's too important."

"I'm not going to argue with you."

"Well, then, that's it."

"I'm glad."

Was it her imagination, or did she detect a little smugness in his expression?

"You're glad about what? That you've had a stadium full of easy women while I've been keeping my legs crossed? Talk about a double standard."

"Hey, I'm not proud of it. It's programmed in those X chromosomes. And it hasn't been a stadium full."

"Let me put it like this: Some people can handle sex without commitment, but it turns out that I'm not one of them, so it would be better if you'd move back into the house."

"Technically speaking, Daph, I've made a pretty big commitment to you, and I'm thinking it's payback time."

"Sex is not a commodity. You can't bargain with it."

"Who says?" His smile turned positively diabolical. "There were lots of nice-looking clothes at that boutique in town, and I can be real free with my credit card."

"What a proud moment this is for me. Bunny-book author turned hooker in one easy step."

He liked that, but his rumble of laughter was interrupted by a couple approaching from the other side of the dining room. "Excuse me, but aren't you Kevin Tucker? Hey, my wife and I are big fans . . . "

Molly settled back and sipped her coffee while Kevin dealt with his admirers. The man made her melt, and there was no use pretending otherwise. If it were just his good looks that attracted her, he wouldn't be so dangerous, but that cocky charm was chipping away at her defenses. As for the kiss they'd shared . . .

Stop right there! Just because their kiss had knocked her off her feet didn't mean she was going to act on it. She'd only begun to pull out of her emotional tailspin, and she wasn't self-destructive enough to throw herself back into it. She simply needed to keep reminding herself that Kevin was bored, and he wanted a little hanky-panky. The grim truth was that any woman would do, and she happened to be handy. Still, she could no longer deny that her old crush was back.

Some women were too dumb to draw breath.

Kevin tossed down the last of the Daphne books Molly had tried unsuccessfully to hide when they returned to the cottage. He couldn't believe it! Half of his recent life lay on the pages she'd written. Expurgated, of course. But still . . .

He was Benny the Badger! His red Harley . . . His Jet Ski . . . That very minor skydiving incident blown *way* out of proportion . . . And Benny snowboarding down Old Cold Mountain wearing a pair of silver Rēvos. He should sue!

Except he was flattered. She was a terrific writer, and the stories were great—kid-hip and funny. Although there was one thing he didn't like about the Daphne books—the bunny generally ended up getting the upper hand over the badger. What kind of message was that to send to little boys? Or big ones, for that matter?

He leaned back on the saggy excuse for a couch and glared toward the bedroom door she'd shut behind her. His good mood from dinner had faded. He'd have to be blind not to know that she was attracted to him. So what was the point?

She wanted to jerk his chain, that was the point. She wanted to make him beg so she could feel like she had her pride back. This whole thing was some kind of power trip for her. She was getting off on being cute and funny around him, making him enjoy her company, fluffing her hair, wearing funky clothes designed just so he'd itch to pull them off her. Then, when it was time to do exactly that, she jumped back and said she didn't believe in sex without *commitment*. Bull.

He needed a shower—a cold one—but there was only that pint-size bathtub. God, he hated it here. Why was she making such a big frickin' deal out of this? She might have said no at dinner, but when he'd kissed her, that sweet little body sure had been saying yes. They were *married*! He was the one who had to compromise himself, not her!

His policy of never mixing business with pleasure had blown up in his face. The trouble he was having keeping his eyes off the bedroom door filled him with self-disgust. He was Kevin Tucker, damn it, and he didn't have to beg for any woman's affections, not when there were so many others standing in line trying to catch his attention.

Well, he'd had enough. From now on he was going to be all business. He'd take care of the campground and step up his work-outs so he was in top shape when training camp started. As for that irritating little brat who happened to be his wife . . . Until they got back to Chicago, it was strictly hands off.

16

"My boyfriend's parents were gone for the night, and he invited me over. As soon as I walked in the door, I knew what was going to happen . . . "

—"My Boyfriend's Bedroom"
for *Chik*

Lilly hated herself for saying yes, but what art lover could turn down an invitation to visit Liam Jenner's house and see his private collection? Not that the invitation had been issued graciously. Lilly had just come in from a Sunday-morning walk when Amy handed her the telephone.

"If you want to see my paintings, come to my house this afternoon at two," he'd barked. "No earlier. I'm working, and I won't answer the bell."

She'd definitely been in L.A. too long, because she almost found his rudeness refreshing. As she turned off the highway and onto the side road he'd indicated, she realized how accustomed she'd grown to meaningless compliments and empty flattery. She'd nearly forgotten that people still existed who said exactly what was on their minds.

She spotted the weather-beaten turquoise mailbox he'd told her to look for. It perched crookedly on a battered metal pole set in a tractor tire filled with cement. The ditch behind the tire held rusted bedsprings and a twisted sheet of corrugated tin, which made the NO TRESPASSING sign at the top of the rutted, overgrown lane seem superfluous.

She turned in and slowed to a crawl. Even so, her car lurched alarmingly in the ruts. She'd just decided to abandon it and walk the rest of the way when the overgrowth disappeared and fresh gravel smoothed the bumpy road surface. Moments later she caught her breath as the house came into view.

It was a sleekly modern structure with white concrete parapets, stone ledges, and glass. Everything about the design bore Liam Jenner's signature. As she got out of the car and made her way toward the niche that held the front door, she wondered where he'd found an architect saintly enough to work with him.

She glanced down at her watch and saw that she was exactly half an hour late for this command performance. Just as she'd intended.

The door swung open. She waited for him to bark at her for not being on time and was disappointed when he merely nodded, then stepped back to let her in.

She caught her breath. The glass wall opposite the entrance had been constructed in irregular sections bisected by a narrow iron catwalk some ten feet from the ground floor. Through the glass she could see the sweeping vista of lake, cliffs, and trees.

"What an amazing house."

"Thanks. Would you like something to drink?"

His request sounded cordial, but she was even more impressed that he'd traded in his paint-stained denim shirt and shorts for a black silk shirt and light gray slacks. Ironically, his civilized clothes only emphasized the Sturm und Drang of that rugged face.

She declined his offer for a drink. "I'd love a tour, though."

"All right."

The house hugged the terrain in two uneven sections, the larger of which held an open living area, kitchen, library, and cantilevered dining room, with several smaller bedrooms tucked into lower levels. The catwalk she'd seen when she'd entered led to a glass-enclosed tower that Liam told her held his studio. She hoped he'd let her see it, but he showed her only the master bedroom below, a space designed with an almost monastic simplicity.

Magnificent works of art were on display everywhere, and Liam talked about them with passion and discernment. An enormous Jasper Johns canvas hung not far from a contemplative composition in blues and beige by Agnes Martin. One of Bruce Nauman's neon sculptures flickered near the library archway. Across from it hung a work by David Hockney, then a portrait of Liam done by Chuck Close. An imposing Helen Frankenthaler canvas occupied one long wall of the living area, and a totemlike stone-and-wood sculpture dominated a hallway. The very best of the world's contemporary artists were represented in this house. All except Liam Jenner.

Lilly waited until the tour was over and they'd returned to the central living area before she asked about it. "Why haven't you hung any of your own paintings?"

"Looking at my work when I'm not in the studio feels too much like a busman's holiday."

"I suppose. But they'd be so joyous in this house."

He stared at her for a long moment. Then the craggy lines of his face softened in a smile. "You really are a fan, aren't you?"

"I'm afraid so. I bid on one of your paintings a few months ago— *Composition #3.* My business manager forced me to drop out at two hundred and fifty thousand."

"Obscene, isn't it?"

He looked so pleased that she laughed. "You should be ashamed of yourself. It wasn't worth a penny over two hundred thousand. And I'm just beginning to realize how much I hate giving you compliments. You truly are the most overbearing man."

"It makes life easier."

"Keeps the masses at a distance?"

"I value my privacy."

"Which explains why you've built such an extraordinary house in the wilds of northern Michigan instead of Big Sur or Cap d'Antibes."

"Already you know me well."

"You're such a diva. I'm certain I've had my privacy invaded far more than you have, but it hasn't turned me into a hermit. Do you know that I still can't go anywhere without people recognizing me?"

"My nightmare."

"Why is it such a big deal to you?"

"Old baggage."

"Tell me."

"It's an incredibly boring story. You don't want to hear it."

"Believe me, I do." She sat on the couch to encourage him. "I love hearing people's stories."

He gazed at her, then sighed. "The critics discovered me just before my twenty-sixth birthday. Are you sure you want to hear this?"

"Definitely."

He stuck his hands in his pockets and wandered toward the windows. "I became the proverbial overnight sensation—on everybody's guest list, the subject of national magazine articles. I had people throwing money at me."

"I remember what that was like."

The fact that she understood what he'd gone through in ways most people couldn't seemed to relax him. He left the windows to sprawl down across from her, dominating the chair he'd chosen in the same way he dominated every space he occupied. She felt a moment of uneasiness. Craig had been overpowering like that.

"It went to my head," he said, "and I started believing all the hype. Do you remember that, too?"

"I was lucky. My husband kept me grounded in reality." Too grounded, she thought now. Craig never understood that she'd needed his praise more than his criticism.

"I wasn't lucky. I forgot that it was about the work, not about the artist. I partied instead of painted. I drank too much. I developed a taste for nose candy and free sex."

"Except sex never is free, is it?"

"Not when you're married to a woman you love. Ah, but I justified my behavior, you see, because *she* was my *true* love and all that other sex was meaningless. I justified it because she was having a tough pregnancy, and the doctor had told me to leave her alone until after the baby was born."

Lilly heard his self-contempt. This was a man who judged himself even more harshly than he judged others.

"My wife found out, of course, and did the right thing by walking out on me. A week later she went into labor, but the baby was born dead."

"Oh, Liam . . . "

He turned away her sympathy with an arch twist of his mouth. "There's a happy ending. She married a magazine editor and went on to have three healthy, well-adjusted children. As for me . . . I learned an important lesson about what is important and what isn't."

"And you've lived in lonely isolation ever since?"

He smiled. "Hardly that. I do have friends, Lilly. Genuine ones."

"People you've known for a hundred years," she guessed. "Newcomers need not apply."

"I think all of us get set in our friendships as we grow older. Haven't you?"

"I suppose." She started to ask why he'd invited her here, since she was definitely a newcomer, but a more important question was on her mind. "Am I mistaken, or didn't you leave something important out of the house tour?"

He sank deeper into his chair and looked annoyed. "You want to see my studio."

"I'm sure you don't make a habit of opening it up to everyone, but—"

"No one goes in there but me and an occasional model."

"Perfectly understandable," she said smoothly. "Still, I'd be grateful if I could just have a peek."

A calculating glint appeared in his eyes. "How grateful?"

"What do you mean?"

"Grateful enough to pose for me?"

"You don't give up, do you?"

"It's part of my charm."

If they'd been at the B&B or by the stream in the meadow, she might have been able to refuse, but not here. That mysterious space where he created some of the world's most beautiful art was too near. "I can't imagine why you'd want to sketch a fat, over-the-hill, forty-five-year-old woman, but if that's what it takes to see your studio, then, yes, I'll pose for you."

"Good. Follow me." He vaulted from his chair and headed for a set of stone steps that led to the catwalk. As he reached it, he glanced back at her. "You're not fat. And you're older than forty-five."

"I am not!"

"You've had work done around your eyes, but no plastic surgeon can cut away the life experience behind them. You're closer to fifty."

"I'm forty-seven."

He gazed down at her from the catwalk. "You're making me lose patience."

"Air could make you lose patience," she grumbled.

The corner of his mouth curled. "Do you want to see my studio or not?"

"Oh, I suppose." Frowning, she swept up the steps, then followed him across the narrow, open structure. She glanced uneasily down at the living area below. "I feel as if I'm walking the plank."

"You'll get used to it."

His statement implied she'd be coming back, an impression she immediately corrected. "I'll pose for you today, but that's all."

"Stop irritating me." He'd reached the end of the catwalk, and he turned toward her so he stood silhouetted against the stone arch. She felt a tiny erotic thrill as he watched her approach with his legs braced and his arms crossed over his chest like an ancient warrior.

She gave him her diva's gaze. "Remind me again why I even wanted to see it."

"Because I'm a genius. Just ask me."

"Shut up and get out of my way."

His laugh held a deep, pleasing resonance. He turned away and led her around a curve of wall into his studio.

"Oh, Liam . . . " She pressed her fingertips to her lips.

The studio sat suspended above the trees in its own private universe. It was oddly shaped with three of its five sides curved. Late-afternoon light glowed through the northern wall, which was constructed entirely of glass. Overhead, the various skylights had shades that could be adjusted according to the time of day. The layers of colorful paint splatters on the rough walls, the furniture, and the limestone floor had turned the studio into a work of modern art all its own. She had the same sensation she experienced when she stood inside the Getty.

Half-finished canvases sat on easels while others leaned against the walls. Several large canvases hung on special frames. Her mind whirled as she tried to take it all in. She might not have had much formal education, but she'd studied art on her own for several decades, and she wasn't a novice. Still, she found his mature work difficult to categorize. All the influences were evident—the teeth-gnashing of the Abstract Expressionists, the studied cool of Pop, the starkness of the Minimalists. But only Liam Jenner had the audacity to superimpose the sentimental over those decidedly unsentimental styles.

Her eyes drank in the monumental, unfinished Madonna and Child that occupied most of one wall. Of all the great contemporary artists, only Liam Jenner could paint a Madonna and Child without using cow dung as his medium, or smearing an obscenity over her forehead, or adding a flashing Coca-Cola sign in place of a star. Only Liam Jenner had the absolute self-confidence to show the cynical deconstructionists who populated the world of contemporary art the meaning of unabashed reverence.

Her heart filled with tears she couldn't let herself shed. Tears of loss for the way she'd let her identity get swallowed up by Craig's expectations, tears of loss for the son she'd given away. Gazing at the painting, she realized how careless she'd been with what she should have held sacred.

His hand curled around her shoulder in a gesture as gentle as the wisps of blue-gold paint softening the Madonna's hair. His touch seemed both natural and necessary, and as she swallowed her tears, she had to resist the urge the curl into his chest.

"My poor Lilly," he said softly. "You've made your life even harder for yourself than I have mine."

She didn't question how he knew, but as she stood before that miraculous, unfinished painting and felt the comforting hand on her shoulder, she understood that all these canvases were reflections of the man—his angry intensity, his intelligence, his severity, and the sentiment he worked so hard to hide. Unlike her, Liam Jenner was one with his work.

"Sit," he murmured. "Just as you are." She let him lead her to a simple wooden chair across the room. He caressed her shoulder, then stepped back and reached for one of the blank canvases near his worktable. If he had been any other man, she would have felt manipulated, but manipulation wouldn't occur to him. He had simply been overcome with the need to create, and for a reason she couldn't fathom, that involved her.

She no longer cared. Instead, she gazed at the Madonna and Child and thought about her life, richly blessed in so many ways but barren in others. Instead of concentrating on her losses—her son, her identity, the husband she'd both loved and resented—she thought of all she'd been granted. She'd been blessed with a good brain and the intellectual curiosity to challenge it. She'd been given a beautiful face and body when she'd needed them most. So what if that beauty had faded? Here beside this lake in northern Michigan, it didn't seem quite so important.

As she gazed at the Madonna, something began to happen. She saw her herb-garden quilt instead of Liam's painting, and she began to understand what had eluded her. The herb garden was a metaphor for the woman who now lived inside her—a more mature woman, one who wanted to heal and nurture instead of seduce, a woman with subtle nuances instead of splashy beauty. She was no longer the person she'd been, but she didn't yet understand the person she'd become. Somehow the quilt held the answer.

Her fingers twitched in her lap as a rush of energy shot through her. She needed her sewing basket and her box of fabrics. She needed them now. If she had them—if she had them right now!—she could find the path that would unlock who she was. She jumped up from the chair. "I have to go."

He'd been completely absorbed in his work, and for a moment he didn't seem to comprehend what she'd said. Then something that almost looked like pain twisted those craggy features. "Oh, God, you can't."

"Please. I'm not being difficult. I have to—I'll come right back. I just need to get something from my car."

He stepped away from the canvas. Left a smudge on his forehead as he shoved a hand through his hair. "I'll get it for you."

"There's a basket in my trunk. No, I need the box that's with it. I need— We'll go together."

They ran across the catwalk, both of them on fire to get this done so they could return to what was essential. Her breath came in little gasps as she raced down the steps. She looked for the purse that held her keys but couldn't find it.

"Why the hell did you lock your car!" he roared. "We're in the middle of godforsaken nowhere!"

"I live in L.A.!" she shouted back.

"Here!" He snatched the purse from beneath one of the tables and began rummaging through it.

"Give it to me!" She grabbed it away and dug herself.

"Hurry up!" He seized her at the elbow, shoved her toward the front door and down the steps. On the way she found the keys. She broke away from him and flicked the remote that opened the trunk.

She nearly sobbed with relief as she grabbed her sewing basket and pushed the box of fabrics at him. He barely glanced at it.

They fled inside again, rushed up the stairs, raced across the catwalk. By the time they got to the studio, they were both struggling to breathe, more from emotion than exertion. She collapsed into the chair. He rushed toward the canvas. They gazed at each other. And both of them smiled.

It was an exquisite moment. One of perfect communication. He hadn't questioned her urgency, hadn't shown the slightest disdain when he'd seen it was only a woman's sewing basket that had made her so frantic. Somehow he understood her need to create, just as she understood his.

Content, she bent to her work.

Gradually it grew dark outside. The studio's interior lights came on, each one exquisitely placed to provide illumination without shadow. Her scissors snipped. Her needle flew in the broad basting stitches that would hold the fabric together until she could get to her sewing machine. Seam met seam. Colors blended. Patterns overlapped.

His fingers brushed her neck. She hadn't realized he'd left his canvas. A streak of scarlet smeared his black silk shirt, and a smear of orange clung to his expensive slacks. His crisp, graying hair was rumpled, and more paint smudged his hairline.

Her skin prickled as he touched the top button on her gauzy, tangerine blouse. Gazing into her eyes, he slipped it free of its buttonhole. Then he opened the next one.

"Please," he said.

She didn't try to stop him, not even when he slipped one side of the blouse down. Not even when his square, paint-smeared fingers brushed the front clasp of her bra. Instead, she bent her head to her sewing and let him unfasten it.

Her breasts spilled free, so much heavier than they'd been when she was younger. She allowed him to arrange the gauzy fabric of her blouse as he wished. He slipped one sleeve down her arm until it caught at the crook. Then the other. Her breasts rested in the nest of fabric like plump hens.

His footsteps tapped the limestone floor as he returned to his canvas.

Bare-breasted, she kept to her sewing.

Earlier she'd believed that her quilt would be about nurture instead of seduction, but now the astonishing fact that she'd allowed him to do this told her the meaning was more complex. She'd thought the sexual part of her had died. Now the hot ache in her body made her understand this wasn't true. The quilt had just unlocked one secret of her new identity.

Without disturbing the drape of fabric at the crook of her arms, she dipped into the box at her side and found a soft piece of old velvet. It was a deep, sensual crimson shaded with darker hues. The color of dark opal basil. The secret color of a woman's body. Her fingers trembled as she rounded the corners. The fabric brushed her nipples as she worked it, making them tighten and bead. She dipped into the box again and found an even deeper hue to serve as the secret heart.

She would add tiny crystals of dew.

A muffled curse made her look up. Liam stared at her, perspiration glistening on the rugged planes of his face. His paint-streaked arms hung slack at his sides, and a brush lay at his feet where he'd dropped it. "I've painted a hundred nudes. This is the first time . . . " He shook his head, looking momentarily bewildered. "I can't do this."

A rush of shame filled her. Her quilt piece fell to the floor as she leaped up, grabbed her blouse, pulled it closed.

"No." He came toward her. "Oh, no, not that."

The fire in his eyes stunned her. His legs brushed her skirt, and he plunged his hands inside the blouse she'd just drawn closed. Gathering her breasts in his hands, he buried his face in the swells. She clutched his arms as his lips closed around a nipple.

Their explosion of passion should have been reserved for youth, but neither of them was young. She felt his hard, thick length. He reached for the waistband of her skirt. Sanity returned, and she pushed his hands away. She wanted him to see her naked as she'd once been, not as she was now.

"Lilly . . . " He breathed her name in protest.

"I'm sorry . . . "

He had no patience for cowardice. He reached beneath her skirt and snagged her panties, then dropped to his knees and drew them off. He pressed his face into her skirt, against her . . . His warm breath seeped between her legs. It felt so good. She separated them, just a few inches, and let his breath touch her secret heart.

He pulled her down beside him on that hard limestone floor. Cupping her face in his hands, he kissed her. The deep, experienced kiss of a man who knew women well.

Together they fell back. Her skirt tangled at her waist. He ran his hands along her legs and pushed them far apart. Then he buried his face between them.

She drew up her ankles, let her knees fall open, and reveled in his lusty, vigorous feasting. Her orgasm was fierce and strong, taking her by surprise. By the time she'd recovered, he was naked.

His body was powerful and fine. She opened her arms, and he plunged inside her. With her fingers curled into his hair, she took his deepest kiss, wrapped her legs around him. Her spine dug into the hard floor beneath. She winced as he plunged again.

He stopped, stroked more gently, then turned them so his body took the punishment of the floor. "Better?" He reached up to cup her breasts as they swung before him.

"Better," she replied, finding a rhythm that pleased them both.

As they moved, the paints on the canvases seemed to swirl around them, the colors growing brighter, turning liquid. Their bodies worked together, awash in hot sensation. Finally neither of them could bear it any longer, and all the colors of the universe shattered in an explosion of bright, white light.

She came back to herself slowly. She was lying on top of him, her blouse and skirt bunched at her waist. She'd fallen under a spell. The man had cast a spell over her as surely as his paintings had.

He groaned. "I'm too old for floors."

She leaped off him, scrambling awkwardly to cover herself. "I'm sorry. I'm—I'm so heavy. I must have crushed you."

"Not this again." He rolled to his side, winced, and slowly rose to his feet. Unlike her, he didn't seem to be in any hurry to get his clothes back on. She refused to look. Instead, she pushed her crumpled skirt down, noticing at the same time that her panties lay on the floor at his feet. She couldn't manage her bra, so she pulled the front of her blouse together, only to have him catch her hands and still them over the buttons.

"You listen to me, Lilly Sherman. I've worked with hundreds of models over the years, but I've never had to stop painting to seduce one of them."

She started to say that she didn't believe him, but this was Liam Jenner, a man with no patience for niceties. "It's—it was crazy."

His expression grew fierce. "Your body is magnificent. It's lush and extravagant, exactly the way a woman's body should be. Did you see the way the light fell on your skin? On your breasts? They're outrageous, Lilly. Big. Fleshy. Bountiful. I couldn't ever get enough of painting them. Your nipples . . . " He settled his thumbs over them, rubbed, and his eyes burned with the same passion she'd seen when he painted. "They make me think of showers. Showers of rich, golden milk." She shivered at the intensity she heard in his husky whisper. "Spilling to the ground . . . turning into rivers . . . sparkling, golden rivers flowing to nourish continents of parched land."

Such an outlandish, excessive man. She didn't know what to do with a vision so outrageous.

"Your body, Lilly . . . don't you see? This is the body that gave birth to the human race."

His words ran counter to everything that the world she lived in preached. Diets. Denial. An obsession with female bone instead of female flesh. The culture of youth and thinness.

Of stinginess.

Of disfigurement.

Of fear.

For a fraction of a moment she glimpsed the truth. She saw a world so terrified of Woman's mystical power that nothing would do but to obliterate the very source of that power—the natural shape of her body.

The vision was too foreign to her experience, and it faded. "I—I have to go." Her heart hammered in her chest. She leaned down and grabbed her panties, threw them into her sewing basket, snatched up her quilt pieces. "This was . . . this was so irresponsible."

He smiled. "Am I likely to get you pregnant?"

"No. But there are other things."

"Neither of us is promiscuous. We've both learned the hard way that sex is too important."

"What do you call *that*?" She jabbed her hand toward the floor.

"Passion." He nodded toward the quilt pieces spilling from her basket. "Let me see what you're working on."

She couldn't imagine permitting a genius like Liam Jenner to see her simple craft project. Shaking her head, she made her way toward the door, but just before she got there, something made her stop and turn back.

He stood watching her. A smudge of blue paint marked his thigh near his groin. He was naked and magnificent.

"You were right," she said. "I'm fifty!"

His soft reply followed her out of the house and down the road.

"Too old to be such a coward."

17

Daphne packed her most necessary things: sunblock, a pair of lollipop-red water wings, a box of Band-Aids (because Benny was going to camp, too), her favorite crunchy cereal, a very loud whistle (because Benny was going to camp, too), crayons, one book for every day she'd be gone, opera glasses (because you never knew what you might want to see), a beach ball that said FORT LAUDERDALE, her plastic bucket and shovel, and a great big sheet of bubble wrap to pop if she got bored.

—*Daphne Goes to Summer Camp*

By Tuesday, Molly was worn out from the ups and downs of working on *Daphne Goes to Summer Camp* as well as trying to keep Kevin entertained. Not that he'd asked to be entertained. In fact, he'd turned surly after their Saturday-night dinner and gone out of his way to avoid her. He even had the gall to behave as if *she* were imposing on *him*. She'd had to threaten to go on strike to get him to come with her today.

She should have left him alone, but she couldn't. The only way she could make him change his mind about selling the Wind Lake Campground was to convince him that this was no longer the boring place of his childhood. Unfortunately, she hadn't been able to convince him of a thing so far, which meant it was time to make her next move. Resigned, she forced herself to her feet.

"Look, Kevin! In the trees over there!"

"What are you doing, Molly? Sit down!"

She gave a jump of excitement. "Isn't that a Kirtland's warbler?"

"Stop!"

All it took was one more small jump and the canoe tipped.

"Aw, *shit!*"

They tumbled into the lake.

As she went under, she thought about the earth-shattering kiss they'd exchanged three days ago. Ever since then he'd kept his distance, and the few times they'd been together, he was barely civil. Once she'd told him she wouldn't sleep with him, he'd lost interest in her. If only . . .

If only what, you dope? If only he were banging his fists on your bedroom door every night begging you to change your mind and let him in? Like that would ever happen.

But couldn't he look as if he were suffering from a little of the lust that had her tossing in her bed the last three nights until she thought she'd scream? It had even affected her writing. This morning Daphne had told her best friend Melissa the Wood Frog that Benny was looking particularly sexy that day! Molly had thrown down her notebook in disgust.

She felt above her head for the capsized canoe's gunwale, then swam beneath it. With a kick she came up into the air pocket beneath the hull, which was just big enough for her head. This drowning thing was going to turn her into a prune.

She knew it would be easy to regain his attention. All she had to do was undress. But she wanted to be something more to him than another sexual fling. She wanted to be . . .

Her mind balked, but only for a moment. A *friend,* that was it. She'd just begun to value their friendship when he'd grown surly. There wouldn't be any chance of reestablishing that relationship if they went to bed together.

Once again she forced herself to remember that Kevin wouldn't be much of a lover. Yes, he was a great kisser, and yes, he'd been asleep during their brief, ill-fated sexual encounter, but she'd already observed that he wasn't really a sensualist. He never lingered over his food. He didn't savor the wine or take the time to appreciate the presentation of the meal on his plate. He ate efficiently and his table manners were flawless, but food wasn't anything more than body fuel to him. Besides, how much energy did a gorgeous multimillionaire pro athlete really need to invest into developing his skills as a lover? Women lined up to please him, not the other way around.

Face it: The sex she wanted to have with him was romantic fantasy sex, and she wasn't willing to sell her soul for that. Despite three nights of tossing and turning, despite the embarrassing heat that made her knees turn goofy at the most inopportune moments, she didn't want an affair. She wanted a real relationship. A *friendship*, she reminded herself.

She'd just begun to imagine how a pair of dripping bunny ears would look peeking out from beneath a capsized canoe when Kevin's head surfaced next to her. It was too dark beneath the hull to see his expression, but the anger in his voice came through loud and clear.

"Why did I know I'd find you here?"

"I got disoriented."

"I swear, you're the most uncoordinated person I've ever met!" He rudely grabbed her arm and yanked on it, pulling her back underwater. They resurfaced in the daylight.

It was a beautiful afternoon on Wind Lake. The sun shone, and the gem-blue water mirrored a single fluffy cloud floating in the sky above like one of Molly's meringue cookies that hadn't gotten burned on the bottom. Kevin, however, looked more than a little stormy.

"What the hell were you thinking of? When you blackmailed me into coming out here, you told me you knew all about canoeing!"

As she treaded water, she was glad she'd remembered to leave her sneakers at the dock, which was more than he'd done. But then, he hadn't possessed her insider's knowledge of where they'd end up.

"I do know about canoeing. My last summer at camp I was in charge of taking out the six-year-olds."

"Are any of them still *alive*?"

"I don't know why you're being so grouchy. You like to swim."

"Not when I'm wearing a Rolex!"

"I'll buy you a new one."

"Yeah, right. The point is, I didn't want to come canoeing today. I had work to do. But all weekend, whenever I tried to get something done, you'd decide a burglar was trying to break into the cottage, or you couldn't concentrate on cooking unless you went cliff diving. This morning you nagged me into playing catch with your *poodle!*"

"Roo needs exercise." And Kevin needed someone to play with.

He hadn't been able to sit still all weekend. Instead of giving in to the spell of Wind Lake and reconnecting with his heritage, he was working out or trying to pound away his restlessness with hammer and nails. Any moment she expected him to hop into his car and drive off forever.

Just the thought of it depressed her. She couldn't leave here, not yet. There was something magical about the campground. Possibilities seemed to shimmer in the air. It felt almost enchanted.

Now he swam toward the stern of the capsized canoe. "What are we supposed to do with this thing now?"

"Can you touch bottom?"

"We're in the middle of a frickin' lake! Of course I can't touch bottom."

She ignored his surliness. "Well, our instructor once taught us a technique to turn over a canoe. It's called the Capistrano Flip, but—"

"How do you do it?"

"I was fourteen. I can't remember."

"Then why did you mention it?"

"I was thinking out loud. Come on, I'm sure we can manage."

They finally righted the canoe, but their technique, which was based mostly on Kevin's brute strength, left the hull full of water and partially submerged. With nothing to use as a bailer, they were forced to paddle back that way, and Molly was gasping for breath by the time she'd finished helping him haul it up onto the beach. She'd never been a quitter, though.

"Look over to the right, Kevin! Mr. Morgan's here!" She hooked a lock of wet hair behind her ear and gestured toward the slightly built, bespectacled accountant setting up a chair in the sand.

"Not this again."

"Really, I think you should follow him—"

"I don't care what you say. He does *not* look like a serial killer!" He yanked off his sodden T-shirt.

"I'm very intuitive, and he has shifty eyes."

"I think you've lost your mind," he muttered. "I really do. And I have no idea how I'm going to explain that to your sister—a woman who happens to be my boss."

"You worry too much."

He spun on her. She saw fire in those green eyes and knew she'd pushed him too far.

"You listen to me, Molly! Fun and games are over. I've got better things to do than waste my time like this."

"This isn't a waste of time. It's—"

"I'm not going to be your *pal*! Can you understand that? You want our relationship to stay out of the bedroom? Fine. That's your prerogative. But don't expect me to be your buddy. From now on you entertain yourself and stay the hell away from me!"

She watched him stomp off. Even though she probably deserved a little of his anger, she still felt disappointed with him.

Summer camp was supposed to be fun, but Daphne was sad. Ever since she'd capsized their canoe, Benny had been mad at her. Now he didn't ask her to spin around in circles until they got dizzy. He didn't notice that she'd painted each of her toenails a different color so they looked like they'd been dipped in a puddle of rainbows. He didn't squish his nose and stick out his tongue to get her attention or burp really loud. Instead, she saw him making stupid faces at Cicely, a bunny from Berlin, who gave him chocolate rabbits and had no flair for fashion.

Molly set aside her notebook and made her way to the sitting room, taking along the newest box of Say Fudge. She dumped it into a milk-glass bowl that still held crumbs from yesterday's fudge. It had been four days since she'd overturned the canoe, and each morning since then she'd found a fresh box sitting on the kitchen counter in the cottage. It sure eliminated any mystery about where Kevin had been the night before. *Slytherin!*

He'd done everything possible to get away from her except the one thing he should do—move back into the B&B. But his aversion to being around Lilly was worse than his aversion to being around her. Not that it mattered much, since they were hardly ever in the cottage at the same time.

Depressed, she shoved a piece of fudge into her mouth. It was Saturday, and the B&B was full for the weekend. She wandered into the foyer and straightened the pile of brochures on the hall console. The job ad had appeared in the paper, and Kevin had spent the morning interviewing the two best candidates, while Molly had shown the B&B guests to their rooms and helped Troy with the new cottage rentals. Now it was early afternoon, and she needed a writing break.

She stepped onto the front porch and saw Lilly kneeling in the shade at the side of the front yard, planting the last of the pink and lavender impatiens she'd bought to go in the empty beds. Even wearing gardening gloves and kneeling in the grass, she managed to look glamorous. Molly didn't bother reminding her she was a guest. She'd tried that a few days ago when Lilly had appeared with a trunk full of annuals. Lilly had said she enjoyed gardening, that it relaxed her, and Molly had to agree that she appeared less tense, even though Kevin continued to ignore her.

As Molly reached the bottom of the stairs, Marmie lifted her head and blinked her big golden eyes. Since Roo was safely inside with Amy, the cat rose and walked over to rub against Molly's ankles. Although Molly wasn't a cat person like Kevin, Marmie was a winning feline, and the two of them had developed a distant fondness. She loved to be held, and Molly bent down to pick her up.

Lilly gave the earth around the seedling a sharp little slap. "I wish you wouldn't encourage Liam to keep showing up for breakfast every morning."

"I like him." *And you do, too,* Molly thought.

"I don't know how you could. He's rude, arrogant, and egotistical."

"Also amusing, intelligent, and very sexy."

"I hadn't noticed."

"I believe you."

Lilly lifted a diva's eyebrow at her, but Molly wasn't intimidated. Lately, Lilly sometimes seemed to forget Molly was the enemy. Maybe the sight of her working around the B&B didn't fit the actress's image of a spoiled football heiress. Molly thought about confronting her again as she'd done in the herb garden over a week ago, but she didn't feel like defending herself.

Each morning, Liam Jenner appeared in the kitchen to have breakfast with Lilly. They bickered while they ate, but they seemed to argue more to prolong their time together than for any other reason. When they weren't bickering, their conversations ranged from art and their travels to their observations about human nature. They had everything in common, and it was obvious they were attracted. Just as obvious that Lilly was fighting it.

Molly learned that Lilly had been to his house once and that he'd started a portrait of her, but Lilly refused his repeated requests to return and sit for him. Molly wondered what had happened at the house that day.

She carried Marmie over to the shade of a big linden tree near where Lilly was planting. Just to be perverse, she said, "I'll bet he looks great naked."

"Molly!"

Molly's devilry faded as she saw Kevin jogging toward the Common from the highway. As soon as he'd finished his interviews, he'd changed into a T-shirt and his gray athletic shorts, then taken off. Even when they served breakfast together, he barely spoke to her. As Amy felt duty-bound to point out, he spent more time talking to Charlotte Long than he spent talking to Molly.

All week he'd been killing Lilly with cool politeness, and Lilly had been letting him get away with it. Now, however, she jabbed her trowel in the ground. "You know, Molly, I've just about run out of patience with your husband."

That made two of them.

Molly watched as he slowed to cool off. He bent his head and rested the palms of his hands on the small of his back. Marmie spotted him and stirred in her arms. Molly gazed at the cat resentfully. She was jealous. Jealous of Kevin's affection for a cat. She remembered the way he stroked Marmie's fur, those long fingers sinking deep . . . sliding down her spine . . . It gave Molly goose bumps.

She realized she was blindly, utterly furious with him! She hated the fact that he'd spent the morning interviewing strangers to take over the campground. And what right did he have to act as if they had a genuine friendship, then dismiss her just because she'd refused to go to bed with him? He might pretend he was angry because of the incident with the canoe, but both of them knew that was a lie.

Impulsively, she turned around and set the cat against the trunk of the linden tree they'd been standing beneath. A squirrel stirred in the branches above. Marmie flicked her tail and began to climb.

Lilly caught the action out of the corner of her eye and spun around. "What are you—"

"You're not the only one running out of patience!" Molly glanced up to see Marmie scramble higher. Then she called out. *"Kevin!"*

He looked over.

"We need your help! It's Marmie!"

He picked up his stride and hurried toward them. "What's wrong with her?"

She pointed into the linden tree, where Marmie had climbed out on a branch high above the ground. The cat yowled her displeasure as the squirrel scampered from sight.

"She's stuck and we can't get her down. The poor thing is terrified."

Lilly rolled her eyes, but she didn't say anything.

Kevin gazed up into the tree. "Hey, girl. Come on down." He extended his arms. "Come here."

"We've been doing that for ages." Molly eyed his sweat-soaked T-shirt and running shorts. The hair on his bare legs was matted. How could he still look so gorgeous? "I'm afraid you'll have to climb up after her." She paused. "Unless you want me to do it."

"Of course not." He grabbed one of the lower branches and pulled himself up.

She couldn't quite contain her relish. "Your legs are going to get ripped to shreds."

He shimmied higher.

"If you slip, you could break your passing arm. This might end your whole career."

He was disappearing into the branches now, and she raised her voice. "Please come down! It's too dangerous."

"You're making more noise than the cat!"

"Let me get Troy."

"Great idea. The last time I saw him, he was down at the dock. And take your time."

"Do you think there are any tree snakes up there?"

"I don't know, but I'll bet you can find some in the woods. Go look." The branches rustled. "Come here, Marmie. Here, girl."

The limb where the yowling cat crouched was fairly thick, but he was a large man. What if it snapped and he really did injure himself? For the first time Molly's warning was genuine. "Don't climb out on that, Kevin. You're too big."

"Would you be quiet!"

Molly held her breath as he threw his leg over the limb about eight feet from where Marmie crouched. He scooted forward, making soothing noises to the cat. He'd just about reached her when Marmie stuck her nose in the air, hopped delicately to a lower branch, then proceeded to pick her way down the tree.

Molly watched in disgust as the traitorous cat reached the ground, then shot toward Lilly, who scooped her up and gave Molly a pointed look. She didn't say anything to Kevin, however, who was climbing back down.

"How long did you tell me she was stuck up there?" he asked as he dropped.

"It's, uh, tough to keep track of time when you're terrified."

He studied Molly, his expression suspicious, then bent to examine a nasty scrape on the inside of his calf.

"I've got some ointment in the kitchen," she said.

Lilly stepped forward. "I'll get it."

"Don't do me any favors." Kevin snapped.

Lilly clenched her teeth. "You know, I'm getting really sick of your attitude. And I'm tired of biding my time. We're going to talk right *now*." She set down the cat.

Kevin was taken aback. He'd grown accustomed to the way she hadn't pressed him, and he didn't seem to know how to respond.

She jabbed her finger toward the side of the house. "We've postponed this long enough. Follow me! Or maybe you don't have the guts."

She'd waved a red flag in his face, and Kevin was quick to respond. "We'll see who has guts," he growled.

Lilly charged toward the woods.

Molly wanted to applaud, but she was glad she didn't because Lilly spun around to glare at her. "Don't touch my cat!"

"Yes, ma'am."

Lilly and Kevin headed off together.

L illy heard the sounds of Kevin's footsteps rustling in the pine needles strewn over the path. At least he was following her. Three decades of guilt began to snuff out the temper that had finally given her the courage to force this confrontation. She was so sick of that guilt. All it had done was paralyze her, and she couldn't stand it any longer. Liam tormented her by appearing every morning for a breakfast she never felt like eating but couldn't seem to avoid. Molly wouldn't fit into the pigeonhole Lilly had assigned her. Kevin looked at her as if she were his worst enemy. It was too much.

In the distance ahead, the trees gave way to the lake. She marched toward it, silently daring him not to follow. When she couldn't stand it any longer, she turned to confront him, not knowing until she spoke what she was going to say.

"I won't apologize for giving you up!"

"Why am I not surprised?"

"Sneer all you want, but have you once asked yourself where you'd be today if I'd kept you? What chance do you think you'd have had living in a roach-infested apartment with an immature teenager who had big dreams and no idea how to make them come true?"

"No chance at all," he said stonily. "You did the right thing."

"You're damn right I did. I made sure you had two parents who doted on you from the day you were born. I made sure you lived in a nice house where there was plenty to eat and a backyard to play in."

He gazed out at the lake, looking bored. "I'm not arguing. Are you about done with this, because I have things to do?"

"Don't you understand? I couldn't come to see you!"

"It's not important."

She started to move closer, then stopped herself. "Yes, it is. And I know that's why you hate me so much. Not because I gave you away, but because I never answered your letters begging me to come to see you."

"I hardly remember. I was—what—six years old? You think something like that is still bothering me?" His air of studied indifference developed a bitter edge. "I don't hate you, Lilly. I don't care that much."

"I still have those letters. Every one you wrote. And they're soaked with more tears than you can imagine."

"You're breakin' my heart."

"Don't you understand? There was nothing I wanted to do more, but it wasn't allowed."

"This I've got to hear."

She finally had his attention. He came closer and stopped near the base of an old gnarled oak.

"You weren't six. The letters started when you were seven. The first was printed in block letters on yellow lined paper. I still have it." She'd read it so many times the paper had grown limp.

Dear Ant Lilly,
I know your my real mom and I love you very much. Could you
come see me. I have a cat. His name is Spike. He is 7 to.
Love,
Kevin
Please dont tell my mom I wrote this leter. She mite cry.

"You wrote me eighteen letters over four years."

"I really don't remember."

She risked taking a few steps toward him. "Maida and I had an agreement."

"What kind of agreement?"

"I didn't give you to them casually. You can't believe that. We talked everything through. And I made long lists." She realized she was twisting her hands, and she let them fall to her sides. "They had to promise never to spank you, not that they would have anyway. I told them they couldn't criticize your music when you got to be a teenager, and they had to let you wear your hair however you wanted. Remember, I'd just turned eighteen." She gave him a rueful smile. "I even tried to make them promise to buy you a red convertible for your sixteenth birthday, but they wisely refused."

For the first time he smiled back at her. The movement was small, the slightest twitch at the corner of his mouth, but at least it was there.

She blinked, determined to get through this without shedding a tear. "One thing I didn't back down on, though—I made them promise to always let you follow your dreams, even if they weren't the same dreams they had for you."

He cocked his head, all pretense of indifference gone.

"They hated letting you play football. They were so terrified that you'd get hurt. But I held them to their promise, and they never tried to stop you." She could no longer meet his eyes. "All I had to do was give them one thing in exchange . . . "

She heard him move closer, and she looked up to see him step into a narrow shaft of sunlight.

"What was that?"

She could hear in his voice that he already knew. "I had to agree never to see you."

She couldn't look at him, and she bit her lip. "Open adoption didn't exist then, or if it did, I didn't know about it. They explained to me how easily confused children can get, and I believed them. They agreed to tell you who your birth mother was as soon as you were old enough to understand, and they sent me a hundred pictures over the years, but I could never visit you. As long as Maida and John were alive, you were to have just one mother."

"You broke your promise once." His lips barely moved. "When I was sixteen."

"It was an accident." She wandered toward a boulder protruding from the sandy soil. "When you started playing high school football, I realized I finally had a chance to see you without breaking my promise. I started flying into Grand Rapids on Fridays to watch the games. I'd strip off my makeup and wrap this old scarf around my head, put on nondescript clothes so no one would recognize me. Then I'd sit in the visitors' stands. I had this little pair of opera glasses I'd train on you for the whole game. I lived for the times you'd take off your helmet. You'll never know how much I grew to hate that thing."

The day was warm, but she felt chilled, and she rubbed her arms. "Everything went fine until you were a junior. It was the last game of the season, and I knew it would be nearly a year before I could see you again. I convinced myself there wouldn't be any harm in driving by the house."

"I was mowing the grass in the front yard."

She nodded. "It was one of those Indian summer days, and you were sweaty, just like you are now. I was so busy looking at you that I didn't see your neighbor's car parked on the street."

"You scraped the side."

"And you came running over to help." She hugged herself. "When you realized who I was, you looked at me like you hated me."

"I couldn't believe it was you."

"Maida never confronted me about it, so I knew you hadn't told them." She tried to read his expression, but he wasn't giving anything away. He nudged aside a fallen branch with the toe of his running shoe.

"She died a year ago. Why did you wait until now to tell me all this?"

She stared at him and shook her head. "How many times did I call and try to talk to you? You refused, Kevin. Every time."

He gazed at her. "They should have told me they wouldn't let you see me."

"Did you ever ask them about it?"

He shrugged, and she knew he hadn't.

"I think John might have said something, but Maida would never have allowed it. We talked about it over the phone. You have to remember that she was older than all your friends' mothers, and she knew she wasn't one of those fun moms every kid wants. It made her insecure. Besides, you were a headstrong kid. Do you really think you'd have shrugged it off and gone about your business if you'd known how much I wanted to see you?"

"I'd have been on the first bus to L.A.," he said flatly.

"And that would have broken her heart."

She waited, hoping he'd come nearer. She fantasized that he'd let her put her arms around him and all the lost years would vanish. Instead, he bent to pick up one of the pinecones lying on the ground.

"We had a TV in the basement. I went down there every week to watch your show. I always turned the volume low, but they knew what I was doing. They never said a word about it."

"I don't suppose they would have."

He rubbed his thumb over the scales. His hostility was gone, but not his tension, and she knew the reunion she'd dreamed of wasn't going to happen.

"So what am I supposed to do about all this now?"

The fact that he had to ask the question showed that he wasn't ready to give her anything. She couldn't touch him, couldn't tell him she'd loved him from the moment of his birth and had never stopped. Instead, she only said, "I guess that'll be up to you."

He nodded slowly, then dropped the pinecone. "Now that you've told me, are you going to leave?"

Neither his expression nor his tone gave her a cue how he wanted her to respond, and she wouldn't ask. "I'm going to finish planting the annuals I bought. A few more days."

It was a lame excuse, but he nodded and turned toward the path. "I need to take a shower."

He hadn't ordered her to leave. He hadn't told her this had come too late. She decided it was enough for now.

Kevin found Molly perched in her favorite spot, the glider on the back porch of the cottage, a notebook on her thighs. It hurt too much to think about Lilly's earthshaking revelations, so he stood in the doorway gazing at Molly instead. She must not have heard him come in because she didn't look up. On the other hand, he'd been acting like such a jerk there was a good chance she was ignoring him, but how was he supposed to behave when Molly kept hatching up all these zany adventures without a clue how being near her affected him?

Did she think it was easy watching her splash around in that skimpy one-piece black bathing suit he'd had to buy her to replace the red one? Did she ever once glance down to see what happened to her breasts when she got *cold*? The legs of the suit were cut so high they practically begged him to slip his hands underneath so he could cup those round little cheeks. And she had the gall to be mad at him because he'd been ignoring her! Didn't she understand he couldn't ignore her?

He wanted to push aside the notebook she was writing in, toss her over his shoulder, and carry her straight to the bedroom. Instead, he headed for the bathroom and filled the tub with very cold water, once again cursing the lack of a shower. He washed himself quickly and slipped into clean clothes. All week he'd been driving himself, but it hadn't done a damn bit of good. Despite the carpentry and painting, despite the daily workouts and the miles he'd added to his run, he wanted her more than ever. Even the game films he'd started watching on the TV in the office couldn't hold his attention. He should have moved back into the B&B, but Lilly was there.

A stab of pain shot through him. He couldn't think about her now. Maybe he'd drive into town for another workout in the tiny health club at the inn.

But no, he found himself moving toward the porch, all his vows to stay away from Molly evaporating. As he stepped through the doorway, he realized he was in the only place he could possibly be right now, in the presence of the only person who might understand his confusion over what had just happened.

She gazed up at him, her eyes full of that generous concern she showed for anyone she thought might have a problem. He couldn't spot even a hint of censure toward him for being so surly, although he knew she'd get around to putting him in his place sooner or later.

"Is everything all right?"

He shrugged, not giving away a thing. "We talked."

But she wasn't impressed by his tough-guy act. "Were you your normal repugnant self?"

"I listened to her, if that's what you mean." He knew exactly what she meant, but he wanted her to pull the story out of him. Maybe because he didn't know what she'd find when she did.

She waited.

He wandered toward the screen. The plant she'd hung from a hook brushed against his shoulder. "She told me some things . . . I don't know . . . It wasn't exactly the way I thought."

"What way was it?" she asked quietly.

So he told her. Leaving out how muddled his feelings were. Just giving her the facts.

When he was done, she nodded slowly. "I see."

If only he did.

"Now you have to adjust to knowing that what you believed about her wasn't true."

"I thinks she wants . . . " He shoved his hands into his pockets. "She wants something from me. I can't—" He whirled on her. "Am I supposed to feel this sudden attachment to her? Because I don't!"

Her expression flickered with something that looked almost like pain, and it took her a long time to answer.

"I doubt she expects that right away. Maybe you could start just by getting to know her. She makes quilts, and she's an amazing artist. But she doesn't know that about herself."

"I guess." He jerked his hands from his pockets and did exactly what he'd been trying to avoid since last Friday. "I'm going stir-crazy. There's this place about twenty miles away. Let's get out of here."

He saw right away that she was going to refuse, and he didn't blame her. At the same time he couldn't be alone now, so he whipped the note-book off her lap and pulled her to her feet. "You'll like it."

An hour later the two of them were soaring over the Au Sable River in a sleek little German-built glider.

18

Sexual daydreams and fantasies are normal. They're even a healthy way to pass time while you're waiting for the right person to come along.

—"My Secret Sex Life"
for *Chik*

I t's nice that Kevin finally decided to spend some time with you. Maybe he'll agree to marriage counseling." Amy finished putting the strawberry jam cake on a Wedgwood plate and regarded Molly with her familiar pitying expression.

"We don't need marriage counseling," Kevin snapped as he came through the door with Marmie padding at his feet. They'd just gotten back from their gliding adventure, and his hair was windblown. "What we need is that cake. It's five o'clock, and the guests are waiting for tea."

Amy moved reluctantly toward the door. "Maybe if you'd both pray . . . "

"The cake!" Kevin growled.

Amy gave Molly a look that indicated she'd done her best but that Molly was hopelessly doomed to life without sex. Then she disappeared.

"You're right," he said. "That kid *is* irritating. I *should* have given you a hickey."

This was a topic Molly definitely didn't want to discuss, and she focused all her attention on arranging the tea tray. She hadn't had time to change out of her rumpled clothes or straighten her own windblown hair, but she forced herself not to fidget as Kevin took a few steps closer.

"In case you were worried, Daph . . . My ears have just about recovered from that scream."

"You were heading right for the trees. And I didn't scream." She picked up the tray and shoved it at him. "I squeaked."

"One hell of a squeak. And we weren't anyplace near the trees."

"I believe that our female guests are anxiously awaiting you."

He grimaced and disappeared with Marmie.

She smiled. She shouldn't have been surprised that Kevin was an experienced glider pilot, although she wished he'd mentioned it *before* they'd taken off. Despite their afternoon together, things weren't much better between them. He hadn't said a word about his interviews that morning, and she couldn't bring herself to ask. He'd also been strangely jumpy. Once she'd accidentally bumped into him, and he'd sprung away as if she'd burned him. If he hadn't wanted her with him, why had he invited her?

She knew the answer. After his confrontation with Lilly, he hadn't wanted to be alone.

The woman who was causing his turmoil slipped into the kitchen through the back door. Uncertainty was written all over her face, and Molly's heart went out to her. During the drive back to the campground, she'd brought up Lilly's name, but Kevin had changed the subject.

She remembered what he'd said earlier at the cottage. *Am I supposed to feel this sudden attachment to her? Because I don't!* It had been a pointed reminder that Kevin didn't like close attachments. She'd begun to realize how skillful he was at keeping people away. Oddly enough, Liam Jenner, for all his obsession with privacy, was less an emotional recluse than Kevin.

"I'm sorry about your cat," Molly said. "It was an impulse. Kevin needs lots of excitement." She traced the edge of the cut glass serving plate. "I want him to enjoy the campground so he won't sell it."

Lilly nodded slowly. Her hands slipped in and out of her pockets. She cleared her throat. "Did Kevin tell you about our conversation?"

"Yes."

"It wasn't exactly a rousing success."

"But not quite a failure either."

A heartbreaking flicker of hope appeared on her face. "I hope not."

"Football is a lot simpler than personal relationships."

Lilly nodded, then toyed with her rings. "I owe you an apology, don't I?"

"Yep, you do."

This time Lilly's smile had something more to it. "I was unfair. I know it."

"Darn right you were."

"I worry about him."

"And the damage a man-eating heiress might do to his fragile emotions, right?"

Lilly looked down at Roo, who'd come out from under the table. "Help me, Roo. I'm scared of her."

Molly laughed.

Lilly smiled then sobered. "I'm sorry I misjudged you, Molly. I know you care about him, and I can't believe you'd deliberately hurt him."

Molly suspected Lilly's opinion would change if she knew the circumstances behind their marriage. Only her promise to Kevin kept her from telling her the truth. "In case you haven't figured it out yet, I'm on your side. I think Kevin needs you in his life."

"You'll never know how much that means to me." She gazed toward the door. "I'm going in for tea."

"Are you sure? The guests will be all over you."

"I'll manage." She straightened her posture. "I've had enough of hiding out. Your husband is going to have to deal with me one way or the other."

"Good for you."

By the time Molly reached the sitting room with a plate of cookies and another teapot, Lilly was chatting graciously with the guests who'd surrounded her. She had her heart in her eyes whenever she looked at Kevin, but he avoided looking back. It was almost as if he believed that any sign of affection toward her would somehow trap him.

Molly's childhood had taught her to beware of people who weren't emotionally open, and his guardedness depressed her. If she were smart, she'd rent a car and drive back to Chicago this very night.

An elderly woman from Ann Arbor who'd checked in earlier that day appeared at her elbow. "I've heard you write children's books."

"Not so much anymore," she replied glumly, thinking about the revisions she still hadn't done and the August mortgage check she wouldn't be able to write.

"My sister and I have always wanted to write a children's book, but we've been so busy traveling that we never can seem to find the time."

"There's more to writing a children's book than just finding the time," Kevin said from behind her. "It's not as easy as people seem to think."

Molly was so startled she nearly dropped the cookie plate.

"Kids want a good story," he said. "They want to laugh or get scared or learn something without having it shoved down their throats. That's what Molly does in her books. For example, in *Daphne Gets Lost . . .* " Off he went, describing with uncanny accuracy the techniques Molly used to reach her readers.

Later, when he appeared in the kitchen, she smiled at him. "Thanks for defending my profession. I appreciate it."

"People are idiots." He nodded toward the baking supplies she was setting out for breakfast the next morning. "You don't need to cook so much. I keep telling you I can order from the bakery in town."

"I know. I enjoy it."

His gaze drifted over her bare shoulders and lacy camisole top. He lingered there for so long she felt as if he were running his fingers over her skin. A silly fantasy, she realized, as he made a grab for the biscuit tin where she'd just deposited the leftover cookies. "You seem to enjoy everything about this place. What happened to all those bad memories of summer camp?"

"This is how I always wanted a summer camp to be."

"Boring and lots of old people?" He bit into a cookie. "You've got strange taste."

She wasn't going to argue with him about this. Instead, she asked the question she'd been postponing all afternoon. "You haven't said anything about your interviews this morning."

He scowled. "They didn't go as well as I wanted. The first guy might have been a great chef once, but now he shows up drunk for interviews.

And the woman I interviewed put so many restrictions on when she could work that she'd have been useless."

Molly's spirits soared, only to sink as he went on.

"I've got one more candidate coming in tomorrow afternoon, though, and she was great on the phone. She didn't even mind a Sunday interview. I figure we can train her on Monday and leave here by Wednesday afternoon at the latest."

"Hooray," she said glumly.

"Don't tell me you're going to miss falling out of bed at five-thirty in the morning?"

Amy giggled in the hallway. "Troy, don't!"

The newlyweds were getting ready to check in before they left. Every afternoon right after tea they raced back to their apartment, where Molly was fairly certain they jumped into bed and made very noisy love before they had to return to the B&B for the night.

"Lucky us," Molly muttered. "Now we can get lectured on our sexual inadequacies by both of them."

"Like hell." With no warning Kevin grabbed her, pushed her against the refrigerator, and crushed his mouth to hers.

She knew exactly what he was doing. And while this might be better than her hickey idea, it was a lot more dangerous.

His free hand caught her leg beneath the knee and raised it. She snaked it over his hip and curled her arms around him. His other hand dipped under her top and covered her breast. Just as if he had the right.

It was all for show. She told herself that as she parted her lips and let his tongue slip into her mouth. He felt as if he somehow belonged here, inside this one small part of her, and she wanted to kiss him forever.

The kitchen door thumped, reminding her they had witnesses. Which, of course, was the whole point. Kevin drew back a few inches, not even far enough for her lips to cool. His eyes never left her mouth, and he kept his hand on her breast.

"Go away."

A gasp from Amy. The thud of the door. The sound of quickly retreating footsteps.

"I—I guess we showed them," Molly breathed against his mouth.

"I guess," he replied. And then he started kissing her all over again.

"Molly, I— Oh! Excuse me . . . "

Another quick thud of the door. More retreating footsteps, this time Lilly's.

Kevin muttered a dark curse. "We're getting out of here."

His voice held the same note of determination she'd heard in television interviews when he promised to dominate Green Bay. He released Molly's leg. His hand slipped more reluctantly from her breast.

She'd gotten herself right back where she wasn't supposed to be. "I really don't think—"

"No more thinking, Molly. I'm your husband, damn it, and it's time you start acting like a wife."

"Like a— What do you—"

But Kevin was fundamentally a man of action, and he'd done enough talking. Shackling her wrist, he hauled her to the back door.

She couldn't believe it. He was abducting her to have . . . *Forced Sex! Oh, jeez . . . Fight back! Tell him no!*

She knew from watching Oprah exactly what a woman was supposed to do in this situation. Scream at the top of her lungs, drop to the ground, and start kicking her assailant as hard as she could. Oprah's authority had explained that not only did this strategy have the advantage of surprise, but it used a woman's lower-body strength.

Scream. Drop. Kick.

"No," she whispered.

Kevin wasn't listening. He was dragging her across the garden and along the path that ran between the cottages and the lake. His long legs ate up the ground just as they did when he was trying to beat the final whistle. She would have stumbled if he didn't have such a tight grip on her.

Scream. Drop. Kick. And keep screaming. She remembered that part. You were supposed to keep screaming the whole time you were kicking.

The idea of dropping to the ground was interesting. Counterintuitive, but it did make sense. Women couldn't compete with men when it came to upper-body strength, but if the male assailant was standing and the woman dropped . . . A shower of hard, fast kicks to the soft parts . . . It definitely made sense.

"Uhm, Kevin . . . "

"Be quiet, or I swear to God I'll take you right here."

Yes, this was definitely Forced Sex.

Thank goodness.

Molly was so tired of thinking, so tired of fighting what she wanted so much. She knew it was a lousy reflection on her personal maturity that she needed to believe that the decision had been taken out of her hands. Even crummier to regard Kevin as a sexual predator. But at twenty-seven she wasn't yet the woman she wanted to be. The woman she intended to be. By the time she was thirty, she was absolutely certain she would have taken charge of her own sexuality. But for right now let him do it.

They were bump, bump, bumping down the path, passing Fairest Lord Jesus, passing Noah's Ark. Lilies of the Field lay right ahead.

She reminded herself of Kevin's shortcomings as a lover and vowed she wouldn't say a word to him about them either during or afterward. He wasn't a naturally selfish person. How was he supposed to know about foreplay when he'd had all those women servicing him? And a little slam, bam, thank you, ma'am would be a good thing. Those feverish nighttime images that had been robbing her of sleep would finally fade in the harsh glare of reality.

"Inside." He jerked open the cottage door and gave her a push.

She had no choice in the matter. No choice at all. He was bigger, stronger, apt to turn violent at any moment.

Even for an imaginative person that was a stretch.

She wished he hadn't let her go, but she liked the way he'd braced his hands on his hips. And his glare definitely looked threatening.

"You're not going to start giving me crap about this, are you?"

This posed a dilemma. If she said yes, he'd back off. If she said no, she'd be giving him permission to do something she knew she should resist.

Luckily, he wasn't done being angry. "Because I'm sick of it! We're not kids. We're two healthy adults, and we want each other."

Why didn't he stop talking and just drag her to the bedroom? If not by the hair, then at least by the arm.

"I'm packing all the birth control we're going to need . . . "

If only he'd said he was packing a gun and he'd turn it on her if she didn't lie there and let him do what he wanted. Except she wanted to do a lot more than just lie there.

"Now, I suggest you march your little butt right to the bedroom!"

The words were perfect, and she loved the way he jabbed his finger toward the door, but the expression in his eyes was beginning to look less like anger and more like caution. He was getting ready to back off.

She hurried to the bedroom. She couldn't make too much of this, couldn't let it be too important. She was a beautiful slave girl forced to give herself to the ruthless (but gorgeous) man who owned her. A slave girl who needed to get her clothes off before he beat her!

She pulled off her top so that she was standing before him in her bra and shorts, which weren't really shorts but gauzy harem pants. Harem pants he was going to rip from her body if she didn't take them off first.

She bent her head and kicked away her sandals. Then she pulled her shorts—harem pants—over her legs and cast them aside. When she looked up, she saw her owner standing in the bedroom door, a slightly befuddled expression on his face, as if he couldn't believe it was going to be this easy. *Ha!* Easy for *him*! He wasn't staring death in the face!

She was wearing only her bra and panties. Lifting her chin, she gazed at him defiantly. He might possess her body, but she'd never let him have her soul!

He moved toward her, his confidence restored. Of course he was confident. She'd be confident, too, if she had an army of guards stationed right outside the door, ready to drag a disobedient slave girl to her death if she didn't submit.

He stopped in front of her and gazed down, his green eyes raking her body. If she'd left her top on, he would have torn it off with his dagger . . . no, his *teeth*!

He burned up her skin with those imperious eyes. What if she didn't please him? Such a merciless master demanded more from her than simple submission. He demanded cooperation! And (she'd just remembered) he'd vowed to have her dearest friend, the gentle slave girl Melissa, tortured to death if he was displeased. No matter how it destroyed her pride, she must satisfy him!

To save Melissa.

She lifted her arms and cradled his magnificent jaw between her hands, desperately trying to gentle this barbarian. She leaned forward and pressed her innocent lips to his cruel ones—cruelly, cruelly . . . sweet.

She sighed and teased him with the tip of her tongue. When he opened his mouth, she invaded. How could she do anything else when she had poor, gentle Melissa's life to protect?

His hands splayed over her bare back, moved up to the clasp of her bra. Her skin quivered. The clasp fell open.

He gripped her shoulders and took over the kiss. Then he tugged off her bra and cast it aside.

His mouth left hers. His jaw scraped her cheek. "Molly . . . "

She didn't want to be Molly. If she were Molly, she'd have to grab her clothes and put them right back on, because Molly wasn't self-destructive.

She was only a slave girl, and she bowed her head submissively as he drew back and gazed down at her naked breasts, now exposed to his predatory emerald eyes. She shivered and waited. Cotton rustled as he drew his T-shirt—his silken robe—over his head and tossed it aside. She squeezed her eyes shut when he pulled her against him, his conqueror's chest pressed to her naked, defenseless breasts.

Tremors swept over the sensitive skin as he began to nibble kisses, like a golden slave's collar, around her throat, then down to the breasts that no longer belonged to her. They were his. Every part of her body belonged to him! Her knees grew weak and sagged. She wanted this so much, but she needed desperately to hold on to her fantasy.

Master . . . Slave girl . . . His to do with as he wished. Mustn't anger him . . . Let him—oh, yes—extend the trail of kisses over her ribs to her navel, her stomach, gliding over her hipbones as his thumbs caught the elastic on her panties.

Concentrate! Envision those cruel lips! Those cutting eyes! The dreadful penalty the slave girl would pay if she didn't ease her legs open so he could slip his hand between them. Her merciless master . . . Her savage owner . . . Her—

"There's a bunny on your panties."

Even the most creative mind couldn't have held a fantasy together against that dark, husky chuckle. She glared at him, then grew uncomfortably conscious that one of them still wore a pair of khaki slacks while the other wore only a sky blue pair of bunny panties.

"What if there is?"

He straightened and rubbed his fingers over the front of the panties, making her shiver as he gave the little bunny a pat. "Just wondering."

"They were a present from Phoebe. A surprise."

"They sure surprised me." He nuzzled her neck while he continued patting her bunny. "Are these the only ones?"

She sucked in her breath. "There . . . might be a few more."

He splayed his other hand across her bottom and massaged. "You got the badger dude on any of them?"

She did. Benny, with his cute little badger mask. "Could you stop . . . talking . . . and get back to . . . ahh . . . conquering."

"Conquering?" He slipped one long finger beneath the elastic leg band.

"Never mind." She sighed as he rubbed. Oh, that was wicked. She eased her legs open and let him go where he wanted.

And he wanted to go everywhere.

Before she knew it, her panties were gone, along with his clothes, and they were naked on her bed, too impatient to pull down the quilt.

Their play turned serious much too soon. He gripped her shoulders and pulled her on top of him—the servicing position. She wiggled up his body, caught his head in her hands, and kissed him again, hoping to slow him down.

"You're so sweet . . . " he murmured in her mouth.

But he was impossible to distract. He caught the back of her knees and spread them over his hips. Here it came. She braced herself for his thrust and bit her lip to keep from yelling at him to *take his time, for Pete's sake, and stop acting as if the ref just blew the two-minute warning!*

She'd promised herself she wouldn't criticize, so she sank her teeth into the hard muscle of his shoulder instead.

He made a low, hoarse sound that might have been pain or pleasure, and the next thing she knew she was on her back and he was hovering over her, those green eyes wicked.

"So the bunny lady wants to play rough?"

With two hundred pounds of muscle? Oh, I don't think so.

She started to tell him she'd only been trying to distract him so he wouldn't be so quick on the trigger, but he shackled her wrists and made a dive for her breast.

Ahhhhh . . . It was torture. Agony. Worse than agony. How could one mouth cause so much havoc? And she didn't ever want it to stop.

He brushed his lips over the slope of her breast. He grazed the nipple, moved to the other breast, where he did the same. Then, without warning, he began to suckle . . .

She writhed against him, but he didn't release the wrists he'd imprisoned in one hand. Leaving the other free to roam.

It meandered from breast to belly, then lower, brushing through the curls. But that proved to be a tease because he quickly moved on to her inner thighs.

They fell open.

He stayed where he was.

She twisted, trying to force those tantalizing fingers away from her thighs to the part of her that throbbed so much she thought she would die.

He didn't take the hint. He was too busy tormenting her, too busy playing at her breasts. She'd heard that women could have orgasms just from this, but she hadn't believed it.

She'd been wrong.

The shock wave caught her by surprise, thundered through her, and pitched her into the sky. She didn't remember crying out, but she heard the echo and knew she had.

He slowed. She shuddered against his chest, breathed him in, tried to understand what had happened to her.

He stroked her shoulder. He kissed her earlobe. His whispered breath tickled her hair. "A little quick on the trigger, aren't you?"

She was mortified. Sort of. Except it had felt so good. And been so unexpected. "An accident," she managed. "And it's your turn."

"Oh, I'm not in any hurry . . . " He picked up a lock of her hair, drew it to his nose. "Unlike some people."

The sheen of perspiration on his skin, the way he pressed against her thigh, told her he was in more of a hurry than he wanted to admit. A very *big* hurry. Funny . . . she hadn't remembered that about him. Not exactly. She remembered that it had hurt. And now that she thought about it, there'd been a moment when she'd thought she might be too small.

No time like the present to find out if that was true.

She scooted on top of him.

He scooted her back off. Dawdled at the corner of her mouth. When was he going to get to the slam, bam part?

"Why don't you just lie back and rest for a while?" he whispered.

Rest? "Oh, I definitely don't—"

He caught her shoulders, nestled his thumbs in her armpits, started that trail of kisses again. Only this time he kept going.

Before long his hands were at her knees, pushing them far apart. His hair brushed her inner thighs, so sensitive now that she quivered. And then he claimed her with his mouth.

The gentle suction . . . the sweet thrusts . . . She couldn't breathe. She caught his head, pleading. Her hips buckled as the waves seized her once again.

This time when she'd calmed, he didn't tease her. Instead, he grabbed the condom she'd forgotten about, eased his body over hers, and gazed down with those green eyes. His skin was hot beneath her hands, and the blaze of late-afternoon sun streaming through the window burnished him with molten gold. She felt his muscles quivering beneath her palms as the effort to hold back became too much for him. Still, he gave her all the time in the world.

She opened . . . stretched to accept him.

He filled her slowly, kissing her, soothing her. She loved him for the careful care he was taking, and slowly, her body accepted his.

But even when he'd buried himself, he didn't ram at her. Instead, he began a slow, silken thrusting.

It was delicious, but it wasn't enough, and she realized she no longer wanted his restraint. She wanted him free and wild. She wanted him to luxuriate in her body, to use it for his pleasure. Wrapping her legs around him, she grasped his hips and urged him on.

The leash he'd held on his self-control snapped. He plunged. She moaned and met his thrust. It was like being burned in a fire of the senses.

He was too big for her, too strong, too fierce . . . Absolutely perfect.

The sun burned hotter until it exploded. They flew together into a brilliant crystalline void.

He'd never made love to a woman with a bunny on her panties. But then, there was a lot about making love with Molly that was different from anything he'd experienced. Her enthusiasm, her generosity . . . Why should he be surprised?

Kevin slid his hand over her hip and thought about how good it had been, even though she'd acted strange at first, almost as if she were trying to convince herself to be afraid of him. He remembered the way she'd stood before him in her bra and bunny panties, with her head high and shoulders back. If an American flag had been waving behind her, she'd have looked like a very sexy Marine Corps recruiting poster. The few, the proud, the cottontailed.

She stirred in his arms and snuffled her nose against his chest, burrowing like one of her storybook pals. But despite the snuffling, the burrowing, and the bunny panties, Molly had been every inch a woman.

And he was in big trouble. In one afternoon, he'd undone everything he'd been trying to accomplish by ignoring her.

She slid her hand from his chest to his belly. Here and there the last shafts of sunlight glazed her hair with little reddish sprinkles like the ones she'd used on yesterday's sugar cookies. He forced himself to remember all the reasons he'd tried so hard to keep her at a distance, starting with the fact that she wasn't going to be part of his life much longer, which could very well piss off her sister, who happened to be the owner of the team he intended to take to the Super Bowl this year.

He couldn't think about all the ways a team owner had of making it tough, even for her star player, not right now. Instead, he thought about how much passion had been locked up inside the small, quirky body of this woman who was and wasn't his wife.

She snuffled again. "You're not a bust-out. As a lover, I mean."

He was glad she couldn't see his smile, because giving her even the smallest advantage generally meant he ended up swimming in the lake with his clothes on. He settled for sarcasm. "I sense a tender moment coming on. Should I get a handkerchief?"

"I just mean that— Well, after last time . . . "

"Don't tell me."

"It was all I had for comparison."

"For the love of—"

"I know it's not fair. You were asleep. And unwilling. I haven't forgotten that."

He tucked her closer and heard himself say, "Maybe it's time you did."

Her head shot up, and she looked at him with a million emotions on her face, the main one being hope. "What do you mean?"

He rubbed the back of her neck. "I mean, it's over. It's forgotten. And you're forgiven."

Her eyes filled with tears. "You mean it, don't you?"

"I mean it."

"Oh, Kevin . . . I—"

He sensed a speech coming on, and he wasn't in the mood for any more talk, so he started making love to her all over again.

19

Yes!

—notes for *Chik* article,
"Do Jocks Only Want One Thing?"

Molly sat in the gazebo staring out at the cottages and daydreaming about last night instead of getting ready for the community tea she'd invited everyone to attend on the Common that afternoon. She'd driven into town after breakfast to buy an extra cake along with some soft drinks, but refreshments were the last thing on her mind. She was thinking about Kevin and all the delicious things they'd done.

A car door slammed, distracting her. She looked up to see the paragon he'd been interviewing settle behind the wheel of an aging Crown Victoria. Molly had caught a glimpse of her as she'd arrived for her interview and hated her on sight. Just one look at the no-nonsense reading glasses dangling from a chain around her neck told Molly this woman's cookies would never burn on the bottom.

Kevin appeared on the front porch. Molly automatically waved to him, then wished she hadn't because it made her seem too eager. If only she were one of those sublimely mysterious women who could control a man with the flicker of an eyelash or a single smoldering glance. But neither flickering nor smoldering was her strong point, and Kevin wasn't a man to be controlled anyway.

Roo saw him coming across the Common and scampered to meet him, hoping for a game of catch. Molly's skin grew hot just watching him. Now she knew exactly what every part of the body underneath his black polo shirt and khaki slacks looked like.

She shivered. She didn't doubt he'd enjoyed making love with her last night—she'd been pretty darned good, if she did say so herself—but she knew it hadn't meant the same thing to him that it did to her. He'd been so . . . everything—tender, rough, thrilling, and more passionate than even her imagination could have invented. This was the most dangerous, the most impossible, the most hopeless crush she'd ever experienced, and last night had made it worse.

Suddenly Kevin stopped walking in midstride. She saw right away what had caught his attention. A nine-year-old boy stood on the edge of the Common holding a football. His name was Cody. His parents had introduced him yesterday when they'd checked in to Green Pastures.

Kevin might not know they finally had younger guests. Between going up in the glider in the afternoon, then locking themselves in the bedroom at the cottage, he wouldn't have seen the children, and she hadn't thought to mention it.

He began walking toward the boy, Roo following along. His stride picked up as he got nearer, until he stopped in front of the child. Molly was too far away to make out what he was saying, but he must have introduced himself because the boy froze up a little, the way kids did when they found themselves in the presence of a well-known athlete.

Kevin rubbed the boy's head to settle him down, then slowly took the football from him. He tossed it back and forth in his hands a few times, spoke to the boy again, then gestured toward the center of the Common. For a moment the boy simply stared at him, as if he couldn't believe what he was hearing. Then his feet flew, and he raced out to catch his first pass from the great Kevin Tucker.

She smiled. It had taken a few decades, but Kevin finally had a kid to play with at the Wind Lake Campgrounds.

Roo joined in the game of catch, yipping at their ankles and generally getting in the way, but neither of them seemed to mind. Cody was a little slow and endearingly awkward, but Kevin kept encouraging him.

"You've got a good arm for a twelve-year-old."

"I'm only nine."

"You're doing great for nine!"

Cody beamed and tried harder. His legs pumped as he ran after the ball, then tried unsuccessfully to duplicate Kevin's form when he tossed it back.

After nearly half an hour of this he finally began to tire, but Kevin was too caught up rewriting history to notice. "You're doing great, Cody. Just relax your arm and put your body into it."

Cody did his best to comply, but he began to dart yearning glances toward his cottage. Kevin, however, focused only on making sure this boy wouldn't suffer the same kind of loneliness he had.

"Hey, Molly!" he called out. "You see what a good arm my friend has here?"

"Yes, I see."

Cody's sneakers were starting to drag, and even Roo was looking tired. But Kevin remained oblivious.

Molly was just getting ready to intervene when the three O'Brian brothers—ages six, nine, and eleven, as she recalled—came running out from the woods behind Jacob's Ladder.

"Hey, Cody! Get your suit on. Our moms said we could go to the beach!"

Cody's face lit up.

Kevin looked thunderstruck. She really should have remembered to tell him that several of the families checking in yesterday had kids. She experienced a sudden, irrational hope that this somehow would make him change his mind about selling the place.

Cody hugged the football to his chest and looked uneasy. "It's been nice playing with you, Mr. Tucker, but . . . uh . . . I have to go play with my friends now. If it's okay?" He edged away backward. "If you . . . can't find anybody else to play with, I guess—I guess I can come back later."

Kevin cleared his throat. "That's okay. You go on with your friends."

Cody was off like a shot with the three O'Brian boys following.

Kevin approached her slowly. He looked so disconcerted that Molly bit her lip to keep her smile within reasonable boundaries. "Roo'll play with you."

Roo whimpered and crawled under the gazebo.

She rose and walked to the bottom of the steps. "Okay, I'll play with you. But don't throw hard."

He shook his head in bewilderment. "Where did all these kids come from?"

"School's finally out. I told you they'd show up."

"But . . . how many are here?"

"The three O'Brian boys, and Cody has a baby sister. Two families have one teenage girl each."

He sank down on the step.

She held her amusement in check as she sat next to him. "You'll probably meet them all this afternoon. Tea in the gazebo will be a nice way to kick off a new week."

He didn't say anything, just gazed out at the Common.

She considered it a tribute to her maturity that only a small bubble of laughter escaped. "Sorry your playmate ran away."

He stubbed the heel of his sneaker in the grass. "I made a fool out of myself, didn't I?"

Her heart melted, and she rested her cheek against his shoulder. "Yes, but the world could use more fools like you. You're a very nice man."

He smiled down at her. She smiled back. And that's when it hit her.

This wasn't a crush at all. She'd fallen in love with him.

She was so horrified, she jerked away.

"What's wrong?"

"Nothing!" She started to chatter to cover up her dismay. "There's another family. More children. Checking in today with . . . some kids. The Smiths. They didn't say how many—how many kids. Amy talked to them."

In love with Kevin Tucker! Please, not that! Hadn't she learned anything? She knew from her childhood how impossible it was to make someone love her, yet she'd once again fallen into that old, destructive pattern. What about all her dreams and hopes? What about her Great Love Story?

She felt like burying her head in her hands and crying. She wanted love, but he only wanted sex. He stirred beside her. She was glad of the distraction, and she followed the direction of his gaze across the Common. The O'Brian boys were chasing each other while they waited for

Cody to change into his swim trunks. Two girls who looked as though they were about fourteen came walking up from the beach carrying a boom box. Kevin took in the kids, the boom box, the old trees, the sherbet-colored cottages.

"I can't believe this is the same place."

"It's not," she managed. "Things change." She cleared her throat and tried to block out her turmoil. "The woman you hired. Is she starting tomorrow?"

"She told me I had to fire Amy first."

"What? You can't! She's finishing all her work and doing everything you ask! Besides, that patronizing little twit's terrific with the guests." She shot up from the step. "I mean it, Kevin. You should make her cover up her hickeys, but you can't fire her."

He didn't respond.

Molly grew alarmed. "Kevin . . . "

"Relax, will you? Of course I'm not going to fire her. That's why that old biddy drove off in a huff."

"Thank God. What was her problem with Amy?"

"Apparently Amy and her daughter went to high school together and never got along. If her daughter's like her mother, I'm on Amy's side."

"You did the right thing."

"I guess. But this is a small town, and I've reached the end of a very short list. The college kids have all gone to work on Mackinac Island for the summer, and the kind of person I need to hire isn't interested in taking a job that's only going to last through September."

"That's your answer, then. Keep this place and make the job permanent."

"That's not going to happen, but I do have another idea." He stood and looked down at her, his eyes doing a sexy dance and his mouth curling in a smile. "Did I mention that you look real good naked?"

She shivered. "What idea?"

He spoke lower. "Do you have any animals on your panties today?"

"I forget."

"Then I guess I'll have to look."

"You will not!"

"Yeah? Who's gonna stop me?"

"You're lookin' at her, jock boy." She jumped from the top step and raced across the Common, glad for the excuse to run off her turmoil. But instead of heading toward the B&B, where the presence of the guests would keep her safe, she darted between the cottages and toward the woods where she'd be . . . unsafe.

Roo loved this new game and scampered after her, yipping with excitement. It occurred to her that Kevin might not be following, but she needn't have worried. He caught her at the edge of the path and pulled her into the woods.

"Stop it! Go away!" She slapped at his arm. "You promised you'd carry those card tables out to the gazebo."

"I'm not carrying anything until I see what's on your panties."

"It's Daphne, okay?"

"I'm supposed to believe you're wearing the same underpants you had on yesterday?"

"I have more than one pair."

"I think you're lying. I want to see for myself." He dragged her deeper into the pines. While Roo circled them barking, he reached for the snap on her shorts. "Quiet, Godzilla! There's some serious business going on here."

Roo obediently quieted.

She grabbed his wrists and pushed. "Get away."

"That's not what you were saying last night."

"Somebody'll see."

"I'll tell them a bee got you, and I'm taking out the stinger."

"Don't touch my stinger!" She grabbed for her shorts, but they were already heading for her knees. "Stop that!"

He peered down at her panties. "It's the badger. You lied to me."

"I wasn't paying attention when I got dressed."

"Hold still. I've just about found that stinger."

She heard herself sigh.

"Oh, yeah . . . " His body moved against hers. "There it is."

Half an hour later, just as they were emerging from the woods, a very familiar-looking Suburban came barreling around the Common. Kevin told himself it was just a coincidence as he watched it screech to a stop in front of the B&B, but then Roo barked and raced toward it.

Molly let out a squeal and began to run. The car doors opened, and a poodle that looked like Roo jumped out. Then came the kids. It seemed like a dozen, but it was only four, all of them Calebows who were rushing his not-so-estranged wife.

Dread pooled in the pit of his stomach. One thing he knew: Where there were Calebow kids, there were bound to be Calebow parents.

His steps slowed as the luscious blond owner of the Chicago Stars slithered from the driver's side of the car and her legendary husband emerged from the passenger side. The fact that Phoebe had been driving didn't surprise him. In this family, leadership seemed to shift back and forth according to circumstances. As he approached the car, he had an uneasy premonition neither of them would like the circumstances at Wind Lake.

What were those circumstances? For almost two weeks now he'd been acting crazed. Training camp was a little over a month away, but he was either laughing with Molly, getting mad at her, freezing her out, or seducing her. He hadn't watched any game film in days, and he wasn't working out enough. All he could think about was how much he loved being with her—this sassy, aggravating kid-woman who wasn't beautiful, silent, or undemanding, but a pain in the ass. And so much fun.

Why did she have to be Phoebe's sister? Why couldn't he have met her in a bar? He tried to imagine her in glitter eye shadow and a cellophane dress, but all he could see was the way she'd looked that morning in her underpants and his T-shirt. Her bare feet had been hooked over the rung of a chair, her pretty hair tousled around her face, and those wicked blue-gray eyes had shot trouble at him over the rim of a Peter Rabbit cup.

Now Molly hugged her nieces and nephew, apparently forgetting that her clothes were rumpled and she had pine needles in her hair. He didn't look much better, and any astute pair of eyes could see what they'd been up to.

There were no eyes more astute than the ones belonging to Phoebe and Dan Calebow. All four of them rotated toward him.

He slipped his hands into his pockets and played it cool. "Hey, there. Nice surprise."

"We thought so." Phoebe's polite response stood in marked contrast to the warm way she used to greet him, while Dan's expression was assessing. Kevin beat back his uneasiness by reminding himself that he was untouchable, the best quarterback in the AFC.

But the Chicago Stars had no untouchables as long as the Calebows were at the helm, and right then it flashed through his mind exactly how this could play out if he wasn't careful. If they decided they wanted to keep him away from Molly, he'd be called into the front office one day soon and hear that he was part of a big-ticket trade. A lot of struggling teams would be more than happy to give up some top draft choices for an All-Pro quarterback, and before he knew what had happened, he'd find himself playing for one of the league's bottom-dwellers.

As he watched Dan taking in the pine needles stuck to Molly's hair, a mental picture flashed through his head of himself barking out signals for the Lions in the Silverdome.

Molly hugged the kids who were chirping around her. "Are you surprised to see us, Aunt Molly? Are you surprised?"

"Roo! Kanga's here to play with you!"

" . . . and Mom says we can go swimming in . . . "

" . . . fell off the monkey bars and got a black eye!"

" . . . this boy calls her every day, even though . . . "

" . . . then he threw up all over the . . . "

" . . . Dad says I'm too young, but . . . "

Molly's attention shifted from one child to the next, her expression flickering from sympathy to interest to amusement without missing a beat. This was her real family.

The sharp ache took him by surprise. He and Molly sure weren't a family, so it wasn't as if he'd been cut out of anything. He was just having a leftover reflex from his childhood, when he'd dreamed about being part of a big, messy crowd like this one.

"Omigosh!" Molly squealed. "*You're* the Smiths!"

The kids squealed back and pointed their fingers at her. *Gotcha, Aunt M!*

Kevin remembered Molly's earlier comment that a family named Smith was checking in today. Meet the Smiths. His sense of dread grew.

Molly gazed at her sister, who was holding Roo the Fierce. "Did Amy know who you really were when she took the reservation?"

Tess giggled. At least he figured it was Tess, because she wore a soccer jersey while her look-alike scampered around in a sundress. "Mom didn't tell her. We wanted to surprise you!"

"We get to stay all week!" Andrew exclaimed. "And I want to sleep with you!"

Way to go, Andy boy. You just tossed good ol' Uncle Kevin right out on his ass.

Molly rumpled his hair and didn't reply. At the same time she reached for the quietest Calebow.

Hannah had been standing a little off to the side, as she usually did, but her eyes sparkled with excitement. "I thought up a whole new Daphne adventure," she whispered, barely loud enough for him to hear. "I wrote it down in my spiral notebook."

"I can't wait to read it."

"Can we see the beach, Aunt Molly?"

As Dan took the keys from Phoebe, he turned toward Kevin. "Maybe you could show me the cottage so I can start unloading."

"Sure." Just what he didn't want to do. Dan was on a mission to assess how much damage Kevin had done to his precious Molly. But when it came to damage, Kevin felt as if he were the one who'd suffered a head wound.

Molly pointed toward the cottage on the other side of the Common. "You're staying in Gabriel's Trumpet. The door's unlocked."

Kevin walked across the grass while Dan drove around. They did a catch-up on the team as they unloaded, but he knew Dan fairly well, and it didn't take the Stars' president long to say what was on his mind.

"So what's going on here?" Dan slammed the tailgate on the Suburban harder than he needed to.

Kevin could be as in-your-face as Dan, but he decided it was smarter using Molly's "dumb" ploy. "The truth is, I've been having a bitch of a time." He picked up a laundry basket filled with beach toys. "I didn't think it was going to be so hard to get someone to run this place."

"Dad!" Julie and Tess came running up, followed by Andrew. "We need our suits so we can go swimming before the tea party this afternoon."

"Except Aunt Molly says I get to drink lemonade," Andrew declared, " 'cause I don't like tea!"

"Look at our cottage! It's so cute!" Julie raced to the door as Molly and Phoebe approached with Hannah.

Molly looked tense, and Phoebe regarded Kevin with eyes as chilly as a Lions uniform in the middle of a losing Detroit November.

"The lake's freezing, girls," Molly called out to the twins on the porch, trying to act as though everything were normal. "It's not like the pool at home."

"Are there water snakes?"

The question had come from Hannah, who looked worried. Something about her had always gotten to Kevin. "No snakes, kiddo. Do you want me to go in with you?"

Her smile flashed a thousand watts of gratitude. "Would you?"

"Sure. Get your suit on, and I'll meet you there." He didn't want to leave Molly alone with the enemy, so he said, "Your aunt'll come along. She loves swimming in that old lake, don't you, Molly?"

Molly looked relieved. "Sure. We can all go swimming together."

And wasn't this going to be a whole new way to have fun?

He and Molly waved cheery see-you-laters to the Calebows. As they walked away, he thought he heard Dan muttering to Phoebe, but he caught only one word.

"Slytherin."

Molly waited until they were far enough away before she let her agitation show. "You have to get your things out of the cottage! I don't want them to know we've been sleeping together."

After the way they'd looked coming out of the woods, he figured it was already too late, but he nodded.

"And don't let Dan get you alone again. He'll just give you the third degree. I'll make sure one of the kids is always around when I'm with Phoebe."

Before he could reply, she took off toward the cottage. He kicked at a clump of gravel and headed for the B&B. Why did she need to be secretive? Not that he wanted her to say anything—things were rocky enough as it was. But Molly didn't have to worry about being traded to Detroit like he did, so why didn't she tell them to go to hell?

The more he thought about it, the more her attitude bothered him. It was okay for him to want to keep this private, but somehow it wasn't okay for her.

20

In olden days a girl who liked a boy always made sure he won
when they played cards and board games.

—"Playing Rough"
article for *Chik*

They changed out of their suits in time for Molly's tea in the gazebo,
which she'd decided to hold at three o'clock instead of five because
it would be better for the kids. She complained to Phoebe that the paper
plates and store-bought cake disqualified her from a photo spread in
Victoria magazine, but Kevin knew she cared more about having a good
time than bringing out the good china.

He nodded at Lilly, who'd walked over with Charlotte Long and Charlotte's friend Vi. He'd already noticed the cottage residents shielding her
from the curiosity of the more transient guests at the B&B. He thought
about going over to talk to her, but he couldn't think of what to say.

Molly kept herself surrounded with scampering poodles and noisy
kids. She had a red heart barrette in her hair, pink jeans, a purple top,
and bright blue laces in her sneakers. She was a walking rainbow, and
just looking at her made him smile.

"George!" Molly bounced up and down waving at Liam Jenner as he
got out of his pickup around four o'clock and walked toward them.
"George Smith! Thanks for coming."

Jenner laughed and walked over to give her a hug. He might be old,
but he was a good-looking son of a bitch, and Kevin wasn't crazy about
the way he and the bunny lady were hanging on to each other.

"You've got to meet my sister. She used to run a gallery in New York, but I won't tell her who you are."

Yeah, right. Molly's eyes flashed the mischief jitterbug, but Jenner was oblivious. *Sucka.*

As the artist headed toward Phoebe, he walked right past Lilly. Maybe Liam had gotten fed up with all her early-morning rejections at the kitchen table. Kevin couldn't figure it out. If Lilly didn't like being around him, why did she keep showing up for breakfast?

He glanced from Lilly to Molly and tried to pick the exact moment when his long practice of surrounding himself with low-maintenance women had exploded in his face. He slammed his ball cap down on his head and promised himself he'd watch game film tonight.

The men wanted to talk football, and Kevin and Dan complied. Around five some of the adults began to drift away, but the kids were still enjoying themselves, and Kevin decided he'd put up a basketball hoop tomorrow. Maybe he'd buy some rubber rafts for the beach. And bikes. The kids should have bikes while they were here.

Cody and the O'Brian boys came running up, their faces sweaty and clothes grimy. Exactly the way a kid should look in the summer.

"Hey, Kevin! Can we play softball?"

He could feel the smile spreading all over his face. A softball game on the Common, right where the tabernacle had once stood . . . "Sure we can. Listen up! Everybody who wants to play softball, raise your hand."

Hands went up all over the place. Tess and Julie raced forward, and Andrew started to yell and hop. Even the adults were interested.

"A softball game is a wonderful idea," Charlotte Long chirped from her lawn chair. "Get everything organized, Kevin."

He smiled at her poking. "You want to be a captain, Cody?"

"Sure."

He looked around for another captain and started to pick Tess, but something about the way Hannah was sitting at her father's feet cuddling the poodles got to him. He'd seen her hand inch up, only to settle back into her lap. "Hannah, how about you? Do you want to be the other captain?"

Kevin was startled to see Dan drop his head and groan.

"No, Kevin!" Tess and Julie cried together. "Not Hannah!"

Molly surprised him most of all—the bunny lady, who was supposed to be so damn sensitive around kids. "Uh . . . maybe it would be better if you picked somebody else."

What was wrong with these people?

Luckily their callousness didn't faze Hannah, who jumped up, smoothed down her shorts, and gave him a smile that looked exactly like her aunt's. "Thank you, Kevin. They hardly ever let me be captain."

"That's because you—"

Phoebe laid her hand over Tess's mouth, but even she looked pained.

Kevin was disgusted with all of them. Nobody was more competitive than he was, but he'd never stooped low enough to make a little kid feel bad just because she wasn't athletic. He gave her a reassuring smile. "Don't pay any attention to them, sweetheart. You'll be a great captain. You can even choose first."

"Thank you." She stepped forward and surveyed the crowd. He waited for her to choose either him or her father. She surprised him by pointing toward her mother, a woman who played so badly that the veterans on the Stars' team had gotten in the habit of scheduling dental appointments just so they'd have an excuse to leave the team picnic before the annual softball game.

"I choose Mom."

Kevin bent closer and lowered his voice. "In case you weren't sure, Hannah, you can choose anybody you want, including guys. That means your dad. Me. Are you sure you want to choose your mom first?"

"She's sure." Dan sighed from behind him. "Here we go again."

Hannah gazed up at Kevin and whispered, "Mom gets her feelings hurt because nobody ever wants her on their team."

Tess cut right to the bone as only an eleven-year-old could. "That's because she sucks."

Phoebe sniffed and patted her team captain's shoulder, conveniently forgetting her earlier lack of support. "Pay no attention, Hannah. A winning attitude is far more important than natural ability."

Unlike Hannah, Cody was no fool, and he chose natural ability over that winning attitude. "I pick Kevin."

Dan rose from his lawn chair and moved closer to his daughter. "Hannah, honey, I'm over here. Don't forget about me. I'll get my feelings hurt if you don't choose me."

"No you won't." Hannah gave him a blazing smile, turned away, and fastened her eyes on Lilly, who'd been talking about gardening with some of the older women, and as far as Kevin could remember, hadn't raised her hand. "I pick you."

"Me?" Lilly looked pleased and stood. "Lord, I haven't played softball since I was a teenager."

Hannah smiled up at her mother. "This is going to be an exc'llent team. Lots of winning attitude."

Cody, not one to let any grass grow under his feet, chose Dan.

Once again Kevin stepped in, trying to help Hannah out by pointing toward the oldest of the O'Brian boys. "I was watching Scott toss the football around earlier. He's a pretty good athlete."

"Save your breath," Dan muttered, and sure enough, Kevin saw Hannah's third choice coming the minute he noticed Andrew's lower lip sticking out.

"I choose Andrew. See, Andrew, just because you're only five doesn't mean nobody wants you on their team."

"I'll take Tess," Cody countered, right on the mark.

"And I'll take Aunt Molly!" Hannah beamed.

Kevin sighed. So far Cody had one current NFL quarterback on his team, one former NFL quarterback, and one of the most athletic little girls in northern Illinois. Hannah, on the other hand, had her mother, the worst softball player in history; her little brother, who had a lot of heart but, at five, not much skill; and Molly, who was . . . well, Molly—the lady who tipped canoes, tried to drown herself, and in general hated sports.

Cody's next choices included the teenage girls who'd been kicking a soccer ball earlier with Tess, the middle O'Brian—who was built like a tank—and both his physically fit parents.

Hannah chose the six-year-old O'Brian, a kid Kevin was fairly certain he'd seen hiding his security blanket in the shrubs. She redeemed herself by picking her sister Julie, who at least was a dancer and coordinated, and then Liam Jenner, although her reasoning wasn't too sound. "Because he drew a beautiful picture of Kanga and Roo for me." While Cody filled in the rest of his team with the younger adults, Hannah chose every oldster who wanted to play.

It was going to be a bloodbath.

The boys ran to their cottages to get the equipment, Mr. Canfield—whose arthritis had been acting up—volunteered to umpire, and everybody soon settled into place.

Hannah's team was up at bat first, and Kevin found himself on the pitcher's mound facing the six-year-old who'd tucked his security blanket in the forsythia. Kevin made the mistake of glancing over at Molly and wasn't surprised to see her give him a look that clearly said, *If you're the kind of man who can strike out Linus, then you're not the man I thought you were, and you can forget all about getting me naked anytime in the foreseeable future,* comprenez-vous?

He walked the kid.

Hannah sent up Andrew next, and Kevin put a soft one over the plate. Andrew missed, but he had a great swing for a little kid, and as Kevin watched an expression of mulish determination settle over his face, he knew he'd just caught a glimpse of what Dan Calebow had looked like at the age of five. Because of that, his next pitch was harder than he intended, but Andrew was game, and he gave it his best.

Molly, on the other hand, shot him a look that had "dickhead" written all over it. *He's five, you idiot! Just a little boy! Is winning so important that you're going to strike out a five-year-old? You're definitely not ever, ever going to see another pair of bunny panties for the rest of your life! No way, no how.* Adiós, muchacho!

Kevin gave him another soft one, and Andrew banged it into short right. The oldest O'Brian kid didn't know how dangerous even a kindergarten Calebow could be, and he was caught napping. As a result, Linus made it to third, and Andrew settled in with his dad on second.

Dan ruffled his hair.

"Kevin?" Hannah called out politely. "Mr. McMullen's up next. He wants to know if it's okay if he uses his walker?"

And didn't that just say it all.

Finally it was Cody's team's turn to bat, and Kevin was up. Near the pitcher's mound he saw Little Hannah Goodheart huddled with the Four Horsewomen of the Apocalypse: Molly, Phoebe, Lilly, and Julie. Finally the females dispersed, leaving their pitcher on the mound.

Molly, the bunny lady.

Kevin couldn't contain his grin. Now, this was more like it. And guess what, boys and girls? Benny the Badger was showing little Daphne no mercy.

Molly tried to stare him down, but he could tell she was nervous. Damn right. All-American. MVP. Heisman candidate. All-Pro. Good reason to be nervous.

He stepped up to the plate and smiled at her. "Just try to keep the ball away from my head, sweetheart. I like my good-looking nose right where it is."

"That," Dan said from behind him, "was a mistake."

Yeah, right . . .

Molly went through a few gyrations that were supposed to pass for a warm-up. Kevin tapped his bat to the ground and waited for the pitch, thinking how cute she looked. Better than cute. Her lips were all rosy where she'd bitten them, and her breasts pressed against her purple top the same way they'd pressed against his chest the night before. As she released the ball, her sweet little rear end wiggled inside those tight pink jeans the same way it had wiggled against—

The ball sailed past him while he was distracted. *Whoa . . . what was that about?*

"Strike one!" Mr. Canfield called out.

A fluke, that's all. A lapse in concentration brought on by too little eye on the ball and too much eye on the doll. He stepped away from the plate.

She knew it was a fluke, too, because she started gnawing at that bottom lip again and looking even more nervous than before. That made this a good time to start playing a few mind games. "Nice pitch, Daphne. Think you can do it again?"

"I doubt it."

She was definitely nervous. Definitely sexy. He loved the way that lady made love, with her whole heart and every part of her body.

Her butt wiggled. Oh, he remembered what that wiggle felt like.

The ball came fast, but this time he was ready for it—except it dropped unexpectedly at the last instant, and his bat met nothing but air.

"Exc'llent, Aunt Molly."

"Thank you, Hannah."

Kevin couldn't believe it.

"Nice going," Dan grumbled from behind him.

Molly stroked the inner slope of her breast with her index finger. The tip of her tongue flicked over that puffy bottom lip. God, she was making him hot! As soon as this game was over, he was dragging her back into the woods, family or not, and then he'd show her a real game.

She wound up, and just as she released the ball, looked right at his crotch. He instinctively stepped away to protect himself. As a result he missed most of it and tapped a feeble roller back to the mound. He started to run. She threw to Julie on first base, who caught it with something that looked like a pirouette from *Swan Lake.*

He was out. *Out!* He looked from the ballerina to the bunny lady and tried to take it in. Molly's eyes flicked from his face to his crotch. And then she grinned. "Did I ever tell you I went to summer camp for nine years?"

"I believe you mentioned it." He couldn't imagine any summer camp teaching that particular trick. The queen of the mischief-makers had thought it up all by herself.

By the end of the first inning Molly had given Cody an easy pitch, walked Dan, and struck out the oldest O'Brian kid, along with his father.

Jocks 0, Last Kids to Be Chosen in Gym Class 2.

She sauntered past him as her team came in from the field. "Nice day."

"I thought you said you weren't any good at sports."

"I said I didn't *like* sports, jock boy." She flicked his chest. "There's a difference."

He couldn't let her get away with that one, so he gave her some prime NFL sneer. "Next time you stare at my zipper, jock girl, you'd better be on your back."

She laughed and ran off to join her team.

Lilly was first up. She was all Guccied in coordinating colors with diamonds flashing from her rings and bracelets. She kicked away a pair of leopard-print sandals, slipped off sunglasses with interlocking C's at the hinges, and grabbed the bat. She took a couple of practice swings, then stood up to the plate as if she owned it. Right then he knew that he hadn't gotten all his athletic ability from the rodeo rider.

She arched an eyebrow at him, and her eyes caught the light. Green like his.

I know your my real mom and I love you very much . . .

He didn't try to burn her. Instead, he sent it nice and easy over the plate. She took a great swing, but she was rusty and didn't catch it all.

"Foul ball!"

He gave her the same pitch again, and this time she caught it clean. The bat cracked against the ball, and as her team whooped, she made it to second. He was startled by the burst of pride he felt.

"Nice going," he muttered.

"Past my prime," she said.

Captain Goodheart was up next, all solemn and serious, with the same worried look on her face he sometimes saw her aunt wearing. Hannah's straight brown hair was a little lighter than Molly's, but they had the same stubborn chin, the same slight tilt at the eyes. She was a serious kid, as well as being neat. Her American Girl T-shirt didn't show any sign that she'd been playing with a couple of poodles and eating chocolate cake. He spotted a tiny notebook sticking out of the back pocket of her shorts, and something inside him melted. She seemed more like Molly's daughter than Dan and Phoebe's. Was this the way his little girl would have looked?

Out of nowhere his throat tightened.

"I'm not very good," Hannah whispered from the plate.

Oh, man, not that . . . He was dead meat. He threw wide.

"Ball one."

She looked even more worried. "I'm better at drawing. And writing things. I'm pretty good at writing things."

"Cut it out, Hannah," her insensitive jerk of a father called from second base.

Kevin had always considered Dan Calebow one of the best parents he'd ever known, which just proved how wrong he could be. He shot him a quelling look and threw a lob so soft, so gentle, that it didn't make it to the plate.

"Ball two."

Hannah bit her bottom lip and spoke in a helpless whisper. "I'll be so glad when this is over."

Kevin melted, and so did his next pitch, just as it passed over the plate.

Hannah bunted it with a choppy little swing.

Kevin went after the ball, but he didn't hurry so he could give her enough time to make it to first base. Unfortunately, Cody missed the catch, and she made it to second.

He heard a chorus of cheers go up and saw Lilly slide home, Gucci pants forgotten.

Last Kids to Be Chosen in Gym Class 3, Jocks 0.

He cocked his head at Hannah.

"I'm not a very good batter," she said in her lost-little-girl voice, "but I can run really fast."

"Brother," Dan said in disgust.

Kevin was about to say something comforting when the little girl exchanged a look with her aunt that just about knocked him off his feet. It was only a smile. But it wasn't an ordinary smile. Oh, no. It was a sly little hustler's smile!

An expression of such perfect understanding passed between niece and aunt that he nearly choked. He'd been conned! Hannah was a world-class mischief-maker, just like Molly!

He turned on Dan, who looked faintly apologetic. "Phoebe and I still aren't sure if she plans it ahead of time or if it just happens."

"You should have told me!"

Dan gazed at his youngest daughter with a combination of irritation and fatherly pride. "You had to see this for yourself."

Sports sometimes had a way of making everything clear, and right then it all fell into place—from Molly's almost drowning and the incident with the canoe to Marmie's uncharacteristic trip up into that tree. Molly had been stringing him along from the very beginning. Cody came forward, clearly unhappy with his pitcher's lackluster performance, and the next thing Kevin knew, he was standing on second base while Dan took over at the mound.

Hannah the Con Artist exchanged a sly glance with Molly, and Kevin saw why. It was Phoebe's turn at bat.

Oh, and didn't the good times just start to roll then? There was more butt wiggling, lip licking, and breast thrusting than anybody under the age of consent should be allowed to witness. Dan started to sweat, Phoebe cooed, and the next thing he knew, the Stars' owner was perched on first while Miss Hannah claimed third.

It had turned into a bloodbath.

The Jocks finally managed to beat the Last Kids to Be Chosen in Gym Class, but only because Captain Cody was smart enough to replace Dan with Tess, who was immune to butt wiggling, plus being nobody's fool. Tess made short work of the nursery set and politely but firmly put the oldsters out to pasture. Even she, however, couldn't stop Aunt Molly from hitting a homer in the last inning.

For someone who hated sports, Molly sure did know how to handle a bat, and the way she ran the bases left Kevin so aroused he had to bend over and pretend he was rubbing away a leg cramp to keep from embarrassing himself. As he rubbed, he remembered how crowded Molly's bed would be this week with all the kids snuggling up against her. The way he understood it, this was Julie's night, tomorrow it would be Andrew's, then Hannah's, then Tess's. Maybe he could sneak into the cottage after bedtime and kidnap Auntie M. But then he remembered her telling him Julie was a light sleeper.

He sighed and resettled his ball cap on his head. Face it. There wasn't going to be any joy in Mudville tonight. Mighty Kevin had struck out.

21

The woods were spooky, and Daphne's teeth chattered. What if no one ever found her? Thank goodness she'd brought along her favorite lettuce and marmalade sandwich.

—Daphne Gets Lost

L illy leaned back into the chaise and listened to the tinkling of the wind chimes hanging from the redbud tree that grew next to the patio. She loved wind chimes, but Craig had hated them and wouldn't let her hang them in her garden. She closed her eyes, glad the guests at the B&B seldom visited this quiet spot just behind the house.

She'd finally stopped asking herself how long she was staying here. When it was time to leave, she'd know. And today had been such fun. When she'd slid into home plate, Kevin had almost seemed proud of her, and at the picnic he hadn't deliberately avoided her the way Liam had.

"Hiding out from your adoring public?"

Her eyes snapped open, and her heart skipped a beat as the man she thought about far too much came out the back door of the B&B. His hair was shaggy, his clothes the same rumpled khaki shorts and navy pocket T-shirt he'd worn earlier at the picnic. Like her, he hadn't yet cleaned up from the softball game.

She gazed into those dark eyes that saw too much. "I'm recuperating from this afternoon."

He sank into the cushions on the redwood chair next to her. "You're a pretty good softball player for a girl."

"And you're a pretty good softball player for a sissy artist."

He yawned. "Who are you calling a sissy?"

She stopped herself from smiling. She did too much of that when they were together, and it encouraged him. Every morning she told herself she'd stay in her room until he left, but she'd go downstairs anyway. She still couldn't believe what she'd done with him. It was as if she'd been under a spell, as if that glass-enclosed studio had been part of another world. But she was back in Kansas now.

She was also mildly irritated by how much he'd enjoyed himself without her. If he hadn't been laughing with Molly, he'd been flirting with Phoebe Calebow or teasing one of the children. He was a gruff, intimidating man, and the fact that they hadn't been frightened of him somehow annoyed her.

"Go get cleaned up," he said. "I'll do the same, then take you out to dinner."

"Thanks, but I'm not hungry."

He gave a weary sigh and rested his head against the back of the chair. "You're hell-bent on throwing this away, aren't you? You're not going to give us a fighting chance."

She eased her legs over the side of the chaise and sat straighter. "Liam, what happened between us was an aberration. I've been alone too much lately, and I gave in to a foolish impulse."

"Just time and circumstances, is that it?"

"Yes."

"It could have happened with anyone?"

She wanted to agree, but she couldn't. "No, not with anyone. You can be attractive when you put your mind to it."

"So can a lot of men. You know there's something between us, but you don't have the guts to see what it is."

"I don't need to. I know exactly why I'm attracted to you. It's an old habit."

"What do you mean by that?"

She twisted her rings. "I mean that I've been there and done that. The alpha male. The stallion who rules the herd. The take-charge prince who makes all Cinderella's troubles go away. Men like you are my fatal weakness. But I'm not a penniless teenager anymore who needs some-one to take care of her."

"Thank God. I don't like teenagers. And I'm too self-centered to take care of anyone."

"You're deliberately minimizing what I'm trying to tell you."

"That's because you're boring me."

She wouldn't let his rudeness distract her, especially since she knew it was calculated to do just that. "Liam, I'm too old and too smart to make the same mistake again. Yes, I'm attracted to you. I'm instinctively drawn to aggressive men, even though it's their nature to run rough-shod over the women who care about them."

"And here I thought this conversation couldn't become any more infantile."

"You're doing it right now. You don't want to talk about this, so you're belittling me to try to get me to shut up."

"Too bad it's not working."

"I thought I'd finally gotten smart, but obviously I haven't, or I wouldn't be letting you do this." She rose from the chaise. "Listen to me, Liam. I made the mistake of falling in love with a controlling man once in my life, and I'll never do it again. I loved my husband. But, God—sometimes I hated him more."

She hugged herself, astonished that she'd revealed something to him she could barely admit to herself.

"He probably deserved it. He sounds like a son of a bitch."

"He was just like you!"

"I seriously doubt that."

"You don't think so?" She jabbed her hand toward the redbud tree. "He wouldn't let me have wind chimes! I love wind chimes, but he hated them, so I wasn't permitted to hang them in my own garden."

"Good judgment on his part. The things are a nuisance."

Her stomach clenched. "Letting myself fall in love with you would be like falling in love with Craig all over again."

"I really resent that."

"A month after he died, I hung a set of wind chimes outside my bed-room window."

"Well, you're not going to hang them outside our bedroom window!"

"We don't have a bedroom window! And if we did, I'd hang as many sets there as I wanted!"

"Even though I've expressly asked you not to?"

She threw up her hands in frustration. "This isn't about wind chimes! I was just giving you an example!"

"You're not getting off that easily. You're the one who brought the subject up." Now he was on his feet. "I've told you I don't like the damn things, but you've said you're going to hang them up anyway, is that right?"

"You've lost your mind."

"Is that right or not?"

"Yes!"

"Fine." He gave a martyr's sigh. "If it's that important to you, go ahead and hang the damn things. But don't expect me not to complain. Bloody noise pollution. And I'll expect you to give in on something that's important to me."

She clutched her head. "Is driving me crazy your idea of seduction?"

"I'm trying to make a point. One you seem unable to understand."

"Enlighten me."

"You're not going to let any man run roughshod over you, not anymore. I just tried, but you wouldn't let me, and if I can't do it, no one can. You see? We don't have a problem."

"It's not that simple!"

"What about me?" He touched his chest, and for the first time he looked vulnerable. "What about my fatal weakness?"

"I don't know what you mean."

"Maybe if you'd think about someone other than yourself, you would!"

His words didn't sting as Craig's would have. Liam's were intended to goad her, not to wound. "You're impossible!"

"What is a man like me supposed to do, tell me that? I don't know how to pull my punches, and I'm too old to learn, so where does that leave me?"

"I don't know."

"Strong women are my weakness. Tough women who don't fall apart just because a man doesn't always say what they want to hear. Except the strong woman I'm falling in love with doesn't want to put up with me. So where does that leave me, Lilly?"

"Oh, Liam . . . You're not falling in love with me. You're—"

"Have a little faith in yourself," he said gruffly. "In the woman you've become."

She felt trapped by his brutal honesty. He didn't know what he was saying. The person he saw when he looked at her wasn't the person she felt like inside.

He moved to the edge of the patio, his hands in his pockets. "You've been slamming doors in my face for long enough, I think. I love you, but I have my pride, too."

"I know that."

"The painting's almost done, and I'd like you to see it. Come to my house on Thursday evening."

"Liam, I—"

"If you don't show up, I won't come looking for you. You're going to have to make a decision, Lilly."

"I hate ultimatums."

"I'm not surprised. Strong women usually do." He walked away.

Kevin spent most of the next two days trying to catch Molly alone, but what with his trips into town for bikes, attending to the guests, and the kids who kept popping up every time he stuck his head out the door, he didn't have the opportunity. Twice Dan tried to talk to him, but the phone interrupted once and a guest's dead car battery the other time. By Tuesday evening he was so grouchy and out of sorts that he couldn't concentrate on the game film he'd stuck in the office VCR. Five weeks to training camp . . . He nudged Roo off his lap and got up to go to the window. It wasn't even seven o'clock, but a few rain clouds had rolled in and it was getting dark. *Where the hell was she?*

Just then his cell phone rang. He snatched it from the desk. "Hello."

"Kevin, it's Molly."

"Where have you been?" he snarled. "I told you I wanted to talk to you after tea today."

"I spotted Phoebe coming up the front walk, so I dodged out the back door. She's getting more persistent. Then I ran into Tess, and she started talking to me about a boy who likes her."

Yeah? Well, what about the boy who likes you?

"The thing is . . . after Tess left, I decided to take a walk in the woods by myself, and I started thinking about this idea I have for Daphne. One thing led to another, and the next thing I knew, I was lost."

For the first time all day he relaxed. "You don't say." As he loosened his grip on the phone, his stomach rumbled. He realized he hadn't eaten anything since breakfast, and he headed into the kitchen to fix himself a sandwich. Roo trotted along.

"Lost in the woods," she said with emphasis.

"Wow." He tried to keep the smile from his voice.

"And now it's getting dark."

"It sure is."

"It also looks like rain."

He glanced out the window. "I was just noticing that myself."

"And I'm scared."

"I'll bet." He tucked the cell phone under his chin and pulled some lunch meat from the refrigerator, along with a jar of mustard. "So you found a nearby convenience store and called me?"

"I happened to bring Phoebe's cell phone along."

He grinned and grabbed a loaf of bread from the pantry. "Smart of you."

"At camp we were taught to wear a whistle around our neck if we went walking alone. Since I didn't have a whistle . . . "

"You took a cell phone."

"Safety first."

"God bless the power of telecommunications." He went back to the refrigerator for some cheese. "And now you're lost. Have you looked for moss on the tree trunks?"

"I didn't think of that."

"It grows on the north side." He began to assemble his sandwich, enjoying himself for the first time all evening.

"Yes, I believe I remember hearing that. But it's a little dark to see."

"I don't suppose you tucked a compass in your pocket, or a flashlight?"

"That didn't occur to me."

"Too bad." He slapped on some extra mustard. "You want me to come look for you?"

"I'd really appreciate it. If you bring your phone along, I might be able to direct you. I started out on the path behind Jacob's Ladder."

"That'd be a good place for me to start then. Tell you what—I'll call you from there."

"It's getting dark fast. Would you mind hurrying?"

"Oh, sure, I'll be there before you know it." He disconnected, chuckled, and settled down to enjoy his sandwich, but he'd barely managed three bites before she called back. "Yeah?"

"Did I tell you I might have sprained my ankle?"

"Oh, no. How'd you do that?"

"Some kind of animal hole."

"Hope it's not from a snake. There are some rattlers around here."

"Rattlers?"

He reached for a napkin. "I'm walking by Jacob's Ladder right now, but somebody must be running a microwave, because I'm getting interference. I'll call you back."

"Wait, you don't have my num—"

He disconnected, gave a whoop of laughter, and headed for the refrigerator. A sandwich always tasted better with beer. He whistled to himself as he popped the cap and settled back to enjoy.

Then it struck him. What the hell was he doing?

He snatched up his cell phone and punched in Phoebe's number from memory. There'd be plenty of time later to teach her a lesson. This was the first chance he'd had in two days to get her alone. "Hey, Molly?"

"Yes."

"I'm having a little trouble finding you." He tucked the phone under his chin, grabbed the beer, along with what was left of his sandwich, and headed out the back door. "Do you think you could scream?"

"You want me to scream?"

"It'd be helpful." He took another bite of sandwich and hurried toward Jacob's Ladder.

"I'm not really much of a screamer."

"You are in bed," he pointed out.

"Are you eating?"

"I need to keep my strength up for the search." He waved at Charlotte Long with his beer bottle.

"I'm fairly sure I'm near the creek. At the end of the path that starts right behind Jacob's Ladder."

"Creek?"

"The creek, Kevin! The one that runs from the woods across the meadow. The only creek there is!"

She was beginning to sound snappish. He took a sip of beer. "I don't remember a creek. Are you sure?"

"Yes, I'm sure!"

"I suppose I'll recognize it when I see it." Kids were running around on the Common. He stopped for a moment to enjoy the sight, then returned to his mission. "The wind's really started to kick up. I can hardly see the path."

"It's not that bad here."

"Then maybe I'm going the wrong way."

"You took the path behind Jacob's Ladder, right?"

He tossed the rest of his sandwich into a trash container and stepped onto that exact path. "I think so."

"You think so? Aren't you paying attention?"

Definitely snappish.

"Just keep talking. Maybe I'll be able to tell how close I'm getting by the reception."

"Can you hear the creek?"

"Which creek is that again?"

"There's only one!"

"I hope I can find it. I don't even want to imagine how terrible it'd be if you had to spend the night in the woods by yourself."

"I'm sure that won't happen."

"I hope not. Whatever you do, don't start thinking about the Blair Witch."

"The Blair Witch?"

He managed a choking noise, then a monster moan, and disconnected.

It didn't take long for his phone to ring again.

"My ribs are aching from laughter," she said dryly.

"Sorry. It was just a squirrel. But it was huge."

"If you don't play right, I'm going home."

"Okay, but you'd better not be wearing anything more than shoes and a hair ribbon when I find you."

"I don't own a hair ribbon."

"That'll be one less thing for you to take off, then, won't it?"

As it turned out, she was still dressed when he spotted her, but that didn't last for long. They tumbled naked into the soft meadow grass, and as the rain began to fall, their laughter faded.

He drugged himself on her kisses, and as he entered her soft, welcoming body, he glimpsed something that felt almost . . . holy. But the illusion was too fragile to survive the primitive demand of his body.

The rain drummed on his back. Her strong fingers dug into his shoulders—demanding. The rain . . . this woman . . . Her pleasure spiraled beneath him, and he lost himself.

As one day slipped into the next, Molly behaved like a woman possessed. On Wednesday she lifted her skirt for Kevin in the office while the guests gathered for tea. That same night she escaped another of Phoebe's arrangements for a private chat and met him in the woods behind the cottage. The following morning he dragged her into the pantry just as Troy was coming through the kitchen door, then had to cover her mouth because she started making too much noise. Later she hauled him into a deserted cottage, but as he lifted her onto the kitchen table, her muscles finally rebelled from the strain of so many awkward positions, and she winced.

He pressed his forehead to hers and took a shaky breath, struggling for control. "This is nuts. You've had enough."

"Are you kidding? I'm just getting started, but if you can't keep up with me, I understand."

He smiled and kissed her. Oh, she loved those slow kisses. He caressed her breasts and her thighs, trying to take more care, but they were dancing with danger, and she wouldn't let him. Before long she forgot all about her aching muscles.

That evening they sidestepped the Calebows' dinner invitation by announcing that they had to drive into town for supplies, but when they returned to the campground, they discovered their luck had run out. Phoebe and Dan were waiting for them on the steps of the B&B.

22

One day this bad guy came to Nightingale Woods. He was realy bad and mean, but he pretended to be Benny's friend. But only Daphne knew he was realy bad. So she told Benny, "Hes not your friend!!!!!"

—*Daphne Meets a Bad Guy*
by Hannah Marie Calebow

Molly heard Kevin's quiet curse and fixed a smile on her face. "Hey, you guys. Escape the kiddies for a while?"

"They're playing flashlight tag on the Common." As Phoebe came down the steps, she took in Molly's rumpled dress.

Molly needed her wits about her, but the fact that she was still missing her underwear put her at a disadvantage. "I hope Andrew's going to be all right. You know how fast he disappears."

"Andrew's just fine," Dan said. "There's not much trouble he can get into around here."

"You have no idea," Kevin muttered.

Phoebe tilted her head toward the lane that led past the beach. Her oversize Stars sweatshirt and jeans didn't quite hide the power player beneath. "Mrs. Long volunteered to keep an eye on all of them. Let's take a walk."

Molly flexed her shoulders. "I think I'll pass. I've been up since five-thirty, so I'm a little tired." From making love three times today. "Maybe tomorrow."

Dan's voice rang with Southern steel. "It won't take long. And there are a couple of things we want to discuss."

"Your vacation is almost over. Why can't you just relax and enjoy the rest of it?"

"It's a little hard to relax when we're so worried about you," Phoebe replied.

"Well, stop worrying!"

"Calm down, Molly," Kevin said. "If they want to talk, I'm sure we can spare a few minutes."

What a suck-up. Or maybe he'd decided it was time to play a risky new game. She'd known from the beginning that he wasn't sneaking around because he was afraid of Dan and Phoebe. He was doing it because he loved taking chances. "You might have the time, but I don't."

Dan reached out for her arm just as he'd done since she was fifteen, but Kevin shot forward and blocked his way. She didn't know who was the more astonished, herself or Dan. Had Kevin interpreted the gesture as a threat?

Phoebe recognized the signs of antlers clashing, and she moved to her husband's side. The two of them exchanged one of their glances, and then Dan set off toward the lane. "Right now. Let's go."

The moment of reckoning was finally here, and there was no escaping it. Molly could imagine the questions they were going to ask. If only she could figure out how to answer them.

They headed silently past the beach and the last of the cottages, then along the edge of the woods. When they reached the split-rail fence that marked the end of the campground, Dan stopped. Kevin stepped slightly away from Molly and rested his hips against a post.

"You've been here for two weeks," Phoebe said as she let go of Dan's hand.

"Two weeks ago Wednesday," Kevin replied.

"The campground is beautiful. Our kids are having a wonderful time."

"It's nice having them here."

"They still can't believe you bought all those bikes."

"I enjoyed doing it."

Dan lost patience. "Phoebe and I want to know what your intentions are toward Molly."

"Dan!" Molly cried.

"It's all right," Kevin said.

"No it's not!" She glared at her brother-in-law. "And what kind of sexist Southern crap is that anyway? What about *my* intentions toward *him*?" She didn't exactly know what those intentions were beyond keeping the real world at bay by staying in Nightingale Woods for as long as she could, but she had to face Dan down.

"You were supposed to be getting an annulment," Phoebe said. "Instead you ran off together."

"We didn't run off," Molly replied.

"What else would you call it? And every time I try to talk to you about it, you dash away." She jammed her hands into the pockets of her jeans. "This is the fire alarm all over again, isn't it, Molly?"

"No!"

"What fire alarm?" Kevin asked.

"Never mind," Molly said hastily.

"No, I want to hear this."

Phoebe betrayed her. "When Molly was sixteen, she pulled the fire alarm at her high school. Unfortunately, she hadn't seen any sign of a fire."

Kevin regarded her curiously. "Did you have a good reason?"

She shook her head, feeling sixteen all over again.

"So why did you do it?"

"I'd rather not go into this now."

He tilted his head toward Dan. "You always talk as if she's perfect."

"She is!" Dan barked.

Molly smiled despite herself, then bit her lip. "It was an aberration. I was an insecure teenager testing Phoebe and Dan to make sure they'd stick by me no matter what I did."

Kevin's eyes took on a speculative gleam. "So did they evacuate the school?"

Molly nodded.

"How many fire trucks?"

"My God . . . " Phoebe muttered. "It was a serious offense."

"It's a Class Two felony," Molly said glumly, "so it got fairly nasty."

"I'll bet." Kevin turned back to the Calebows. "Fascinating as this is—and I'll admit it's pretty fascinating—I don't think that's what you want to talk about."

"This isn't a big deal!" Molly exclaimed. "Two weeks ago Kevin showed up at my place because I'd missed an appointment with the attorney. I hadn't been feeling well, and he decided some fresh air would do me good, so he brought me up here."

When Phoebe wanted to, she did sarcasm better than anyone. "You couldn't just take her for a walk?"

"Didn't think of it." Unlike Phoebe, Kevin wasn't going to tell Molly's secrets.

But Molly had to be truthful about this part. "I've been seriously depressed, but I didn't want you to know how bad it was. Kevin's a fairly dedicated do-gooder, even though he tries to fight it, and he told me if I didn't go with him, he'd drive me out to your place and dump me on the two of you. I didn't want you to see me like that."

Phoebe looked crestfallen. "We're your family! You shouldn't have felt that way."

"I'd already upset you enough. I'd been trying to pretend I was all right, but I just couldn't do it any longer."

"She wasn't all right," Kevin said. "But she's gotten better since she's been here."

"How long are you planning to stay?" Dan's expression was still suspicious.

"Not much longer," Kevin replied. "Another couple of days."

His words made Molly's chest hurt.

"Do you remember Eddie Dillard?" Kevin went on. "He used to play for the Bears."

"I remember him."

"He wants to buy the place, and he's driving up tomorrow to check it out."

Molly's stomach turned over. "You didn't tell me that!"

"Didn't I? I guess I was preoccupied."

Preoccupied having sex with her. But there'd been plenty of time between their erotic workouts for him to have mentioned this.

"We can leave right after that," he said. "I just talked to my business manager this afternoon, and he finally found someone in Chicago to take over for the rest of the summer, a married couple who've done this before."

He might as well have slapped her. He hadn't even told her he'd asked his business manager to look in Chicago. She felt more betrayed than when Phoebe had mentioned the fire alarm. He knew she'd hate this, so he'd neglected to mention it. There was no real communication between them, no common goal. Everything she didn't want to accept about their relationship was right there in front of her. They might share sex, but that was all.

Phoebe nudged a clump of chicory with her toe. "And then what happens?"

She couldn't stand hearing Kevin say it, so she said it for him. "Nothing happens. We file for a divorce and go our separate ways."

"A divorce?" Dan asked. "Not an annulment?"

"Grounds for an annulment are limited." Molly tried to sound impersonal, as if this had nothing to do with her. "You need to prove misrepresentation or duress. We can't, so we'll have to get a divorce."

Phoebe looked up from the chicory clump. "I have to ask . . . "

Molly knew right away what was coming and tried to think of a way to stop it.

"The two of you seem to get along . . . "

No, Phoebe. Please don't.

"Have you considered staying married?"

"No!" Molly jumped in before Kevin could respond. "Do you think I'm crazy? He's not my type."

Phoebe's eyebrows shot up, and Kevin looked annoyed. She didn't care. She was filled with an awful desire to hurt him. Except she couldn't do it. Phoebe was Kevin's boss, and his career meant everything to him.

"Kevin didn't have to bring me up here, but he did it anyway because he knew I needed help." She took a deep breath and reminded herself he'd forgiven her and that she owed him this. "He's been wonderful, extremely kind and sensitive, and I'd appreciate it if the two of you stopped being so suspicious of him."

"We aren't—"

"Yes you are. It's put him in a difficult position."

"Maybe he should have thought about that when he was dragging you into the woods on Sunday," Dan drawled. "Or was he too busy being kind and sensitive?"

Kevin got that tight look around his jaw again. "Exactly what are you trying to say, Dan?"

"I'm saying that if helping Molly was just a humanitarian gesture on your part, you shouldn't be sleeping with her."

"That's it!" Molly exclaimed. "You just crossed the line."

"It's not the first time, and I'm sure it won't be the last. Phoebe and I watch out for our family."

"Maybe you should watch out for somebody else in your family," Kevin said quietly. "Molly's asking you to respect her privacy."

"Is it her privacy you're worried about or your own?"

Antlers were clashing again, but Molly didn't care. "You keep forgetting that I'm not accountable to you any longer. As for my relationship with Kevin . . . In case you haven't noticed, we're not even sleeping under the same roof."

"And I wasn't born yesterday," Dan said stubbornly.

Molly could no longer hold back. "How about some simple courtesy, then? I've spent the past twelve years pretending I don't see the two of you grope each other, pretending I don't hear the two of you at night when you make—believe me—*way* too much noise. The fact is, Kevin and I are married at the moment. We'll be getting a divorce soon, but we don't have one yet, so whatever is or isn't going on between us isn't a topic for discussion. Do you understand me?"

Phoebe was looking increasingly upset. "Molly, you're not the kind of person who can take sex lightly. It needs to mean something."

"You're damn right it does!" Dan whirled on Kevin. "Did you forget that she just had a miscarriage?"

"Back off." Kevin's lips barely moved.

Dan saw he wasn't getting anywhere there and zeroed in on Molly. "He's a football player, and it's part of the mentality. He may not intend to, but he's using you."

Dan's words stung. He understood what it was to love a woman, so he recognized how shallow Kevin's feelings for her were.

Kevin shot forward. "I told you to back off."

Molly couldn't let this go on any longer, so instead of crying as she wanted to, she went on the attack herself. "Wrong. I'm using *him*. I lost a baby, my career's in the toilet, and I'm broke. Kevin's my distraction. He's my reward for twenty-seven years of being a good girl. Now, do you have any more questions?"

"Oh, Molly . . . " Phoebe chewed her bottom lip, and Dan looked even more upset.

Molly lifted her chin and glared at both of them. "I'll give him back when I'm done with him. Until then leave me alone."

She'd almost reached Lilies of the Field before Kevin caught up with her. "Molly!"

"Go away," she snapped.

"I'm your *reward*?"

"Only when you're naked. When you have your clothes on, you're a cross to bear."

"Stop being a wise-ass."

Everything was falling apart. Eddie Dillard was showing up tomorrow, and Kevin had found someone else to run the campground. Even worse, there was nothing that could make him care about her in the same way she cared about him.

He touched her arm. "You know they mean well. Don't let them get to you."

He didn't understand that they weren't the ones who were tearing her apart.

Lilly refused to look at the clock as she moved away from the window. The Calebows had finally managed to corner Kevin and Molly, but she couldn't imagine that the confrontation had been productive. Her son and his wife didn't seem to know what they wanted from their relationship, so she doubted they could explain it to her family.

Lilly had liked the Calebows immediately, and their presence these last five days had helped lift her heavy heart. They obviously loved Molly and, just as obviously, saw Kevin as a threat, but Lilly was beginning to suspect that Kevin was as big a danger to himself as he was to Molly.

Nine-thirty . . . She headed for the armchair in the corner where she'd left her quilting but picked up a magazine instead. She hadn't been able to work on her quilt since Sunday, when Liam had issued his ultimatum. And now it was Thursday.

Come to my house on Thursday evening. . . . If you don't show up, I won't come looking for you.

She tried to build up some resentment against him, but it didn't work. She understood exactly why he'd done it, and she couldn't blame him. They were both too old to play games.

9:34 . . . She thought about Kevin taking over the bedroom downstairs. She liked falling asleep knowing they were under the same roof. When they passed each other in the hallways, they smiled and made small talk. At one time that would have been more than she could have hoped for. Now, it wasn't enough.

9:35 . . . She concentrated on flipping through her magazine, then gave up and paced the floor. What good were life lessons if you didn't pay attention to them?

At ten-thirty, she forced herself to get undressed and put on her nightgown. She got into bed and stared at the pages of a book she'd been enjoying only a week earlier. Now she couldn't remember anything about it. *Liam, I miss you so* . . . He was the most remarkable man she'd ever met, but Craig had been remarkable, too, and he'd made her miserable.

As she reached across the bed and turned off the light, her world had never seemed smaller or her bed lonelier.

E ddie Dillard was big, genial, and coarse, the kind of man who wore
a gold chain, burped, scratched his crotch, carried a wad of bills
held together with a big money clip, and said . . .

"You duh man, Kev. Isn't he, Larry? Isn't Kev here the man?"

Oh, yes, Larry agreed, Kev was definitely the man.

Dillard and his brother had shown up late that morning in a black
SUV. Now they were sitting around the kitchen table eating salami sandwiches and belching beer while Eddie gloated over the prospect of own-
ing his own fishing camp and Larry gloated over the prospect of running
it for him. To Molly's dismay, they all seemed to regard it as a done deal.

This would be a place, Eddie said, where a man could put up his feet,
relax, and get away from being "pussy-whipped by his wife." This last
was uttered with a wink, clearly signaling (one man to the other) that
no woman pussy-whipped Eddie Dillard.

Molly wanted to throw up. Instead, she jammed a tiny bar of French-
milled soap into one of the bird's-nest baskets they used in the bathrooms to hold toiletries. She didn't know whom she disliked more,
Eddie or his revolting brother Larry, who planned to live upstairs in the
house while he ran the fishing camp.

She glanced over at Kevin, who was leaning against the wall sipping
from a longneck. He didn't burp. When Eddie had arrived, Kevin had
tried to get rid of her, but she wasn't going anyplace.

"So, Larry," Eddie said to his brother, "how much you figure it'll cost
to paint these frou-frou cottages?"

Molly dropped one of the tiny, frosted-glass shampoo bottles. "The
cottages were just painted. And they're beautiful."

Eddie seemed to have forgotten she was there. Larry laughed and
shook his head. "No offense, Maggie, but it's gonna be a fishing camp,
and guys don't like fruit colors. We'll just paint everything brown."

Eddie pointed at Larry with his longneck. "We're only painting the
cottages in the middle, the ones around that whadyacallit?—that Common. I'm gonna tear down the rest of them. Too much upkeep."

Molly's heart stopped. Lilies of the Field wasn't on the Common. Her
pink, blue, and yellow nursery cottage would be torn down. She aban-

doned the toiletry baskets. "You can't tear those cottages down! They're historic! They're—"

"The fishing's real good around here," Kevin cut in, shooting her a frown. "Large- and smallmouth bass, perch, bluegill. I heard a guy in town talk about a seven-pound pike he pulled out of the lake last week."

Eddie patted his stomach and belched. "I can't wait to get out on that boat."

"This lake is too small for what you want," Molly said desperately. "There's a strict limit to how big an outboard motor you can use. You can't even water-ski."

Kevin shot her a pointed look. "I don't think Eddie plans to cater to the water-skiing crowd."

"Nah. Just fishermen. Roll out of bed in the morning, give everybody a coffee thermos, a bag of doughnuts, and some beer, then send 'em out on the lake while the mist is still on the water. Come back after a coupla hours for brats and beer, take a nap, play some pool . . . "

"I think we should put the pool table out there." Larry pointed toward the front of the house. "Along with a big-screen TV. Once we tear down all the walls between the rooms, everything will be together—the pool table, TV, the bar, and the bait shop."

"*Bait shop!* You're putting a bait shop in this house!"

"Molly." Kevin's voice sounded a warning note, and Eddie tossed him a pitying look. Kevin narrowed his eyes at her. "Maybe you'd better go check on Amy."

Ignoring him, she zeroed in on Eddie. "People have been coming here for years. The campground needs to stay the way it is, and the bed-and-breakfast, too. The house is filled with antiques, and it's in wonderful condition. It even runs at a profit." Not much of one, but at least it paid for itself.

Eddie gave an open-mouthed laugh that revealed too much of his salami sandwich. He jabbed his brother. "Hey, Larry, you want to run a bread-and-breakfast?"

"Yeah, sure." Larry snorted and reached for his beer. "As long as I can have a pool table, satellite TV, and no women."

"Molly . . . out. Right now." Kevin jerked his head toward the door.

Eddie chuckled as the little woman was finally put in her place.

Molly clenched her teeth, then drew her lips into a stiff smile. "I'm leaving, darling. Just make sure you clean up after your friends. And last time you washed dishes, you splashed—so don't forget to wear your apron."

Now *that* was pussy-whipping!

After dinner Molly pleaded an upset stomach to the munchkins and told them they'd have to sleep in their own cottage. Since it was their last night here, she felt guilty, but she didn't have any choice. She changed into jeans, turned out the lights, and curled up in the chair by the open window. Then she waited.

She didn't worry about Kevin dropping in. He'd gone to town with the Dillards, where, if there was any justice, he'd get drunk and end up with a world-class hangover. Also they hadn't spoken all afternoon.

During tea she could see right away that he was angry with her, but she didn't care because she was angry right back. *You duh man . . . You duh big dumb jerk!* Selling the campground was bad enough, but selling it to somebody who intended to destroy it was unconscionable, and she'd never forgive herself if she didn't at least try to put a stop to it.

Lilies of the Field was too isolated for her to be able to see the men when they returned from town, but the campground was quiet enough that she knew she'd hear them. Sure enough, a little after one in the morning the sound of a car engine drifted through the window. As she straightened in the chair, she wished there weren't so many loopholes in her plan, but it was the best she had.

She pulled on her sneakers, grabbed the flashlight she'd swiped from the house, and left Roo behind so she could set to work. Forty-five minutes later she let herself inside Lamb of God, where Eddie and Larry were spending the night. She'd checked it out earlier, right after the men had left for town, to see which bedroom was Eddie's. Now it smelled like stale liquor.

Moving closer, she gazed down at the big, dumb, drunken lump under the covers. "Eddie?"

The lump didn't move.

"Eddie," she whispered again, hoping she didn't wake up Larry, too, since it would be easier dealing with only one of them. "Eddie, wake up."

Fumes came off him as he stirred. Someone this gross shouldn't be allowed in Nightingale Woods. "Yeah . . . yeah?" He wedged open his eyes. "Whatzu . . . "

"It's Molly," she whispered. "Kevin's estranged wife. I need to talk to you."

"Whadya . . . whatzabout?"

"About the fishing camp. It's very important."

He started to lever himself up, then fell back into the pillow.

"I wouldn't bother you if it weren't important. I'll just step outside while you put some clothes on. Oh, and you don't need to wake Larry."

"Do we hafta talk now?"

"I'm afraid so. Unless you want to make a terrible mistake." She hurried from the room, hoping he'd get up.

A few minutes later he stumbled out the front door. She put her fingers to her lips and gestured for him to follow. Sweeping her flashlight across the ground, she cut across the edge of the Common, then headed back toward Lilies of the Field. Before she got there, however, she turned into the woods and headed toward the lake.

The wind had picked up. She felt a storm brewing and hoped it didn't hit until she was done with this. He loomed next to her, a big, hulking shape.

"What's going on?"

"There's something you need to see."

"Couldn't I see it in the morning?"

"That'll be too late."

He swiped at a branch. "Shit. Does Kev know about this?"

"Kev doesn't want to know."

He stopped walking. "What do you mean by that?"

She kept her flashlight pointed at the ground. "I mean that he's not deliberately deceiving you. He's just ignored some things."

"Deceiving me? What the hell're you talking about?"

"I know you thought I was being silly today at lunch, but I was hoping you'd listen to me. Then we could have avoided this." She started walking again.

"Avoided what? You'd better tell me what's going on here, lady."

"I'll show you instead."

Eddie stumbled a few more times before they finally reached the water. The trees whipped in the wind, and she braced herself. "I hate being the one who has to show you this, but there's a . . . problem with the lake."

"What kind of problem?"

She slowly swept the flashlight beam along the edge of the water, just where it lapped the shore, until she found what she was looking for.

Dead fish floating in the water.

"What the hell . . . ?"

She played the light over the silver bellies of the fish before turning the beam back onto the bank. "Eddie, I'm so sorry. I know you have your heart set on a fishing camp, but the fish in this lake are dying."

"Dying?"

"We have an environmental disaster going on. Toxins are leaking into the water from a secret underground chemical dump. It'll cost millions to fix the problem, and the town doesn't have the money. Since the local economy depends on tourists, there's a big cover-up going on, and no one will publicly admit there's a problem."

"Fuck." He grabbed the flashlight and shone it back on the floating fish. Then he snapped it off. "I can't believe Kev would do this to me!"

This was the most glaring loophole in her plan, and she tried to overcome it with dramatic presentation. "He's in denial, Eddie. Terrible, terrible denial. This was his childhood home, his last link with his parents, and he simply can't face the fact that the lake is dying, so he's convinced himself it isn't happening."

"How does he explain the damn dead fish!"

A very good question, and she gave it her best shot. "He stays away from the water. It's so sad. His denial is so deep that—" She gripped his arm and went into full Susan Lucci. "Oh, Eddie, I know it's not fair to ask you to do this, but do you think . . . ? Could you just tell him you've changed your mind and not confront him about this? I swear he wasn't deliberately trying to deceive you, and it'll tear him apart if he thinks he's destroyed your friendship."

"Yeah, well, I'd say he has."

"He's not well, Eddie. It's a mental problem. As soon as we get back to Chicago, I'll make sure he gets psychotherapy."

"Shit." He sucked in his breath. "This is gonna blow the hell out of his passing game."

"I'll find a sports psychotherapist."

Eddie wasn't a complete fool, and he asked her about the underground dump. She expanded her story to include as many buzz words from *Erin Brockovich* as she could still remember and made up the rest. When she was done, she dug her fingernails into her palms and waited.

"You sure about all this?" he finally said.

"I wish I weren't."

He shuffled his feet and sighed. "Thanks, Maggie. I 'preciate it. You're all right."

She slowly released the breath she'd been holding. "You, too, Eddie. You, too."

The storm hit just after Molly collapsed in bed, but she was so tired she barely heard it. It wasn't until the next morning when a series of thuds on the front steps awakened her that she forced open her eyes. She blinked and looked at her clock. It was after nine! She'd forgotten to set her alarm, and no one had awakened her. Who'd fixed breakfast?

"Molly!"

Uh-oh . . .

Roo scampered into the room, and then Kevin appeared looking like a gorgeous storm cloud. So much for hoping the loopholes in her plan wouldn't come back to haunt her. Eddie must have confronted Kevin after all, and now there was going to be hell to pay.

She sat up in bed. Maybe she could distract him. "Just let me brush my teeth, soldier boy, and then I'll take you to paradise."

"Molly . . . " His voice sounded a low warning note, the same note she'd heard on Nick at Nite when Desi confronted Lucy. Molly had some 'splainin' to do.

"I have to pee!" She jumped up, flew past him to the bathroom, and shut the door.

The flat of his hand smacked the panel. "Come out here!"

"In a minute. Did you want something?"

"Yeah, I want something, all right. I want an explanation!"

"Oh?" She squeezed her eyes shut and waited for the worst.

"I want you to explain why there's a frickin' *tuna* in my lake!"

23

It's true. Guys don't think the same way girls do, and this can lead to trouble.

—"When Guys Won't Listen"
for *Chik*

Oh, boy . . . Molly stalled as long as she could—brushing her teeth, splashing water on her face, straightening her tank top, and retying the drawstring on her pajama bottoms. She half expected him to charge in after her, but apparently he didn't see the need, since the window had been painted shut and the only other way out was through him.

A bath was too much to hope for. Besides, it was way past time to face the music. She'd edged open the door and saw him leaning against the opposite wall ready to pounce. "Uh . . . what were you saying?"

He carved out the words with his teeth. "Would you care to explain why, when I walked down to the beach after breakfast this morning, I found a *dead tuna* floating in the lake?"

"A change in fish migration patterns?"

He grabbed her arm and pulled her toward the front room. Another bad sign. At least in the bedroom she'd have had a fighting chance.

"I seriously doubt that migration patterns are going to change enough for a saltwater fish to end up in a freshwater lake!" He pushed her down onto the couch.

She should have gone back to the lake last night and fished out the fish, but she'd assumed they'd stay where they were until they sank. They probably would have if it hadn't been for the storm.

Okay, enough messing around. Time for some righteous indignation. "Really, Kevin, just because I happen to be brighter than you doesn't mean I know everything about fish."

Probably not her best strategy, because his words bristled with splinters. "Are you going to look me in the eye and tell me you don't know anything about how a tuna got in that lake?"

"Well . . . "

"Or that you don't know why Eddie Dillard came up to me this morning and told me he wasn't going to buy the campground after all?"

"He did?"

"And what do you think he said to me before he drove away?"

"Just a guess: 'You duh man'?"

His eyebrows shot up and his voice grew as soft as an assassin's footsteps. "No, Molly, he didn't say that. What he said was 'Get some help, man!' "

She winced.

"Now what do you suppose he meant?"

"What was it he said again?" she croaked.

"Exactly what did you tell him?"

She fell back on the Calebow kids' technique. "Why do you think *I* told him something? There are lots of people here who could have said something to him—Troy, Amy, Charlotte Long. It's not fair, Kevin. Every time something happens around here, you blame me."

"And why do you think that might be?"

"I have no idea."

He leaned down, braced both his hands on her knees, and brought his face inches from hers. "Because I've got your number. And I've got all day."

"Yes, well, I don't." She licked her lips and studied his earlobe, perfect just like the rest of him, except for a small red tooth mark she was fairly sure she'd put there. "Who fixed breakfast this morning?"

"I did." He spoke softly, but the pressure on her knees didn't ease. He definitely wasn't letting her up. "Then Amy came in and helped me. Are you done stalling?"

"No . . . yes— I don't know!" She tried to move her legs, but they weren't going anywhere. "I didn't want you to sell the campground, that's all."

"Tell me something I don't know."

"Eddie Dillard is a tool."

"I know that, too." He stood up, but he didn't back away. "What else have you got?"

She tried to stand herself so she could let him have it, but she was pinned in by his body. It made her so agitated she wanted to scream. "If you know that, how could you have done this in the first place? How could you have stood there and let him talk about painting the cottages brown? About tearing down *this* cottage—the cottage you're standing in right now!—and then turning the B&B into a bait shop?"

"He could only do those things if I sold the campground to him."

"If you—" She whipped her legs around him and jumped up. "What are you saying? Omigod, Kevin, what do you mean?"

"First I want to hear about the tuna."

She gulped. The moment she'd conceived her plan, she'd known she'd have to tell him the truth. She'd just hoped it wouldn't be quite so soon. "All right." She backed away a few steps. "Yesterday I bought some fish at the market, and last night I put them in the lake, and then I woke up Eddie and took him to see them."

A pause. "And you told him *what* exactly?"

She made eye contact with his elbow and talked as fast as she could. "That an underground chemical dump was leaking into the lake and killing all the fish."

"An underground chemical dump?"

"Uh-huh."

"An underground chemical dump!"

She took another quick step backward. "Could we talk about something else?"

Oh, jeez, that made his eyes flash fourteen different shades of mad. "Eddie didn't happen to notice that some of those fish shouldn't have been in a freshwater lake?"

"It was dark, and I didn't let him have a really good look." Another quick step backward.

Countered by a quick step forward from him. "And how did you explain away my trying to sell him a fishing camp on a *contaminated lake*?"

Her nerves snapped. "Stop looking at me like that!"

"Like I might wrap my hands around your neck and squeeze?"

"Except you can't, because I'm your boss's sister."

"Which only means I need to come up with something that doesn't leave marks."

"Sex! There are couples who think that having sex when they get really angry with each other is a turn-on."

"And you know this how? Never mind, I'm going to take your word for it." He reached out and snared the front of her top.

"Uh . . . Kev . . . " She licked her lips and gazed up into those glittering green eyes.

He splayed his hand across her bottom. "I seriously suggest you don't call me that. And I seriously suggest you don't try to stop this either, because I really, *really* need to do something physical to you." He shoved himself against her. "And everything else I'm thinking about will put me in jail."

"O-okay. That's fair." As soon as she was naked, she'd let him know what else she'd said to Eddie.

But then his mouth crushed hers, and she stopped thinking altogether.

He didn't have the patience to take off his own clothes, but he stripped her, then slammed and locked the bedroom door in case any little Calebows decided to come visit their Auntie M.

"On that bed. Right now."

Oh, yes. As fast as she could get there.

"Open your legs."

Yes, sir.

"Wider."

She gave him a couple of inches.

"Don't make me have to ask you again."

She slid up her knees. It would never be like this for her again. Never again would she feel so absolutely safe with a dangerous man.

She heard the sound of his zipper. A rough growl. "How do you want it?"

"Oh, shut up." She reached out and opened her arms. "Shut up and come here."

Seconds later she felt his weight settling over her. He was still angry, she knew that, but it didn't stop him from touching her in all the places she loved to be touched.

His voice was low and husky, and his breath stirred a lock of hair near her ear. "You're making me crazy, you know that, don't you?"

She pressed her cheek to his hard jaw. "I know. I'm sorry."

His voice grew softer and tighter. "It can't—we can't keep . . . "

She bit her lip and held him tight. "I know that, too."

He might not understand that this was going to be the last time, but she did. He drove deep and high inside her, just the way he knew she liked. Her body arched. She found her rhythm and gave him every-thing. Just once more. Just this one last time.

Usually, when it was over, he drew her onto his chest, and they cud-dled and talked. Who'd been more magnificent, her or him? Who'd made the most noise? Why *Glamour* was superior to *Sports Illustrated*. But this morning they didn't play. Instead, Kevin turned away, and Molly slipped into the bathroom to clean up and dress.

The air was still damp from the storm, so she pulled a sweatshirt over her shorts and top. He was waiting on the screen porch, Roo at his feet. Steam curled from his coffee mug as he gazed out into the woods. She huddled deeper into the warmth of the sweatshirt. "Are you ready to hear the rest of it?"

"I guess I'd better be."

She made herself look at him. "I told Eddie that even though you were selling this place, you were still emotionally attached to it, and you couldn't stand the thought of something happening to the lake. Because of that, you were in denial about it being contaminated. I said you weren't deliberately deceiving him; you couldn't help it."

"And he believed this?"

"He's stupider than dirt, and I was pretty convincing." She trudged through the rest of it. "Then I said you had a mental problem—I'm really sorry about that—and I promised I'd make sure you got psychiatric help."

"A mental problem?"

"It was all I could come up with."

"Other than butting out of my business?" He slammed down his mug, sending coffee sloshing over the table.

"I couldn't do that."

"Why not? Who gave you permission to run my life?"

"No one. But . . . "

His temper had a long fuse, but now it fired. "What's *with* you and this place?"

"It's not me, Kevin, it's you! You've lost both your parents, and you're determined to keep Lilly at arm's length. You don't have any brothers and sisters—any extended family at all. Staying connected with your heritage is important, and this campground is all you have!"

"I don't care about my heritage! And, believe me, I have a lot more than this campground!"

"What I'm trying to say is—"

"I have millions of dollars I haven't been stupid enough to give away—let's start with that! I have cars, a luxury house, a stock portfolio that'll keep me smiling for a long time. And guess what else I have? I have a career that I wouldn't let an army of self-serving do-gooders steal from me."

She clenched her hands together. "What do you mean by that?"

"Explain something to me. Explain how you justify spending so much time minding my business instead of taking care of your own?"

"I do take care of it."

"When? For two weeks you've been plotting and scheming over this campground instead of putting your energy where it belongs. You have a career that's going down the toilet. When are you going to start fighting the good fight for your rabbit instead of lying down and playing dead?"

"I haven't done that! You don't know what you're talking about."

"You know what I think? I think your obsession with my life and this campground is just a way of distracting yourself from what you need to be doing with your own life."

How had he managed to turn the conversation? "You don't understand anything. *Daphne Takes a Tumble* is the first book on a new contract. They won't accept anything else from me until I revise it."

"You don't have any guts."

"That's not true! I did all I could to convince my editor she'd made a mistake, but Birdcage won't budge."

"Hannah told me about *Daphne Takes a Tumble*. She said it's your best book. Too bad she'll be the only kid who gets to read it." He gestured toward the notepad she'd left on the couch. "Then there's the new one you're working on. *Daphne Goes to Summer Camp*."

"How do you know about—"

"You're not the only sneak. I've read your draft. Other than some blatant unfairness to the badger, it looks like you've got another winner. But nobody can publish it unless you follow orders. And are you doing that? No. Are you even forcing the issue? No. Instead, you're letting yourself drift along in some never-never land where none of *your* troubles are real, only mine."

"You don't understand!"

"You're right about that. I never did understand quitters."

"That's not fair! I can't win. If I make the revisions, I've sold out and I'll hate myself. If I don't make them, the Daphne books are going to disappear. The publisher will never reprint the old ones, and they sure won't publish any new ones. No matter what I do, I'll lose, and losing's not an option."

"Losing isn't as bad as not fighting at all."

"Yes it is. The women in my family don't lose."

He gazed at her for a long time. "Unless I'm missing something, there's only one other woman in your family."

"And look what she did!" Agitation forced her to move. "Phoebe held on to the Stars when everybody in the world had written her off. She faced down all of her enemies—"

"Married one of them."

"—and beat them at their own game. Those men thought she was a bimbo and wrote her off. She was never supposed to have ended up with the Stars, but she did."

"Everybody in the football world admires her for it. So what does this have to do with you?"

She turned away. He already knew, and he wasn't going to make her say it.

"Come on, Molly! I want to hear those whiny words come out of your mouth so I can have a big cry."

"Go to hell!"

"Okay, I'll say it for you. You won't fight for your books because you might fail, and you're so competitive with your sister that you can't risk that."

"I'm not competitive with Phoebe. I love her!"

"I don't doubt that. But your sister is one of the most powerful women in professional sports, and you're a screw-up."

"I am not!"

"Then stop acting like one."

"You don't understand."

"I'm starting to understand a lot." He circled his hand over the back of one of the farmhouse chairs. "As a matter of fact, I think I've finally got it."

"Got what? Never mind, I don't want to know." She headed for the kitchen, but he moved in front of her before she could get there.

"That thing with the fire alarm. Dan talks about what a quiet, serious kid you were. The good grades you got, all the awards you earned. You've spent your whole life trying to be perfect, haven't you? Getting to the top of the honor roll, collecting good-conduct medals like other kids collect baseball cards. But then something happens. Out of nowhere the pressure gets to you, and you flip out. You pull a fire alarm, you give away your money, you jump in bed with a total stranger!" He shook his head. "I can't believe I didn't see it right away. I can't believe nobody else sees it."

"Sees what?"

"Who you really are."

"Like you'd know."

"All that perfection. It's not in your nature."

"What are you talking about?"

"I'm talking about the person you'd have been if you'd grown up in a normal family."

She didn't know what he was going to say, but she knew he believed it, and she suddenly wanted to run away.

He loomed in the door between her and escape. "Don't you see? Your nature was to be the class clown, the girl who ditched school so she could smoke pot with her boyfriend and make out in the backseat of his car."

"What?"

"The girl most likely to skip college and—and run off to Vegas to parade around in a G-string."

"A G-string! That's the most—"

"You're not Bert Somerville's daughter." He let out a bark of rueful laughter. "Damn! You're your mother's daughter. And everybody's been too blind to see it."

She sagged down on the glider. This was silly. The mental meanderings of someone who'd spent too much time inside an MRI machine. He was trying to take everything she understood about who she was and turn it topsy-turvy. "You have no idea what you're—"

Just like that, she ran out of air.

"What you're—" She tried to say the rest, but she couldn't because deep inside her something finally clicked into place.

The class clown . . . The girl most likely to ditch school . . .

"It's not only that you're afraid to take a risk because you're competing with Phoebe. You're afraid to take a risk because you're still living with the illusion that you have to be perfect. And, Molly, trust me on this, being perfect isn't in your nature."

She needed to think, but she couldn't do it under those watchful green eyes. "I'm not— I don't even recognize this person you're talking about."

"Give it a few seconds, and I bet you will."

It was too much. *He* was the bonehead, not her. "You're just trying to distract me from pointing out everything that's screwed up about you."

"There's nothing screwed up about me. Or at least there wasn't until I met you."

"Is that right?" She told herself to shut up, this wasn't the time, but everything she'd been thinking and trying not to say spilled out. "What about the fact that you're afraid to make any kind of emotional connection?"

"If this is about Lilly . . . "

"Oh, no. That's way too easy. Even someone as obtuse as you should be able to figure that out. Why don't we look at something more complicated?"

"Why don't we not?"

"Isn't it a little weird that you're thirty-three years old, you're rich, moderately intelligent, you look like a Greek god, and you're definitely heterosexual. But what's wrong with this picture? Oh, yeah, I remember . . . You've never had a single long-term relationship with a woman."

"Aw, for the . . . " He sprawled down at the table.

"What's with that anyway?"

"How do you even know it's true?"

"Team gossip, the newspapers, that article about us in *People*. If you ever did have a long-term relationship, it must have been in junior high. Lots of women move through your life, but none of them gets to stay around for long."

"There's one of them who's been around way too long!"

"And look at what kind of women you choose." She splayed her hands on the table. "Do you choose smart women who might have a chance of holding your interest? Or respectable women who share at least a few of your—and don't even *think* about arguing with me about this—a few of your rock-bottom-conservative values? Well, surprise, surprise. None of the above."

"Here we go with the foreign women again. I swear, you're obsessed."

"Okay, let's leave them out of it and look at the American women the PK dates. Party girls who wear too much makeup and not enough clothes. Girls who leave drool marks on your shirts and haven't seen the inside of a classroom since they flunked dummy math!"

"You're exaggerating."

"Don't you see, Kevin? You deliberately choose women you're predestined not to be able to have a real relationship with."

"So what? I want to focus on my career, not jump through hoops trying to make some woman happy. Besides, I'm only thirty-three. I'm not ready to settle down."

"What you're not ready to do is grow up."

"Me?"

"And then there's Lilly."

"Here we go . . ."

"She's terrific. Even though you've done everything you can to keep her at arm's length, she's sticking around, waiting for you to come to your senses. You've got everything to gain and nothing to lose with her, but you won't give her even a little corner of your life. Instead, you act like a petulant teenager. Don't you see? In your own way you're as freaked by your upbringing as I am about mine."

"No I'm not."

"My scars are easier to understand. I had no mother and an abusive father, while you had two loving parents. But they were so different from you that you never felt connected to them, and you still feel guilty about it. Most people could push it aside and move on, but most people aren't as sensitive as you."

He sprang from the chair. "That's bullshit! I'm as tough as they come, lady, and don't you forget it."

"Yeah, you're tough on the outside, but on the inside you're so soft you squish, and you're every bit as scared of screwing up your life as I am."

"You don't know anything!"

"I know that there's not another man in a thousand who would have felt honor-bound to marry the crazy woman who attacked him in his sleep, even if she was related to the boss. Dan and Phoebe might have held a shotgun to your head, but all you had to do was place the blame where it belonged. Not only wouldn't you do that, but you made me swear not to either." She pulled her cold hands into the cuffs of the sweatshirt. "Then there's the way you behaved when I was miscarrying."

"Anybody would have—"

"No, anybody wouldn't have, but you want to believe that because you're afraid of any kind of emotion that doesn't fit between a pair of goalposts."

"That's so stupid!"

"Off the field you know something's missing, but you're afraid to go looking for it because, in your typically neurotic and immature fashion, you believe something's wrong inside you that'll keep you from finding it. You couldn't connect with your own parents, so how can you ever make a lasting connection with anyone else? It's easier to focus on winning football games."

"Lasting connection? Wait a minute! What are we really talking about here?"

"We're talking about the fact that it's time for you to grow up and take some real risks."

"I don't think so. I think there's a hidden agenda behind all this mumbo jumbo."

Until that moment she hadn't thought so, but he sometimes saw things before she did. Now she realized he was right, but it was too late. She felt sick.

"I think you're talking about a lasting connection between us," he said.

"Ha!"

"Is that what you want, Molly? Are you angling to make this a real marriage?"

"With an emotional twelve-year-old? A man who can barely be civil to his only blood relative? I'm not that self-destructive."

"Aren't you?"

"What do you want me to say? That I've fallen in love with you?" She'd meant to be scathing, but she saw by his thunderstruck expression that he'd recognized the truth.

Her legs felt rubbery. She sat on the edge of the glider and tried to think of a way out, but she was too emotionally battered. And what was the point when he'd see through it anyway? She lifted her head. "So what? I know a one-way street when I run into it, and I'm not stupid enough to drive down it in the wrong direction."

She hated his shock.

"You are in love with me."

Her mouth was dry. Roo rubbed against her ankles and whimpered. She wanted to say this was just another variation on her crush, but she couldn't. "Big deal," she managed. "If you think I'm going to cry all over your chest because you don't feel the same way, you're wrong. I don't beg for anybody's love."

"Molly . . . "

She hated the pity she heard in his voice. Once again, she hadn't measured up. She hadn't been smart enough or pretty enough or special enough for a man to love.

Stop!

A terrible anger filled her, and this time it wasn't directed at him. She was sick of her own insecurities. She'd accused him of needing to grow up, but he wasn't the only one. There wasn't anything wrong with her, and she couldn't keep living her life as if there were. If he didn't love her in return, that was his loss.

She shot up from the glider. "I'm leaving today with Phoebe and Dan. Me and my broken heart are skulking back to Chicago, and you know what? We'll both survive just fine."

"Molly, you can't—"

"Stop right now, before your conscience gets cranked up. You're not responsible for my feelings, okay? This isn't your fault, and you don't have to fix it. It's just one of those things that happened."

"But . . . I'm sorry. I—"

"Shut up." She said it quietly because she didn't want to leave in anger. She found herself moving toward him, watched her hand go to his cheek. She loved the feel of his skin, loved who he was despite his all-too-human frailties. "You're a good man, Charlie Brown, and I wish you all the best."

"Molly, I don't—"

"Hey, no begging me to stay, okay?" She managed a smile and stepped away. "All good things come to an end, and that's where we are." She made her way to the door. "Come on, Roo. Let's find Phoebe."

It's a bunny-eat-bunny world.
                                    —Anonymous children's book editor

Only the presence of the kids made the trip back to Chicago bear-able. It had always been difficult for Molly to hide her feelings from her sister, but this time she had to. She couldn't taint Phoebe and Dan's relationship with Kevin any further.

Her condo was musty from having been closed up for nearly three weeks and even dustier than when she'd left. Her hands itched to start scrubbing and polishing, but cleaning chores would have to wait until tomorrow. With Roo scampering ahead, she carried her suitcases to the sleeping loft, then forced herself back down the steps to her desk and the black plastic crate that held her files.

Sitting cross-legged on the floor, she pulled out her last contract with Birdcage and flipped through the pages.

Just as she'd thought.

She gazed up at the windows that stretched all the way to the ceiling, studied the mellowed brick walls and cozy kitchen, watched the play of light on the hardwood floors. *Home.*

Two miserable weeks later Molly stepped from the elevator onto the ninth floor of the Michigan Avenue office building that held the offices of Birdcage Press. She retied the cardigan around the waist of her red-and-white checked gingham sheath and made her way down the corridor to Helen Kennedy Schott's office. Molly had long ago passed the point where she could turn back, and she only hoped the concealer she'd dabbed under her eyes hid the shadows.

Helen rose to greet her from behind a desk cluttered with manuscripts, galleys, and book covers. Even though the weather was muggy, she was dressed in her customary editorial black. Her short gray hair lay neatly against her head, and although she wore no makeup, her nails shone with slick crimson polish. "Molly, it's wonderful to see you again. I'm so glad you finally called. I'd nearly given up trying to get hold of you."

"It's good to see you," Molly replied politely, because no matter what Kevin said about her, she was, *by nature,* a polite person.

A strip of the Chicago River was visible through the office window, but the colorful display of children's books on the shelves drew Molly's attention. As Helen chatted about the new marketing manager, Molly spotted the bright slender spines of the first five Daphne books. Knowing that *Daphne Takes a Tumble* would never join them should have felt like a stab in the heart, but that part of her was too numb right now to feel anything more.

"I'm so glad we're finally having this meeting," Helen said. "We have lots to talk about."

"Not so much." Molly couldn't prolong this. She opened her purse, drew out a white business envelope, and set it on the desk. "This is a check reimbursing Birdcage for the first half of the advance you paid for *Daphne Takes a Tumble.*"

Helen looked stunned. "We don't want the advance back. We want to publish the book."

"I'm afraid you won't be able to. I'm not making the revisions."

"Molly, I know you haven't been happy with us, and it's time to sort this out. From the beginning we've only wanted what was best for your career."

"I only want what's best for my readers."

"We do, too. Please try to understand. Authors tend to look at a project only from their perspective, but a publisher has to look at the larger picture, including our relationship with the press and the community. We felt we had no choice."

"Everybody has a choice, and an hour ago I exercised mine."

"What do you mean?"

"I published *Daphne Takes a Tumble* myself. The original version."

"You published it?" Helen's eyebrows shot up. "What are you talking about?"

"I published it on the Internet."

Helen erupted from her chair. "You can't do that! We have a contract!"

"If you check the fine print, you'll see that I retain the electronic rights to all my books."

Helen looked stunned. The larger publishing houses had plugged this hole in their contracts, but some of the smaller presses like Birdcage hadn't gotten around to it. "I can't believe you did this."

"Now any child who wants to read *Daphne Takes a Tumble* and see the original illustrations will be able to do it." Molly had planned a big speech, complete with references to book burning and the First Amendment, but she no longer had the energy. Pushing the check forward, she rose from her chair and walked out.

"Molly, wait!"

She'd done what she needed to, and she didn't stop. As she headed for her car, she tried to feel triumphant, but she mainly felt drained. A college friend had helped her set up the Web site. In addition to the text and drawings for *Daphne Takes a Tumble*, Molly had included a page that listed some of the books various organizations had tried to keep out of children's hands over the years because of their content or illustrations. The list included *Little Red Riding Hood*, all the Harry Potter books, Madeleine L'Engle's *A Wrinkle in Time*, *Harriet the Spy*, *Tom Sawyer*, *Huckleberry Finn*, as well as the books of Judy Blume, Maurice Sendak, the Brothers Grimm, and Anne Frank's *Diary of a Young Girl*. At the end of the list, Molly had added *Daphne Takes a Tumble*. She wasn't Anne Frank, but she felt better being in such wonderful company. She only wished she could call Kevin and tell him that she'd finally fought for her bunny.

She made a few stops to pick up supplies, then swung onto Lake Shore Drive and headed north to Evanston. The traffic was light, and it didn't take her nearly long enough to get to the moldy old brownstone where she now lived. She hated her second-floor apartment with its view of the Dumpster behind a Thai restaurant, but it was the only place she could afford that would take a dog.

She tried not to think about her little condo, where strangers had already moved in. Evanston didn't have many loft conversions available, and the building had a waiting list of people anxious to buy, so she'd known it would sell quickly. Even so, she hadn't been prepared for it to go in less than twenty-four hours. The new owners had paid her a premium to sublease while they waited for the final paperwork, so she'd had to scramble to find a rental, and here she was in this dismal building. But she had the money to repay her advance and settle her bills.

She parked on the street two blocks away because her Slytherin landlord charged seventy dollars a month for a parking spot in the lot attached to the building. As she climbed the worn steps to her apartment, the El tracks shrieked just outside the windows. Roo greeted her at the door, then scampered across the worn linoleum and began to bark at the sink.

"Not again."

The apartment was so small that she had no place for her books, and she crawled over the packing boxes on her way to the kitchen sink. She gingerly opened the door, peered inside, and shuddered. Another mouse quivered in her Hav-A-Heart trap. The third one she'd caught, and she'd lived here for only a few days.

Maybe she could get another *Chik* article out of this—"Why Guys Who Hate Small Animals Aren't Always Bad News." Her cooking piece had just gone into the mail. At first she'd called it "Breakfasts That Won't Make Him Puke: Scramble His Brains with Your Eggs." Just before she'd slipped it into the envelope, she'd come to her senses and substituted "Early-Morning Turn-ons."

She was writing every day. As devastated as she was about everything, she hadn't given up and gone to bed the way she'd done after her miscarriage. Instead, she was facing her pain and doing her best to live through it. But her heart had never felt emptier.

She missed Kevin so much. Each night she lay in bed staring at the ceiling and remembering how his arms had felt around her. But it had been so much more than sex. He'd understood her better than she'd understood herself, and he'd been her soul mate in every way but the one that counted. He didn't love her.

With a sigh that came from the bottom of her being, she set aside her purse, slipped on the gardening gloves she'd bought along with the trap, and warily reached under the sink for the handle on the small cage. At least her bunny was hopping free and happy in cyberspace. Which was more than she could say about the rodent.

She let out a squeak as the frightened mouse started scampering around the cage. "Please don't do that. Just be quiet, and I promise I'll have you in the park before you know it." Where was a man when you needed one?

Her heart contracted in another achy spasm. The couple Kevin had hired to take over at the campground would be in place by now, so he was probably back in town partying with the international set. *Please, God, don't let him be sleeping with any of them. Not yet.*

Lilly had left several messages on her answering machine wanting to know if Molly was all right, but she still hadn't returned them. What could she say? That she'd had to sell her condo? That she'd lost her publisher? That her heart had suffered a permanent break? At least she could afford an attorney now, so she had a shot at being able to get out of her contract and sell her next Daphne book to another publisher.

She held the cage as far away as she could and retrieved her keys. She was on her way to the door when the buzzer sounded. The mouse had given her the heebie-jeebies, and she nearly jumped out of her skin.

"Just a minute."

Still holding the cage at arm's length, she stepped around another book box and opened the door.

Helen charged inside. "Molly, you ran out before we could talk. Oh, God!"

"Helen, meet Mickey."

Helen pressed her hand to her heart, the color bleaching from her face. "A pet?"

"Not exactly." Molly set the cage on a packing box, but Roo didn't like that. "Quiet, pest! I'm afraid this isn't the best time for a visit, Helen. I have to go to the park."

"You're taking it on an outing?"

"Releasing it."

"I'll—I'll come with you."

Molly should have enjoyed seeing her sophisticated former editor so discomposed, but the mouse had discomposed her, too. With the cage held far from her body, she led the way outside and began winding through the back alleys of downtown Evanston toward the park by the lake. Helen, in her black suit and heels, wasn't dressed for either the heat or stumbling around potholes, but Molly hadn't invited her to come along, so she refused to take pity.

"I didn't know you'd moved," Helen called from behind. "Luckily, I ran into one of your neighbors, and he gave me your new address. C-couldn't you release it somewhere closer?"

"I don't want him to find his way back."

"Or use a more permanent trap?"

"Absolutely not."

Although it was a weekday, the park was filled with bicyclists, college students on Rollerblades, and children. Molly found a grassy area and set the cage down, then hesitantly reached for the latch. As soon as she sprang it, Mickey made his leap for freedom.

Straight toward Helen.

Her editor gave a strangled cry and leaped up on a picnic bench. Mickey disappeared into the shrubbery.

"Beastly things." Helen sagged down on the tabletop.

Molly was feeling a little wobbly-kneed, too, so she sat on the bench. Beyond the edge of the park, Lake Michigan stretched to the horizon. She gazed out and thought of a smaller lake with a cliff for diving.

Helen pulled a tissue from her purse and dabbed at her forehead. "There's just something about a mouse."

There were no mice in Nightingale Woods. Molly'd have to add one if she ever found a new publisher.

She gazed at her old editor. "If you've come here to threaten me with a lawsuit, you're not going to get much."

"Why would we want to sue our favorite author?" Helen pulled out the envelope that held Molly's check and set it on the bench. "I'm giving this back. And when you look inside, you'll see a second check for the remainder of your advance. Really, Molly, you should have told me how strongly you felt about the revisions. I'd never have asked you to make them."

Molly didn't even try to respond to that piece of Slytherin crapola. Nor did she pick up the envelope.

Helen's tone grew more effusive. "We're going to publish *Daphne Takes a Tumble* in its original version. I'm putting it on the winter schedule so we have time to line up promotion. We're planning an extensive marketing campaign, with full-page ads in all the big parenting magazines, and we're sending you on a book tour."

Molly wondered if the sun had gotten to her. "*Daphne Takes a Tumble* is already available on the Internet."

"We'd like you to remove it, but we'll leave the final decision up to you. Even if you decide to keep the Web site, we believe most parents will still want to buy the actual book to add to their children's collections."

Molly couldn't imagine how she'd been so magically transformed from a minor author to a major one. "I'm afraid you'll need to do better than this, Helen."

"We're prepared to renegotiate your contract. I'm sure you'll be pleased with the terms."

Molly had been asking for an explanation, not for more money, but she somehow got in touch with her inner tycoon. "You'll have to deal with my new agent about that."

"Of course."

Molly had no agent, new or old. Her career had been so small that she hadn't needed one, but something had definitely changed. "Tell me what's happened, Helen."

"It was the publicity. The new sales figures just came out two days ago. Between the press coverage of your marriage and the SKIFSA stories, your sales have soared."

"But I was married in February, and SKIFSA went after me in April. You're just noticing?"

"We spotted the first rise in March and another in April. But the numbers weren't all that significant until we got our end-of-the-month report for May. And the preliminary June figures are even better."

Molly decided it was a good thing she was sitting down, because her legs would never have held her. "But the publicity had died down. Why are the numbers shooting up now?"

"That's what we wanted to find out, so we've spent some time on the phones taking with booksellers. They're telling us that adults originally bought a Daphne book out of curiosity—either they'd heard about your marriage or they wanted to see what SKIFSA was so upset about. But once they took the book home, their kids fell in love with the characters, and now they're coming back to the stores and buying the whole series."

Molly was stunned. "I can't believe this."

"The kids are showing the books to their friends. We're hearing that even parents who've supported SKIFSA's other boycotts are buying the Daphne books."

"I'm having a hard time taking this in."

"I understand." Helen crossed her legs and smiled. "After all these years you're finally an overnight success. Congratulations, Molly."

Janice and Paul Hubert were the perfect couple to run a bed-and-breakfast. Mrs. Hubert's eggs were never cold, and none of her cookies burned on the bottom. Mr. Hubert actually enjoyed unstopping toilets and could talk to the guests for hours without getting bored. Kevin fired them after a week and a half.

"Need some help?"

He pulled his head out of the refrigerator and saw Lilly standing just inside the kitchen door. It was eleven at night, two weeks and one day since Molly had left. It was also four days since he'd fired the Huberts, and everything had turned to crap.

Training camp started in a couple of weeks, and he wasn't ready. He knew he should tell Lilly that he was glad she'd stayed to help out, but he hadn't gotten around to it, and it made him feel guilty. There'd been something sad about her ever since Liam Jenner had stopped showing up for breakfast. Once he'd even tried to mention it, but he'd been clumsy, and she'd pretended not to understand.

"I'm looking for rapid-rise yeast. Amy left a note that she might need some. What the hell is rapid-rise yeast?"

"I have no idea," she replied. "My baking is pretty much limited to box mixes."

"Yeah. Screw it." He shut the door.

"Missing the Huberts?"

"No. Only the way she cooked and the way he took care of everything."

"Ah." She gazed at him, amusement temporarily overriding her unhappiness.

"I didn't like how she treated the kids," he muttered. "And he was making Troy nuts. Who cares if the grass gets mowed clockwise or counterclockwise?"

"She didn't exactly ignore the kids. She just didn't pass out cookies to every scamp who showed up at the kitchen door like Molly did."

"That old witch shooed them off like they were cockroaches. And forget about taking a few minutes to tell the kids a story. Is that too much to ask? If a kid wants to hear a story, don't you think she could put down her damn Lysol bottle long enough to tell 'em a story?"

"I never heard any of the kids actually ask Mrs. Hubert to tell them a story."

"They sure as hell asked Molly!"

"True."

"What's that supposed to mean?"

"Nothing."

Kevin opened the lid on the cookie jar, but closed it again when he remembered the ones inside were store bought. He reached into the refrigerator for a beer instead. "Her husband was even worse."

"When I heard him tell the kids not to play soccer on the Common because they were ruining the grass, I figured he might be doomed."

"Slytherin."

"The B&B guests did love the Huberts, though," she pointed out.

"That's because they don't have kids here like the cottage people do."

He offered her a beer, but she shook her head and got a water tumbler from the cupboard instead. "I'm glad the O'Brians are staying for another week," she said, "but I miss Cody and the Kramer girls. Still, the new kids are cute. I saw you bought more bikes."

"I forgot about the rug rats. We needed some Big Wheels."

"The older kids all seem to be enjoying the basketball hoop, and you did the right thing hiring a lifeguard."

"Some of the parents are a little too casual." He carried his beer over to the kitchen table, took a seat, then hesitated. But he'd already put this off long enough. "I really appreciate the way you've been helping out."

"I don't mind, but I do miss Molly. Everything's more fun when she's around."

He felt himself growing defensive. "I don't think so. We've had lots of fun without her."

"No, we haven't. The O'Brian boys keep complaining, the old folks miss her, and you've been grouchy and unreasonable." She leaned against the sink. "Kevin, it's been two weeks. Don't you think it's time to go after her? Amy and Troy and I can take care of the place for a few days."

Didn't she realize he'd already thought about this from a hundred different angles? There was nothing he wanted more, but he couldn't go after her, not unless he wanted to settle down forever as a married man, and that was something he couldn't do. "It wouldn't be fair."

"Fair to whom?"

He poked at the label on the bottle with his thumbnail. "She told me . . . She has feelings."

"I see. And you don't?"

He had more feelings than he knew what to do with, but none of them were going to make him lose sight of what was most important.

"Maybe in five or six years things will be different, but I don't have time right now for anything but my career. And let's be realistic—can you see Molly and me together long-term?"

"Without any trouble."

"Come on!" He shot up from his chair. "I'm a jock! I love being active, and she hates sports."

"For someone who hates sports, she's an excellent athlete."

"She's okay, I guess."

"She swims beautifully and dives like a champ."

"That's just from summer camp."

"She plays an excellent game of softball."

"Summer camp."

"She knows everything about football."

"That's only because—"

"She plays soccer."

"Just with Tess."

"She's studied martial arts."

He'd forgotten about that kung fu move she'd put on him last winter.

"And she told me she'd played on her high school tennis team."

"There you go. I hate tennis."

"Probably because you're no good at it."

How did Lilly know that?

Lilly's smile looked dangerously sympathetic. "I'd say you're going to have a hard time finding a woman who's as athletic and adventurous as Molly Somerville."

"I'll bet she wouldn't go skydiving."

"I'll bet she would."

Even to his own ears he sounded sulky. And Lilly was right about the skydiving. He could almost hear the sound of Molly's screams when he pushed her out of the plane. But he knew she'd love it as soon as her chute popped.

He still felt queasy about her falling in love with him. And angry, too. This had been temporary right from the beginning, so it wasn't as if he'd led her on. And he sure hadn't made any promises. Hell, half the time he'd barely been civil.

It was the sex. Everything had been fine up until then. If he'd kept his pants zipped and his hands to himself, she'd have been fine, but he hadn't been able to do that, not when they were together day after day. And who could blame him?

He thought of the way she laughed. What man wouldn't want to feel that laughter under his lips? And those blue-gray eyes with their wicked tilt were a deliberate sexual challenge. How could he have thought about anything except making love when they were turned his way?

But Molly knew the rules, and great sex wasn't a promise, not in this day and age. All that crap she'd handed out about his not making emotional connections couldn't have been more wrong. He had connections, all right. Important ones. He had Cal and Jane Bonner.

Whom he hadn't talked to in weeks.

He gazed at Lilly. Maybe because it was late and his defenses were down, he found himself telling her more than he intended. "Molly has some opinions about me I don't share."

"What kinds of opinions?"

"She thinks . . . " He set down his beer bottle. "She says I'm emotionally shallow."

"You are not!" Lilly's eyes flashed. "What a terrible thing to say!"

"Yeah, but the thing is—"

"You're a very complicated man. My God, if you were shallow, you'd have gotten rid of me right away."

"I tried—"

"You'd have given me a few pats on the shoulder and promised to send me a Christmas card. I'd have been satisfied and driven off into the sunset. But you're too emotionally honest to do that, which is why my being here has been so painful for you."

"That's nice of you to say, but—"

"Oh, Kevin . . . you mustn't ever think of yourself as shallow. I love Molly, but if I ever hear her say anything like that about you, she and I are going to have words."

Kevin wanted to laugh, but his eyes were starting to sting, and his feet were moving, and the next thing he knew, his arms just opened up.

Leave it to a man's mother to come to his defense when the chips were down, even if he didn't deserve it.

He gave her a fierce, possessive hug. She made a sound that reminded him of the mew of a newborn kitten.

He hugged her closer. "There are some things I've been wanting to ask you."

A shaky sob against his chest.

He cleared his throat. "Did you ever have to take music lessons and stink at the piano?"

"Oh, Kevin . . . I still don't know one note from another."

"And do you ever get a rash around your mouth when you eat tomatoes?"

Her grip on him tightened. "If I have too many."

"And what about sweet potatoes?" He heard a hiccuped sob. "Everybody likes them but me, so I wondered . . . " He stopped because it was getting hard for him to speak. At the same time, pieces inside him that had never quite fit began to come together.

For a while they simply held each other. Finally they began to talk, trying to catch up on three decades in one night, stumbling over their words as they filled in the blanks. By unspoken consent they avoided only two topics: Molly and Liam Jenner.

At three in the morning, when they finally parted at the top of the steps, Lilly stroked his cheek. "Good night, sweetheart."

"Good night—" *Good night, Mother.* That's what he wanted to say, but it felt like a betrayal of Maida Tucker, and he couldn't do that. Maida might not have been the mother of his dreams, but she'd loved him with all her heart, and he'd loved her right back. He smiled. "Good night, Lilly Mom."

The waterworks really opened up then. "Oh, Kevin . . . Kevin, my sweet little boy."

He drifted off to sleep with a smile on his lips.

When the alarm forced him out of bed a few hours later to start breakfast, he thought about the night before and the fact that Lilly would be a permanent part of his life now. It felt good. Exactly right.

But nothing else did.

As he made his way down to the gray, empty kitchen, he told himself there was no reason to feel guilty about Molly, but that didn't seem to matter to his conscience. Until he figured out some way to make amends, he'd never be able to stop thinking about her.

Then it came to him. The perfect solution.

Molly stared at Kevin's attorney. "He's giving me the campground?"

The attorney shifted his weight closer to the center of the packing box that held Molly's computer. "He called me first thing yesterday morning. I'm finalizing the paperwork now."

"I don't want it! I'm not taking anything from him."

"He must have known you'd react that way, because he said to tell you if you refused, he'd let Eddie Dillard bulldoze the place. I don't think he was kidding."

She wanted to scream, but it wasn't the attorney's fault that Kevin was high-handed and manipulative, so she controlled her temper. "Is there anything to prevent me from giving the campground away?"

"No."

"All right, I'll accept. And then I'm giving it away."

"I don't think he'll be too happy about that."

"Hand him a box of tissues."

The attorney was young, and he gave her a halfway-flirtatious smile, then gathered up his briefcase and made his way through the furniture to the door. In deference to the July heat, he wasn't wearing a suit coat, but her apartment didn't have air conditioning, and there was a damp spot on his back. "You might want to get up there fairly soon. Kevin's left, and there's no one in charge."

"I'm sure there is. He hired someone to take over."

"They didn't seem to work out."

Molly wasn't a swearing person, but she could barely hold back a big one. She'd had only forty-eight hours to get used to being a successful children's book author, and now this.

As soon as the attorney left, she crawled over the couch to retrieve her phone and call her new agent, the best contract negotiator in town. "Phoeb, it's me."

"Hey, big-time author! Talks are going well, but I'm still not satisfied with the up-front money they're offering."

She heard the relish in her sister's voice. "Just don't bankrupt them."

"It's so tempting."

They chatted about the negotiations for a few minutes before Molly got to the point, doing her best to say it without choking. "Kevin's just done the sweetest thing."

"Walked blindfolded in front of speeding traffic?"

"Don't be like that, Phoebe." She was definitely going to strangle on this. "He's a great guy. As a matter of fact, he's given me the campground as a surprise."

"You're kidding."

Molly gripped the receiver tighter. "He knows how much I love it there."

"I understand that, but . . . "

"I'm going to drive up tomorrow. I'm not sure how long I'll stay."

"At least this will get you out of that fleabag apartment until we finish negotiating your contract. I suppose I should be grateful."

It had been humiliating telling Phoebe that she'd been forced to sell her condo. To her sister's credit, she hadn't offered to bail Molly out, but that didn't mean she'd kept quiet.

Molly got off the phone as soon as she could and glanced over at Roo, who was trying to keep cool under the kitchen table. "Go ahead and say it. My timing sucks. If I'd waited two weeks, we'd still be in our old place basking in air-conditioning."

It might have been her imagination but Roo looked censorious. The traitor missed Kevin.

"Let's get our chores done, pal. First thing tomorrow we're taking off for the North Woods."

Roo perked up.

"Don't get too excited, because we're not staying. I meant it, Roo, I'm giving the place away!"

Except she wouldn't. She kicked a dish box aside, wishing it were Kevin's head. He'd done this out of guilt. This was his way of trying to make it up to her because she'd fallen in love with him and he didn't love her back.

A great big pity present.

25

Daphne wasn't speaking to Benny, and Benny didn't care, and Melissa couldn't find her movie-star sunglasses, and it had started to rain. Everything was a big mess!
—*Daphne Goes to Summer Camp*

Lilly stopped just inside the B&B's kitchen door. Molly had fallen asleep at the table. Her head rested on her arm, her hand lay by her sketch pad, and her hair spilled across the old oak tabletop like over-turned syrup. How could Lilly ever have believed she was a dilettante?

Since Molly had returned to the campground ten days ago, she'd finished the illustrations for *Daphne Goes to Summer Camp*, started a new book, and written an article for *Chik*, all that in addition to cooking and tending to guests. She couldn't relax, even though she'd told Lilly her new contract had finally given her financial stability. Lilly knew she was trying not to dwell on Kevin and understood her quiet suffering. She could have strangled her son.

Molly stirred and blinked, then looked up and smiled. There were shadows under her eyes. They probably matched the shadows under Lilly's own. "Have a nice walk?"

"I did."

She sat up and tucked her hair behind her ears. "Liam was here."

Lilly's heart skipped a beat. Other than catching a glimpse of him in town a few days after he'd issued his ultimatum, she hadn't seen him in weeks. Instead of growing easier, their separation had become more painful.

"He brought something for you," Molly said. "I had him put it in your room."

"What is it?"

"You probably should see for yourself." She picked up a pen that had fallen to the floor, then began to fiddle with it. "He asked me to tell you good-bye."

Lilly felt chilled, even though the kitchen was warm. "He's leaving?"

"Today. He's going to live in Mexico for a while. He wants to experiment with the light."

She shouldn't be shocked. Had she expected him to sit around waiting for her to change her mind? Anyone who understood Liam Jenner's art knew he was fundamentally a man of action. "I see."

Molly rose and gave her a sympathetic look. "You've screwed up so bad."

"So badly," she retorted, in one of those leftover reflexes from life with Craig.

"Not that I could survive without you, but, with Kevin gone, why are you still here?"

Lilly had made plans to meet Kevin in Chicago soon. Neither of them wanted to keep their relationship a secret, and Kevin had already flown to North Carolina to share the news with his friends, the Bonners. He'd also told Cal's brothers, their wives, and the guy sitting next to him on the plane, according to their last phone call.

Lilly yearned to see him again, but she couldn't bring herself to leave the campground yet. She told herself she was staying because of Molly. "I'm hanging around to help you out, you ungrateful little twit."

Molly carried her water glass to the sink. "Other than that."

"Because it's peaceful here, and I hate L.A."

"Or maybe because you can't make yourself walk away from Liam, even though you've treated him like crap and you don't deserve him."

"If you think he's so wonderful, take him yourself. You have no idea what it's like being married to a controlling man."

"Like you couldn't have him eating out of your hand if you wanted."

"Don't you take that tone of voice with me, young lady."

"You're such a dork." Molly smiled. "Go upstairs and see what he left you."

Lilly tried to sweep from the kitchen in a diva's huff, but she knew that Molly wasn't buying it. Her son's wife had the same kind of open, honest charm as Mallory. Why couldn't Kevin see what he'd turned his back on?

And what about the man she'd turned her back on? She still couldn't work on her quilt. All she could see now when she looked at it were scraps of fabric. There were no more surges of creative energy, no more glimpses of the answers to life's mysteries.

She made her way past the second-floor landing to the narrower flight of stairs that led to the attic. Kevin had tried to get her to move into one of the larger rooms, but Lilly liked it up here.

As she slipped inside, she saw a large canvas, taller than it was wide, leaning against the end of her bed. Even though it was wrapped in brown paper, she knew exactly what it was. The Madonna she'd admired so much that afternoon in his studio. She fell to her knees on the braided rug and, holding her breath, pulled away the paper.

But it wasn't the Madonna at all. It was the painting Liam had done of her.

A sob rose in her chest. She pressed her fingers to her mouth and scrambled back. He'd been brutal in his depiction of her body. He'd shown every sag, every wrinkle, every bulge that should have been flat. The flesh of one thigh lapped the edge of the chair where she was seated; her breasts hung heavy.

And yet she was glorious. Her skin was luminous with a glow that seemed to come from deep inside, her curves strong and fluid, her face majestically beautiful. She was both herself and Everywoman, wise in her age.

This was Liam Jenner's final love letter to her. An uncompromising statement of feelings that were clear-sighted and fearless. This was her soul exposed by the brilliant man she hadn't been courageous enough to claim as her own. And now it might be too late.

She grabbed her keys, flew down the stairs, and ran outside to her car.

One of the children had drawn an elaborate rabbit in the dust on the trunk. Then she realized that the drawing was too sophisticated. More of Molly and her mischief.

Too late, too late, too late . . . The tires hissed as she sped from the campground toward his glass house. While she'd been putting up barriers against a dead husband she hadn't loved in years, he'd gone after what he wanted.

Too late, too late, too late . . . The car jolted over the ruts at the top of the lane, then steadied as the house came into view. It looked empty and deserted.

She jumped out, rushed to the door, and leaned on the bell. There was no answer. She banged it with her fists, then raced to the back. *He's going to Mexico* . . .

The glass-enclosed studio rose above her, a tree house for a genius. She could see no signs of life inside, none in the rest of the house either.

Behind her the lake sparkled in the sunlight, and the sky floated blue and cloudless above, the perfect day mocking her. She spotted a door off to the side and rushed toward it, not expecting it to be open, but the heavy knob turned in her hand.

Everything was quiet inside. She moved through the back of the house into the kitchen, then made her way to the living room. From there she mounted the catwalk.

The arch at the end beckoned her toward his sacred space. She had no right to enter, but she did.

He was standing with his back to the door packing tubes of acrylics into a carrying case. Like the other time she'd been here, he was dressed in black—tailored slacks and a long-sleeved shirt. Dressed for traveling.

"Do you want something?" he growled without looking up.

"Oh, yes," she said breathlessly.

He finally turned, but she saw by the stubborn set of his jaw that he wouldn't make it easy.

"I want you," she said.

If anything, his expression grew more arrogant. She'd badly dented his pride, and he needed much more.

She reached for the hem of her linen sundress, pulled it over her head, and tossed it aside. She unsnapped her bra and discarded it, slipped her thumbs beneath the waistband of her panties, pushed them down, and stepped out of them.

He watched her silently, his face revealing nothing.

She raised her arms and slid her hands into her hair, lifting it from the nape of her neck. She crooked one knee, turned slightly from the waist, and eased into the pose that had sold a million posters.

With her age and her weight, standing before him like this should have been a travesty. Instead, she felt powerful and fiercely sexual, just as he'd painted her.

"You think that's all you have to do to get me back?" he scoffed.

"Yes. I do."

He jerked his head toward an old velvet couch that hadn't been here last time. "Lie down."

She wondered if he'd posed another model on it, but instead of feeling jealous, she felt a stir of pity. Whoever the woman might have been, she hadn't possessed Lilly's powers.

With a slow, certain smile, she made her way to the couch. It sat beneath one of the studio's skylights, and light showered her skin as she lay upon it.

She wasn't surprised to see him grab a palette and tubes from the case. How could he resist painting her? Resting her head against one of the rolled arms, she settled with perfect contentment into the soft velvet while he worked, squeezing out the paint. Finally he gathered brushes and came toward her.

She'd already noted his quickened breath. Now she saw the fire of desire burning behind the genius in his eyes. He knelt before her. She waited. Content.

He began to paint her. Not an image on canvas. He painted her flesh.

He drew a soft brush fat with cadmium red across her ribs, then added Mars violet and Prussian blue at her hip. He dappled her shoulder and belly with orange, cobalt, and emerald, clamped a discarded brush between his teeth like a pirate's dagger and stippled her breast in ultramarine and lime. Her nipple beaded as he swirled it with turquoise and magenta. He pushed open her thighs and adorned them with aggressive patterns of viridian and blue-violet.

She felt his frustration growing along with his desire and wasn't surprised when he tossed the brushes aside and began to use his hands on her, whorling the colors, claiming her flesh until she could no longer bear it.

She sprang to her feet and pulled at the buttons on his shirt, smearing it with the stigmata of Renaissance gold he'd dabbed in her palms. No longer content to be his creation, she needed to re-create him in her image, and when he was naked, she pressed against his flesh.

The hot pigments blended and fused as she imprinted herself upon him. Once again there was no bed, so she pulled the cushions from the couch and kissed him until they were both breathless. Finally he drew back far enough so she could open herself to him. "Lilly, my love . . . " He entered her as fiercely as he created.

The paint made her inner thighs slip against his hips, so she gripped tighter. He plunged harder and faster. Their mouths melded with their bodies until they stopped being two people. Together they tumbled off the edge of the world.

Afterward they played with the paint and exchanged deep kisses along with all the love words they needed to say. Only when they were in the shower did Lilly tell him she wouldn't marry him.

"Who asked you?"

"Not right away," she added, ignoring his bluster. "I want to live together for a while first. In perfect bohemian sin."

"Just tell me I don't have to rent a cold-water flat somewhere in lower Manhattan."

"No. And not Mexico either. In Paris. Wouldn't that be lovely? I could be your muse."

"My darling Lilly, don't you know you already are?"

"Oh, Liam, I love you so. The two of us . . . an atelier in the Sixth Arrondissement owned by an old lady in ancient Chanel suits. You and your genius and your wonderful, wonderful body. And me and my quilts. And wine and paint and Paris."

"They're yours." He laughed his great lusty laugh and soaped her breasts. "Did I remember to say that I love you?"

"You did." She smiled the depth of her feelings into those dark, intense eyes. "I'll hang a set of wind chimes under the eaves."

"Which will keep me awake, so I'll have to make love to you all night."

"I do love wind chimes."

"And I do love you."

With a sense of detachment Kevin watched the indicator on the Ferrari's speedometer climb. *Eighty-seven . . . eighty-eight.* He shot west on the tollway past the last of Chicago's suburbs. He'd drive all the way to Iowa if he had to, anything to make this restlessness go away so he could concentrate on what was important.

Training camp started tomorrow morning. He'd drive until then.

He needed to feel the speed. The sizzle of danger. *Ninety . . . ninety-one.*

Next to him the divorce papers that had arrived that morning from Molly's lawyer slid off the seat. Why hadn't she talked to him before she'd done this? He tried to steady himself by remembering what was important.

He had only five or six good years left . . .

Playing for the Stars was all that counted . . .

He couldn't afford the distraction of a high-maintenance woman . . .

On and on he went, until he was so tired of listening to himself that he pressed the accelerator harder.

It had been one month and four days since he'd seen Molly, so he couldn't blame her for the fact that he hadn't stepped up his workouts as he'd planned or watched all the game film he'd intended to. Instead, he'd gone rock climbing, run some white water, done a little paragliding. But none of it satisfied him.

The only time he'd felt remotely content was when he'd talked to Lilly and Liam a few days ago. They'd both sounded so happy.

The wheel vibrated beneath his hand, but he'd felt a bigger rush going cliff diving with Molly.

Ninety-five. Or what about the day she'd flipped the canoe? *Ninety-six.* Or when he'd climbed the tree after Marmie? *Ninety-seven.* Or just watching the mischief flash in her eyes.

And when they'd made love. That had been the rush of a lifetime.

Now all the fun was gone. He'd gotten more thrills riding a bike at the campground with Molly at his side then he was getting going ninety-eight in a Ferrari Spider.

Sweat trickled under his arms. If he blew a tire right now, he'd never see her again, never have a chance to tell her she'd been right about him all along. He was exactly as afraid as she'd said.

He'd fallen in love with her.

Just like that the empty spaces inside him filled up, and he took his foot off the accelerator. As he sagged back in the seat, he felt as if his chest had caved in. Lilly had tried to tell him and so had Jane Bonner, but he hadn't let himself listen. Molly was right. He'd secretly believed he couldn't measure up as a person in the same way he measured up as a player, so he hadn't tried. But he was way too old to keep living his life underneath leftover shadows.

He slipped into the right lane. For the first time in months he felt calm. She'd told him she loved him, and now he knew exactly what that meant. He also understood what he had to do. And this time he intended to do it right.

Half an hour later he rang the Calebows' doorbell. Andrew answered wearing jeans and an orange inner tube. "Kevin! Do you want to go swimming with me?"

"Sorry, buddy, can't do it today." Kevin slipped past him. "I need to see your mom and dad."

"I don't know where Dad is, but Mom's in her office."

"Thanks." He ruffled Andrew's hair and made his way through the house to the office in the back. The door was open, but he knocked just the same. "Phoebe?"

She turned and stared at him.

"Sorry for barging in like this, but I need to talk to you."

"Oh?" She kicked back in her chair and extended her chorus-girl legs—longer than Molly's but not nearly as enticing. She wore white shorts and pink plastic sandals printed with purple dinosaurs. Despite that, she looked more formidable than God, and when it came to the world of the Stars, she was just as powerful.

"It's about Molly."

For a moment, he thought he saw speculation in her expression. "What about her?"

He stepped into the room and waited for an invitation to sit down. It didn't come.

There was no way to ease into this, and no reason he should. "I want to marry her. For real. And I want your blessing."

He didn't get the smile he expected. "Why the change of heart?"

"Because I love her, and I want to be part of her life forever."

"I see."

She had a perfect poker face. Maybe she didn't know the way Molly felt about him. It would have been just like Molly to try to protect him by hiding her feelings from her sister. "She loves me."

Phoebe didn't look impressed.

He tried again. "I'm fairly sure she's going to be happy about this."

"Oh, I'm sure she will be. At first anyway."

The temperature in the room dropped ten degrees. "What do you mean by that?"

She rose from the desk, looking much tougher than someone wearing plastic dinosaur sandals should. "You know we want a real marriage for Molly."

"So do I. That's why I'm here."

"A husband who'll put her first."

"That's what she's going to get."

"The tiger's changing his stripes awfully quickly."

He didn't pretend not to know what she meant. "I'll admit it's taken me a while to figure out that my life needs to be about more than playing football, but falling in love with Molly has readjusted my viewpoint."

Her expression of cool skepticism as she came around the side of the desk wasn't encouraging. "What about the future? Everyone knows how you feel about the team. You once told Dan that you'd like to coach after you retire as a player, and he got the idea you eventually want to move into the front office. Do you still feel that way?"

He wasn't going to lie. "Putting the game into perspective doesn't mean I want to throw it away."

"No, I don't imagine it does." She crossed her arms. "Let's be honest—is it Molly you want or is it the Stars?"

Everything inside him went still. "I hope you don't mean what I think you do."

"Marrying into the family on a permanent basis seems like an efficient way to make sure you eventually get to the front office."

The chill that crept through him went all the way to his bones. "I said I wanted your blessing. I didn't say I needed it." He began to walk away, only to have Phoebe's next words slap him from behind.

"If you go near her again, you can kiss the Stars good-bye."

He turned, not believing what he heard.

Her eyes were cold and determined. "I mean it, Kevin. My sister's been hurt enough, and I won't let you use her to fulfill your long-term plans. Stay away from her. You can have the team or you can have Molly, but you can't have both."

26

Daphne was in a very bad mood. It followed her around while she baked her favorite oatmeal-strawberry cookies, and it stuck to her side when she talked to Murphy Mouse, who'd moved into the woods a few weeks before. Even the big pile of shiny new coins jingling in her pink backpack didn't make her feel better. She wanted to run to Melissa's house for cheering up, but Melissa was planning a trip to Paris with her new friend, Leo the Bullfrog.

Most of all Daphne was in a very bad mood because she missed Benny. He made her angry sometimes, but he was still her best friend. Except she wasn't his best friend anymore. Daphne loved Benny, but Benny didn't love her.

She sniffed and wiped her eyes with the strap from her electric guitar. His new school started today, and he'd be having so much fun that he wouldn't even think about her. He'd be thinking about touchdowns instead, and all the girl rabbits who'd be hanging out by the fence wearing tube tops and trying to entice him with foreign phrases and puffy lips and bouncy breasts. Girls who didn't understand him like she did, who were impressed with his fame and money and green eyes, and didn't know that he loved cats and needed entertaining sometimes and didn't hate poodles nearly as much as he thought, and that he liked to sleep cuddled around her with his hand—

Molly ripped the paper from her yellow pad. This was supposed to be *Daphne's Bad Mood*, not *Daphne Does Dallas*. She gazed out across

Bobolink Meadow and wondered how some parts of her life could be so happy and some parts so sad.

The sweatshirt she'd spread in the grass had bunched under her bare legs. It was Kevin's. As she straightened it, she tried to concentrate on the happy parts of her life.

Thanks to her new contract, she was financially secure for the first time since she'd given away her money, and she was bursting with ideas for new books. The campground and B&B were filled to capacity, and the more responsibility she gave Amy and Troy, the more they were able to handle.

Their feelings toward the place had become as proprietary as her own, and they'd asked her to consider converting the attic into an apartment where they could live year round. They wanted to keep the B&B open all winter for cross-country skiing and snowmobile enthusiasts, as well as city people who simply felt like enjoying winter in the country. Molly had decided to let them do it. When Kevin had been searching for someone to run the campground full-time, he'd overlooked the obvious.

She hated how much she missed him. He probably didn't even think about her. She knew now that was his loss. She'd offered him her most precious possession, and instead of holding on tight, he'd thrown it away.

She snatched up her writing pad. If she couldn't work on *Daphne's Bad Mood,* she could at least make a list of groceries for Troy to pick up in town. Amy was baking her new specialty for tea—dirt cupcakes, which were chocolate cupcakes topped with green coconut frosting and Gummi Worms. Molly was going to miss Lilly's help with the guests, although not nearly as much as she'd miss her companionship. Her mood lifted a little as she thought about how happy Lilly and Leo the Bullfrog were.

She heard a movement behind her and set aside the notepad. One of the guests had found her hiding place. So far that morning she'd made restaurant reservations, drawn maps to antique stores and golf courses, unstopped a toilet, taped up a broken window, and helped the older kids organize a scavenger hunt.

Giving in to the inevitable, she turned—and saw Kevin coming around the fence at the bottom of the meadow.

She forgot to breathe. The frames of his silver Rēvos glinted, and the breeze tousled his hair. He wore a pair of khaki slacks with a light blue T-shirt. Only as he came closer did she see a picture of Daphne printed on the front.

Kevin stopped where he was and stood there simply gazing at her. Molly sat crossed-legged in the meadow with the sun shining on her bare shoulders and a pair of yellow butterflies fluttering like hair bows around her head. She was all the dreams he'd lost at dawn—dreams of everything he hadn't understood he needed until now. She was his playmate, his confidante, the lover who made his blood rush. She was the mother of his children and the companion of his old age. She was the joy of his heart.

And she was gazing at him as if a skunk had just wandered out of the woods.

"What do you want?"

What had happened to *Kiss me, you fool?* Riiiight . . . He pulled off his sunglasses and tried a little of the old playboy smile. "So how's it going?"

Had he really said that? Had he really said "how's it going?" He deserved everything she was going to throw at him.

"Couldn't be better. Nice T-shirt. Now get off my property."

So much for the woman who'd wished him all the best the last time they'd been together. "I, uh . . . heard you might be selling the place."

"When I get around to it."

"Maybe I'll buy it back."

"Maybe you won't." She stood up, and a few blades of grass stuck to the side of one of those legs he loved to touch. "Why aren't you at training camp?"

"Training camp?" He slipped his sunglasses into his shirt pocket.

"Veterans are supposed to report this morning."

"Damn. I guess I'm in trouble then."

"Did Phoebe send you here?"

"Not exactly."

"Then what's going on?"

"I wanted to talk to you, that's all. Tell you some things."

"You're supposed to be at training camp."

"I think you already mentioned that."

"One phone call and I can find out why you're not there."

He hadn't wanted to do this yet, and his hands found their way into his pockets. "First, maybe you'd better hear what I have to say."

"Give me your cell phone."

"It's in the car."

She grabbed a sweatshirt he seemed to remember belonged to him and marched toward the fence at the bottom of the meadow. "I'll call from the house."

"I'm AWOL, okay? I'm being traded!"

She spun around. "Traded? They can't do that."

"They're crazy, and they can do just about anything they want."

"Not without throwing away the season." She twisted the arms of his sweatshirt into a knot at her waist and charged toward him. "Tell me exactly what happened. Every word."

"I don't want to." His throat felt tight and his tongue clumsy. "I want to tell you how pretty you are."

She regarded him suspiciously. "I look just like I did the last time you saw me, except my nose is sunburned."

"You're beautiful." He moved closer. "And I want to marry you. For real. Forever."

She blinked. "Why?"

This wasn't going the way he'd planned it. He wanted to touch her, but the frown marks between her eyebrows made him think twice. "Because I love you. I really do. More than I ever could have imagined."

Perfect silence.

"Molly, listen to me. I'm sorry about what happened, sorry it's taken me so long to figure out what I want, but when I was with you, I was having too good a time to think. After you left, though, things weren't so good, and I realized that everything you said about me is right. I was afraid. I let football become my whole life. It was the only thing I was sure of, and that's why I got so reckless this year. There was something missing inside me I was trying to fill up, but I went about doing it the wrong way. But there sure isn't anything missing inside me now because you're there."

Molly's heart was pounding so loudly she was afraid he could hear. Did he mean it? He looked as if he meant it—worried, upset, more serious than she'd ever seen him. What if he really meant it?

As a child who'd been emotionally abused, she had a strong survivor's instinct, and it kicked in. "Tell me about the trade."

"Let's not talk about that now. Let's talk about us. About our future."

"I can't talk about the future until I understand the here and now."

He must have known she wasn't going to let it go, but he still tried to sidestep. "I've missed you so much. Without you, I stopped being happy."

It was everything she'd wanted to hear. And yet . . . "All I have to do is call her."

He wandered toward the fence. "All right, we'll do it your way." He braced a hand on the top rail. "I wanted to try to set things right with them once and for all, so I went out to the house. Dan wasn't around, but I saw Phoebe. I told her I loved you and that I was going to ask you to marry me for real. I said I wanted her blessing."

Molly needed something to hold on to, but there wasn't anything around, so she sank down in the weeds, drew her knees to her chest, and concentrated on sucking in air.

He gazed down at her. "You could look a little happier."

"Tell me the rest."

"Phoebe didn't like it." He pushed himself away from the fence, the lines around his mouth deepening. "As a matter of fact, she hated it. She accused me of using you as an insurance policy toward my retirement."

"I don't understand."

"Everybody knows I want to coach eventually, and I've talked to Dan about his front-office work."

Molly finally got it. "She said you were using me to guarantee your future with the Stars. Is that it?"

He erupted. "I don't need a guarantee! I proved myself a long time ago! There's not a player in the league who knows more about the game than I do, but she looked at me like I was a no-name parasite. Molly, I understand that you love your sister, but football's a game about winning, and I have to tell you right now that I've lost all respect for her."

Her legs had regained enough strength for her to stand. "There's more, isn't there?"

His expression was a mixture of anger and confusion, as if he couldn't comprehend how a life made of gold could have developed any tarnish. "She said I could have you or the Stars, but not both. She said if I saw you again, my career with the team was over. If I stayed away, I still had my job."

Something warm opened up in Molly's heart. "And you believed her?"

"You're damn right I believed her! And it's her loss! I don't need the Stars. I don't even want to play for them anymore."

Her loving, interfering sister . . . "She was scamming you, Kevin. This whole thing's a scam."

"What are you talking about?"

"She wants me to have a Great Love Story like she had with Dan."

"I saw her face. This wasn't any scam."

"She's very good."

"You're not making sense. What do you mean that she wants you to have a love story? I'd already told her I loved you."

"She's a romantic. Almost as much as me. An ordinary love story isn't good enough. She wants me to have something I'll remember my whole life, something to pull out and examine if you forget to send flowers on our anniversary or get mad because I put a dent in the car."

"I'm sure you understand what you're talking about, but I don't have a clue."

"If you were a woman you would."

"Well, excuse me for having a—"

"Words are wonderful, but every once in a while a few women are lucky enough to have something extra, something unforgettable." This was so basic to her that she had to make him understand. "Don't you see? Dan saved her life! He was willing to give up everything for her. Because of that, Phoebe always knows she comes first with him—ahead of football, ahead of his ambition, ahead of everything. She wanted me to have the same thing with you, so she convinced you that you had to choose."

"I'm supposed to believe that she jeopardized the entire team just to force me into making some kind of grand romantic *gesture?*" He was starting to shout. "I'm supposed to *believe this?*"

Kevin loved her! She could see it in his eyes, hear it in his frustration. He'd been willing to give up the team for her, and her heart sang. But the sound was almost drowned out by another noise—one as unexpected as it was inevitable.

The clang of a fire alarm.

She tried to ignore it. Even though she knew Kevin's career with the Stars was as secure as ever, he hadn't known it, and the fact was, he'd been willing to make the sacrifice.

Yes, her heart was definitely singing. Yes, this was a moment she could spend her entire life reliving. A moment that was perfect.

Except for the fire alarm.

She refused to listen to it. "You seem a little angry."

"Angry? Now, why would I be angry?"

"Because you thought Phoebe kicked you off the Stars."

"You forget that I don't *care* about the Stars anymore. You forget that I want to play for a team with an owner who understands that the point of the game is *winning*, not jeopardizing millions of dollars in revenue so her star quarterback can play Sir Galahad!"

The fire alarm clanged louder. "Then you didn't make much of a sacrifice."

He was a champion, so he could spot the blitz coming from a mile away, and his expression grew wary. "This is important to you? This whole romantic-gesture thing?"

Clang . . . Clang . . . Clang . . . "I have to get ready for tea."

"I haven't done enough? You want something more?"

"Not at all."

A muffled curse, and then he swept her into his arms and began carrying her toward the woods. "How's this for a romantic gesture?"

She crossed her arms over her chest, crossed her ankles, a perfect portrait of petulance, but she felt sick. "If this involves naked bodies, it's sex, not romance."

Unfortunately, he set her down instead of kissing her until he'd drowned out the sound of a thousand fire alarms. "You think I don't know the difference between sex and romance? You think because I'm male, I'm obtuse."

Her Great Love Story was on a downhill spiral because of a fire alarm that had grown so loud she wanted to cover her ears. "I guess only you can answer that question."

"All right, here's what I'm going to do." He took a deep breath and met her gaze straight on. "I'll win the Super Bowl for you."

She realized he meant it, and little starbursts of happiness exploded inside her—each one punctuated by the noise of the alarm. Right then she understood that she was facing the fundamental question of her life, a question that had its roots in the heart of a little girl who'd been emotionally abandoned when she was much too young. Kevin Tucker was strong enough to slay dragons for her and strong enough to win the Super Bowl for her, but was he strong enough to love her even when she wasn't lovable? She needed an answer that would quiet the fire alarm forever.

"It's only July, loser," she sneered. "By Super Bowl Sunday I'll have forgotten your name."

"I seriously doubt that."

"Whatever." She scratched a mosquito bite, looked bored, and spoke the ugliest words she'd ever said. "My mistake. I really don't think I love you after all."

Horrified, she began to snatch it back, then stopped because he didn't look upset, only calculating.

"Liar. Have you ever heard of the Saxeten River Gorge?"

"Can't say as I have." Had the fire alarm lost a few decibels? "It sounds boring. Did you hear me say I didn't love you?"

"Yeah. Anyway, it's in Switzerland, and it's as treacherous as they come. But I'm prepared to rappel to the bottom, and once I get there, I'll carve your initials in the rock."

Yes, definitely not as loud. She tapped her foot in the grass. "Touching, but Switzerland's almost as far away as the Super Bowl. Besides, when it comes right down to it, all you're talking about is a little graffiti, right?"

"There's a sport called parapenting. You parachute off a mountain peak—"

"Unless you're going to write my name in the sky on your way down, don't bother."

His eyes lit up.

"On second thought," she said hastily, "you'd probably misspell it. And the closest mountains are on the other side of the state, so what about the here and now? Okay, maybe I do love you, but truth is, champ, all this Iron Man stuff might impress the guys in the locker room, but it won't get you babies and home-cooked meals."

Babies and home-cooked meals! A family that was all hers. And a man who satisfied her to the very depths of her soul.

Just like that, the fire alarm went still forever.

"So we're going to play hardball," he said.

Kevin understood her better than anyone on earth. He understood her so well that he still hadn't thrown up his hands and stomped away. She listened to the glorious silence inside her and wanted to weep with the joy of knowing that this man's love didn't have to be earned with perpetual good behavior.

"I was willing to give up the Stars for you," he reminded her, his expression shrewd. "But I guess that's not good enough . . . "

"Oh, yes . . . " Kevin without the Stars was unthinkable.

He didn't take his eyes off her. "So I'll have to give you something more."

"Not necessary." She smiled her love at him. "You passed the test."

"Too late." He grabbed her hand and began pulling her back toward the campground. "Come on, sweetheart."

"No, really, Kevin. It's all right. I was just— It's the fire-alarm thing. I know it's neurotic, but I wanted to be sure you really loved me. I—"

"Could you walk a little faster? I'd like to get this over with so we could start working on one of those babies you mentioned."

A baby . . . And this time it would be all right. She realized he was pulling her toward the beach. "You don't have to—"

"We'd better take one of the rowboats. Not that I don't trust you in a canoe, but let's face it, you've got a spotty record."

"You want to go out on the lake? Now?"

"We have unfinished business." He led her onto the dock. "You're still looking for that great romantic gesture."

"No I'm not. Really! I've already had the most romantic gesture you could possibly make. You were willing to give up the Stars for me."

"Which didn't impress you."

"More than you can imagine. I've never been so impressed."

"Could have fooled me." He stepped down into the rowboat tied to the end of the dock, then pulled her in with him. "Apparently I still haven't met the Dan Calebow Standard."

"Oh, but you have." She sat on the seat. "I was just being . . . careful."

"You were being neurotic." He untied the line and picked up the oars.

"That, too. So do we really need to take to the high seas?"

"Oh, yeah." He began to row.

"I didn't mean it. When I said I didn't love you."

"You think I don't know that? And you can tell me how romantic I am when we get to the middle of the lake."

"I'm not being critical, but I don't imagine you'll be able to do anything too romantic out there."

"That's what you think."

She loved him so much that it wasn't hard to humor him. "You're right. Rowing us to the middle of the lake is a very romantic gesture."

"I do know my romance."

He didn't have a clue about romance, but this sweet-talking son of a preacher man knew everything there was about love. Daphne rippled on his chest with the movement of his muscles as he rowed. "I like your T-shirt."

"If you're right about your sister—which I hope you are, even though I swear I'm going to report her to the commissioner—I'll have them made up for all the guys on the team."

"Maybe not your best idea."

"They'll wear 'em." He smiled. "I'll make a concession to the defense, though, and put Benny on theirs. And congratulations on saving your books. Lilly told me all about it over the phone. I'm sorry you had to sell your place, but it would have been too small for both of us anyway."

Molly thought of the big old Victorian farmhouse on the outskirts of Du Page County she'd heard Phoebe mention was up for sale. It would be plenty big enough.

"I think we're about in the middle," she said.

He looked behind him. "Just a little farther. Did I tell you how deep it was out here?"

"I don't think so."

"Really deep."

She could feel her smile spreading all over her face. "I'm hopelessly in love with you."

"I know that. It's my own hopelessly-in-love feelings that are in question."

"I promise I won't ever question them again."

"Let's make sure of that." He shipped the oars, and they drifted for a while. He looked at her and smiled. She smiled back.

Her heart felt as if it had somehow gotten lodged in her throat. "You're the most steadfast man I've ever known, Kevin Tucker. I can't imagine why I thought, even for a moment, that I needed to test you."

"Every once in a while you go crazy."

"Phoebe calls them 'incidents.' And today was the last one. I risked throwing away the most important thing in my life, but I won't make that mistake again." Her eyes filled with tears. "You gave up the Stars for me."

"I'd do it again. Although I sincerely hope I don't have to."

She laughed. He smiled, then looked serious. "I know you don't love football the same way I do, but, driving up here, I kept thinking about coming out of the huddle and looking over toward the fifty-yard line." He touched her cheek. "I saw you sitting there just for me."

Molly could see it, too.

"The wind's picked up," he said. "It's getting colder."

The sun shone in the sky as well as in her heart, and she knew she'd never be cold for the rest of her life. "I'm fine. Perfect."

He nodded toward the sweatshirt that was still wrapped around her waist. "You'd better put that on."

"I don't need it."

"You're shivering."

"That's from excitement."

"Can't be too careful." The rowboat wobbled a bit as he stood and drew her up in front of him, where he unfastened the sweatshirt and pulled it over her body. It was so large it came to her knees. He pushed a lock of hair behind her ear. "Do you have any idea how precious you are to me?"

"Yes, I really do."

"Good." Quick as a flash he crossed the empty sleeves in front of her like a straitjacket and tied the cuffs in the back.

"What are you—?"

"I love you." He brushed a kiss across her lips, picked her up, and dropped her over the side.

She was so astonished that she took a mouthful, then had to kick furiously to get to the surface. With her arms imprisoned, it wasn't easy.

"There you are," he said when she bobbed up. "I was getting worried."

"What are you doing?"

"Waiting till you're ready to drown." He smiled and eased back down on the seat. "And then I'm going to save your life. Dan did it for Phoebe, and I'm going to do it for you."

"Dan didn't try to *murder her first!*" she screamed.

"I go the extra mile."

"Of all the stupid—" She caught another mouthful, coughed, and tried to say more. Unfortunately, she was sinking back under.

He was in the water waiting for her when she came up—hair dripping in his eyes, Daphne plastered to his chest, his green eyes dancing with the sheer pleasure of being alive, in love, and having such a good time. There was no woman on earth who could entertain him the way she could. And no woman who would ever love him more.

Which didn't mean she was giving in without a fight. "By the time you save me," she pointed out, "I'll be too tired to do anything but sleep."

Seconds later she watched the sweatshirt sink to the bottom of the lake without her.

"That was fun." Kevin's smile was a mile wide, and his eyes were misty with something other than lake water.

"Not in front of the children." Her eyes were misty, too, as she tugged off his Daphne T-shirt.

They made love in the shadow of the rowboat, holding on to the gunwale and each other, choking and gasping, first one of them underwater and then the other, two daredevils who'd found their perfect mate. Afterward they gazed into each other's eyes, not saying anything, just feeling peaceful and absolutely perfect.

EPILOGUE

Found in a notebook tucked under the gazebo at the Wind Lake Campground. Author unknown—although there are suspicions.

All the animals in Nightingale Woods gathered for the christening. Daphne wore her second-best rhinestone tiara (she'd misplaced her best at a road rally). Benny polished his mountain bike until it shone. Melissa dazzled with a swirly scarf from the rue Faubourg Saint-Honoré, and her new husband Leo the Bullfrog created a beautiful painting in honor of the occasion.

The ceremony took place under a shady tree. The animals waited until it was over to scurry out from the shadows of the gingerbread cottages and move among the guests, invisible to all but the very smallest of humans.

Victoria Phoebe Tucker blinked down at Benny from her perch on her father's shoulder, her green eyes alive with curiosity. *What's up, dude?*

"What's up yourself?"

Hey, you look familiar.

"I know your dad pretty well."

Daphne hopped forward. "*Bonjour,* Victoria Phoebe, and welcome to Nightingale Woods." She cast an admiring glance at the frothy confection of white lace and pink ribbons that enveloped the baby and draped her father's large, tan arm. Victoria Phoebe already had an eye for fashion. "I'm Daphne, and this is Benny. We stopped by to introduce ourselves."

"And see if you wanted to play some football," Benny added.

Victoria Phoebe stuffed a pink ribbon from her christening cap into her mouth. *You might have noticed I'm sort of tied up right now.*

"Sarcastic like her mother," Murphy Mouse noted.

Victoria Phoebe's father reached up to retrieve the ribbon. She went after his hand and took a few chomps on her favorite teether, his brand-new Super Bowl ring. He kissed her forehead and exchanged a special smile with her mother, who stood at his side. Nearby her Aunt Phoebe gazed happily at the new family that her special talent for deception had helped create.

"I don't recognize all of the big people," Leo the Bullfrog said, "but I sure know the little ones—the Calebows and Bonners, the Denton children from Telarosa, Texas, and isn't that a Traveler over there?"

Victoria Phoebe liked being in the know, and she abandoned the Super Bowl ring to point out some of the adult guests. *All those giant men are Daddy's playmates. And over there are Uncle Cal's brothers with the mommies and kids. Aunt Jane is talking to Uncle Dan right now. She's pretty nice, but she tried to write something on my leg last night when she was holding me, and Daddy had to take her pen away.*

"We've had complaints before," Daphne said. "Your mother looks particularly fetching."

And she smells totally awesome—like flowers and cookies. I love my mom. She tells the best stories.

"Like, duh," Benny said.

Daphne poked him, but Victoria Phoebe was snuggling into her father's neck and didn't notice. She peeked back up. *This is my daddy dear. He says I'm his very special girl, but not to tell Mommy, except he always says it in front of her, and then they laugh.*

"You have very nice parents," Melissa observed politely.

I know, but they kiss my cheeks too much. I'm getting chapped.

"I remember Rosie Bonner used to complain about the same thing."

Rosie Bonner! Victoria Phoebe grew indignant. *Last night she tried to hide me in the litter box because I was getting too much attention, but Hannah distracted her with a cookie. I loooove Hannah.*

"She's always been our special friend," Daphne said. "We played with her a lot when she was your age."

Don't you play with her now?

The animals exchanged glances. "Not in the same way," Benny said. "Things change. Stuff happens."

Victoria Phoebe was a future summa cum laude, so not much got past her. *What kind of stuff?*

"Children can only see us when they're very young," Melissa explained kindly. "As they get older, they lose the power."

That bites.

"But they can read about us in books," Murphy Mouse added, "which is nearly as good."

"Books that are making your mother a ton of money," Leo pointed out. "Although not as much as my paintings."

Victoria Phoebe grew huffy. *Forgive me very much, but reading doesn't hold a lot of appeal at the moment. I'm still trying to cope with diaper rash.*

"Definitely sarcastic," Celia the Hen clucked.

Daphne, who appreciated sarcasm, decided it was time for more explanation. "Even though you won't be able to see us as you get older, Victoria Phoebe, we'll be around watching out for you and all your brothers."

Brothers?!

"We're sort of like guardian angels," Melissa interjected hastily.

"Furry ones," Benny added.

"The point is," Daphne said patiently. "You'll never be alone."

Exactly how many brothers? Victoria Phoebe asked. And then, *Oops! Gotta go!* as her father passed her over to her mother.

The creatures watched Kevin pick up a glass of lemonade from the table under the trees. "I'd like to propose a toast," he said. "To all our friends and the family that means so much to me. Especially to my mother, Lilly, who came into my life at just the right time. And my sister-in-law, Phoebe, who is almost as good at matchmaking as she is at running a football team." He turned, cleared his throat, and sounded sniffy. "And to my wife . . . the love of my life."

Victoria Phoebe peered around her mother's arm. *Here they go with the kissing again. Right now it's just each other, but they'll get to me and my cheeks next.*

Sure enough, they did.

Daphne gave a blissful sigh. "Now we're at the very best part of being in the book business."

"The happy ending." Melissa said, nodding in agreement.

"Way too much kissing," Benny grumbled. And then he brightened. "I got an idea. Let's go play some football!"

Which they did. Right before happily ever after.